Dying for It

TALES OF SEX AND DEATH

Edited by Mitzi Szereto

THUNDER'S MOUTH PRESS • NEW YORK

Dying for It: *Tales of Sex and Death*

Published by
Thunder's Mouth Press
An Imprint of Avalon Publishing Group, Inc.
245 West 17th Street, 11th floor
New York, NY 10011

AVALON
publishing group incorporated

Compilation and introduction copyright © 2006 by Mitzi Szereto

Page 389 serves as an extension of this copyright page.

first printing, August 2006

Library of Congress Cataloging-in-Publication Data is available.

ISBN: 1-56025-857-8
ISBN-13: 978-1-56025-857-5

9 8 7 6 5 4 3 2 1

Book design by Bettina Wilhelm

Printed in the United States of America
Distributed by Publishers Group West

Contents

Introduction

*The difference between sex and death is that with death you
can do it alone and no one is going to make fun of you.*

—*Woody Allen*

Sex and death have long been connected themes in literature, poetry,
music, film, and the visual arts. One of the most famous examples
is undoubtedly William Shakespeare's *Romeo and Juliet*, a tragic tale
of star-crossed lovers who die in each other's arms. Around this
same historical period, the English metaphysical poet John Donne
penned "The Apparition," featuring the "ghost" of a jilted lover
who visits the bed of the woman he loves so he can scorn her and
her new lover. Fast-forward to the dusk of the Victorian Age and
we have Bram Stoker's gothic novel *Dracula*, where seduction leads
to death and, for some, immortality. Not long afterward the
German author Thomas Mann wrote *Death in Venice* (interpreted
into a cinematic masterpiece in 1971 by Luchino Visconti), the
story of a repressed man's longing for the androgynous beauty of a
young boy, which leads him to risk death (and eventually succumb
to it) rather than abandon his obsession. The late twentieth century brings the arrival of J. G. Ballard's controversial novel (and film)
Crash, about a subculture of people who become sexually aroused
by car crashes. In music, Georges Bizet's famous opera *Carmen*
(first staged in 1875) involves a classic love triangle, with the sultry
Carmen seducing and discarding men until her fickleness results in
her death at the hands of a dejected suitor. The world of the visual
arts hasn't been immune to the sex-and-death connection, either.

Many famous works pertain to such subject matter, often inspired by religion and mythology. In fact, the twentieth-century Surrealist painter Salvador Dalí's formative boyhood experience of finding a book containing explicit photos of people suffering from advanced stages of untreated venereal diseases prompted him to associate sex with putrefaction and decay, and had a lasting influence on his future works.

Why this fascination with sex and death? And why is sex so often connected with death? There's clearly a demonstrated link between the two, even if only in philosophical and thus unverifiable terms. Aristotle held that each sex act had a direct life-shortening effect. (That certainly holds true for the male praying mantis, which is eaten by his bride during the act of copulation.) The Victorians likewise believed that a man's climax depleted his physical strength and moral resolve and brought him closer to death. Even language expresses this connection, with the French describing orgasm as *la petite mort* (the little death). Some language scholars maintain that the root of the old English word for "orgasm" is the same as that for death. And in Sanskrit, *nirvana* means annihilation. Think about this the next time you slip into bed with your lover.

Whether on a conscious or unconscious level, perhaps we've all experienced sex and death in one way or another. One of the most shared human experiences is the longing to die when thwarted in love—when being prevented from possessing the object of our desire is so painful we'd prefer not to live   than go without the consummation of our love. Then there are those who cross over to the opposite extreme of the sex-and-death duet, with the desire to combine the two so overwhelming that the transition from sex *to* death actually takes place, as was the case with the late Michael Hutchence (from the rock band INXS), who died of autoerotic asphyxiation in 1997.

Sex and death are both experiences of transcendence, which take us from one dimension to another. Perhaps through sex we confront our own mortality—or, indeed, defy it. It's a way to escape death, even if only for a few moments. Sex brings us together, death rends us apart—the evanescence of one versus the finality of the other. Through sex we are offered an experience of ecstasy—that sense of being swept away, of losing awareness of time and space, of being swallowed up by blackness. Many believe that to know ecstasy is also to die. By contrast, it might be argued that the fear of death prevents some from being able to let go, to become lost in the sexual experience. Either way, the tie between sex and death is still there.

Of the various anthologies I've edited and for which I have solicited contributions, no other topic has matched the overwhelming response of this subject. This theme has really struck a chord with those wielding writing quills around the world, lending itself to interpretation in an astonishing variety of ways. Included here are authors from the USA, Canada, Australia, Great Britain, Greece, Germany, Thailand, and Kenya. In *Dying for It: Tales of Sex and Death*, we run the gamut from the subversive, provocative, and poignant to the bizarre, humorous, and visceral. Be warned: This collection contains a lot of sharp edges.

Mitzi Szereto
Leicestershire, England
March 2006

Like Friendship Set on Fire

Niall Griffiths

God, he said in a whisper, I really love your body, but she couldn't make out what he said over the drone of the engines, so she asked him to repeat himself and he did: —I really fucking love your body.

And she raised her arms over her head the better for him to lift her shirt up over her breasts and her knuckles knocked against the low ceiling of the cramped cubicle they'd twisted their bodies into. He bent his legs to lower his trousers and his knees struck the toilet seat and he accidentally head-butted her in the belly, her dark flat belly, and she laughed and went "Oof" and one of his elbows struck the door and the other struck the back wall right next to the flush button. Such a small space they were in. The two of them in such a small space and the weak yellow light on their bodies, the paleness of his and the darkness of hers and their arms wrapped around each other both making zebras of their backs.

She reached down for his penis, stroked it to make it hard. He reached down between her legs, too, made her moisten and they leaned back away from each other as much as the crushed conditions would allow so that they could see each other's eyes. Hers so brown as to be almost black and his as blue as the sky outside the thin metal skin of the fuselage.

—Think we're a mile high yet?

A gasping in her voice.

—Does it matter?

A gasping in his, too, and then a groan from both as she guided him into her. They stood a moment locked like that to savor as they always did the first event of that good joining. He kissed her neck and she nuzzled his. They held each other tightly, very tightly, due in a small part to the constricting space they were in and in a large part to the fact that they loved each other dearly and had done so for two years. The plane they were on was taking them to L.A. In L.A. they were going to get married, and then they were going to honeymoon in California, too, and then they were going to fly home to Liverpool to tell their parents of their marriage and then, as they'd envisioned it happening many times over, they were going to stand and watch helpless as their parents roared and called to their respective gods to cast curses down on their children and hex their marriage and generally rend and split and separate. It was a scene they knew would occur because they knew their parents, and how they would react. It was a scene they knew would happen because they'd seen it happen before.

—Feel good?

Her answer was to bite his neck and moan into the muscle. He began to thrust. She began to thrust back. Their knees and hips and elbows knocked against walls and shelves and the bowl of the toilet. So many hard surfaces pressing in around them and their conjoined softnesses the center of it all, the steel and plastic and glass.

Face pressed to face they smelled deeply each other's hair. Smelled deeply each other's skin. He saw in close-up the whorl of her ear, even the infinitesimal downy hairs on the golden lobe, and he licked it. She saw the forest of his eyebrow, the blond hairs almost pure white at that resolution and she nibbled it softly. She ran her hands over the muscles of his back and he would've held her breasts with his but couldn't because of their confinement so he held the back of her head with one and wrapped the other tightly so tightly around her waist to keep her very close to him, to ensure that they didn't disengage, to keep him deeply in.

As good on the plane as it had been last night in the Boston hotel bed. As good on the plane as it had always been the six hundred times they'd done it.

Turbulence thrummed in their feet. Slight shock waves of some impacts in the main cabin outside the toilet were felt in their legs. Turbulence rattled the walls of the cubicle and jostled their bodies and he began to soften and slip out of her.

—What's wrong? she said.

—It's just a wee bit of turbulence. Not to worry about.

But he thought that he could hear screams. Behind the muted roar of the engines it seemed he could hear some screaming and he looked at her, looked into her face so beautiful to him that he thought he'd never tire of looking at it and he was about to tell her that he thought something was wrong when the plane lurched so violently to the left that all their internal organs lurched with it and they were thrown to that side and then back to the right as the plane lurched that way and their soft bodies collided with hard surfaces and bruises bloomed instantly and a small cut opened on his head and she tore a muscle in her neck and when the plane leveled out after a few more lurches each less pronounced than the last they'd become wedged together in a corner by the door each with their arms wrapped around the other's head for the scant protection that might've offered. The noise of the engines had resettled and the tiny toilet was filled with panting.

—Jesus Christ, he said. —What was that?

They let each other go, regarded each other with huge eyes.

—Are we crashing?

—I don't think so. But that wasn't just turbulence, was it?

And now it seemed that she could hear screaming, too. It seemed like a lot of screaming was going on in the main cabin outside and was filtering in through the locked toilet door.

—That wasn't right, he said. —Something's wrong.

She nodded and felt the side of her neck where the muscle had ripped and he touched his head gingerly and his fingertips came away smeared red and then a voice came over the intercom and said just seven words:

—Everybody stay calm. We have some planes.

She saw his blue eyes then as she'd never seen them before and indeed she looked out of her own in a wholly unprecedented way. Eye to eye for a few moments the same thought occurring behind each set and she gave that thought voice: —Oh, God. It's a hijack. What the *fuck* are we going to do?

A wobble to the plane again, a jerk and then a wobble. The pilot must be nervous, flying erratically, not surprising given that someone was probably holding a gun to his head or something. She couldn't blame him for his wobbling airplane.

She said it again: —What are we going to do?

He shook his head. —Dunno. I'm thinking.

Peculiar straining sound to the engines now, juddering the flat surfaces in the tiny toilet. The mirror shimmered, striped with jelly-ish squirtings from the smashed soap dispenser, releasing a smell that approximated cherries into the poky space. A small blood spot dotted red the door to the immediate left of the ashtray with the NO SMOKING sign on it and there was a shallow dent in the surface of the paper-towel holder. The plane was not flying steadily anymore and their bodies swayed with its movements, the whiteness of his, the darkness of hers, their two skins rocking in unison to match the side-to-side movements of the aircraft.

—D'you think we're going to die?

It was a question she had to ask.

And he had to answer it. —No. Don't be daft. It's just a hijack; they'll force the pilot to land somewhere, and keep us hostage till their demands have been met or until special forces storm the plane or something like that. Remember what happened in Germany? In 1972?

—No. I wasn't born then.

—Nor was I. But I saw a program about it and we're not going to die. I don't think it's going to be very nice but I don't think we'll die either.

He found a smile from somewhere and said, —It just adds to the adventure, doesn't it?

—What adventure?

—Y'know. This. Me and you.

She also trawled a smile from somewhere within, and what surprised her was how easy it had been to find, even here on this rocking hijacked airplane high in the bright blue American sky. It had only been basking just below the surface, as it had been doing, it seemed, for every second of every day of the past two years.

—So we'll just stay in here, then?

—I think so, he said, nodding. —Unless you want to go out there and see what's happening.

—Do you?

—No.

—Then nor do I.

—So we'll just stay in here and wait till we land. See what happens then.

—Yes.

—Fine by me.

—Me, too.

Silence for a moment, just the straining engines. So small the space they were in that they must touch each other, must stand face to face, their hands on each other's shoulders.

—We're still going to get married, aren't we?

—God, yes, of course we are. Nothing's ever going to stop that. Not even a fucking hijack.

—And at least we saw Boston.

—Yes, and we'll still see L.A. as well, cos that's where we're going to get married. Maybe not tomorrow, now, but it'll still happen. I promise it will.

She kissed him then, just once on the cheek. Smelled his aftershave and he her shampoo.

—When will we tell our mums and dads? Wait till we get home or call them from L.A.?

—Oh, Christ, I don't know. Let's not worry about that till after the ceremony, okay? Either way, they're going to go mad. I can hear me dad already, going on about what Father Mulcahy will say. How I've disgraced the church and all that shite, marrying a heathen. Twenty-first century, Dad, Jeez.

—Yeh. Mine are . . . they'll be shattered. Dread to think what they'll do, me tying the knot with an infidel, like. The way me dad freaked out when me sister told him she didn't want the arranged marriage. It was awful. Smashed every window in the spare bedroom, he did. Completely flipped. Scared me. But arranged marriages! In two thousand and one!

—Aye, I know. Friggin' stupid. I love me folks and all that, but . . .

—So do I. But I love you more. Or in a better way.

—Same with me. From when I first saw you.

—What, that first time we met at Larks in the Park? You loved me then? At first sight?

—No, not really. But it didn't take long. Just a week or two and I knew you were the one. Only one ever.

—What, out of the hundreds?

—Yes. So? I shagged around a bit, so what? You did, too.

—Not as much as you. A few times, maybe. Not like I was a virgin or anything.

—Doesn't matter, does it? All the others in the past, for both of us, they're just not important. It's just you and me, now.

—Just us two.

—Yes.

—That's what's important.

—That's all that counts.

—That's all that's ever mattered, *ever.*

Quiet for a second then she remembered something. —Ey, remember that song we heard the other day, at Heathrow? Can't remember who it's by or what it's called but it said something about love being like friendship set on fire. Remember it?

—Yes.

—Well it's true, isn't it? That's exactly what it's like, isn't it?

A meeting of lips. Then a mingling of tongues, the two wet muscles in a rigorous wrestle. Two breaths suddenly heavier.

—God, can you believe this? I'm getting horny. Stuck in the bog of a hijacked plane and I'm getting a friggin' hard-on.

She looked down and laughed.

—What's so funny?

—We've still got our trousers down, look.

He looked down and laughed, too, and then was thrown against her as the plane tipped suddenly forward, nose down.

—What's happening?

—I think we're descending.

—The plane might be. But you're not.

She tugged a groan from him. The straining of the engines became a scream.

—I don't care what's happening out there. I'd be happy to stay in here forever.

—Me too.

Nothing but groans for a bit. Then, from her, —Say, just say, that these are our last moments alive. How would you want to spend them?

—Guess, he said, and then was inside her, and whatever was going to happen was in a moment gone and all there was was her and him and the linking of their bodies and the touching of their flesh and the pounding of their hearts felt deep within each other's diaphragm and the swapping of their breath from mouth to mouth and the exchange of souls from eye to eye. And the contrasting colors of those eyes and the contrasting colors of their skins but never a clashing in such opposites.

The plane descended. It descended at so steep an incline that they were forced even closer together, even deeper together and they had to hold each other even tighter, clutching, clasping, tighter than they'd ever held each other before. And what nobody saw—not the plane's other passengers nor the hijackers themselves nor those on the city streets below with their necks craned upward nor those in the offices of the towers nor even the billions who would gape aghast at their TV screens across the entire planet—what none of these people saw as the plane hit the building and cracked apart, was a couple ejected from the tail area of the aircraft upward into the clear blue sky with incredible force and at incredible speed and, despite the violence of their expulsion, continued to remain linked as they rocketed up into the blueness because *that's* how very, very tightly they were holding each other.

Must Bite

Vicki Hendricks

I thought I'd seen everything and survived it—and I was fucking sick of it. I'd been dancing in Key Largo for four years, since age twenty-one, and men were nothing but work to me. I enjoyed women's company—but women being a dead end economically, I was looking for a dick with major dollar signs flashing. I was ready to pack up for Miami because summer in the Keys was such poor pickings. Then came my lucky night, so I thought, the night Rex turned up at the club.

Sleaze, the manager, came into the dressing room to get me, so I knew he'd got a tip.

"He wants the monkey," Sleaze told me. "That be you."

"The monkey?" I caught my breath. "Who is he?" Spunky Monkey was the nickname Pop had given me back home in Indiana, but he was long dead, and nobody in the Keys knew the name.

"Guy in his forties. Big guy. Wad of cash."

"He asked for Monkey?"

"Yeah. You used the trapeze last number, right?"

I nodded.

Sleaze jerked his thumb toward the bar.

"Cool." I tossed on a robe over my bare shoulders and moved my ass out. I had a real acrobatics performance and I felt appreciated when it wasn't wasted on a bunch of drooly burnouts. The usual crowd didn't care if you could keep time with the music, as long as they could smell your cunt. Tips were lean at Reefers, and a special request meant I could set my own price, the best kind of reward.

It was odd hearing the name Monkey again. I was compact and muscular, and kept up my gymnastic skills from junior high, so it was a compliment. Although being a redhead, I had less body hair than most of the girls, and with my big blue eyes, I didn't really look like a monkey.

He was facing toward me from the bar, catching my tit action as I walked, what little there was. Attractive, considering he was close to fifty. Had a tan face, salt-and-pepper hair, and a hard, smooth jaw. About twice my size, sitting down. I was barely a hundred pounds, the smallest chick during the off-season. I took my stance in front of him, legs wide, hands on hips, robe thrown back on my arms. It was how I met all the big boys.

"I'm Darlene. Lap dance?"

"Let me look and decide."

He'd seen all there was, since I'd already swung naked with my legs wide open a foot over his head, but I turned around and bent over, lifting the robe to my waist. The thin chain of the G-string didn't cover my little shaved mound from behind, and I got wet, feeling his eyes home in. Pop always told me it was a good thing to enjoy your work because that's mostly what life is made of. Too bad I didn't enjoy it quite enough.

I bent farther and looked between my legs. His mouth was part open, and I got a sudden need for his tongue, like I could come the instant it split me.

"I'd like a date," he said.

I stood up and turned around. "I don't do dates." I always lied to get the price up.

"Never?"

"Not much."

He grabbed my arm as I started to walk and showed me three hundreds. I asked for four. His place. After work. He'd wait outside.

When I came out a little after two, it was raining and smelled like a jungle, musty and thick, mosquitoes swarming around the light under the awning, waiting to bite, tree frogs with their creepy grunts. There was one car, sparkling under the low, streaming palms, headlights shining through the downpour, beacons to my fate. He pulled up, and the passenger side opened. I slung my ass on the leather seat.

"Cool Mercedes." He smiled at my thin wet shirt.

He held out his hand for me to shake. "Rex."

He turned left behind Shell World, and we passed the Blue Fin Marina, then snaked down a long private drive. It was dark. Dripping vines and fronds dragged across my window, and the Mercedes bumped along slow. He pulled up under a two-story concrete-block house on stilts, and when I got out I could hear the lapping of water out back, either a bay or the ocean, and caught the scent of rotten eggs that reminds you when it's low tide in the Keys.

He motioned me up the stairs on the side and flicked on a light. We passed sacks of feed and huge empty cages, scratched mirrors, a rope ladder, chewed-up rubber toys, and a large doll. Her eyes followed me, or so I thought. Rex crooked his finger at me and I climbed the stairs, wondering if I'd get a chance to see what this was all about. He seemed to have a rule about not talking. I could handle it.

Rex opened the door to a Florida room with a built-in bar, lots of shiny bottles on the shelves, sparkling mirror tiles. He picked up a glass. I shook my head. I'd had too much of that sickening champagne at the club. He put his finger to his lips, and I followed him past two closed doors with small barred windows, tiptoeing. Sounds of huffing, snoring, and heavy movement came from inside. Must be renting out rooms to crazy old farts, I thought. He led me upstairs to the loft. The rain had stopped, and clouds drifted over the moon outside the balcony window.

It wasn't the usual trick. He didn't act cool and order me around. He took me in his arms and kissed my neck, breathing hot, and holding back my hair to uncover more skin. Normally, I would have broken it off and set some rules, but I was geared up to think that something interesting could come of this, with his bucks. I dropped my snotty whore act and let myself go. He held my head back and planted the softest kisses on my mouth. His breath was sweet, no garlic, no rotten teeth, no cigarettes. I wondered how he was with mine. I kissed him back and he had to cut it off to get a breath. Then he stripped me down so softly, I felt like I was the one who paid. I held onto the dresser as he knelt in front of me, his fingers opening me up, and tongued my clit. I came hard, and he pulled me on top of him into the bed.

I let him do everything he wanted, not even thinking so much of the money. In all the years since Pop turned me out, I'd never felt so appreciated by a man. I was loose as a rag doll when he flipped me over and got on top, but he kept pumping strong and even, until I actually came from his cock, and that didn't happen often.

That night he made sure I'd want to see more of him. He knew how good he was, and the attention I needed. Looking back, I'm sure he'd searched for a girl like me in all the local places, my athletic build and helpful personality, my need to get out of that disgusting club. And the nickname Monkey. When I told him how he hit on that, I saw the light come into his eyes. I was a perfect fit. Life would've been so good if was that simple.

The next morning I opened my eyes to bright sun sneaking through the blinds. I was surprised at the clean tropical style of the bedroom. No sign of mismatched pieces of furniture with broken arms or rings from glasses, no scary stained sheets, not even a scratchy couch with burn holes, like most Key Largo guys seemed to own. The bed and nightstands were heavy-duty bamboo, stuff I'd buy if I saw it in the thrift shop. The curtains and sheets were a leafy pattern with light green and beige. He had orchids and other plants outside on the balcony, all stuff that blended nice and looked happy. I thought he might have hired a decorator, but later I realized it was his talent, knowing just what fit together.

"Nice place," I said when I saw his eyes open.

"Want to stay?"

I tried to calculate a price for the day, not sure how long he meant.

"Come on. Let me show you around."

I started to climb out of bed, but my foot got tangled in the sheet and he caught me before I fell. His hands went straight to my hips, and then I couldn't resist that tongue. He dug right into the pussy, and it was an hour before we dragged ourselves out. I was set up good. If I hadn't been looking at the situation through the blur of sex, I might have had better sense. Then again, it was a wonderland to me.

"Now you stand behind me when I open the door," he said. We were outside of one of the two doors on the first floor. I stepped back so I could only see his big body. "Hey, guys," he said, "I have somebody for you to meet." He turned to me. "It's okay. They're relaxed."

He stepped aside. I knew these were not going to be humans from the sounds I could hear. There they were, four monkeys, two of them nearly my size, looking at me. The smallest one had a finger in its mouth, like a child. The ceiling was high, must have been two stories, and there were monkey-sized trapezes mounted on beams. The windows were barred. A few piles of shit were off to the sides, and one wall had a hole punched through the plasterboard, exposing more bars inside the wall. I could see through a barred door in the middle of the wall that there was a bigger monkey in the next room. A weird feeling ran through me. I didn't know what my purpose was, but being there was no accident.

"Hear No Evil, Think No Evil, and Speak No Evil?" I asked, pointing one, two, three. "I'm not sure of the order."

"They're not quite that well behaved."

Two of them came over and I reached down to take the hand held out to me. The long fingers were warm and light, like a good pair of leather gloves.

Rex touched their heads gently. "These are spider monkeys, females, Itsy and Bitsy."

"Went up the waterspout?"

"You got it, but don't give me credit for those names, either. The other two are Mack and Sweetums, male and female."

I could see what seemed to be penises hanging from three of their asses, but no balls. "Females?"

"Spider monkeys have elongated vaginas. It makes mating impossible, except when they're fertile, every four years. Rape-proofing."

"The boys must get horny."

"Mack masturbates often—although not as much as Big Man." He pointed into the next room.

Sweetums stayed back, but Mack came up and took my hand, putting my fingers into the coarse hair on his back. I started to scratch and he leaned into it. "Don't let him get carried away," said Rex. I took my hand off, and sure enough Mack grabbed my wrist and forced my hand back between his shoulder blades.

"They're willful." Rex pried the long fingers from my wrist and disentangled the legs and tail clutching my thigh. He took Mack's wrists in one hand and pushed his body back with his shoulder. Mack arched and squirmed, making shrill shrieks. Rex tossed him into the mattress in the corner.

"Dash."

I broke for the door and Rex pushed it almost closed behind us, but not quite, because he had to stop and tuck a small hand inside. "They like you," he said. "A lot. I knew it. Be careful what you start."

"Don't they usually like people?"

"Not really."

"So where did you get all these monkeys?" I could hear the other one rumbling around, wanting attention.

He locked the door and opened the next room. The monkey was waiting for us and took my hand in his warm grip. "This is the chimp, Big Man. He's an ape, not a monkey. He was named when I got him. You'll see why."

"I do already," I said. "He's as tall as me."

"That's not what I mean." He used his fingers to sign words as he spoke to Big Man. "Darlene friend," he said as he signed. Big Man puckered up, but I couldn't quite bring myself to kiss him.

Rex took my hand and motioned me to walk out in front of him. Big Man glared but didn't move. Rex turned and spoke as he signed. "Bye-bye. Breakfast time." He shut the door and locked it.

"You taught them sign language?"

"No, when we bought Big Man they told us he understood signs. I learned some words so I could sign to him, but he never signs back. I think he understands, though."

"What about the spiders?"

"He taught them, I think, but they don't pay much attention."

"Big Man must be bored."

"I entertain him. One chimp is hard enough to handle. Come on. I'll get their breakfast."

Rex led me into the kitchen. It was huge, with two stainless-steel refrigerators. He opened one filled with vegetables. "I knew they'd take to you."

"I like them, too," I said.

I was starving, but I didn't say anything because the animals were waiting. They were hungry and dependent on Rex, and it was my fault that breakfast was late. I insisted on helping. We set everything out on the long preparation table and sink. I washed pounds of carrots and celery and bags of apples, while Rex rinsed heads of lettuce. Then we divided the vegetables onto two trays and poured the monkey chow into the five bowls with their names.

Together we served them, first Big Man, then Itsy and Bitsy, Sweetums and Mack. I stood outside the window and watched them eat. Big Man sat and stuffed his face with a head of lettuce, pieces falling from his open mouth, making a big wet mess on the floor as he chewed, showing us how he was starved because we were upstairs fucking. Itsy and Bitsy chowed down too, occasionally glancing over their shoulders at me. I knew the feeling, your meals being in someone else's control. Been there.

Mack started on the carrots, gnawing them down like a buzz saw, and Sweetums crunched celery, holding it a stick at a time, nibbling, just like a person.

Rex sponged up the water and dirt we'd left on the countertop, while I made the coffee.

"So where did you get them?" I asked him.

"It was a business."

"Monkey business?"

He laughed. "You got it."

"Circus?"

"No, a petting zoo of sorts, with some shows. The stage and big cages are still outside. It was my ex's idea, Julia. She taught them the tricks and it was fun—for a while. We never made money, all spent on food and vet care, but she had money anyway. The Monkey Hut was her hobby. You want some bacon and eggs?"

"Sure. And then she split?"

"She left me the place and investments so I could take care of the monkeys."

"Ouch," I said.

"She was generous. It was my fault. We never talked."

"She never complained?"

"She might have."

He put a skillet on the stove and went into the second refrigerator and pulled out a package of bacon and a carton of eggs. "They'll smell this," he said. "Ignore the noise. I don't give them meat. Spider monkeys are vegetarian, and Big Man gets too wild. He wants it all."

The bacon had barely started to sizzle when there was a loud howl. Others took up the scream and then there was pounding, like one was beating a tray. The screeching got louder and one of them started banging on the door.

"Metal doors?" I asked.

"Yeah, don't worry. They'll settle down in a minute."

It took about five minutes, but I thought, fuck, Rex is a kind man to care for all these animals, and I could live in a place like this. He could even make me come, unusual for a man. By then I didn't have any romantic notions. I'd settle for a nice home, some monkeys to play with. I was sure I could still get out now and then with my girlfriends. So Rex was devoted to monkeys, and I was the new monkey. That must have flickered in his mind when he saw me, and I had nothing against it—if enough money came my way.

Over the next month, I got on well with everybody. Rex and I took care of their meals together, and I scratched backs and gave treats, and they brightened up every time I came into their rooms. At dusk, I fixed the strawberry yogurt, oatmeal, and flan combination that filled out their dietary needs. They'd stick their little faces into it or squeeze it through their fingers and lick it off. I felt appreciated, more than I'd ever have expected, more than most of my life.

I told Rex if he installed a big trapeze in the spiders' room, I would come by and swing with them. He had it up in two days, no surprise. I climbed up naked and went into my act, swinging with my ass on the bar, then dropping to hang by my knees, but before I got any farther, Mack swung over and whipped past me, switching from hands to feet to tail and flinging himself to the other trapezes and back again. I couldn't compete. He scared me by coming so close, but he was perfect in his moves. Sweetums joined in and soon they were both swinging fast and switching hands, feet, and tails, synchronizing with each other. I pulled myself up to watch.

"Don't stop," Rex hollered. "I want to see you, not them."

I hung by my arms and swung a little and pulled up my legs above my body in a split across the bar, like I'd done that first night, twisted around under it.

Rex stood up and came over. The trapeze was just high enough that his tongue could lick my pussy, no accident, and he licked it a couple of times as I swung toward him and then he grabbed me. The monkeys kept cavorting around us, but he ate me like a starving man, ignoring them, and I hung limp on the trapeze, all feeling concentrated in my clit. When I opened my eyes, all four spiders were watching, and Big Man was grunting in the next room. I didn't mind giving the show.

I wasn't sure who thought of marriage first, but things moved fast. A captain friend of Rex's married us on his sailboat, and we put on a party at Reefers. Sleaze got in some decent champagne specially for me. It was a nice party with chicken wings and nachos, but I was glad to be saying good-bye to that place, and all the sucking up to creeps that went with it.

We'd planned on a honeymoon in the Bahamas for a few days, but on the morning after the wedding, Bitsy got sick, and we had to cancel. Rex was afraid to leave her with the sitter, a teenage boy that was supposed to stop by. She didn't look that sick to me, no puking or diarrhea, but she just lay on the mattress and held her stomach instead of eating her breakfast. Rex said that was a sure sign. After we'd canceled our flight we looked in on her, and she had gotten up and was eating the remains from Itsy, and I thought sure she'd faked her illness, but it was too late to worry about it. Rex promised we could try again soon, but "the kids" didn't like everyone, and they needed lots of human interaction every day, so it was tricky. I never counted on things until they happened—it wasn't any big deal. I had my own island there separated from outsiders. The monkeys were more fun than most people I knew, and honest in their needs.

I had them spoiled in the first week. I started giving them an extra treat or two each day, a cookie or a few crackers. They really liked the crunchy stuff. They loved French fries, too, but I was careful not to go too far with the grease. None of them would keep a diaper on. I hadn't counted on so much shit, but it seemed to pile up more and more, maybe from the treats, or else Rex was falling down on the cleaning. I hadn't bargained on it, but I started pitching in on shit detail. They were mine now, too, and they would cuddle and kiss me when I sat with them.

"Why not use the big cages outside?" I asked Rex one day. "We could squirt them out easier."

"We used to. You can't keep neighborhood kids from sneaking around, sticking their arms inside."

"The monkeys seem so tame, even Big Man."

He shook his head. "One time Mack grabbed a handful of a girl's hair. He just wanted to smell her shampoo—he does that—but he's so strong. She told her parents he tried to scalp her. The father came back with a gun. Lucky I was home."

"That's crazy."

"Yeah, but they get that look, like a war going on inside. One second everything is nice, nice, love, love, and the next, 'Must bite! Must bite!' flashes in their eyes."

"They're always sweet to me."

"So far. You can't predict when somebody will get jealous or want one of us for himself. Especially Big Man."

Within a couple months, I was doing more than my share of the work, but hey, it was appreciated. By the third month, things started to get a little tedious. Rex had been unemployed for a couple of years, living on the investments. Now with me around, or so he said, we were running short. I wondered why he hadn't figured that out earlier. He didn't ask me to go back to work, but the Mercedes was on lease, and it had to be turned in. We were stuck with the old pickup that was used for carting the monkeys in cages to the vet and bringing home bags of feed.

Rex started giving sailing lessons at the yacht club. Seems that was his job when he met Julia, and they were always after him to come back and teach. Now he was gone most of the day, and every morning during prime feeding time. Not working was far more labor than I had imagined. I didn't know his finances were so tight or I might have had second thoughts about the deal. Still, I got to drink piña coladas and lay around in the sun all afternoon on my own private beach, and sometimes my best girlfriend from the club would come by to keep up her all-over tan, and we'd order pizza or sushi. Rex knew it, and must've figured we fooled around, being dancer types, but he never said anything. I always gave him whatever he wanted, and he did his part in that area.

At first, we went out to dinner most nights. There was so much food prep for the monkeys that he said the whole day would be taken up by food if we cooked dinner. There were lots of nice seafood places, and we had our favorites. At night, we'd sit at the huge window overlooking our bay and listen to music, gazing out at the stars and the water. He had a light behind the house so we could see the palms blowing and the sparkle of waves. On the first night of a full moon, he turned the light off and we sat there in the dark and waited for the moon to come up. It cast its glittery trail across the water, and I thought it was a magic road leading right to me, where I had found my jackpot.

Sometimes we'd put on Mack's leash and take him out behind the house, where he could be fastened to a rail left from the tourist attraction days. He really enjoyed the fresh air, and he would sit in a palm that slanted near the edge of the water. Sometimes he flirted, throwing me kisses, and I'd unhook him and let him cuddle next to me and pick through my hair.

Our eating at nice places and star gazing got less and less over the weeks and months. Rex started to watch TV sports in the den a few nights a week. Sometimes he went out with his buddies, leaving me there to sip my drink and count the stars alone and listen to the grunting and banging. It was eerie.

One night I thought one of the spiders was being used for a punching bag. When I opened the door, Itsy and Bitsy were grooming each other, Mack and Sweetums were swinging, and Big Man was racked out in the other room playing with his toe, the door between the rooms closed as we generally left it. They all looked up at me, like, "What's your problem?" I think they could hear my footsteps, or see me in their mirrors, and it was all a trick to get my attention. I started to suspect they knew more than they let on.

These ruckuses started to break out often in both rooms, and I'd go in to check on them and scratch backs, bring treats. Mack or Big Man would often sit there and masturbate, looking at my face. Sometimes the females would be fingering themselves.

I'd sign a few phrases I'd learned to Big Man, but he just stared at me. He was stubborn. They were bored, poor things, him especially, because he was smarter and more isolated. I wanted to swing with them and get some exercise, but when I mentioned it to Rex he said that was too dangerous if he wasn't home, and I knew he was right. I saw them when the softness in their eyes turned flat and hard, like there was something wild ready to break out, the sudden animal impulse that came over them for no reason. That's when I'd race for the door.

Rex went out two nights in a row one week and I was really pissed. He had a friend down from Miami, but I was almost mad enough and bored enough to head over to Reefers and see some of the regulars. I started to get dressed and then I thought about them—the regulars—and remembered the smell of that place, and I wasn't that bored. I realized I had a better friend in the next room.

Big Man was calm, and he knew what the leash meant, so it was no problem to hook him up and lead him to the back patio to sit with me in the cool evening air. After he sat for a while in his palm, he came down to sit on the bottom of the lounge chair and I gave him pieces of ice from my drink. Then he stood behind my back and groomed me. I don't know what he found there, but his cool fingers picking through my hair was like a massage, and we both enjoyed it. I wasn't sure if Rex would like the idea, so I didn't mention it. Big Man knew if he acted up, he would never get out with me again. It wasn't like he'd try to escape. He'd been born in captivity and he knew where his meals came from. He was more civilized than some of those regulars at Reefers. It became our little secret. Every time Rex went out, Big Man got out.

As the nights turned cooler toward Christmas, Big Man would sit next to me and doze off with his head on my chest. He'd wake up drowsy and look at my face. "Nice, nice," glowed in his round eyes. But the animal was always close. Sometimes he'd jump, as if I'd hit him, and his lips would curl back. "Must bite, must bite," was fighting to take over his brain. I'd get out of his way until he settled down. But he wasn't so different from the guys at the bar overall. You never knew with men.

Around this time, I started to get suspicious of Rex. He didn't have much time for sex or monkey tricks, and started spending every day at the yacht club and helping out at the bar four or five nights a week. Since the snowbirds were down, it made sense that he had more work, but I thought he might be seeing another woman. If you think it, it's true, they always say. Follow your instincts. Maybe she was a snowbird, and this was a yearly rendezvous. I was split in my head because on one hand I had my own girlfriend, but I didn't like that Rex was sneaking around and leaving me home bored at night and peeling bananas all day. I wondered if that was his plan all along, find some sucker for the monkeys so he could be with his girlfriend. Maybe she didn't like monkeys and I was his chance to make a break. Maybe that was what his wife did to him.

The difference was that Julia had money. She left him with investments and the house, and still had enough to take off. He was pretty much stuck with me, unless he wanted to leave with nothing. I started to think I could do without him fine, but even if he left me with everything, finances would still be lousy. I'd have to take care of the monkeys and go back to spreading my ass besides.

Finally, one night Rex stayed home with me, and we were having a drink on the patio like the old days. Big Man was making a ruckus inside, and I knew why, but Rex ignored it. I was unhappy, having picked up shit all day and made dinner, and he walked in and made himself comfortable without a word of thanks. I tried to act normal and talk about all the cute things the monkeys did. Then I asked the important question.

"What will the monkeys do if something happens to us?"

"I guess you'll be here when I'm gone," he said.

"Great. I can't handle them."

He took a drink of his scotch. "Don't worry. I have a big life insurance policy. You can get any extra help you need. These guys could live to be forty."

"Forty! How much money?"

"A million. My wife set that up, too, so the monkeys would be taken care of, no matter what."

"That was pretty generous, but if they live till forty—"

"She has plenty of money. She felt responsible for these guys, even though she hated them."

"Hated them?"

"Yeah, I don't know why. Big Man scared her one day, and she never forgave him. After that she didn't want to be near any of them."

"What did he do?"

"Nothing. She said he was going to do something."

I figured Julia just wanted out, and that was the easiest way. If you had money everything was easy.

We both kept drinking. That was the only thing we enjoyed together anymore, but it made me hostile.

"So what are the monkeys and me supposed to do all the time when you're gone?"

"Shh. You're too loud."

"So what? Nobody around here."

"You'll wake them."

I got louder on purpose. "Well, they're in this, too. You don't spend any time with them."

He whispered. "I have to work. Somebody has to."

"You don't make much."

"I don't wave my naked ass in anybody's face."

"You sure?"

He gave me a disgusted look. I didn't ask again. It didn't matter what he was doing. It was how he tricked me, setting me up to think he had money, forcing me into the boring, shit job he was sick of. I almost left right then, but I'd have been right back where I started.

After that night, the million bucks wouldn't leave me alone. It taunted me every morning when I cut vegetables and afternoons when I scrubbed shit off the walls and windows, slimy lettuce from the floor, washed sour soggy monkey biscuit out of all the water bowls, and scraped yogurt and oatmeal from the windowsill. After about a week I realized that although Rex was a lot older, I couldn't hold out till he died. Nothing was the way it was supposed to be. I was a cheap slave to a man, trapped with wild children that would never grow up. I was angry that he'd tangled my emotions into the mess.

I started my training plan. I concentrated on Big Man because he could do the job alone, and the others would follow his lead. I had our wedding picture blown up huge, and I cut Rex's face out of it and mounted it with a stick inside a shirt and jeans that I got out of the dirty laundry and stuffed with Rex's underwear. I padded the stick with foam rubber so it looked like a neck and put an X on the left side where the jugular would be. I sewed sets of cocks and balls out of foam to stuff inside the pants.

I fried up a pound of bacon, and put it into the refrigerator, knowing the shit was going to fly if I had to do much rewarding, but I could handle it. I coaxed Big Man into the kitchen on his leash, signing. "Bacon, bacon, Big Man." I had a strip inside the oven, and I stood in front of it with the dummy. "Big Man, bite," I said and signed it to him. I pointed to the X and signed it again and again. "Big Man, bite."

His head moved high and low from side to side. He sniffed to find the bacon, but the whole room was filled with the smell. I held the dummy near his face and signed "Bite," pointing to the X. "Bite." I signed "I give bacon." I signed "bite" and "bacon," "bite" and "bacon," but he didn't get it, or pretended not to. I was aggravated. I took the dummy and bit it on the X, shaking my head like a shark in a frenzy. I opened the oven and grabbed the bacon and flopped it on the neck. I shoved the dummy at Big Man and he bit lightly—all he wanted was the bacon—but it was a start.

I opened the refrigerator to get another piece. Big mistake. Big Man grabbed the platter and pushed me down. The leash came right out of my hand. He sat on the floor and ate the whole pound in twenty seconds. I realized I had little control. That night the shit was beyond anything I would have believed, but I got most of it cleaned up before Rex came home.

The next day I hooked Big Man outside. I wanted him to know that the bacon was all mine and he would only get it if he did what I said. I brought out the bacon and set it on a table outside his reach. He went wild. He jerked at the chain and his eyes bounced from me to the bacon and back. He drooled. I dug into the back of the broom closet and got the dummy and stood there signing and saying, "Big Man, bite. I give bacon."

He started making his hooting chimp noises, trying to coax me, full of glee.

"What does Big Man want?" I said. "Tell Darlene," I signed.

He continued to hoot and I held the dummy near him. "Kill Rex, get bacon," I said. "Kill Rex!" I handed him the dummy but not the bacon. "Bite Rex!" I held out a strip. "Kill Rex!"

Finally, he curled back his lips and ripped a chunk out of the rubber. I grabbed two strips of bacon and stuck them at him. He grabbed them with his hand and shoved them into his mouth. Then he grabbed the dummy and ripped every shred of rubber off the neck.

We went on half the day that way, with several repaired necks, moving down to the genitals, until I could barely say the word *bite* and he'd have his teeth on the dummy, tearing the rubber away. After he'd shredded all the parts, I let him rip out the stuffing and toss it around. I knew I had a load of shit coming that night, but Big Man would do his job when I asked him.

I could tell he was into it. His animal nature was taking control. He must have known that Rex had let him down, and I played up my role as his pal, chaining him in the kitchen one day, giving him all my attention. He sat on a chair, and watched me wash and cut fruit and vegetables all morning. After a while, I heard him making a familiar grunt and when I turned, he was pumping his cock. His eyes were soft and his lips were curled in a smile as he came on the seat of the kitchen chair. He was with me all the way.

I decided the best way to do it was in one big rush. I'd unlock the doors while Rex was having his coffee, and wait for Big Man to find his way into the kitchen when I started frying the bacon. I'd sign "Kill Rex," behind his back, and in the few seconds that Rex had to live, he'd think he was meeting his natural fate, the fate he deserved for betraying his children. The county would take all the monkeys away, most likely destroy them, and I tried not to think of that, but I'd be free with the million. Nobody would suspect me, because it would be so clear, an accident waiting to happen. The crazy guy with the monkeys had been asking for it for years.

I didn't waste any time. That afternoon I put the dummy clothes in the wash and threw the foam rubber in the trash, burned the photo face. Nobody could put all that together.

The next morning Rex was sitting at the kitchen table, reading the paper as usual. I'd unlocked the cage doors while the monkeys were still asleep. I told Rex I felt like making some bacon and eggs. When I said the word, the hooting started. Big Man went wild and the others followed. Rex shook his head and kept reading.

The bacon barely started to crackle when Big Man came leaping through the door. I don't think he even saw me sign. He knocked Rex to the floor and bit into his throat, tearing away flesh, much easier than he had the rubber. Blood shot out and he kept on biting and spitting out the pieces. Rex dropped, unconscious in seconds. It was more horrible than I had imagined. Big Man moved down and tore up his cock and balls, yanking them off with his hand, ripping the sack with his teeth. I was frozen watching.

Big Man didn't forget the bacon. He looked at me and I jumped aside, and he picked up the half-cooked pieces three at a time and stuffed them into his bloody mouth. Mack, Sweetums, Itsy, and Bitsy were in the doorway watching, excited. I knew I had no control over the situation and I started toward the door to make my break down the stairs. Big Man had already finished with the bacon, and he leaped to block the way, with more "must bite" in his eyes. I grabbed a sharp vegetable knife off the sink, but he reached for my wrist and twisted. The knife fell to the floor. "Bacon!" I yelled and pointed toward the stove. He turned and let loose, and I ran the opposite direction into the monkey rooms and slammed the door to wait until they'd all settled down. I didn't count on Big Man locking me in.

I was at their mercy, caged for hours, had to pee in the corner. I wasn't anywhere near as strong as they were, and obviously no smarter, so there was no hope unless somebody came to the house. That didn't happen often. I thought they might get bored eventually and let me out, take care of me, as I had taken care of them—or better—but they seemed to take no interest.

They were banging around in the kitchen—no doubt, eating all the food, tossing pans, breaking dishes, and yanking out drawers. After a long time, things got quiet. I woke up at dusk. Big Man's face was at the window. Maybe he wanted me to fix the yogurt and oatmeal or sit with him, the way we did in the evenings. I went to the door. "Big Man, let Darlene out," I said and signed. "Big Man, unlock door."

He looked at me and got a big grin, pulling his lips out, snorting and mocking me. His hands came close to the window and he moved his fingers. I couldn't believe it. He was signing. He'd known how to do it all along. "Darlene kill Rex," he signed.

"No!" I signed, "Big Man kill Rex!"

He started with that chimp laugh that made my skin crawl, a piercing, mocking hoot that went on and on. "Darlene kill Rex," he signed while he laughed. He bent down then, and I thought he was unlocking the door. I wasn't sure I wanted out. But that wasn't it. His face came back up and he was holding the sharp knife in his teeth by the blade. It was covered in Rex's blood. He signed, "Darlene kill Rex."

My guts froze. The handle of the knife had my prints on it. But it was impossible that he could know that, a coincidence how he was holding it. I had to get that knife. I kicked the door and banged with my fists, and he ran off. I sat down on the floor, drained and horrified. In a few minutes the door was unlocked. I looked out. Nobody there. No knife. Now I didn't think the police knew sign language or would listen to a chimp, but they would take the knife for evidence. As the beneficiary of a million bucks, I was in trouble.

The spiders were lounging all over the couch and chair in the living room, groggy, greedy monkeys, limbs dangling. Liquor fumes were thick, and bottles broken, so they might have been drinking. There were piles of shit on the carpet. I walked past it all into the kitchen. Garbage, blood, and shit were everywhere. The refrigerator was open and empty, milk and orange juice cartons smashed, pickles and ketchup and lettuce trampled on the tile floor. They'd eaten at least two days, worth of carrots, celery, bananas, oranges. A fifty-pound bag of monkey biscuit, was dumped in the corner and somebody had peed on it. A package of raw bacon was ripped open and tossed into a pan still in the wrapper.

A river of blood showed that Rex's body had been dragged under the table. I looked and held my breath. Besides the torn and bitten flesh there were clearly knife wounds, the throat slit from the right ear to the mangled, stringy part on the left, the head nearly severed. I gagged up the small amount of food in my stomach. Everything was wrong. I wanted Rex back. He hadn't been so bad. I heard something behind me and stood up. Big Man walked in and signed, "Darlene kill Rex."

"Where's the knife, Big Man?"

He started to laugh, and I knew by then that none of this was coincidence. He'd been waiting for his chance, playing me, just like I'd thought I was playing him, and Rex had played me. Predator and prey, back and forth. I bent over and gagged some more, and then pulled myself up, steadying on the wall. Big Man was staring at me. He kept laughing until that animal look came into his eyes. He pulled his cock and it grew out long and hard. I jerked with the impulse to run, but he looked down at himself. He sat on the chair and worked his pud, and I looked around for the knife. All I had to do was find it and wipe off my prints. Without evidence, nobody would believe a freaking monkey. I could tell the cops I was locked in the monkey rooms, and that's why it took me so long to call. I'd collect my million and leave them all to rot.

I got down on my hands and knees and raked through the slimy trash with my fingers. The knife could be anywhere in the house or even outside. I tried to think like an ape, but my brain was dead. I would never find it like that. He was too smart. The only way was to convince Big Man to show me. I didn't have much time.

Big Man was rocking and grunting, and I watched his come squirt out onto the chair. He would be calm for a while. It was my chance for one last bargain. I looked at him and signed, "Darlene wants knife." I turned my back to him, slipped my shorts and panties down, and bent over. It always worked with men—or so I'd thought. "Darlene loves Big Man." I bent farther and watched him from between my legs. He grinned and hooted, showing his mouthful of long yellow teeth and dark gums. I had his attention.

Smelling of Roses

Clare Colvin

I hear them as they move about the house. I hear their laughter, the squalling of a child, feet running up- and downstairs. Sometimes the wife comes into the bedroom and places a posy of flowers on the dressing table, which signals the arrival of a guest. I am aware of people moving around the room, of the bed creaking, of curtains being drawn and undrawn. I cannot see them distinctly, for that requires more energy than I possess. I feel no empathy with the wife, she seems too far removed from me. But occasionally a person arrives whom I recognize. I am aware of them before they even enter the room. I can scent them. It happens rarely, once in a decade perhaps, and I wait, and hope. Today I can smell the difference in the air. It is happening again.

Juliet was standing at the front door, in her hand a Harrods carrier bag containing a few clothes and cosmetics. There were bruises around her neck and a discolored swelling over her eye. As Laura opened the door, Juliet burst into tears. Laura put her arms around her, guided her to the kitchen, and sat her down in a chair. "Don't try to explain," she said. "Let me get you some tea, take your time."

Once she had poured the tea, Laura's curiosity could be

contained no more. She said in a soothing voice, though with a hint of avidity, "Tell me what happened."

"He's mad," said Juliet. Her eyes had the blankness that comes with shock. "He's certifiable, he's paranoid with jealousy. Look!"

She drew out of the Harrods bag a cardboard placard with a string loop attached. On it was written in capital letters with a black felt-tip: I AM A FAITHLESS BITCH.

"He told me to wear it around my neck and when I refused he beat me up."

Her shoulders shook with sobs. Laura, patting her hand and fighting back the feeling of mirth that welled up inside her, said, "There, there, you're safe now," and then, momentarily alarmed, "He doesn't know where you are, does he?"

"I went upstairs, shoved a few things in the bag, then made a run for it when he had to answer the phone. I was in the car starting the engine by the time he got to the door, and he couldn't do anything because there was a policeman going by."

"Could you have told the police?" asked Laura, but Juliet cried all the more.

"I'm so ashamed . . . I'm so tired . . ."

Laura got to her feet, accepting the inevitable. "Come, I'll show you to the spare room and then you can rest as long as you like. And I don't want you to worry about where to go next. Think of this as your sanctuary for a while."

As Laura drove to school to fetch Benjie she rehearsed in her mind what she would say to Mark that evening. The conversation ran as she had feared.

Mark: How long will this lame duck of yours be staying?
Laura: She's a friend and she's in trouble. You know that Brian is an absolute bastard.

Mark: So he is, but she didn't have to marry him. Was she unfaithful?

Laura (heatedly): Why should it matter? Is that a reason for beating her up?

Mark: Well, was she?

Laura: She was vague, but I think the answer is probably no.

Mark: What is the point of living quietly in the country if we're going to get involved in messy metropolitan dramas?

Laura: I promise that she won't stay for long.

She is resting and I can hear her breathing evenly now that the crying has subsided. I am aware of her every movement, though she is not yet aware of me. She turns in bed and I feel myself turning. The sheets were always so smooth, so cool. Such fine linen—I can feel them now wrapping me in their white drifts.

Juliet stretched her hands above her head. She touched the polished mahogany of the headboard, and felt the smoothness of the newly laundered sheets against her body. She got out of bed and walked over to the window to draw back the curtains. The room filled with the golden light of early evening and the walls glowed with an abundance of roses. They were not the scattered sprigs or bunches that you see in contemporary versions of old-fashioned wallpaper but a dense mass of blooms without background space. She looked more closely at the astonishing detail of the paper. The flowers were painted like eighteenth-century Dutch still lifes, with a sensitivity to lighting, each petal lit in the sunshine of the artist's imagination. And as with the Dutch masters, there was a mass of insect life. Every few feet of the length of the wallpaper a blue butterfly hovered and a little fly with glinting wings settled at intervals on a damask rose from which one petal floated earthward.

She ran her hand over the wallpaper, feeling the smoothness of what seemed at first sight to be a surface painted in oils. She smiled to herself. Laura was such a genius at interior decoration, but then she excelled in everything to do with the home. She had chosen a loving and sensitive husband to father her children. She had chosen this spacious Georgian house in a north Oxfordshire village, close enough to Oxford for Mark to feel part of the college where he was a fellow, but removed from the claustrophobia of university life. Laura had spent all her free time before the arrival of Benjie traveling to London to select materials and wallpapers, had gathered furniture from country house sales, or had had it bequeathed to her by relatives. Whenever anyone in the family died, Laura's inquiries, after the preliminary expressions of grief, would turn to the disposal of the furniture. Her house had become her work of art and she strove toward its perfection.

As Juliet sat at the dressing table, toning down the bruise over her eye with foundation cream, she reflected on the difference in their lives. They had begun with the same advantages, yet where Laura had planned and had chosen, Juliet had floundered uncertainly and had been chosen. Brian was erratic, he drank, but she had been overwhelmed by his love, until he stopped caring. Their house in Kilburn was a reflection of their marriage. Door handles fell off, window sashes broke, the patio that they were going to whitewash and line with trellis and bay trees developed algae, damp crept up the walls. Chaos and incompatibility around them and within. She had thought a discreet affair would do her good, but Brian had tipped from aggression to paranoia. He had sensed her thoughts before anything happened. The bruises from having her head smashed against the wall were for nothing.

She examined her face in the mirror. The foundation had diminished the bruise to a shadow, but her face was still pale. A pale moth, a moth with dark eyes, Brian had said in the days before he became angry. She put on some more foundation and blackened her lashes with mascara. She would not dream of appearing in company with naked eyes.

In the small living room next to the kitchen, Laura and Mark were sitting with their drinks while supper simmered in the oven. Benjie watched television in his pajamas. The only clue that all was not harmony was Mark's glass of whiskey in preference to sherry. He had erected a newspaper before his face as a barrier against further communication with Laura. As Juliet entered the living room he lowered the newspaper slowly and folded it before rising to his feet. She smiled at him uncertainly, but Mark's politeness forbade him from letting her feel ill at ease. He kissed her on the cheek and said, "This is a welcome surprise. You must flee London more often."

Laura looked relieved. She glanced at Juliet and noticed how carefully she had disguised the bruise over her eye, yet at the same time had left the bruises on her neck uncovered, almost like trophies, Laura thought, of her disaster.

It is only my will that keeps me here like a small black bat clinging to the hangings of this room. I will not let go until I have lived. I am beginning to breathe again, I feel the blood running through my veins.

At first I could only hear her as she invaded the room. Her shoes being dropped near the bed, the creaking of the springs, the sound of her bare feet on the carpet, of her brushing her hair at the dressing table. Now I begin to see, dimly, then more distinctly, the arm moving, the hand clasped around a black-handled brush. I wait in stillness, I wonder whether she can hear my heart beating. Her hair is dark and it lies loosely on her shoulders. She is putting some colored ointment on her face, then she brushes her eyelashes with a stick. She is pretty, though she does not possess my beauty. The way my hair looped and coiled about my head, with the long curling tendrils around my face . . . and then I would take out one pin and another and it would cascade to my waist.

This is my favorite room, for the roses remind me of the rose garden, and it is as peaceful as I can be on my own. Dr. Hislop was sympathetic when I tried to explain, and besides, I do not think he cares much for Alfred. He agreed any disturbance to my equilibrium would worsen my nervous condition and he said as much to my husband. So I am allowed to enjoy ill health. I stay in bed till ten, rest in the afternoon, and retire again soon after dinner. Alfred remains downstairs with the port. Nowadays he goes to town during the week and stays at his club. Occasionally I look in the mirror at the healthy young woman masquerading as an invalid, and feel ashamed.

Is she aware of me yet? I am reaching out to her yet she seems unconscious of me. She exists outside this room, she can walk and talk, can commune with people. She can do the things I long to, but this room, which is my haven, also confines me. The rose garden must be in full bloom by now, its borders shading from deepest crimson to the faintest blush on white. Swagged garlands on the pergola, petals like shells on the grass. Petals that I gazed at with downcast eyes while I listened to the outpouring of another soul. Has she memories like mine?

"Do you mind if I retire to bed now?" asked Juliet. "I'm feeling completely exhausted."

"Of course you are," said Laura. "And get up as late as you like. Apart from the school run, I'll be around tomorrow."

Juliet impulsively kissed both Laura and Mark. "You're wonderful people. I love you."

At the threshold of the bedroom she paused, gazing into the darkness. She sensed, in a curious denseness of the atmosphere, that someone was there. She hesitated, then switched on the light, but the room was occupied only by the wallpaper and the furniture. For the first time in weeks, she thought, she would be able to sleep peacefully. She put on the nightdress Laura had lent her and got into bed. This room, she thought, is my haven.

This room is where I can be at peace for the first time since I left my parents' house. I remember the carriage at the door, our two grays in their best harness, proudly aware of the occasion. Mama embraced me in tears and said, "Please remember that whatever happens in your married life is God's will. The way to happiness is to obey your husband."

I wore white silk with roses at the neck and hem, and carried a garland of roses and lilies. When I lifted my veil Alfred looked at me with the light of worship in his eyes. It was not until that night when we were finally alone that I remembered Mama's words.

"Will you get undressed and come to bed?" Alfred's eyes had seemed like gray pebbles and his voice was cold. His kisses, which were not at first unwelcome, became frenzied. I struggled against them. Hold still, he said, and then there was the pain, and his uncontrolled spasms. I tried to love him after that, as a wife should, but he always was angry as if I had failed him. It is a memory that I have tried to put aside, but now the room is full of unhappiness.

Laura sat at the kitchen table, a cup of coffee in her hands. She glanced at Juliet's shadowed face and asked, "How did you sleep?"

"Fitfully," said Juliet. "I had nightmares about Brian when he had had too much to drink. I hope he doesn't guess where I am and come here and create a scene."

"I sincerely hope not." Laura looked worried, and Juliet felt annoyed with herself. She said, "You chose the most beautiful wall-paper for the bedroom. Where did you find it?"

"It's original late Victorian and was here already. You'd never find anything like it nowadays."

"In one of the dreams I was wearing a white silk ball gown and Brian was tearing at it. I woke up sweating with fear."

Laura sighed. "Let's forget about Brian for today. Why don't you just go and have a lazy morning by the pool? I'll join you later."

The swimming pool was set in an enclosed garden to the left of the house. The surrounding stone walls, covered by Virginia creeper, provided a sheltered sun trap. Behind the far wall an ash tree cast its shade over part of the garden. Two white-painted sun beds were left haphazardly where the weekend bathers had been catching the last light of the evening. Juliet wheeled one around to face the sun, and found some cushions in the glass house, by the wall. She lay back in her borrowed swimsuit and closed her eyes.

As she drifted half awake, she was aware of the chuckling of a blackbird and the hum of many insects. A small animal rustled in the Virginia creeper. Under the surface peacefulness the air was alive with the sounds of unnoticed creatures about their daily business of living. She heard the gate creak and assumed Laura was about to join her.

No one approached and she continued to let her thoughts drift in the sun. She closed off past and future and free-floated in the present. There was a rustling noise again, not from the creepers but nearer at hand, then a faint but perceptible gasp. A voice that seemed to be both by her ear and inside her head, said clearly, "This will not do." Startled into wakefulness, she sat up and looked around, her first thought being of Brian. But the walled garden was empty and the voice was not his, in fact it was hard to divine whether it was a man or woman. The voice of my conscience, she thought. My mind won't let me rest, it's sending me messages. Now she felt ill at ease in the walled garden and alert to the slightest sound. She was relieved when Laura appeared at the gate.

Later, during lunch on the terrace, Laura, believing it was now time, began to encourage Juliet to put some order into her life. She talked of injunctions, of suing for divorce, of property matters.

"You have to be practical and take the initiative, otherwise you'll find the ground cut from under your feet," she said. "And what about the time off you're having? Have you told your office?"

Juliet confessed, and it was worse than Laura had thought. Her company had embarked on redundancies and Juliet was working out her notice. No job, no marriage. At times like these Laura was at her best. In a few minutes she laid out a blueprint for Juliet. She was to ring her lawyer about the divorce and her office to say that she was staying with friends and would they forward her papers here. No, said Laura, to Juliet's halfhearted protests, she would be doing them a favor. Their au pair had left, they were coming up to the summer holiday and they needed someone to baby-sit and generally help out. Juliet could stay for a month or two until she sorted herself out.

Juliet murmured gratefully, feeling ever more hopelessly adrift. Minnie the tabby cat had been watching her with large amber eyes and now, as if she sensed Juliet's isolation, jumped onto her lap and, after turning around several times and kneading with her paws, settled down with her chin tucked into her chest and an audible purr. Laura watched the cat indulgently, with the selfsame expression of tucked-in contentment. She had put on weight since having Benjie and her fair hair was beginning to fade. Behind her the herbaceous border shimmered with the azure spires of delphiniums, the pinks and creams of lupines, and the white and gold of marguerites. Juliet looked around her and sighed, saying Laura was so lucky.

"Luck had nothing to do with it, dearie," said Laura crisply. "You should have seen the state of the place when we bought it. Garden rampant with weeds, moss all over the lawn, dry rot in the rafters. The house had been neglected for years, but we could see that it had once been beautifully cared for. The swimming pool was our final effort. We had to clear the walled garden, which was overgrown with mildewed rosebushes and brambles. And now we can collapse beside it, but not for long. Even now I know that I should be weeding the herbaceous border."

"And lucky with Mark, too."

"That wasn't luck, either. That was choice, and fortunately, he felt the same." Laura's voice had acquired a certain edge.

• • •

Juliet's exhaustion gathered on her in the evenings and she usually retreated early to the rose bedroom. On the second evening she took with her Minnie the cat, who had been reluctant to leave her lap after dinner, but as she opened the door, Minnie struggled violently, leaped from her arms, and ran downstairs. Juliet shut the door, feeling the room gathering around her. The silence should have been calming, but her mind was filled with images of Brian—Brian standing over the bed, shouting at her, his hair in a wispy halo around his head, his face contorted with rage. Juliet reached out for the transistor radio and switched it on. A Radio 3 commentator was discussing the work of Johann Strauss. Juliet listened to the chords of the "Blue Danube Waltz." Soothing, heart-lifting Strauss. She thought of park bandstands, people in deck chairs, of operetta at Sadler's Wells, singers circling to the strains of the waltz in dresses with taffeta swags. They whirl around close to her, and she is among them, one hand on a smooth alpaca-clad shoulder, her fan swaying in time to the dance.

It lifts you out of yourself, out of your daily life, bringing an atmosphere in which for a few hours you bloom. I feel freer, more light-hearted with a glass of champagne in my hand as I watch the dancers swirling around the ballroom to the polka. A succession of scents catches at my nostrils. Jasmine, lavender, bay rum, an undertone of perspiration. Their faces are flushed, their eyes alight with excitement. I watch with the matrons, my feet tapping under my gown to the music. Alfred does not dance. He has adjourned to the smoking room with the men who wish to absent themselves from their obligations.

I watch with envy a man talking to a girl who is dressed in ingénue white sprigged with flowers. He has the self-contained sleekness of a cat. His evening suit is well cut, his shoulders broad, his waist narrow. He turns as I watch and his eyes look straight into mine. How strange that I did not recognize him at first in his transformation.

Another man approaches them to claim the girl for the "Blue Danube Waltz." Now he is on his own and he walks toward me. He smiles warmly at me and bows. "How extraordinary," I say. "I did not recognize you in your evening wear, Dr. Hislop."

"That is the point of parties, to display facets of yourself that aren't everyday," he says. "And I have never seen you look as elegant as tonight. Would you do me the honor of accepting this dance?"

Now we are whirling around in the center of the gathering. A man bumps against me, Dr. Hislop's arm holds me more firmly to save my balance. "How well you dance," I remark.

"Only because you dance so well," he replies. "And what a pity you have danced so little this evening."

The "Emperor Waltz" has finally done for me and the band is striking up a mazurka. We leave the party and wander through the conservatory. The hard edges of palm leaves brush against my arms, my feet tread the petals of gardenias into the tiles. I am feeling breathless. There are two wicker chairs in a glade of ferns and orchids. The air is warm and humid, moonlight slants through the glass. In this seclusion, everything we say is heightened with significance. I feel as if I have been starved of conversation, and now I can talk forever.

It may be an hour later that I suggest we have been here rather too long. Surely Dr. Hislop should be squiring the young girls who are, after all, searching for husbands, and a bachelor is supposed to be in need of a wife.

He laughs and says, "They only have eyes for our hostess's eldest son. I'm not high on the list of eligible men. Besides," and he looks into my eyes, "I would rather be here with you."

It is too late to turn the remark lightly, for he has leaned forward, looking into my eyes as he asks earnestly, "Would you allow me to call on you—as a friend?"

"Please do," I whisper, then try to retrieve the situation. "Alfred would be delighted to see . . ." but he raises one hand and says, "Enough. I'll visit you next Wednesday afternoon."

How strange, a few words, and one's life is changed. We return to the party. He dances with the flower-sprigged maiden, I sit with the matrons. Alfred returns from the smoking room, his clothes exuding cigar smoke, his breath smells of port. In the carriage on our way home, he senses a change in my mood and asks, "With whom did you talk tonight?"

"With Mrs. Earnshaw, Mrs. Jopling, Lady Carstairs, for the most part," I reply. "I should have liked to dance with you, but you were not there."

The carriage rolls on. In the dim light I feel his eyes watching me. I look straight ahead, immersed in a world of my own.

A light breeze ruffled the curtains. Juliet stretched out to pick up her watch from the bedside table. The aftermath of sleep remained and as she looked at her arm extended toward the watch she remembered its smooth whiteness in the dream. She got out of bed, and the "Emperor Waltz" lingered as a refrain in her mind. She hummed it to herself as, half awake, half asleep, she made her way to the bathroom, tying the sash of her kimono. She brushed against Mark in the corridor. He put out his arm in support as she stumbled.

"I'm sorry, I'm still half asleep," she said.

For a few minutes afterward she felt the impression of his arm on hers—an invisible warmth.

The ringing of a telephone during a meal has an urgency as though the caller can't wait. Laura was serving out *spaghetti alle vongole* for dinner.

"What a time to choose . . ." Mark said and picked up the phone. Irritation turned to concern as he heard the voice of the caller.

"Why, hello, Brian, yes it's Mark . . . Is who here? . . . Look, could you hang on for a moment . . ." and turning to Laura with one hand over the mouthpiece, "Bloody Brian is demanding to know if we have Juliet staying here. What shall I say?"

Laura took the phone from him and answered in her most soothing tones, "Yes, hello, Brian . . . What were you asking about Juliet? . . . Oh, her office said that, did they? Well, yes, she is staying here. She's exhausted and needs to be out of town for a while. . . . No, I don't think it would be a good idea for you to come here. She needs absolute quiet. . . . No, she can't, she's gone to bed early, we're having dinner, she's really not well. . . ."

And so on, the raging at the other end met by a soothing stone wall. Finally Laura put down the phone, and Juliet, staring at her, demanded, "Why did you tell him I was here?"

"I could hardly pretend you weren't and let him report you to the police as missing. But you really need to get things moving with your solicitor now."

"I'll do it tomorrow," Juliet said. "I'll be feeling less tired. I promise."

The pool sparkled with points of light in the midday sun. Juliet applied her mind to the absorbing task of massaging the shining tracks of sun cream into her skin. Against the blue towel her legs glistened. She looked up to see Mark, stretched out on a sun bed a few yards away, watching her. In the sunlight his eyes were amber, and she noticed, as if in a picture, the shape of his face, the light brown hair with one strand that fell forward, the nose she always likened to that of an Arab horse, concave and wide-nostriled.

Mark's eyes shifted from her legs to her face.

"Were you unfaithful?" he asked.

Her hands were slippery from the sun cream. She rubbed them against her cheeks, obscuring her face from him.

"He thought I was. He became paranoid with jealousy over imagined things."

She gave Mark a brief end-of-conversation smile, lay back on her sun bed, and closed her eyes. She felt the peacefulness around her invaded by the unease that comes from being watched.

"Were you?" he asked quietly.

She opened her eyes and saw he was still watching her face.

"I could have been, possibly. I didn't have time to find out. He turned imagination into reality. Does it matter?"

"Of course not. And now you're free anyway, aren't you?"

"Yes." She heard the change in her voice and felt the bonds of complicity between them. Her skin registered invisible sensations and she thought, Not Mark, surely? She was aware of a vacuum into which she was being drawn, an area without rules to keep you secure from anarchy and emptiness.

This won't do, she thought, and tried to fill her mind with everyday matters. She breathed in deeply and caught an unmistakable perfume in the air she had not noticed before. Her nostrils filled with the scent of roses.

"Don't the roses smell beautiful?" she said. "The sun has brought them out in full strength."

"What roses?" asked Mark. "There's only the one by the gate."

The scent faded and now she could smell the coconut sun cream and an undertone of swimming pool chlorine.

"It must have been carried on a breeze," she said. "It's gone, but for a moment it was lovely."

"You have a sensitive nose," said Mark. "And sensitive skin. Would you like me to put lotion on your back?"

The touch of him remains with me, lingering as an awareness on the skin. The warmth of his handshake when we first meet, the tentative guiding hand on the small of my back as I ascend the stone steps that reminds me of his hand on my back when we danced. He is no longer Dr. Hislop, for I said to him: We are friends and should not be formal. Now he is my Edgar, my dear friend, my confidant. If he were not here to lighten the day I would despair.

His head is dark and sleek as he bends to smell the roses.

"This one has a scent as rich as its ruby petals," he says. His hand touches mine as I draw the rose to my face.

"Do you know its name?" I ask him. "It's called the 'Empereur du Maroc.'"

"And this mass of sugar pink here?"

"The 'Bourbon Queen.' And here is a white moss rose. Isn't it delicate?"

His head bends toward the flowers. I see strands of his dark hair overlapping his starched collar. The cloth of his coat is taut across his shoulders. He turns his head from the roses and meets my eyes. He smiles at me in the sweetest way and says, "You know so much about roses."

"They are my favorite flower. I have decorated my bedroom with the most beautiful rose paper that makes me feel as if I am in my garden again."

"I should love to see that paper," he murmurs, still gazing at me. We are standing close together in the warmth of the sun. There is a midday hush in the air. I can hear his breathing and see the rise and fall of his chest against his jacket. I feel the color come to my cheeks and dare not look at his face. I turn away and he follows me silently along the path. The scent of the roses is overwhelming.

He says, and his voice has a constraint in it as if he has not talked for some time, "And what is the name of this rose which is growing so profusely?"

I feel my color heighten as I say, "It's called 'Maiden's Blush.'"

He laughs and says, "It's your own rose, my dearest, for you're blushing so prettily."

His hand touches my burning cheek, then he bends his head so quickly that I do not have time to draw back and he kisses me.

"I have longed to do that ever since I met you," he says. We gaze at each other, and now at last I understand all the verses I have read, all the extravagant words of the poets, for I, too, am fathoms deep in love. I am alight with love, flooded and on fire with it.

"This will not do," I tell him, but the words mean nothing to either of us. I hear behind me the sound of the gate creaking, but no one comes into the garden. No one exists but the two of us.

The rose wallpaper gathers around to form a barrier of flowers against the outside world. She longs for that blotting out of her life, that forgetfulness that comes to her only in this room. The roses slide and blur as her eyes close, and on the edge of her mind hovers the question: What is happening between me and Mark?

Sometimes when she gets out of bed at night she has the sensation of being detached from her body. Her feet, reaching for her slippers, seem not part of her. It's like watching the feet of a stranger. Her hand reaches out to switch on the lamp and yet it is not her hand. She watches her arm as if it is someone else's, pale in the lamplight. As she sits on the edge of the bed she is watching herself, a young woman, dark-haired and slight, half dreaming, half awake. And the dream was something to do with Mark. He was close to her, smiling at her. It is fading already, but she remembers the scent of the roses.

At night it is easy to reach her, when she is drifting to sleep and the watchguards of the mind sleep, too. I can feel the bedclothes as she turns, as I turn. My feet reach for the slippers she left by the bed. I switch on the lamp and she picks up her book but she cannot read, I cannot read, our mind is elsewhere. His smile in the garden, and all those years I have waited since, with only my will to exist. I place the book back on the table. Look at my hand, how slim and small it is. I have always admired fine hands.

The house was quiet in the mornings after Mark departed for the day and Laura took Benjie to school. Juliet sat at the kitchen table over a cup of coffee, glancing at the headlines of *The Times*. The ringing of the telephone was raucous as it broke into the silence. She picked up the receiver and as she did so, she knew it was Brian.

She could not remember the conversation afterward, but they seemed to be talking in circles for hours. First he pleaded, then he threatened, then after an emotional appeal to remember their happier times, he said, "I'm coming down to sort this out. It's useless talking on the phone."

She could hardly speak for the dryness in her mouth. "Please don't. I don't want you to come here."

That set him off into a morass of suspicion. Why did she not want him there? Who was she with? His voice heightened its pitch. He shouted, "You can't stop me seeing you. You're still my wife."

"What do you mean, Brian? I really must go, I'm too tired to talk anymore."

This provoked another outburst and she put down the phone. It began to ring again and she went out into the garden until it stopped. As she returned to the house she heard the front door slam, and froze in alarm, but it was only Laura back from the school run.

Laura looked at her in concern. "Are you all right, Juliet?"

"It was just Brian on the phone being difficult." Juliet sat down at the kitchen table. "Do you think I should go? I don't want him coming down here and making a scene. It's not fair on you because you'll get involved."

Laura put an arm around her shoulder. "Don't worry about that, but I do think you should be sorting things out. What did your solicitor say?"

Juliet confessed that he was away when she rang and she hadn't yet rung him back.

"You should," said Laura. "It's exhausting being in limbo as you are. Sometimes you look as if you're not quite in this world. You must try to get a grip on things again."

"Not quite in this world," Juliet repeated softly, for it described how she had felt for several days.

"I'll pull myself together," she promised. "I'll ring up this afternoon."

Laura looked pleased, as if something positive had been achieved, and now she could get on with other matters.

The university's long vacation had begun and Mark was more often at home than in Oxford. He worked in his study in the mornings, then spent the afternoons gardening and swimming. Laura continued her part-time job in Oxford three days a week, dropping Benjie at play school on the way. The household timetable was leisurely, the summer turning out to be one of the good years when the garden was more lived in than the house.

"Do you know how lucky you and Laura are?" Juliet watched Mark clipping the hedge that shielded the kitchen garden from the main lawn. Laura was in Oxford and Mark had given up work for the day.

"I've got a shrewd idea," said Mark. "If you rake up the clippings and put them in the wheelbarrow, that'll be a great help."

Juliet raked and piled the twigs into the wheelbarrow.

"I weeded the entire herbaceous border this morning," she said.

"I think we both deserve a rest." Mark turned to smile at her, the blades of the shears poised immobile, several twigs in their grip.

"As soon as I've finished this." He drew the handles together, the twigs fell to the ground. Juliet raked and watched as he clipped the rest of the hedge. He put the shears down on the barrow and said, "That's enough for the moment. Let's take a walk around the estate and then have a swim."

There is an orchard at the end of the garden where Mark has planted new trees at intervals, spindly and straight among the craggy, lichen-fringed branches of the old trees. As they walk through the orchard, Juliet feels the sensation of aliveness on her skin, of the closeness of him, of being drawn closer. She looks sideways at him and catches in his eyes a speculative awareness. His hand slides around her waist, and he guides her toward the great beech tree at the edge of the orchard. Its branches sweep toward the ground, forming a canopy. Stepping through the drooping branches, they are in a hushed and vaulted space, the tree's trunk like a stone pillar extending into a filigree of arches. Dry leaves and beech husks rustle beneath their feet. They turn to look at each other and the tension can only be broken if one turns away. But neither does, and slowly, inevitably their faces draw closer. They pause, breathing in each other, then Mark touches Juliet's lips with his. She sighs, her lips part, and the tentative kiss becomes mouth-searching and long. Eventually Mark draws back, his mouth shining as if covered with sweat. He says, "This won't do."

"Won't it?" asks Juliet.

"You know that I find you attractive. But I have to think about Laura as well."

"There'll be no trouble," says Juliet. "Just a little affection—that's all I need."

"It's not as easy as that," says Mark. "I wish that it were."

He takes her hand and leads her back into the garden. A little while later they are by the swimming pool. Mark is massaging sun lotion onto Juliet's back.

"You smell of coconut," he says, bending forward and kissing the back of her neck. His hand slides around and touches her breast. Juliet thinks: It is beginning to happen at last.

And yet it was there from the start. He was so restrained, so delicate, his feelings betrayed only by the ardor in his eyes, by the way his hands would find a reason to touch me. Since that day he first kissed me, the village has never had such an attentive doctor, and if no one is ill, he arrives in any case. I no longer make any excuses for his being here. What the servants may think is not my concern.

Sometimes he will look at me and sigh, "If only . . ."

Ah yes, if only . . . If only I were not married, if only my husband were dead . . . How happy I would be living here with Edgar.

"If only . . ." he sighs and then exclaims, "Oh, if you knew how difficult this is for me. How I burn to be close to you, to be part of you, to love you fully. If you truly loved me, you would let me love you."

We are sitting in our favorite bower in the rose garden, on the wooden bench under the archway of climbing roses. It is late summer, the petals are scattered like confetti over the grass, the rose hips are ripening.

"You do not love me," he says.

"Oh, I do, my dearest. Don't be so cruel as to doubt me."

"Then show me." His lips touch mine, gently at first, then more firmly, and suddenly I am no longer myself. I am dizzy, my soul melts toward him, I am drowning in love. He crushes me to him and cries out as if in pain.

We are half lying on the bench. The armrest is a ridge against my back, thorns are entangled in my hair.

"Will you let me come to you tonight?" he asks.

"Not tonight, Alfred will be back. Next week when he returns to London. I promise you then."

"Love does not make appointments," he says.

"Love that is married does."

He laughs and kisses my hand. "Till next week, then."

I watch him depart, eloquent with love, and wait in the garden until I feel composed enough to go in. As I enter the house from the terrace, I hear the front door close. Alfred comes in. He stares at me, coldly suspicious.

"What was the doctor doing here?" he asks.

"He was attending someone in the village and called in to see if we were well. He particularly asked after you."

Alfred is looking at me strangely. His eyes take in my disheveled hair.

"He rode by hell for leather and nearly collided with my hansom."

"Oh, tut," I say lightly, but Alfred grasps my wrist, twisting me around to face him, and says, in a low voice, "Don't you ever play false with me."

I hear the venom in him, see the hatred in his eyes, and a chill goes through me.

"How dare you! Let go of me." I pull away from him. He loosens his hold and I walk toward the stairs. I hear him call, "Stop, I haven't finished," but I pay no heed. Then I hear his voice behind me, its harsh, deliberate tone: "I warn you, my dear, if you will not love me, you will love no one."

I bow my head from the force of his words, which sound like a curse. I can feel his eyes at my back, I can feel without seeing them their malign strength. It seems to take an eternity to reach the top of the stairs.

How quiet the house is without Laura and Mark. Benjie is tucked up in bed. Juliet is baby-sitting for the evening while they go to a dinner in Oxford.

"Will you be all right on your own?" Laura asked. Juliet seemed to be growing more nervous by the day.

"I'll be fine. I'm glad to be able to help you. Enjoy your evening, don't worry about me."

"Don't answer the phone if it rings, and double lock the door."

Over Laura's head, Mark's eyes met Juliet's. As he left the room, his hand touched hers.

Now they are gone and Juliet is alone. The evenings have begun to draw in. The light fades from the garden and the air grows cool. As dusk gathers, first in shadows in the depths of the garden, then spreading like a dark mist toward the house, she walks from room to room, drawing the curtains to keep the darkness at bay. Laura's curtains, lined and padded, sweeping pinch-pleated from under their pelmets down to the floor, insulate her from the outside. She ascends the curved staircase, her feet cushioned by Wilton carpeting, and feels the uneasiness that has come to her sometimes in the evening on the staircase, a feeling that she is being watched. She turns but sees nothing below except the stone-flagged floor with the rose-colored Persian carpet, hears nothing but the ticking of the grandfather clock. She walks more swiftly toward the landing and her heart begins to race. She reaches her room, switches on the light, and closes the door. She feels the curious thickness of the atmosphere, a density almost as if there were another dimension to the room. She goes to draw the curtains and looks out at the garden, over which the rising moon casts its indistinct light. In the stillness she sees, or perhaps it is a trick of her eyes, a shadow that seems to move near the walled garden. Quickly drawing the curtains, she sits for a while on the bed, trying to control her breathing. She tells herself it is only because Mark and Laura are out that she feels threatened by being alone. She goes to Benjie's room and looks in through the half-open door. A night-light casts a soft glow. She can hear the child's breathing and see the small shape in the bed, peacefully asleep. She feels reassured.

Downstairs in the kitchen she puts the pan of lasagna Laura has left for her into the oven and switches on the radio. It is playing atonal music. She switches it off. She retreats to the living room and switches from one television channel to another while she waits for the lasagna to heat. Thank heavens for television, for the sheer mind-numbing inanity of it. A fat man is making hammy expressions and flapping his hands, to an outburst of studio laughter. She lets it wash over her until the kitchen timer pings.

The lasagna is burned at the edges. She has a glass of the red wine they opened last night. She thinks about Mark. What is he up to? What is she playing at? She thinks: I could live here very happily with Mark. She switches on the radio again. Someone is talking about Goethe in self-satisfied tones. She switches it off.

She returns to the living room. Minnie the cat is curled up in a chair. Juliet watches the almost imperceptible movement of her breathing. One paw is stretched over the nose, shading the closed crescents of her eyes. Juliet feels affection toward Minnie and scoops her up into her arms. Minnie glares at Juliet and struggles out of her grasp. She streaks from the room. Juliet is left feeling alone and rejected.

There is nothing to watch on television so she picks up her book and begins reading. One part of her mind reads, the other listens to the sounds of the house. Her heightened senses hear murmurs and creaks that would otherwise have gone unnoticed. It's the house settling at night, she tells herself, turning a page. It's because of the absolute stillness she is hearing these sounds. The stillness seems to deepen, to become tangible. Then in the hushed room she hears a scratching at the window and suddenly all her senses screech an alert. She imagines fingernails running along the glass. She waits, listening, then switches off the light beside her and cautiously approaches the window. She stands to one side and draws back the edge of the curtain. Through the gap she glimpses the dark outline of a spray of leaves from the rambling roses trained on the wall outside. It must have brushed against the window in an evening breeze. That was all, she tells herself. Her nerves heightened the sound.

She reads on without concentration until the grandfather clock strikes ten. As the final stroke fades, the telephone rings. She sits on the edge of the chair, resolving not to answer it. She waves the remote control at the television and it comes in with *News at Ten*. A politician's voice resounds through the room. The phone rings on; she turns the television's volume higher till it assails her ears. Now a distraught woman with wild gray hair is sobbing at the camera, "Please bring her back to us, please don't harm her." The pain on the tormented face is unbearable to watch. Juliet switches off the screen. The phone still rings. She reluctantly picks up the receiver and listens to silence at the other end. She says "Hello," but no one answers. She listens for breathing and cannot even hear that. She replaces the receiver and picks it up again. There is no dial tone, only silence. He has not hung up. His listening presence fills the room. She shuts the phone into the drawer of Laura's desk and goes to the front door to make sure it is double-locked. It is. The kitchen door is locked and bolted. Minnie is nowhere to be seen. She decides to retire to her bedroom and shut away the rest of the house.

At the foot of the stairs she pauses. In her mind she hears the thought that is so clear it might almost have been spoken. "If I ascend these stairs it will be irrevocable." She does not know what that can mean, but as she walks up the stairs she feels as if there is a space parting around her, as if she is walking a predestined course. One foot in front of the other, she moves without volition. She reaches her room and shuts the door behind her. A curious sense of detachment descends on her. She goes through the motion of brushing her hair, at the same time feeling it is not her arm that is moving. She puts on her nightdress and as the soft lawn folds around her the voice that is both inside and outside her mind says, "So it is tonight then."

She sits before the mirror and as she listens and waits, she looks at the wallpaper. The flowers have such a freshness and aliveness about them that she would not be surprised if the wings of the painted butterflies quivered. She thinks: I do believe this room is haunted. At the same time she doesn't wish to leave the room for the uneasiness she feels in the rest of the house, for the vulnerability of the tall ground-floor windows to the outside, the disconnected phone with its silent caller. She continues to brush her hair and listen, then she gets into bed and reads for a while. She switches off the light and switches it on again, for in the darkness she is suddenly on edge. The switching on and off of the light is repeated several more times. Her eyes, heavy-lidded with sleep, demand rest, though her mind races. She tells herself that Mark and Laura will be back soon, and the house is securely locked. She pulls the bed-clothes over her ears and turns toward the wall. She falls asleep.

She dreams. In her dream she hears the sound of footsteps on the flagstones in the hall. They are walking back and forth in slow and heavy deliberation. There is quietness now, for the feet are ascending the carpeted stairs. She can hear movement outside on the landing, then the sound of a door handle turning. She is aware that she is dreaming, and yet at the same time she's half awake. Whoever is outside has paused for a moment, as if listening. The door begins to open. She whispers, "Mark?" There is only silence and now, in her waking dream, she reaches her hand out to the lamp. It falls to the floor and, wide awake, heart pounding, she cries out. Just before the hands grasp her throat she senses a malignity that fills the room.

She is struggling against the hands, against the body whose weight lies over hers, and at the same time nothing is there to struggle against. She feels its force and solidity, yet as she tries to ward it off, her hands touch only the air. She wrenches at the hands on the throat and she is grasping at her own hands. In the emptiness a sour smell of whiskey fills her nostrils. Someone is there and not there. She screams out, tearing at the bedclothes as she fights against the weight that overwhelms her.

Why is he here? What has happened? I fight him with all my strength. I will not give in. I will not be cheated of life. I will live for my love . . . I shall live . . .

With the final days of September comes an autumnal coolness. Mark and Laura are glowing with un-English tans from their fortnight on a Greek island. In the pale surroundings of the hospital their health shines all the more robustly. A nurse in white starched cotton and dark stockings leads them to a small, sunny room. They can see Juliet sitting in an armchair by the window, wearing a gray track suit.

"She's been up and about for several days," said the nurse. "She's quite energetic at times."

Juliet smiled politely at Mark and Laura. "How nice of you to come and see me again. You are looking well, though you have caught the sun."

Laura sat down on the bed and told Juliet about their holiday, about the beaches, the tavernas, the ferryboat rides. Juliet smiled, though she seemed not to be taking it in. When Laura paused, she said, "I would find Greece far too hot at this time of year."

Laura glanced at Mark, who looked bored and embarrassed.

"How are you getting on here, anyway?" asked Laura. "You're looking so much better."

"I'm safe here," said Juliet. "There's a nice young doctor looking after me. We get on very well."

Mark made signs at Laura. She got up from the bed.

"The doctor won't let Alfred come and see me," said Juliet. "Even though he shouted and stormed."

"Brian," Laura gently corrected her. "Your husband, Brian."

Juliet looked at her blankly.

As they reached their car in the hospital yard, Laura said to Mark, "Well, that's over for another week. And they won't keep her in much longer, anyway. Even raging schizos get thrown back on the streets."

Mark drove along the Oxford bypass to their turning and the miles of deep, winding lanes that led to their house. He said, "Let's hope we don't have another of your friends in a mess descending on us."

"My friends?" asked Laura. "I thought she was your friend as well."

She turned to watch his face. "You know, at one moment I even thought she was making a pass at you."

Mark glanced at her, but he was wearing dark glasses and she could not see his eyes.

"How fanciful you are," he said.

Back at the house, Laura gathered a spray of late roses to put on the dressing table for their weekend guest. She paused on the threshold of the room. The wallpaper was beginning to look faded and old. The time might have come, she decided, to redecorate.

On the bedspread a bundle of tabby fur was asleep, one paw stretched over its face. Dear little Minnie, thought Laura, always looking for a quiet and comfortable spot to curl up in. Of late, this room seemed to have become her favorite place.

Back to Mother

Michael Mahoney

I'm sitting in the back of a taxi, my cheek on the cool glass, losing myself in the faces that bustle and bob through the wet city streets—I could be any one of them; the old Asian raising the shutters on the kiosk, the yuppie with the hands-free kit, or the goth kid with the spikes and buckles, snapping bubblegum between black lips. I see a young mother at the bus stop shielding her toddler from the drizzle with her coat, and now I'm being sucked back behind the glass, remembering who I am: a middle-aged man on the way to his mother's cremation, and it all seems so random, I want to cry.

The cab stops in front of the pebble-dashed crematorium. I pay the driver, go inside, and wait in the foyer.

The foyer: hidden lighting, sprays of dried flowers in glazed terra-cotta vases.

It's all contrived, a comforting veneer of normality, like the powder and blush they painted on my mother's face; underneath, it's all dead flesh.

Doors swing open and a sullen procession files out, withdrawing pocket makeup kits, hurriedly dabbing away mascara runs. By the time they reach the exit, they're smiling again. A short, balding man who is too big for his suit is acting out a joke with big, sweeping hand gestures.

I feel the hot swell of tears but fight them back. I cry for myself when I'm alone, but not in public. Out here I'm an actor, like everyone else. As long as I have my role and my costume, my job and my suit, my performance is competent enough not to attract suspicions. And my mother, I wish I still had my mother.

Shit, my mobile's ringing.

"Hello?"

"Hi Dan, this is Jack Frask . . . we met at the office party last year."

Oh, yes, the middle-management man with the dandruff who danced around with the traffic cone on his head.

"Of course! Jack! I've been meaning to call you, but you know, busy busy busy—"

"Yeah well, some bad news, I'm afraid. Head office gave me a list of people to notify. . . . We've been bought out, and there will be cutbacks. Unfortunately, well, your position has been made redundant."

I'm not hearing this.

I'm not hearing this.

A vacuum cleaner is switched on somewhere.

"But the company will offer you a settlement, and the pension plan is still intact and . . . Dan? Are you still there?"

That vacuum noise, louder, then quieter, closer, then farther away.

Slowly at first, then faster, I bang the phone off my face. The louder the vacuum sounds, the harder I bang. A hand grabs my wrist.

I look up.

"Mum?" I hear myself say. I blink the tears out of my eyes, and it's not Mum, it's a cleaner, with an alarmed expression. The vacuum is on the floor, slurping at the valance on the bottom of the settee.

I end the call. The cleaning lady rests her hand on my shoulder. I look up at her, sniffling.

"If you would like to come this way, sir," says the undertaker. He gives me a look of understanding, so effortlessly; it must've been stamped into his brow by force of repetition. He gestures toward the swinging doors. "We'll be with you shortly."

I glance back at the woman, who smiles slightly as she squeezes my shoulder. I get up, nod politely, and walk through the doors.

I take a seat at the front of the room next to the aisle. My every movement echoes on the polished floor and sparse décor of the room. Before me, the conveyer belt waits.

A small organ sits in the corner on a raised platform. Gold-sprayed pipes cling to its face, but they're just decoration to hide the chipboard. Mum didn't want any hymns, though, no religious ceremony, she was adamant about that. But as I stare into the sliver of darkness between the curtains that cover the incinerator, I wish she had given me at least one mythic system for comfort. In all my years of service as personnel manager to Victor P.L.C., I only had the Staff Code of Practice, and that was merely the wrapping paper on my efficient dealings with the workforce. A little ribbon tied on the top and it was ready to deliver. *Position made redundant*; no, not position, *people*, real people, like me. Every time I had to sack an employee, the only advice the Staff Code of Practice dictated to soften the blow was to draw the subject's attention to the prospect of a few weeks' rest before they found a position better suited to their skills. So, I'm expendable, too, they've sacked me now. They can't do this. I want to scream—I'm boiling over.

I check my watch—4:58. Two minutes before my mother is to be committed to the flames, and no one but me is here as witness. It seems fitting, though. Except the doctors, it was just the two of us when I came into this world. No one to hold her hand during the fourteen hours of labor—no one to dab her forehead when they finally used the forceps.

Ever since I was forced into this world, I've wanted to crawl back whence I came.

The doors open, and the casket is being rolled down the aisle on what appears to be a wood-paneled catering trolley. One of the wheels seems to be broken; it screeches on the waxed floor. The attendants struggle to keep the trolley from veering off into the chairs while trying to remain composed. That's Mum, awkward to the last.

The men link arms under the casket and slide it onto the conveyor belt.

"Would you like a moment alone?" one asks as they turn the trolley. I nod.

The casket: I wonder if it's a good fit, or did they have to curl back her toes and angle her neck? I'm sure she was tall when I was younger, but as I grew against her in height she became more stooped. Must have been all the times that her back arched to load the washing machine, or clean school dinners off the floor at work. When she hugged me, her forehead rested on my chest, my upper weight bore down on her shoulders. It hurt her, but she hugged me all the same. I kind of wish that I could have been more supportive of her, but I can just about hold myself upright, I admit.

But that's not my fault. I'm a product of an environment that I did not choose, and therefore, I accept no responsibility for how it has shaped me. Surely it is enough that I must suffer, that I had to feel her grow dry and brittle under my embraces, shrink and yellow at the edges; watch her eyes fade under cataracts, see the person behind them drift farther and farther away.

I'm crying now, sobs punctuated by sharp sniffs. I wipe my nose with my handkerchief, and notice the little initial *D* that she embroidered on it. On the way out every morning, I always found a fresh one sitting under my keys on the little oak table by the front door. Now I press it to my eyes, let my face burrow into its folds. The soft lighting behind it gives it a pinkish tinge, like the lining of a womb.

The conveyor belt whirs into motion. It's like she's been lying on it since birth, assembled, used, and now the ride is over she'll be melted down and recycled. I let the hankie fall from my eyes to my mouth, where I suck and gnaw at it, as the head of the casket penetrates the slit in the curtain, and inches its way into the darkness. Life and death are one long joyless fuck, and there she is, taking her last thrust, and the casket's going in, and I can't take this—I've had enough!

I spit the rag from my mouth, run over to the conveyor belt, climb up, and straddle the coffin. The incinerator door opens. The red heat blisters the wood around my fingers. I cry out, feeling my nose hairs singe. Hands are gripping my legs and pulling me back into the coolness against the motion of the belt that rolls up my shirt and friction-burns my belly. They force me to the floor, and I can hear the roar of flames consuming my mother. I imagine the collapse of the charred casket, the flames licking her flesh—her skin turning brown and crinkling up like a crisp packet in a fireplace, her subcutaneous fat boiling and spitting.

I lie motionless between their weight and the cold floor. The crush squeezes a tear from my eye, and I feel it roll down my cheek. How like me, this acting out. Such relief I feel on the surface of my movements, controlling my gestures, the inflections of my voice. If only I could stay there, floating on the surface of my mind, seeing only my reflection like a Jesus bug on a pond. But my pond is too deep, and the fish within have mutated in its depths. I need to drag them out, let them gasp and die in the air, so I can skitter across the surface, a little Jesus bug, without fear of being eaten.

I clear my throat.

"I want to get up now. I'm all right."

They back off. I get up and pat the dust off my pants, walk across the room, stoop, and pick up my handkerchief, glance up and they're staring at me like I'm a strange insect.

"I'm okay, a little upset, that's all," I say.

The men look at each other; the oldest steps forward.

"There's a doctor on the way. If you'd like to take a seat, he'll be here shortly," he says, gesturing toward a chair.

"No, really, I just want to go home."

"Please sit down, sir."

The old man's lips are clamped tightly, his face red as he points toward the seat. I walk abruptly out of the room. Bursting through the swinging doors, my eyes immediately lock with the cleaning lady's.

She reminds me of Mother; the same slight build, the same sad hazel eyes, the same line of the mouth, pinched at the bow, tapering off in a frown that puffs her jowls. I resist the urge to touch her skin to feel if it is also roughly pitted, and coated in a fuzz of tiny transparent hairs. I've made eye contact, so now I've got to speak.

"Margaret," I say after a quick glance at her name badge, "I need your help."

"Umm." She coughs and scans the reception area, smiling nervously. "I think there's a doctor coming for you."

Behind me, the doors open, and the little old man is upon me again, trying to measure his professionalism with the need to communicate that what I did was an offensive breach of protocol. I just stare at him until I see the cleaning lady behind him, holding up a set of keys, motioning toward a small, dimly lit side exit.

"The toilet."

"Pardon?" says the funeral director, clearly angry at the interruption.

"The toilet, where is it, please?"

"Down the corridor, first on the right."

I leave him standing there.

It's almost dark outside. The rain that had sputtered and threatened during the day now falls steadily. I stand in the small car park, looking around for any sign of the cleaner. An engine starts somewhere, tap of a car horn, then headlights. I run toward them squinting against the rain, first to the driver's side of the Ford

Fiesta, then, realizing my error, the passenger side. While I'm sitting down, closing the door, and fishing around for my seatbelt, she's looking at me.

"Where to?" she asks, putting the Fiesta gingerly into reverse.

"Home."

"Where's home?"

"I'll direct."

Driving home. The wipers slay raindrops on the windshield. I sense her looking at me, and take care to appear composed but troubled. Composed: stiff lip, no tears. Troubled: watching the war on the windshield, eyes glazed and vacant, shell-shocked. And I am, but my emotions, thoughts, and actions never connect properly. It's how you feel when you're an infant school kid with your arm in a sling and the class is singing: "If you're happy and you know it clap your hands . . ."

"Well, here you are," she says as the car stops.

"Here I am," I sigh.

I don't want to be alone now, not in the house with all Mum's things. I've got to talk her into staying.

Scanning the contents of the car for any objects that will give me an angle. There're no coloring books or packets of fizzy sweets stuffed in the seats; doubt she has any young children. No wedding ring on her finger, either.

"I . . ." I hesitate for effect, as if my words pain me. "I am very lonely." Silence; a car passes making a *sssshhhh* sound on the wet street.

"Sorry, I don't know where that came from. Thanks for driving me home. Here, I'll give you some petrol money."

"No need."

"At least let me fix you a drink, I mean tea or coffee or something."

She locks me in her gentle scrutiny.

I hold my breath.

She turns the engine off.

"Lead the way," she says.

In the front hall, I take her denim jacket and drape it over the hat stand. I guide her into the kitchen by the shoulders, glad to have established physical contact.

"Tea, coffee, something stronger?"

"Something stronger?" she says, cocking an eyebrow. "What do you have in mind?"

I reach into the cabinet under the sink and shuffle some bottles around before withdrawing a large bottle of whiskey. I shoot her a questioning glance.

She meets my eyes and smiles. "Go on then."

We sit in the small living room overlooking the street. She's cleared a space among the dolls that sit on the hard sofa, and after half a bottle, she shares the dreamy look of their porcelain heads, staring into the middle distance, eyes bobbing gently when she moves. Conversation is awkward at first. We run through all the talk that might be shared among strangers, like the traffic system, and the weather. But through her superficial chitchat, I sense a tremendous weight pushing forward, as if her words are just controlled leaks in a floodgate straining to remain closed. Just a little pressure in the right place, and I'm sure she'll burst.

"Won't you want to be getting home? I'm sure your family must be thinking you've joined the Foreign Legion or something."

"No," she sighs, "I'd best be going, you've had a tough day, and I'm sure you're not in the mood for guests."

"No, not at all. I . . . I enjoy your company . . . very much, but um, I don't want to keep you, I'm sure you've got responsibilities."

"Well, not really, I'm not working tomorrow. Just bringing my aunt to Bingo tomorrow night," she says, putting her eyes up in the air. I laugh my gentle laugh, and she smiles.

"Have time for another drink?"

"I think so," she says.

I top up her glass. She blushes a little, and toys with the golden locks of hair on one of the dolls.

"Out on the town this weekend?" I ask.

"Me?" she says, as if confused, "No . . . uh . . . no plans."

She winds the strand of doll hair more tightly around her finger.

"How would you and me like to—"

Snap.

The lock of hair comes away from the hole in the doll's head. Her face knots in anxiety. She's probably scolding herself in her mind, going: *Stupid Margaret stupid Margaret stupid Margaret.*

And then she opens her mouth and starts to stutter.

"I—I—I—I'm really sorry. Oh, shit. I'll replace it. I should go. I'm sorry," she says, getting up and staggering aimlessly around the room. I jump to my feet and intercept the path of her pacing. She's inches away from me, eyes wide and wary. I close the gap with a quick stride, slip my arms around her waist, and rest my chin on her shoulder, cheek against cheek. Her short-cropped hair smells of sweat.

"Margaret," I whisper, "I don't care about the doll, it's nothing a bit of Super Glue won't fix. I want to get rid of them anyway, eventually. Maybe I'll give them to the orphanage on East Road. To be honest, they give me the creeps."

I feel her relax. Her arms fall from her chest and her hands work their way up to my shoulders. I squeeze her close, and she reciprocates. Her breasts are small and flat, and I can almost feel the bones beneath, gripping the spaces in my rib cage like cog teeth, as we rock back and forth, my weight on her, her weight on me, rhythmically.

"They were your mother's?" she asks.

"Yes. She collected them—peopled the house with them. They kept her company, I suppose. When her eyesight went I would take one every now and then and put it in the loft, but she'd always notice. She was sharp that way."

Surely I hadn't intended to spill myself out this way. She's listening, though. It's nice when someone listens.

"She had names for them. Some were the names of childhood friends, I think, but some, were like, how do I say, different parts of her. Some she'd talk to when she was happy, some when she was lonely, and sometimes when I found one of the porcelain ones smashed, I knew it was one she talked to when she was angry.

"Then, a few years ago, she began to express an interest in beauty products. She'd leave catalogs open on tables, usually around her birthday, Christmas, Mother's Day, and the like, as if casually, with certain products ringed, or a pen or pencil on top with the tip pointing to a certain thing. Now of course I went out and bought her the stuff, and she'd act surprised when I gave it to her, but she never wore it. She never wore makeup. But still, time after time, the same catalog was left on the table.

"Then," I gulp, "the other day, when I came home from work and called her name, there was no answer. I thought she might be on the loo or taking a shower, but when I got to the top of the landing I saw the door to her bedroom was open, which was unusual, because she always kept it locked. So I went in and I saw . . . her legs . . . sticking out of the wardrobe, and she was lying there . . . dead. Inside the wardrobe sitting on a throne of pillows and discarded containers of makeup and antiaging cream was this doll. Its face was caked in all this cream and makeup that had dried and cracked on the surface of its head. Above it was a little sign written in my mother's scratchy writing; it said 'Lucida the Beautiful.' "

She's hugging me, desperately, as if to silence me. I respond with long, hard strokes from the base of her back to her buttocks, cup them in hands and pull her to the swelling warmth of my groin. Kissing the sinews of her neck, I whisper, "Let's go upstairs, we'll be more comfortable."

I feel her smile and turn her head to find my lips. I put my index finger against them.

"Wait," I say, because Mummy never kissed me on the lips.

I hug her close, wanting nothing more than to fuse with the body of this woman, burrow into it, lose myself. Slowly, an image begins to take shape in my head as to how this might be accomplished, and as much as I try to dispel it, it lingers, fueled by the warm passivity of her embrace.

"I have a friend who lives in Italy," I say, "in the hills above the bay of Naples. Have you ever been?"

"No," she says, "but a few years ago I went on a day trip to a hypermarket in Calais to pick up some cheap drink. Must have strained myself. I had a miscarriage aboard the hovercraft."

She's not making this easy; she needs to stay a cardboard cutout.

"Well," I say, "you might have gained some appreciation of the Mediterranean climate, and you might understand, when I talk about the cool breeze that blows off the sea on hot summer afternoons. And how nice it was, to be in my friend's vineyard at such a time, plucking bunches of grapes and washing them in the cold brook that flowed between the olive groves. And the best part— putting them all in a big vat, taking our shoes off, just Antonio and me, and squishing the grapes down with our feet. I recommend you do that someday. It's a wonderful feeling . . ."

"I'm sorry for telling you that, about the miscarriage, I mean. You have enough problems right now, so—"

I want to grab her tongue.

"It's okay. I have some wine that I took home from his vineyard. It was his parting gift, and in nearly twenty years, I have never opened it. I was waiting for the right time . . . or the right person to share it with, and well, would you like me to uncork a bottle?"

"Um, well you've been saving it for such a long time . . ."

"I want to."

"Well, in that case, yeah, that would be great."

"Good. I'll just go get it. Why don't you go upstairs and draw yourself a bath. I bet you could do with a good soak, and I'll be up shortly."

"Ooh, that would be nice," she says, getting all girly again.

"There's a bathrobe on the back of the door, some towels on the drying rack, and the bath salts are on the windowsill. The boiler's been on all day so there should be plenty of hot water."

"Thanks," she chirps, and with a little bounce, begins to pad up the stairs. Halfway up, she seems to remember something, slows, and looks back, worried.

"I'll turn the light on," I say. "The bathroom is the second door on the right."

I flick the switch, and she continues on her way, cautiously.

I wait in the kitchen, fiddling with a can opener until I hear the swish of the pipes that means she's running a bath. Then I reach into the cabinet under the sink, pull out a bottle of Happy Shopper Value Red Wine, and run the label under the hot tap. When the glue softens, I peel it off and put it in the bin.

I search the medicine chest in the downstairs bathroom for the bottle of barbiturates. I've done this before, when Mother worked herself into frenzies of excitement at antisocial hours. I'd often lock her in the bedroom until she tired herself out, but I soon discovered that chemicals were her best baby-sitter. Hypnocil, at first—a few tablets crumbled in with her hot chocolate before bed, but then there was the vomiting when she woke up. That was no good. The Valium didn't work, either—she could taste it. But then I remembered my student days, when my flatmate nicked Ketamine from his dad's veterinary surgery. We'd line it up on a mirror, and snort until our bodies were so anesthetized that our minds could float to higher planes. Not that it ever did me any good; I only got those nightmarish introspective trips, but Mother took to it well—so well, in fact, that she requested her hot chocolate several times a day.

Yes, K will do the trick just nicely.

I put the sleeping pills back in the cabinet, unlock the bottom drawer, fish out the little Ziploc bag of the stuff, and set to work cutting it on a vanity mirror, reducing the little crystals to a fine powder with a straight razor. I take it into the kitchen and set it down on the table, then get out two wineglasses from the cupboard and place them on a metal tray, grab a drinking straw, and with one ear on her movements upstairs, snort an eighth of the mirror's contents. The rest I pour into the wineglass on the right.

I can already feel a numbing sensation wash over my body as I twist the corkscrew. The bottle opens. I fill the glasses, stir the spiked one with the straw, pick up the razor, blow the remaining powder from the blade, snap it shut, slip it in my pocket, get the tray, and head for the stairs.

I'm listening outside the bathroom. She's singing, sweetly, but otherwise badly, over the whine of the hairdryer that Mother persisted in using even after the radiation treatment. She'd burn her bald scalp with it, drying her phantom hair. Then she'd put the wig on as if nothing were amiss.

The wig, that's an idea.

I knock on the door.

"Just a sec," comes the reply.

The door opens, and there she is, wearing Mother's floral bathrobe, holding it closed at the waist. Her skin is rosy with the water's warmth, and beads of moisture glisten on her neck, but beneath her attempt at an alluring smile, I can't help seeing the objective fact of this creature; her receded gums and stained teeth, her flaccid skin, and the ochre goo that slumbers in the corners of her eyes.

"Wine, madame?" I ask with a low growl of a French accent.

"*Oui oui, garçon,*" she replies, locking eyes with mine and narrowing them to half-mast. I nearly laugh, but instead pick up the glass on the right and hold it out to her. She lets go of the bathrobe and takes it.

"Oops," she says, staring down at her exposed body, her small breasts, flabby midsection, and nest of pubic hair.

I grip her free hand and lead the way to the cold, dark bedroom at the end of the hall. I leave her standing in the middle of the room while I light the beeswax candles that Mother put on the chest of drawers for ornamentation. Burned sulfur stings my nose as I extinguish the flame between my fingertips.

"Is this your room?" she asks, hugging the robe to her body.

"No," I reply. "But this room is better."

"It's a bit chilly."

"Finish your wine, and I'll see what I can do."

She giggles, and drinks.

"Mmm, this wine is great," she says, licking her lips.

"I'm glad you think so."

When she's finished every last drop, I remove the empty glass from her hand and set it down on the chest of drawers. I extend my hand to her neck, and trace a line with the tip of my finger, from the hollow below her larynx, to the cleft of her chin. She sighs as I sweep the line of her jaw, slip into her ear, and navigate its contours, pretending it's a labyrinth. She grips my back and then leans on me, small tremors shaking through her body. It's working, the muscle spasms are starting already.

"We should go to Italy. Would you like to go to Italy?" I ask, caressing her hair.

"Yeah," she moans. "But I have to take my Aunty Beatrice to Bingo tomorrow."

She's going under. Not long now.

"We can go and see my friend Antonio. You can walk out of the spare bedroom, onto a balcony. You can sit there in the morning and watch the boats leaving the harbor. Would you like to do that?"

"After Bingo?"

Her arms fall limply at her side.

"Yes, and we can even take your Aunt Beatrice, after Bingo, of course."

"No," she flails her arm weakly. "I don't want her to come."

"Why ever not?"

"Because," she slurs, "she's a smelly old bitch."

Her knees buckle beneath her. I catch her weight, and let her fall on Mum's bed. Her eyes roll in her head and she makes goldfish movements with her mouth.

I walk down the corridor into the warm, moist air of the bathroom. I try to unbutton my shirt, but my fingers are too numb, so I pull it open, sending buttons pinging off the tiled walls. I remove my pants, socks, and shoes, and follow her wet footprints over to the sink, where I pick up a pair of scissors, raise them to my head, and begin cutting. I let the strands of hair fall past my eyes until my head is a mass of uneven stubble. I squirt a quantity of shaving cream into my palm, and rub it into a thick white lather on my scalp. I use the straight razor to shave my head clean. I grab a jar of Vaseline and return to the bedroom, where Margaret's body is still sprawled on the bed, bathed in shadows that flicker with the candle's flame. I lie down beside her, look into her glazed eyes, and feel her warm breath against my face. Her eyes narrow slightly and refocus on some invisible object.

"Gimme back my baby," she groans. "I want my baby."

Her body tenses up as if to move, but the drug keeps her paralyzed.

"Shhh . . . Baby's here," I whisper, mapping the contours of her body with my touch. I kiss her softly on the cheek and raise myself from the bed.

"Baby?" she dribbles.

"Baby's here," I repeat, crossing the room to the wardrobe. I turn the skeleton key and the door creaks open, accompanied by the scent of talc and makeup. Lucida sits on her throne at the bottom of the wardrobe, and I take care not to look at her as I pull a couple of belts from the hook on the back of the door.

Margaret's trying to sit up. I fluff up the pillows under her head, and gently coax her back to their softness. I loop the belts around her ankles, pull her legs apart, and tie each belt to its corresponding bedpost.

When I return to the wardrobe to find Mum's wig, Lucida seems to smile at me.

At the mirror, I unscrew the cap on the Vaseline, slap a dollop on my scalp, and cake my head in the translucent gel.

"Baby?" bleats Margaret as I slip the wig over her hair.

I approach the foot of the bed, crawl between her legs, grip her hips, and begin pushing my head against her vulva.

"Baby's coming," I assure her.

The Solo Sadomasochist

K. L. Gillespie

I check my watch for the third time in five minutes, I'm eager to get home, it's been a long day and I'm sick of being Daniel and eager to become someone else. It is a minute past six so I knock the computer off, shove an anonymous black shiny carrier bag into my briefcase, and hurry out of my executive office toward the lift. I try my best to avoid eye contact with everyone I pass; I never could look anyone in the eye. Even as a child I had things to hide and was convinced that people would know what was going on in my mind if I let them look inside for long enough.

Predictably, Helen, my PA, corners me outside the lift. She's had romantic designs on me since I started here. To the outside world I am a good catch, exactly the type of man these women bother to turn up to work for, but I'm not interested. She pinions me to the wall with a dozen probing questions, delivered in staccato, about my plans for the weekend, but I fob her off with well-practiced ease and soon I am squashed in the lift with half of the fifteenth floor. The tingle of apprehension runs through my veins as more people squeeze in, forcing me up against the back wall.

Ground floor, I apprehensively leave the confines of the lift and make a dash for the door and the great big outside world that is my connection between here and there. I pull the collar of my cashmere overcoat up to my ears and shuffle through the sea of cigarette ends at the entrance to the building, where smokers huddle to puff their way out of this life, and make a beeline for the tube station.

I always catch the tube; I've never liked buses and taxi drivers are too intrusive in London. I like the anonymity the tube affords; as soon as I hit the escalator I can stop pretending. The LED readout says that the train is a minute away, which could mean anything down here, so I fill my mind thinking about the weight of London pressing down above my head. The train arrives and I force my way on with a herd of other dead-eyed commuters.

The Misery Line is living up to its name tonight, and as the carriage jolts from side to side I reach up and grab hold of the sprung stirrup hanging from the ceiling. My cuff draws back to reveal the faint yellow rings of bruised flesh around my wrist, souvenirs from a now-fading memory. I reach up and run my fingertips over the skin until I notice a woman opposite me, watching. I remember where I am and cover the bruises as quickly as I can.

The train drags itself into my station, the doors slide open, and I am swept along by a crowd of people with somewhere to go and someone to meet. I allow the escalator to carry me upward, where the night air bites my skin, and I head for the bright lights of the supermarket around the corner.

One ready meal for one and a pint of milk later and I am back outside, heading for home. The High Street is buzzing with couples holding hands, but I try to push the thought of them from my head by filling it with my plans for the evening. Two minutes later and I am standing outside my house. I've got a nice house, really nice—if Helen saw it I would never get rid of her. I climb the steps and put the key in the lock.

I breathe a sigh of relief as I shut the door behind me. This is one of my favorite parts of the day, but I cannot relax yet. There are still a couple of things to do. Most important, the keys, they are the foundation for the rest of the night and the first step in a carefully thought-out scene. There are four keys in all: a tiny black one, two small fiddly ones made from stainless steel, and a larger, ornate brass belt swinger. I methodically seal them in a manila padded envelope and address it to myself before sticking a selection of stamps in the top corner. I check my watch again; I've got eight minutes to catch the last post or I will have to postpone, so I hurry out of the house and plunge myself back into the night air.

I am cutting it really fine, so I break into a jog. As I round the final corner I can see the post office van pulling up and a tremor of panic emanates from the pit of my stomach, so I run as fast as I can, shouting like a banshee for them to wait. I reach the mailbox panting and with the greatest relief I deliver the package safely into the familiar hands of the waiting postman.

On the way home the chill night air cools my body, but I am starting to sweat with anticipation now as I run the scene planned for tonight around and around in my head. I am already thrilled by my own daring because I have never pushed myself to this sort of extreme before.

As soon as I get in I throw my processed lasagna into the microwave and jump in the shower while the meal cooks. While I am in the shower I check on old friends, scars that have become a permanent feature on my well-toned body. I touch each one gently, proudly.

When I get out of the shower I look at my naked body in the mirror and I like what I see, but there are improvements to be made. I've been thinking about this scene for weeks now, but I've been working toward it for years. I have planned it like a military operation and now the first stage is complete. I am eager to move on because I know what awaits me, and me alone.

The microwave pings, reminding me to eat, so without dressing I sit down in the kitchen. I push the food around the plate, eating only a mouthful or two because it is not advisable to enter into serious bondage on a full stomach. Anyway, I can eat like a pig tomorrow to make up for it. As I eat I think about Helen and wonder what sort of lover she would make and I laugh out loud at the thought of her bound and gagged.

Nevertheless, it would be nice to have someone to share this with. Sometimes I yearn to be half of a whole, and I am sure that one day I will be, but for now I have to be both halves, the top and the bottom, the left and the right, the good and the bad, the sadist and the masochist.

I put some music on, Wagner, and it has never sounded better; the heightened state of my senses allows me to experience each note with every fiber of my being, and momentarily I am the music. I do listen to contemporary music; I won't list what—I'm not in a Brett Easton Ellis novel—but it does not set the scene as well as Wagner.

With the excitement of a five-year-old at Christmas I remember the black bag in my briefcase. I open it up and a smile stretches across my face: my new hood, black and shiny with its own brilliant red ball gag built in. Impatience gets the better of me and I pull it over my head as quickly as I can, adjusting it so that I can breathe through my nose. It's perfect, better than I could have hoped, but it's not time yet, so I take it off on the way to the bedroom and place it on the corner of the bed. Under the bed is a black metal chest that I pull out and unlock. Inside lives my equipment: handcuffs, padlocks, ropes, gates of hell, nipple clamps, three harnesses, size 11 stiletto shoes, latex pants, latex hoods, latex bodysuits (I like latex), and my prize collection of bondage photos.

The dictionary defines bondage as serfdom, slavery, confinement, constraint. I know that because I looked it up when I was eight. But as we all know, it goes much deeper than this. For some people it's simply a way of life, a way of being, and when I look into this chest I can see my whole life lying in front of me. I take out my latex boiler suit, bury my face in it, and breathe deeply, filling my nostrils with every drop of its essence. They say smell is the most evocative of the senses, and when I smell rubber I am overwhelmed and can barely stop myself from getting an erection.

Everyone has fetishes, whether they are consciously aware of them or not, and whether the fetishes are sexual or nonsexual, fetishism is a natural and necessary part of living as a human. For me, if I remember back, the desire to be restrained first became apparent when I was a child playing cowboys and Indians and I would secretly hope to be caught and tied up, and when I was I inevitably came.

At the bottom of the chest is a latex G-string, I bought it for Lauren, an old girlfriend, but she was horrified at the thought of wearing it. We split up not long after, but I kept it, partly in the hope that I will meet someone one day who will relish wearing it and partly because on nights like tonight if I wear it I sometimes feel like I am not alone.

I cover my lower body with baby talc and pull the G-string on. It is a tight fit and I know it will get tighter as the night goes on, but the thought thrills me. I run a soft cloth over the bodysuit to buff the shine and sit on the edge of the bed to tease it on. As I'm pulling it up inch by inch over my legs, wishing I'd shaved them every time the rubber grips the hairs and pulls, my thoughts drift back to Lauren, who was the love of my life. We nearly got married, until she found out and I never saw her again. I don't know why, I don't hurt anyone, I pay my taxes, I give to charity, I love my mum—but we all love our mum; she gave us all our first taste of confinement, after all, in the womb. Which reminds me, I should give my mother a ring about seeing her on Sunday. It's Mother's Day, and she likes to have a fuss made.

I laugh to myself as I pick up the phone to dial her, and I imagine her reaction if she could see me sitting here half dressed for a night of hard-core bondage and autoerotica. Her phone rings three times and then her answering machine kicks in, so I leave her a message but tell her I am going out so I will ring her in the morning. I hang up and attach two silver clamps to my nipples.

Back in the bedroom I sprinkle talc over my arms, back, and chest and pull the bodysuit over my shoulders. It is a struggle and I breathe a sigh of relief when it snaps into place. Already I can feel the rubber chafing my nipple clamps and I press down on them to accentuate the divine pain.

I have a pain lust; algolagnia, the experts call it. I get high on the endorphins that are released by my brain when my body suffers pain and if it is focused and channeled it can take me to peaks of ecstasy that make everything else fade away.

Before I start on the restraints I take a wheeled cart from my wardrobe and attach a long chain. I put the cart under the letter-box, where it will wait patiently for tomorrow's post, and I drape the chain along the floor, back through the hall to my bedroom, all the time making sure there is nothing lying about for it to catch on when I pull the cart and the keys toward me in the morning.

Next step, I clear my dressing table and remove the blanket, which is draped over it, revealing a four-foot-square reinforced stainless-steel cage. My breathing quickens as I lovingly run my hands over it, seducing it. It is my pride and joy and the setting for some of my greatest scenes.

In order to fully submit, I create a frame around my actions which suspends reality. It helps to create expectations and set the scene apart from other parts of my life. Once inside the frame, I am free to act and feel in ways that I cannot at other times. Naturally, fantasies play a huge part in the whole thing. Often I dream of being a dominatrix's sex slave—she would look like 50s pin-up model Bettie Page or the woman I followed at Bond Street tube last year. Her beauty and poise struck me so hard I have been unable to get her image out of my head, and she has been in the frame with me in nearly all of my scenes ever since.

Nearly there, but the preparation is part of the whole experience so it is not to be rushed. I position a mirror opposite the cage and momentarily climb inside to make sure it is in the right position, giving a perfect view, but it will look better when I am fully dressed.

I pull on my new hood and take a deep breath before snapping the padlock shut on the zipper, sealing my head in. I adjust it slightly so the gag fits in my mouth, and I close my teeth over it. I can see out of it through two slits and there are holes for my nostrils so that I can breathe. Once it is in position, I take a squirt of nasal spray to open my nose and reach for my restraints. I step into my custom-made high-heel shoes and cuff the first set of restraints around my ankles, which immediately restricts me to a five-inch totter as I try to move toward the cage.

I wait until I am there before I cuff my wrists. I am careful to put the restraints on the right way around with the keyholes facing down to my fingers because I know when the morning arrives my fingers will be numb and I want to make it as easy as possible to unlock them when the time comes. I fasten my hands in front of me; I'd prefer to fasten them behind my back but I do have some safety concerns and I need to be able to open the envelope in the morning.

When I do this I am taking a breather from myself, from work, from Helen, from the treadmill, from life. I know what people think, but it's not just about sex; it is a spiritual discipline practiced by shamans for centuries. Nevertheless, I keep it a secret because people wouldn't understand. I'm afraid of being condemned by people, especially my mother; she'd never be able to hold her head up at bridge club again, but if I'm honest, part of me likes the thought of that.

Once I lock the door to the cage I know that I am trapped until the morning when the keys will drop through my letterbox and fall onto the trolley, which I can pull toward the cage and release myself. I usually have some safeguards in place, such as an emergency number programmed into my phone, but I stopped doing that three months ago in an attempt to push things further and further.

As I climb into the cage and pull the door closed behind me I hesitate; it's only natural and always happens. What if I get stuck, what if I can't get out? I stop myself midthought and go through a familiar dialogue in my head. What is the worst that can happen if I can't release myself? It's an enormous risk to depend on an unknowing third party for release. Anyone will tell you: when it comes to release mechanisms, it's best to rely on very basic things—ice melts, gravity makes things drop—but that's not enough for me anymore. Where is the thrill in reliance? I need more than that. I need to completely submit, and I am a harsh master. I ignore all good sense in my head, close the door to my prison, and snap the padlock shut. I chain my wrists to the bottom of the cage, and a glazed, peaceful look washes over my face. I am no longer Daniel Johnston, thirty-nine, type A personality, in control, hardworking, intelligent, demanding. Now I am powerless, and it is bliss.

I crane my neck to look in the mirror, where I gasp in awe at the sight that presents itself to me with such vulnerability. I slowly move my eyes over my latex-bound body and groan in pleasure through my gag as the veracity of the situation hits me fully for the first time.

The walls of reality are just beginning to dissolve and my first imaginary scenario is approaching, when the phone rings. I curse myself for forgetting to unplug it but I didn't and I have no choice but to listen as the shrill bell cuts through the air three times before the answering machine kicks in. It is my mum; she says she will ring back later, and I groan at the prospect of being interrupted all night by my mother, of all people. I try to wipe the sound of her voice from my head and regain my concentration.

Surrender and vulnerability, surrender and vulnerability, surrender and vulnerability, surrender and vulnerability, surrender and vulnerability, surrender and vulnerability. I say it over and over in my head like a personal mantra.

Some people have to be tied up to be free. For me, losing myself in my imagination is an escape from a life of adding up numbers and profits. An accountant with an imagination—you wouldn't think it, would you. You wouldn't believe it, either.

I am losing track of time but it is not important, so I allow it to slip from my grasp for now . . .

I don't know how long I've been here; it's starting to get really hot and my limbs are aching, but amid the pain and discomfort another fantasy presents itself, and I drift into it body and soul. What else can I do?

The phone rings again, tearing me from my experience, and I am angry as I suspend my scene until the message has been recorded. Mother again. If she's not careful she will not be getting a Mother's Day present this year. As she hangs up I wonder what she would say, how she would react, if she knew. She would be horrified, probably, and she definitely wouldn't understand. Sometimes I'm not even sure I do myself. Some experts say it is because I was a cesarean birth and missed out on the restriction and compression of the birth canal. That's experts for you, always trying to pigeon-hole, always trying to explain, but some things are more compli-cated than science, some things like men and their compulsions.

More time passes and my arms and legs are numb. I twist about as much as the iron bars will let me and I strain against my restraints, allowing the shards of searing pain to shimmy up and down my spine. When I am tied up I am forced to be entirely sex-ual and no guilt can come in the way. It's not completely guilt-free, but that can wait until tomorrow and for now I allow myself to be swallowed up by a total emotional release. The clamps on my nip-ples are piercing my flesh, and tears from my eyes mix with drool from my gagged mouth. Believe it, this is the best bit for me: when the restraints are biting and I'm reaching the limit of my reserves— this is when I really lose myself for hours on end . . .

Time is running out; the sun is nearly up and experience tells me the post will be here soon. Part of me is relieved but part of me wishes this could go on forever. I always wish that, but I don't dwell on it. I want to make the most of the time left and my mind goes hunting for the perfect experience . . .

I am exhausted and would kill for a drink of water. The post should have arrived by now, I'm sure of that, but then again my mind could be playing tricks on me. The restraints seem tighter on my wrists and ankles and my face feels like it is being split in two by the gag. The blood has rushed to my head and my face is burning up but I'm sure it won't be long now so I settle into my pain.

I begin to wish I had engaged a backup plan, but the body compels even when the mind rebels, and sometimes I lose control over this compulsion. I've been tying myself up since I was a teenager. The complexity of the bondage has increased with time—I've become more daring, more extreme—but nothing has ever gone wrong before; the postman is just late. He'll be here by lunchtime and it's Saturday, so I don't have to worry about work. I always was an eternal optimist.

A fly has entered the room and it is buzzing around inside the cage. I try to swat it away as best I can with my heavily restrained arm, but it taunts me, unknowingly becoming my tormentor. It watches me from its cubist eyes and I squirm uncomfortably under its judgmental gaze. I catch a glimpse of myself in the mirror and the opinions of the outside world start to seep into my mind, but I struggle to keep them out and the illusion in place. I concentrate on the aches and pains that dance up and down my body and I spend the next hour indulging my wildest thoughts . . .

There is still no sign of the post and I know I've been here too long now. I'm beginning to panic, but I force myself to calm down. If I panic it will be even harder to breathe and—oh, fuck, it hits me for the first time, I could die like this and I panic more, I throw myself against the side of the cage, but my restraints prevent me from making any impact.

All of a sudden a million scenarios flog my brain. If my mother finds me will her heart stand the shock? Will she tidy the death scene away to make it look like suicide, as so many other embarrassed families do? If the police find me will my corpse become a laughing-stock? Will they think I am sad and lonely and that I had to do this through desperation? I want to leave a note telling them that I did this because I wanted to because it is my life, the life I chose. I'm not dirty, I'm proud.

I am half scared, half exhilarated; this is the best trip I have ever had, the most death-defying roller coaster of an experience. I'm taking things to the limit, the very limit . . .

I haven't had a drink in nineteen hours and I gave up holding my pee in sometime around midday. The sun is going down and I have to accept that the postman is not going to come, not today anyway, but tomorrow is nearer than it was. Then I realize it is Sunday tomorrow; no post.

I'm going to die. Nobody knows I am here and there is no way of freeing myself without the keys. This thought sends a wave of fear through my body. I knew I was taking a risk, but a hard cock has no conscience. It also doesn't have any common sense.

The fly appears in front of me again, and in a hypnagogic daze I ask him the time. For a moment I am genuinely surprised that he does not answer me and then I am angry, angry with the fly because he can't answer me and because of all the living things to spend my last hours with I'm stuck with a filthy, shit-eating housefly. It probably knows I am on the verge of death and it's waiting to lay its eggs and fill my body with maggots.

I remember reading somewhere that a good scene does not end in orgasm, it ends in catharsis and what in life could be more cathartic than death. This thought offers me short-lived comfort, and the pain becomes too much for me. I am weakened by dehydration and I black out just as the phone starts ringing again . . .

I think it is Sunday, or Monday, or Christmas Day; I'm not sure anymore. My head is swimming and I feel as weak as water. I can't stop thinking about water, but thoughts don't feed my thirst, they just aggravate it, and I feel like a rabid dog in a cage.

This is the longest I have ever been bound and gagged and I know I've exceeded any notion of a safety zone. They say you should always be careful what you wish for because it might come true. The words wade around and around in my head but I am too weak to remember why by the time the thought is finished.

And so here I hang, my soul suspended between this life and the next, neither offering much comfort at the moment.

I long for a safe word that would release me, one magic utterance that would unlock my bondage. My mind becomes obsessed and when I see the fly land nearby I desperately whisper to it over and over again, "Red, red, red . . ." but it does not understand the universal concepts of bondage and I am still here, trapped by my own obsession.

I must have blacked out again, I now have no concept of time passing, and it could be anytime between sunrise and sunset. I try to judge by the shadows cast by the sun, but my thick, concealing curtains keep the light out as well as they do prying eyes. Even the fly has deserted me now.

Wave after wave of anxiety washes over me. The panic I feel is the only difference between being awake and blacking out. I have not felt my arms or legs in hours, my body has already left me, all that remains is my mind and now that is growing dim.

Epilogue

Monday morning arrives and at 8:35 precisely the postman climbs the steps to Daniel's house and pushes the manila envelope with the keys in through the letterbox, where it lands in the trolley cart. The trolley does not move and the chain attached to it is lifeless.

Later in the day a key turns in the lock and the front door opens. Daniel's mother appears and picks up the uncollected post from the trolley. She rattles the manila envelope and hears the keys jangling inside before putting it on the hall table. She calls her son's name out and while waiting for an answer she notices the chain leading from the cart and she follows it into the bedroom. She does not notice the cage at first and busies herself tidying the room. She opens the curtains and the sun's brutal rays pour in, illuminating the latex-clad, lifeless body in the cage. Shock sets a scream off in her chest but it sticks in her throat when she realizes that the monster in front of her is her only son.

Reflex Doll

Teresa Lamai

Test.

First of all, let me tell you how despicable I find this whole project. You heard me.

I didn't ask you to leave out of modesty. I wanted to be alone with your recorder, for as long as I like, saying what I need to say without your peevish interruptions. Can I tell you that your voice is arguably the most detestable thing about you?

But it's your face that makes me want to hit something. Oatmeal-colored, round with a jutting, bratty chin and a hateful little nose.

And did you dye your hair that same oatmeal color to match? No, aspiring professors don't usually dye their hair. You do wear those sporty boiled-wool clogs, don't you? Wearing girly clothes and heels would probably feel as foreign to you as wearing this safety-orange jumpsuit.

I caught you staring at it when we first met. I have to wear these handcuffs, too—either that or sit on the other side of some Plexiglas. The cuffs add a touch of timeless pathos that Plexiglas lacks.

Before I was sentenced to life, I had never met any women grad students. Isn't that funny? But since I've been here, whoa! Every goddamn week, a new grad student—even a couple of ballsy under-grads. Not that I mind, normally. The psychology students are more fucked up than I am, poor things. The social work students are nuts, too, but more fun. One of them tried to bring me weed.

But with you sociologists, there's this slavering avarice, like vampires or zombies who need human misery to survive. No, really. It's like you want to be taken as seriously, and probably funded as extravagantly, as the hard sciences, so you're all obsessed with finding the most problematic specimens of humanity and reducing them to data points.

And I saw that article about you in the *Globe*. Front page of the metro section! "Women and Life: Harvard Sociologist Dares to Connect." And a big-ass photo of you, looking all soulful and earnest. Good move. I don't think anyone's done an ethnographic study of women with life sentences. The more our cases drag on, the more we lose it, bit by bit—solitary confinement, rapes, failed appeal after failed appeal—the more edgy and relevant your research will seem.

Shit, you could milk your whole dissertation out of us, possibly a book, then tenure.

I doubt you'll listen to this whole recording. I already know you'll ultimately claim to have lost it, or tell your adviser I was unin-telligible—because it won't fit in your outline. Your type is almost pathologically devoid of curiosity; simply, you manage the world until it meets with your expectations, and any anomalies are lanced like boils.

But I bet there's a part of you that needs to know how I under-stand you so well.

No, I'm still here. I'm just wondering if I should bother. Well, fuck, this is for me, anyway.

Do you realize I didn't start working as a prostitute until col-lege? Now, that's a data point that won't fit in your chart, I'm sure. I hadn't even kissed a boy who wasn't related to me until I was seventeen. Although my father never faltered in his conviction that I was a slut, holding forth on that topic since I was a toddler. I think "slut" was the first word I learned.

I believe my father may have been in a way disappointed that I wasn't actually a slut. Or maybe he really did believe I was, you know, meeting my pimp during study hall, and turning tricks in the late afternoon, between AP physics and the debate club. Or perhaps giving hand jobs on the two-hour commute into school each day, the long bus ride from gray-towered Brockton to the Beacon Hill Academy and their pilot program for gifted low-income kids.

I never really thought I was gifted, but I was determined to be good. So desperately good all the time, at everything. Oh, I learned to read teachers so closely that I could produce whatever they wanted.

Even when the busing program stopped, my school counselor gave me a ride to school every morning so I could continue in the college prep program. It was quite the gauntlet to get to her car. My dad once followed me out to the sidewalk in his underwear, shrieking that I was a slut, that he hoped I enjoyed the ride with my john. Because as a former cop, he would know that's how it goes down—a sixteen-year-old hooker carrying eight textbooks gets in a minivan with her pudgy schoolmarm of a john at 5:30 A.M. I mean, I'm surprised we didn't get busted.

Mrs. Ito was silent on that drive, bless her. The last thing I needed was a mess with Child Protective Services and some whacked hippie foster parents.

Dad flipped when I got into Tufts, on scholarship. Of course I had to forge his signature on all the application stuff; he's typically too drunk to hold a pen. He found out when he was invited to Freshman Parent Welcome, an unbelievably swank affair in the Faculty Club. The Alumni Association fawned over new students and their parents, nearly swooning at what was typically a fresh crop of wealth and influence for the school. Dad actually showed up halfway through the keynote address, barely clothed, reeking of Everclear, shoving his way through the ushers. By the time campus security arrived, he'd shaken me till I broke a tooth. It took several hours for my vision to clear.

I'm sure you read about that in the papers.

Shit. No, I'm not crying, I'm laughing. Some people have issues; my dad has a lifetime subscription. All psychotic, all the time. You have to admire his stamina, in a way.

But that's an entirely different inquiry. Maybe some sociologist will find him in a homeless shelter once he's out of the hospital.

Back to me.

I really thought I would love college. It started out okay. But I just got so fucking broke after the first two months. The scholarship paid for tuition, but once I got a room and bought my books, all my savings were gone. I got a job as a waitress, but still. The worst was this "freshman enrichment" seminar, where the professor wanted us to become well rounded and sophisticated by attending different theater shows around the city, or taking field trips to New York City to see the Met. I mean, fuck, there goes my food budget till February. I tried to talk to him but he just said freshman year is always a shock to kids who have never budgeted before and I should cut down on the shopping and pizza.

But you know what? It wasn't only that I was broke. I was slipping under the stress. I was freaking out. And for some reason I kept hearing my father's voice, even louder and more shrill than when I was living with him. Slut, slut, and slut. I would try to force it down, grabbing my elbows and rocking in the bed. But it was still the one word that rattled around in my skull until I couldn't hear anything else.

How can I explain this? Have you ever driven on a bridge so narrow and slippery that it seemed only a matter of time until you veered off? You can feel the roaring, empty air sucking at you from all around; you can feel your car twitching on the dark, ice-slick pavement. You train your eyes on the road, you force yourself to keep driving straight, but the fear swells in your chest like a bloated, hot parasite, inching its way up your throat, to your tongue.

And it would be a relief to just crank the steering wheel and let the whistling darkness claim you completely.

So I woke one morning with the clarity of thought that comes with fasting, and I concluded that prostitution was the most viable option for me.

I cut classes that day and rented some porn to get myself started. I bought a dildo while I was at it, the largest model. I felt my jaw clench as I picked it up.

Then I had my own Freshman Enrichment seminar at home. I wondered if I should write a paper on those films; revelatory and revolting, kind of like watching close-ups of people eating or going to the bathroom, but grosser. Almost put me off the whole endeavor, but then I'm the determined type.

It took me twenty minutes to force the dildo in. I'd never had anything quite so big all the way inside me before. I didn't know about lube then, but the blood actually made it easier. It still burned like a motherfucker. I forced myself to watch a feature-length film with it in. By the end my whole pelvis was numb. After that, I figured, anything else would be cake.

That weekend, I took the subway to the Golden Tent, a topless dancing bar in Roxbury. I sat outside by the exit and drank coffee to stay warm. Toward midnight, the first men came stumbling out, grimacing in the bitter cold, squinting at me. I smiled at them until one finally came near, eyes huge, chin lowered, like a starving coyote sniffing poisoned meat.

He jumped when I spoke. "Are you a cop?"

"What? No."

"You know it's entrapment if you lie."

"N—no, I'm not a cop."

"Want to have some fun?"

"Jesus. How old—?"

"I'm not a minor. Is that your car?"

It was much more low-key than the porn films. Although he grossed me out a little when he licked his hand. That clued me in to the whole concept of lube, as I watched his glistening cock bulge out of his fist, then under my own smaller fingers. It clenched on itself and quivered, flushing scarlet, like a colicky alien baby.

I didn't have to do much. It wasn't even strictly necessary for me to lean over and take it in my mouth. I kind of enjoyed how it smelled, like a tide pool.

I swallowed instinctively when he came, terrified of ruining my one good coat. It was a gift from Mrs. Ito.

He lay back gasping afterward. The windows of his station wagon were fogged solid white. A dog's chew toy and a Barbie doll rolled under my feet.

He started to moan with each breath, his lips trembling. "Oh. God. Oh. God. I've never—" His shoulders hitched.

I offered him some gum. "One hundred dollars."

I made five hundred dollars that night. I still cannot believe I was able to get that much without undressing, but I had taken them all by surprise, and I was really young and fresh-looking then. Beginner's luck.

I never worked the same place twice, although some bars were more profitable than others. I did have to start fucking them, eventually, but even that was fine. Over surprisingly fast. And I had an unlimited supply of condoms from the campus health office.

I quit my waitressing job and had time for homework, for writing. I did really well in my classes. I found more business close to campus, with wealthier clients. I started giving out my number and scheduling follow-up appointments in hotels, thinking I could make some more money that way, maybe get to where I was working only one day a week.

But that turned out to be a total time-suck. I mean, a guy in a car will come in like thirty seconds. Then he'll hurry to pay and drive off, because you're lying on his baby's blankie.

But get a guy in a hotel room with a hooker, and sweet Jesus, it's a psychodrama marathon. Their eyes would glaze over and I knew they were seeing someone else, some proto-mama who ruled their hind brains. They would punish me or idolize me in someone else's stead, compulsively reenacting whatever trauma haunted them, over and over and over.

Most wanted to insult me or degrade me. Yes! Shocking as that may sound. I would never let anyone tie me, no matter how much they insisted I wanted it, but I did make a big deal of struggling and sobbing when they beat me. They seemed satisfied.

Then there were the ones who begged me to hit them. The meaner I was, the more they shivered with pleasure. I'll never forget this one portly doctor who undressed without a word and got on the floor, raising his clotted-cream buttocks to me. With his forehead pressed into the carpet, he fumbled for his discarded belt and shook it imperiously until I snatched it up. His fuzzy ass started to gleam, green-tinted in the clock-radio's light. When he moaned, it trembled. It looked like a swamp monster. I smacked it out of sheer fright.

But the worst were the ones that wanted to talk to me, wanted me to be their mom or sister. God, they'd hang out in a hotel room for hours on end, drinking tea, telling me about their classes, how stressed out they were about their dissertations. Then when I finally did get them in bed, they'd paw me all over and then slobber around my cunt until I pretended to come. And only then would they let me put the condom on them and finish them off. I finally had to draw the line when they wanted me to stay and take a goddamn nap with them. Christ, waste a whole afternoon for one hundred and fifty bucks.

If you're still listening, I commend you. Because this isn't quite what interests you, is it? You want to know about Ryan Croyden. Specifically, how I met him, and how I killed him.

Well, you already know *how* I killed him. That's in the coroner's report, public record. Rather, you want to hear about my motive, the thoughts that wormed their way through my black, shriveled, felonious little mind.

What is this need to romanticize criminals? You really believe that I approached all of this with some fantastically intricate plan, that I orchestrated every last detail? I didn't know I would kill him until the astonishing moment when it happened. And in that moment there are worlds and worlds of mystery—I'll relive it with each blink, until I die here. I will never understand how he could have been alive one moment, then gone the next.

But I can tell you what I remember.

I was in the English program, and I was starting to be known as a strong writer. Some people told me about the summer creative-writing workshop, a course for real writers from all over the world. Anyone could apply and the prospect made me giddy with terror. Before I could lose my nerve, I e-mailed to the program director, Professor Croyden in the French Lit Department, and asked for an appointment. He responded right away, gracious and welcoming as if I were another professor. Ryan was like that.

It was the first truly warm day of the year. I'd never seen the campus looking so bright, the air sparkling and silky. The apple blossoms in the quad were full-blown, downy, and gleaming against the limpid, flawless sky. I just had to sit in the grass and watch the petals drift like enchanted warm snow. Even through my jacket I could feel the fresh moss, like a balm on my constantly inflamed labia. Everything seemed so new and delicious; the bike racks looked sugary and brittle as ribbon candy, the buildings were gingerbread edged with spiced cream.

I read idly, killing time before my appointment. Sun-blinded, I lay back. It's funny how the sun always feels warmest on your face. Especially when you close your eyes.

Suddenly I was turning my head to follow a flock of starlings.

The sun had moved. The tower bells were ringing. I'd fallen asleep. I stood, gasping. "Fuck."

My panting was loud in the murky corridor. A tall man was locking his door and heading toward the opposite stairwell.

"Um. Professor Croyden."

I don't know if he smiled at the sight of me or if he always wore that placid, gently bemused smile. His fine hair was slightly grown out, the color of ancient wood, filled with copper and topaz lights. His eyes were earthy brown, tinged with deep crimson like very old wine.

"Call me Ryan."

"I'm so sorry. I brought some stories. I'm never late."

"You must be Brenna. You're hardly late—oh, you're all out of breath. Look at you."

He seemed even taller up close, lean and broad-shouldered. I willed myself to lift my eyes from his shirt buttons. He stared at my cheek, my hair. His hand stirred, starting to lift, then he cleared his throat. I ran my palms over my head and some petals fell, glimmering, to the floor.

"Really, not even five minutes late, Brenna, it's fine. I just needed a caffeine fix. Why don't you come with me?"

And five minutes later I was sitting at the library café with him. He suggested a table on the patio, as if we were old friends enjoying an afternoon off. Before I could stop myself, I ordered a double cocoa with whipped cream and sprinkles. The waitress smiled indulgently and my heart sank. Way to be sophisticated.

His smile was radiant. His skin was smooth, satiny as apricots. I couldn't help smiling back.

"All right, so you brought some of your work? Let me take a look."

I stared as he leaned over my portfolio. His lashes were long as a girl's. Looking at him, you'd think he was always sunlit, that even in the middle of winter he would be glowing faintly with amber and dappled green shade. The sun found seams of gold in his hair, painfully bright.

We were so still that greedy sparrows started hopping around our table. I kept watching, wary now. I drank as quietly as I could. His smile faded and his cheeks collapsed, paled.

He looked up, finally. His pupils were dilated. "You wrote this?"

"Well, that one—that's not so good, I know. I really wanted to show you this other piece—"

"I mean. Brenna. How old are you?" A dry, uncertain laugh burst out of him. "I'm sorry, it's just so intense."

I felt the blush start as two burning pinpoints on my cheeks. I should have known better than to make an ass of myself like this. Just because a story is creepy and shocking doesn't mean it has merit. That's what I get for being so desperate for attention.

I swallowed. "Well, I appreciate your looking at them in any event." I kept my voice low, even. "I've got to get to class—Oh. Oh."

His hand settled on mine. I gazed at it, open-mouthed. The warmth crawled up my arm until my shoulders tingled.

"Brenna. This is truly—" He lifted his hand away and I exhaled. "I think, truly some of the most remarkable writing I've seen. And I don't say that lightly."

His smile returned. He cocked his head as if he were listening to something far away.

"My God, Brenna. You know, I'm always secretly hoping to find something so utterly unique. Where have you been, you little wonder child?" I searched his face but his smile was guileless, blissful, his eyes sparkling like warm cider.

My feet twitched happily under the table. "I don't know, I've just been here." I didn't know where to look so I drank the rest of my cocoa.

It's really impossible to describe the breathless, surreal moments when friendly strangers become lovers. It's as much a mystery as his death. Although, with lovers, both know from the beginning that it's going to happen, even when it seems the most improbable, far-fetched thing.

We started meeting at that café every week, me bearing a new chapter and him shaking his head with gentle wonder. Soon the cherry blossoms faded and lilacs took their place, then finally pearl-bright clusters of wisteria, with their heady, cloying scent. I would watch Ryan speak and find myself thinking, *When we're lovers we'll talk much more quietly. We'll walk close together when it's cold out, arm in arm for warmth.*

My body thought we already were lovers. My palms would tingle until I found an excuse to touch him. I'd feel my eyes narrowing as I imagined how his skin would smell under his starched white shirt, under his cologne and his grassy-scented soap. My breasts would sting until I nearly winced. It was like electricity running through me; like dying and being jolted to life every ten seconds.

I think Ryan convinced himself for a long time that he was my surrogate older brother. He would cajole me, rolling his eyes at my diffidence, punching my shoulder with exaggerated gentleness until I squealed. He confessed that he felt like a fraud and an outsider at Tufts; he'd only just got his doctorate, and was barely breaking even as an adjunct professor. He didn't know how long he could keep up the illusion of being a real academic.

Once we met on a Sunday, and found the café was closed.

"I know." He squeezed my forearm. "Let's take the T into town. I want to show you something."

As soon as we left the irrigated glades of campus, the day's heat was suffocating. The sky was fitful and hazy, diffusing the sunlight into a sick glare. The T station was like an overheated Dumpster; the crowded car smelled of vinegar and blood.

"I'm sorry, Brenna." I was already sweating, my hair clinging along the back of my neck. We stood close, but his voice was quieter than it needed to be. "It's never this packed on a Sunday." He held the strap next to mine, his lean biceps near enough to cushion my head if I fell. When the seat in front of us became free, he bustled me into it. Both his arms were stretched over his head. I could have rested my temple on his hip. My tongue moved restlessly behind my teeth as he smiled down at me.

I let him pull me up by my elbows. His arm coiled around my waist, squeezing briefly, leaving an imprint of sweat, as we pushed off the train.

"You've probably been here many times before, right?"

We entered a cold, high-ceilinged foyer with the bitter, earthy scent of a church. The darkness soothed my eyelids. The air was heavy with incense. It was a museum, but built more like a palace, vaulted with soaring arcs of medieval filigreed stone. The courtyard garden glinted with ancient, dark-watered fountains. Roman gods smiled serenely from pastel mosaics. Under the rosy filtered sunlight, ferns and orchids shimmered with dew, their tiny leaves forming an emerald-green mist.

"I haven't been here." I stretched, breathing deep. My dress still smelled like the subway.

His arm slid around my waist again.

"Come on, let's walk." His voice was softer now than I'd ever heard it, but intent, focused. I couldn't think of how to answer. A pool of silence spread between us. Our footsteps were loud in the half-private cloister; portraits lolled and smirked from their pools of lush, aged color.

"Can you imagine this was once someone's house? This crazy, filthy-rich harpy who really had no clue about art, just traveled over the world picking up anything that caught her eye. It's like a pirate's cave, isn't it? Full of unimaginable treasures, strewn about as if they were toys. It almost enhances their worth, the way you feel you're the first person to truly notice them."

The benches on the second-floor balcony looked down on the birdless garden. I sat with my head on his shoulder, snuggling into him because I was chilly. His hand strayed around my waist to my hip, lingering where he felt the line of my panties. My shoulders drew together and I shivered.

"Brenna." Each time he said my name, he kissed the top of my head. His kisses dropped swiftly, glancing at first, then heavier and warm. He turned his head, resting his cheek on my hair. When he sighed, chills washed over my neck, my shoulders, like trickles of ice water. My nipples burned unbearably, like two hot embers I wanted to shake off.

"Do you know how much I think of you, you little genius?" His voice was so faint I could barely hear it.

One palm rested on my hip, the other on my temple, holding me to his chest. I closed my eyes and there was only his voice.

"You remind me of those old French tapestries, those pale young virgins, with their enormous solemn eyes and tight, determined little mouths. That kind of fierce innocence that brings people to their knees."

He kissed my head again, and spread his slender fingers through my hair.

"It's not willful, affected naïveté, but an intense purity, the kind of innocence that is fearless. The kind of innocence that persists, untouched by any experience."

I couldn't focus on what he said. I let my arms wind around his waist. My dress crept up my thighs and the stone bench was smooth as glass. He cupped my cheek in his palm.

"I can't stop thinking of you, Brenna. I see your mouth and I just want to taste it, feel it swell under mine." His thumb brushed my lips and I cried out. The sound ricocheted softly, dropping down into the courtyard. I bit the inside of my cheek.

"Shh. Close your eyes. There are only a few people here; now and then a pair of eyes will glance toward us from the foyer below, or from the balconies above. It's so cool and quiet, everyone thinks you're just dozing against my shoulder. They can't see my hand under all your hair, stroking your pretty neck, feeling the goose bumps rise."

I couldn't stop shaking. My heart thudded, tight and hot.

His hand trailed down my arm. The hairs stood on end. "Do you think of me, Brenna?"

"No," I murmured into his collar. He laughed quietly, his chest lifting.

"Not at all?"

"I stop. I stop thinking when I'm with you. I can't think at all, I just feel. I just take it in. I can't imagine anything beyond what you're saying, how you look, what you're doing in that instant. What you're doing now."

His fingertips traced along my collarbone, slow and pensive, light as moth wings. His other hand slid low on my hip, the palm just grazing my ass. He took hold of my dress and pushed the silk over my bare skin, resting his damp lips on my forehead.

"But I want you to imagine. I know that if you let yourself imagine, you'll surprise both of us with what you want, how much you want. Brenna, I'm afraid that if I kiss you now, if I bring you to my apartment and undress you and lay you down on my bed, that you'll just follow whatever I do, letting yourself be led. That my own need will flare up and blind me. And we'll never discover what you really want."

His embrace tightened and the room went dim around me.

"Listen. I want you to imagine us making love, can you do that? After I bring you home today, I want you to undress. Spread lotion over your skin, lie where it's cool. I want you to be alone with your thoughts. Imagine what you want, no limits, whatever makes everything in your body connect and your blood start humming. Touch yourself the way you want me to touch you, soft at first, then insistent, forceful, nails digging crescents until you jump with the pain."

My back writhed softly. I sneaked one hand to my mouth and bit my fingertips, as hard as I dared.

"Shh, shh. Are your eyes still closed? You like that, don't you, Brenna?" His touch on my throat was so gentle I started to pant. "Shh. Imagine how you want me to kiss you, where you need to be kissed and cuddled and where you need that swift shock of pain to sear all the thoughts from your mind. Imagine the kind of touch that would make you wet and so swollen your legs can't help falling open."

I lifted one hand as if to shush him. Footsteps fell along the corridor behind us, echoing over the parquet. Ryan kept murmuring into my hair.

"I want you to take a small mirror and look at yourself. Look at your breasts, watch your indigo-black hair snaking over them. I imagine your nipples are the same pale violet color as your lips."

His thumb brushed my mouth again.

"Look at your cunt. Spread your thighs and watch the glossy, matted hair pull away from your slit. Oh, what a gorgeous little flower. Touch the outer labia and watch them react. Do they contract like a sea anemone or do they pout, becoming so hot it seems they've melted? Run your fingertips along the dark inner lips. Pinch them, nip them with your fingernails. I know it hurts. Watch your cunt react to the pain."

"Ryan." I was panting. My hands were clenching and twisting, grabbing handfuls of his shirt. My hips slid forward.

"I can smell you, Brenna, such a sweet, rich smell. Touch your clit lightly at first. Find the rhythm you need, and watch your small white fingers disappear under those black curls. Keep touching it, tracing unhurried circles with just the barest pressure. Then stop and look at it."

"Ryan, fuck." I was alarmed now. A voice shouldn't be able to penetrate your skull and your rib cage like that, as if you'd never been solid to begin with. A voice shouldn't be able to drop into your center and detonate through your heart and mind.

"Shh. Shh. I want you to look at yourself and know that's what you'll look like to me when you're naked, slick with oil and sweat and tied to my bed. When you're just about to come and you've lost control and you're begging for my cock."

"Ah." I jumped to my feet. Two older women turned from a painting and gazed at me. I gulped and sat again, straight-backed.

Ryan and I shared a cab, stopping at my building first. I was speechless, gripping his hand. His eyes were dark with shock but his smile was tender. He walked me to my door, wrote his address on the back of my museum ticket, and brushed my lips with his.

My apartment was clammy and dank. I undressed and padded about restlessly. The living room was full of neglected homework. My bed was still sweaty from the night before. I ran a shallow bath and sat in the dim, rippling light. Giggling, I reached for a mirror.

I usually got myself off in the dark, wedged between my mattress and the wall, my legs pressed so tightly together that my knuckles left bruises on my inner thighs. But now I spread my legs wide, resting my dusty feet on either side of the tub, brushing my hands over my waist, my breasts. My hair still smelled like Ryan and I smoothed it across my face.

I was laughing to myself when I put the mirror between my feet and raised my legs straight to the ceiling. With my blurred, foreshortened thighs and my hair set free underwater, I looked like a mermaid. I stopped laughing when I saw my cunt—fluted, raw flesh, unfinished and shockingly vulnerable, a mollusk torn from its shell.

When I started touching it, my legs collapsed and the mirror splashed into the water. My body squirmed, thrashed in the small tub. Ryan's voice filled my head. I came quickly, screaming as if something were being ripped from me, my thoughts scattering like pearls from a broken string. One hand worked my clit and the other twisted, seized, clutched at the empty air. I lay twitching for a long time afterward, blinking at the ceiling.

I smiled to myself, then a small laugh fluttered up my spine. "Ryan."

Hold on. You have to understand something. This is not a rehash of a million poorly written gothic novels; I wasn't intending to keep my unspeakable secret life from Ryan. I wasn't at all ashamed of being a prostitute. I've never been ashamed of anything—I don't have that kind of self-worth. My part-time job had been simply irrelevant to our conversations thus far; if I'd been waitressing, for example, I wouldn't have interrupted our talks to say, "Oh, I just want to make sure you know that I'm working as a waitress." I mean, who cares?

And, yes, I know that prostitutes, even in the abstract, inspire this salacious fascination—like as soon as you take some money for sex you stop being human and start being some stock character in an adult fairy tale. But I knew Ryan; he wasn't fucking stupid that way. Ryan would understand that working as a prostitute was just one of life's indignities, something to endure and quickly forget.

Anyway, after all that splendor in the bathtub I dozed off. I woke several hours later with a sore neck, sweating where my body wasn't submerged. The phone was ringing.

Shit. I had an appointment. It was one of my regulars, Graham. As I dressed, his voice rang sharp and tinny through the answering machine:

"Well, here I am waiting. You let me down, sister. Since I'm here I might as well smoke out—but fuck me, I'm not going to waste my whole evening waiting for you."

He was still speaking as the door slammed shut behind me.

Graham was in his sixth year as an art student. He seemed to believe that if he cultivated the worst traits of the archetypal artist-rebel—sloth, filthy dreadlocks, a sustained, unfocused aggression—people wouldn't notice that he had no eye for art, no talent. He was convinced that his work was rejected by commercial galleries only because it was too edgy, too daring. He preferred to be shown, he claimed, in his friends' cafés, where the audience wasn't afraid of his shamanistic vision. I think he also believed that patronizing a prostitute was another statement, full of irony and nihilism—when in fact he was just too obnoxious to get laid otherwise.

"Well, fuck, Brenna. Hookers don't get to be late." He lay naked on his belly on the anonymous beige bedspread. The room was nearly dark, and the smoke around his head gleamed phosphorescent in the TV's shifting colored light. His back fat jiggled when he moved. He raised his head to me, arching like a sea lion.

"What, Graham, I'm five minutes early. We said seven-thirty."

"Nuh-uh."

I had a sudden image of him as a kid, maybe at Disney World. I bit back a smile. It was impossible to dislike Graham completely.

"Ya-huh, Graham. I had seven-thirty written down in my little calendar. And a gold star next to your name."

"Fuck you," he chuckled. He rolled on his back, his furred belly swelling. He had new silver nipple rings. He covered his eyes with his meaty forearm.

"Brenny?"

"What-y?" I approached the bed and he smiled at my footsteps.

"Want to take off your dress for me?" He reached toward his rosy cock. I watched him grab it, his black nail polish making the skin seem even more fragile and tender.

When I worked my dress over my hair and let it fall beside me, his eyes were wide.

"Jesus, you came here like that, wearing just that dress?"

I got on the bed but he moved away, rising to his knees.

"Brenna, look at you. What's so different?"

He reached toward me and I bit my lip, cursing. I usually put Anbesol on my nipples before an appointment—I've found it dulls the feeling and tastes bad enough that it discourages a lot of sucking. But that night I forgot. When he touched the underside of my breasts, my nipples crinkled tight, tiny knots forming. They tingled and my shoulders twitched.

I shouldn't have closed my eyes. He ran his fingertips down my belly and my lonely skin was suddenly flooded with sweetness. I moaned. His fingers found my swollen cunt at the same time his wet mouth closed around my right nipple. I grabbed his woolly head, panting. Then I jumped off the bed.

His breathing was hoarse, strained. Veins bulged in his neck. He struggled off the bed, cock casting about blindly as he moved. He groped for my hips.

"Goddamn, Brenna, I've never seen you like this. You're ready for me, aren't you? Your skin is just on fire."

He slumped to his knees and ran his tongue over my stomach. Two chubby fingers slipped in my cunt. "So wet," he hissed.

I backed away, wiggling to dislodge his hand. I was shaking so hard I could barely pick up my dress.

"You know what, Graham? The thing is, I don't feel that great. I've—I've got a stomach bug. I'm sick."

"Come on, now, Brenna, don't fuck around." I froze when his hands found my ass, caressing in slow circles, lifting slightly so my wet, aching labia were stretched. My knees trembled.

"No, really, Graham. I promise a rain check." I stepped away and managed to get the dress over me. Please God, I prayed, don't let him have a tantrum about this. The insides of my thighs were slippery; my clit pulsed furiously. I had to get out of there.

Do you understand how important it was for me to escape then?

I think it's generally understood that prostitutes rarely enjoy sex with clients. But here's the thing: They *must not* enjoy it. They must never let themselves go—ever.

True, you'll find some girls who just go for it, who get off compulsively with their johns. For them, sex is all about fury. They chase that rage and then come hard to exorcise it, even for a few moments. But those girls don't last long. That shit is exhausting. And it's dangerous—you lose your focus even for a second and you could find yourself in handcuffs.

I never felt anything. That's why I was so good at it. Until I met

Ryan, until his voice starting resonating up and down my spinal cord. All my nerves were becoming alive and hungry.

And I knew if I had an orgasm with Graham or someone like him, that would be the end. I wouldn't have been able to live with myself afterward. Just the thought of it makes me shudder. Being so wet and mindless with lust and reduced to this slack-eyed reflex doll. Just—ah, God.

When I look back on it, I think Graham just meant to toss me onto the bed. He was giggling, stoned, oblivious. But I struggled so hard when he hefted me that he lost his grip. I dropped to the floor. My skull knocked against the end table.

I saw stars. I thought I would throw up. When my vision cleared, he was leaning over me. That's when I freaked.

I grabbed for the nearest solid thing—the desk chair. I screamed and hurled it toward his head.

The next thing I knew, I was standing with my back against the door. My hand was closing and unclosing over the handle. My teeth chattered and I moaned to myself, "no, no," over and over.

Graham lay on the floor. Blood pooled around his head, sticky and black as tar in the dim light. A sitcom was on TV and the room filled with raucous laughter.

When he moved, I gasped and ran to him. He stared at me, one eye swollen shut.

"Bitch."

I grabbed a towel off the bed and held it toward him. He clambered away.

"Crazy. Goddamn. Bitch." When I moved closer, he shrieked.

He pulled his jeans on, hopping frantically, nearly falling over the upturned table. His shirt was streaked with blood once he got it over his head.

"Graham. You need—" I stuttered. I couldn't quite believe he was able to move. "You're hurt really, really bad."

He hurried to the door.

"Trick-ass fucking slut." He gurgled blood, spat on the carpet. "Kill you."

He left. I looked around the empty room. "Think," I whispered. "Think."

Twenty minutes later I was at Ryan's town house, ringing the buzzer. The doorman scowled at me from inside the lobby.

The intercom crackled. "Yes?"

I almost sobbed with relief. "Ryan, it's me, Brenna. Can I—? Can I come—?" My breath was shuddering, breaking.

The door clicked and I fell through. He burst from the stairwell.

His mouth fell open when he saw me. He took off his dinner jacket and wrapped it over my shoulders, glancing toward the street as he hurried me into the elevator.

He practically carried me into his apartment. With his arms around me, I was suddenly so tired. I fought to keep my eyes open.

He sat me on an antique sofa and disappeared into the bathroom. His apartment was cool, humming with air conditioning and a Bach concerto, playing low.

"Okay. Okay. I'll drive you to Mass General and you can tell me what happened." He raised his voice over the sound of running water.

I closed my eyes for longer than a blink. I jumped to see him sitting beside me, a damp washcloth in his hand.

"Brenna, you're in shock. I'm calling an ambulance." He moved the cloth to my cheek and I leaned away, confused. I looked down at myself. Oh, Jesus. Blood on my hands, down the front of my dress. I grabbed his wrist.

"It's not my blood. I need—I need your help, Ryan." Focus. Focus, just a little longer, I told myself, then you can sleep.

He held my cheeks in his palms, staring. His eyes filled with tears. "You are in shock. God, Brenna, your eyes—did you hit your head? Can you tell me what happened?"

I swallowed. My eyelids felt so heavy. "Ryan. It's not my blood. I need to hide out here for a while, a couple of weeks."

"Whose blood—" He shook his head, scowling. "Someone attacked you?"

I nodded. "He said he'd kill me. Or, no, he wouldn't. I don't know. But I'll be okay if I can just hide out here. Or, or, can you help me get out of Boston for a while? I have a cousin in New York, I can—" I stopped, suddenly dizzy. I just wanted to rest my head on something.

"Jesus." He stood. "I'll call the police, and tell them to send an ambulance, too. You came here first because you were in shock, weren't you? Someone must have broken into your place, and you just came here half-dressed. . . . It'll be okay, Brenna."

I stood, clenching my fists, and grabbed the phone from his hand. It landed in the fireplace, cracking open, and we both jumped with the noise.

"Ryan. Okay, I'm sorry. I'm not myself. Do not call the police."

His glance darted about the room. He looked toward the door and I ran to it, pressing my ass into the wood and facing him.

"Ryan. A guy attacked me and I hit him, harder than I meant to. I—I panicked. You can't call the police because he's one of my clients. He pays me to have sex with him. 'Cause that's what I do, and I cannot get busted. He's not going to the police but he said he'd—I don't know, I don't know what he'll do. I'm scared."

Ryan sat, his mouth working silently. He ran his hands through his hair until it stood on end, curling wildly over his temples.

"Ryan! You understand? That's why I just need to hide out here. Or, no, better yet, just go to New York. Can you help me? Just let me use your phone, let me stay here till the next train leaves. I didn't want any of this."

He stared out the window. He was wearing a spotless white shirt and a dove-gray tie, probably going out to dinner. I hadn't left any bloodstains on him.

"I can't," he finally managed. He stared up at me, plaintively.

"If even part of what you're saying is true, I can't get involved in all this."

"Ryan!" I bellowed. I thought he'd been listening. "No, I'm sorry, I won't yell. I won't. But I am not asking you to get involved. I want to make one phone call and sit on your couch until I can catch a train to New York!"

He kept murmuring, as if to himself. "How could I do this? How could I get involved in this kind of nightmare?" He held his head, rocking.

"Ryan. Have you heard a word I said? There'll be no scandal. I won't—bother you again after tonight."

"How could I be so stupid?" he muttered, tugging absently at his hair.

"I didn't mean to yell, Ryan. I didn't mean—" I started to cry in sharp, bleating sobs, alarming both of us.

He rose, shaking. "Brenna, the only thing that's plain to me right now is that you're not well. You're probably on something. You need to get out of the way."

I braced myself against the door. He gripped my shoulders and I stumbled away, breaking my fall with my palms. I heard the door open.

Do you think he meant to be cruel? Or was his heart so delicate that it couldn't help collapsing, retracting into itself like a snail? Before that moment, I had always thought that brutality and cruelty were the same thing. But at the sight of his retreating shoulders, it hit me: only the tenderhearted have the grace—the finesse— necessary for true cruelty. They put you at ease, they make you melt, they tease out all your defenses, so that when they decide they've had enough, you don't have any means of surviving.

But you still shouldn't infer that I suddenly decided to kill him. I didn't. The coroner's report implies that Ryan was tripped and pushed down the stairs. This story was corroborated by the police reports, character witnesses, psychologists—everyone who wasn't there.

You know what I was actually doing? Following him on my hands and knees, clutching at his ankles, wailing like an orphan.

His feet slipped from my grasp. There was a sickening thud and crack and he was at the bottom of the concrete stairwell, motionless.

There's nothing to tell after that. I knew it was over and I sat and waited for the police to come. Since then, it's all just been a nightmare that I can't wake up from.

Yeah, I'm still here. I'm going to erase this file. You don't deserve to know any of this. Well, you just wouldn't get it. It would go completely over your head. Or, worse yet, I'll find my words written into a novel, maybe a screenplay. Some horrid TV movie of the week that I'll watch in the prison rec room ten years from now. You'll retire on the royalties.

Fuck you. I'm erasing this and recording over with some bull-shit. Maybe I'll make something up about hearing voices, or aliens invading my brain.

Or maybe I'll just leave it blank.

Good Morning, John

Jendi Reiter

January 14

I think this time it'll be the fire again. The swimming-pool drowning got a good reaction yesterday, but I'm not sure if all the details were convincing. It explained Betsy's death, which is the main thing, of course, but not my own injuries. In the end I had to make up an entirely separate story about a rusty nail. I have to remember not to get too creative.

I sit up on the bed, strap on my prosthesis, and pull myself upright by holding on to the night table. Even though I do this every morning, my body, like John's brain, keeps resetting to the time before all this happened, stumbling over the absence of a member. The difference is that in a moment I'll get my bearings, as always.

After I make breakfast it's time to wake my husband. I used to enjoy making fancy gourmet breakfasts for us. Now I don't bother. Sometimes he notices that things have changed before he eats and he gets too upset to have breakfast. That could be why he's getting so much thinner. As for me, I have more important projects than cooking for myself.

"Good morning, John," I say. He says good morning and gets out of bed. He follows me downstairs to the kitchen. Since I'm wearing a long skirt today, he doesn't notice my leg until we're sitting at the table finishing our muffins and coffee. I cross my legs and the skirt falls away, exposing the unnatural gleam of smooth beige plastic.

"My God, what happened to you?" he cries. Startled, he drops his unlit cigarette into his coffee cup, where it floats like drowned Ophelia.

I get up and turn away, hobbling a little, even though I actually feel quite sure of my footing by this point. He grabs me and tries to make eye contact but I refuse to look at him.

"What is it? Did I do something to you? How come I can't remember?" He's starting to panic.

Showing reluctance, I murmur, "You didn't mean it." Now he looks truly desperate, knowing he's somehow guilty even without free will or memory. The specific act doesn't matter.

Finally I seem to drag forth the words, "We were at our country house last weekend. You fell asleep in bed with your cigarette lit. There was a fire. . . . A beam fell on my leg as I was carrying you out."

It sounds like I'm struggling to break the news to him. In fact, this is a story I've told him several times over the past two months. The part about my rescuing him is new, though. I wonder how he'll react. Will it seem too melodramatic?

"Why can't I remember?" he yells.

"You had a concussion. You were unconscious for days. They just let you out of the hospital."

Accepting this explanation without further thought, he collapses on the couch. I sit across from him in the armchair, resigned and patient. Very patient.

Suddenly he looks up, terrified that an even worse blow is about to fall on him. "Where's Betsy? She's all right, isn't she?"

"I'm sorry, John. Our daughter's dead," I say gently, almost suppressing a sob. I lean forward and put a hand on his knee. He shakes it off. His face crumples into tears like a photo on a wadded-up sheet of newspaper.

I watch him wail and tear around the house for a while. My worries that he'd see through my melodramatic embellishments were unfounded. Whatever noble feats I supposedly performed, his tears and apologies are not for me. When he's tired himself out, I give him a tranquilizer and help him back up to bed. He'll probably sleep for the rest of the day, as usual.

Then I go to work. Another day.

January 15

Just a quick one today with John. I have a lot to do this morning. The sooner he notices my leg and asks for today's story, the sooner I can get going.

When I go into his room, I'm still in my short nightgown. He's tossing and turning in his sleep. I remember when I used to have those nightmares of grief and remorse, before I embarked on this project. I sleep better now because I'm doing what needs to be done. It's been a long time coming.

I wonder whether John remembers in his dreams what really happened. The doctors all agreed that the head injuries he suffered permanently damaged his hippocampus, the part of the brain that forms new memories. No matter how many times we told him about the accident and its consequences, he'd forget it all when he woke up the next morning. Still, no one knows exactly how the brain creates its dreams.

On a sudden inspiration, I remove my leg before lying down next to John. The stump of my knee is exposed because I'm lying on top of the blankets. I shake his shoulder to bring him out of the dream.

"Good morning, John," I say. I don't have to fake the troubled look on my face. If I'm not wearing the leg, I feel the ghost of the real one aching. The plastic leg supplants the useless phantom, just as efficient rage drives out despair.

"What's the matter?" he asks. He's not used to seeing me in his bed. I moved to my own room six months ago.

"I couldn't sleep," I say. "I was having nightmares about the accident."

"The accident?" he gasps, almost as if he half remembers, which worries me. Then he notices my leg, and his uncomprehending horror is so real that I relax.

"What happened?" he demands, trying to pretend that he's recoiling from the sight out of shock and grief alone, not disgust. But long before the incident, I learned to see through all the ways he hid his physical aversion to me.

"Don't you remember?" I demand plaintively. "You took us all out skating on the pond—I didn't think the ice was thick enough but you said it was fine—and Betsy and I fell through. By the time the paramedics got us out, my leg was so frostbitten that they had to amputate it."

"Was Betsy hurt?" He's starting to understand that something that matters may have been lost after all.

"She drowned," I whisper, and bury my face in the pillow.

His grief is sharp this morning. He bangs his head against the wall and tears at his face with his nails. "Oh, Betsy, oh, my beloved Betsy," he moans.

It's enough to make me sick.

Tranquilizers. Toast and coffee. Another day's work.

January 16

I've never thought of myself as a particularly inventive person. Perhaps it's just that no one ever gave me confidence in my own talents. For whatever reason, I'm running out of plausible disasters. My specifications are somewhat confining. Natural catastrophes like avalanches are out, as are violent crimes by other people: the essential feature of the story is that John must be blamed. Obviously, because of his memory impairment, I could tell the same story every day and still inspire the pain of fresh bereavement, but I'd get bored and eventually become unconvincing. Instead, I'm trying to develop a few effective fantasies which I repeat and embellish with new details and variations each time, like sketched studies for a masterpiece.

I'm feeling like taking risks today. The story I tell him will be closer to the truth than it's ever been.

When I go down to the kitchen, John is already sitting at the table. He's prepared the coffee and muffins. As usual, he must have noticed the day of the week on his fancy bedside clock radio, and started to follow his Saturday routine of getting up early to make breakfast and take Betsy to gymnastics class.

I used to think he had offered to help in this way in order to ease his guilt over some affair, perhaps with Betsy's gymnastics teacher. It wouldn't have been the first time. Why else would he seem so excited to go over there? If only the truth were that simple.

"Good morning, John," I say. He's too distraught to return my greeting.

"Where's Betsy?" he asks, rising from his chair. "I waited for her to come down, and then I looked all over the house for her, but she's not here. Do you think she crept out last night to see that Wilson boy? She's only fourteen—I'll kill him—"

"John, don't you remember? Not that I blame you. I'm still in shock myself. You just have to keep telling yourself that it wasn't your fault. I know you couldn't have seen that patch of ice on the road in time."

"Were we in an accident?"

"Oh, God—you were driving us home from McDonald's last night and the car swerved on the ice and hit a tree. Oh, it was awful!" I hide my face in my hands so he can't see my expression. I'm recalling what it really felt like to fly down that dark, shining road, the freedom, the power . . .

"And Betsy? She's in the hospital, right? I should be there!"

"Oh, John, Betsy's dead!" I cry, keeping my hands over my face and turning away from him.

"My God—Betsy, my darling—" He stumbles to the couch, weeping, and snatches up Betsy's gym leotard, which I left there last night so he would see it this morning. Clutching it to his chest, he covers it with kisses: the straps, the breast, the crotch . . .

He loved to watch her tight young body in that outfit. Her and the other girls. That's why he was so helpful on Saturdays, so eager to go.

I couldn't say how long it had been going on. I didn't find out until six months ago. My bridge club ended an hour earlier than expected. Upon coming home, I went upstairs to her room to say good-night. The lights were out, but the hallway light shone in through the half-open door. I saw them both in Betsy's bed. John was on her, crying out her name just like he's doing right now. I could tell she was enjoying it, too.

I could have stopped them, but I didn't. They never knew I'd seen them. I bided my time.

What I did, I did for Betsy. I couldn't let him corrupt her like that, turn her into someone who enjoyed her own destruction.

I took the wheel that night, not John. I knew the ice was there, and welcomed the bright, smooth path it made on the black road I'd been driving on for so long. The tree reached out its gnarled many-fingered arms to me, and I flung us all into its embrace.

Unfortunately, not everything worked out as planned. Only John was supposed to die. Still, in a sense it's for the best. This way I can make sure he gets what he deserves. And for the first time people value me. They exclaim how nurturing and noble I am, taking care of John all by myself instead of putting him in a home, and with my crippled leg, too. It's not really a lie. I could have been that person if they'd loved me sooner.

Poor Betsy. Even if she'd lived, she was already lost. I hope she's in a better place, one where she's learning to love me because I've done so much justice in her name.

Death Dealer

Kelley Armstrong

I shuffled the deck of fortune-telling cards. Eyes closed, I mentally ticked off each card as it passed, reading the minute scratches and dents that told my fingers which one it was. Then I dealt the spread in front of Thomas, my fingertips double-checking each as I flipped it facedown on the table. It wouldn't do to make a mistake, particularly not with the one slightly notched in the bottom left corner. The Death card.

As a child, I'd learned the mark on that one first. I'd learned it so I could avoid it. My grandmother had picked up on that trick quickly enough.

"Do you fear the Death card, Dani?" Nonna had asked, her dark eyes boring into mine.

She'd flipped the card over and my breath had caught at the hooded skull grinning up at me.

"Here," she said, taking my hand. She guided my fingers across the words below the death's head. "See these words? *'Carpe diem.'* That's Latin. It means 'Seize the day.' It reminds us to enjoy life while we can. Used right, this is the most powerful card in the deck."

She was right, though she couldn't have imagined the use I'd find for it.

All the cards were powerful, each in its way. They told no fortunes, but could add a touch of destiny to uncertain lives, signposts pointing the way. Some needed those signs more than others. Like Thomas. His problems? The usual life letdowns of a thirtysomething, single, corporate-ladder climber—stress in his worklife, loneliness in his personal life, and frustration in both.

As I laid out the cards, Thomas talked about his week. Under the table, his foot tapped the floor, his leg brushing mine.

"—he gets up and presents it as his idea. *His.* After we spent weeks working on it together."

I looked up into Thomas's face. An average face—nothing to catch the eye or turn it away.

"So what did you do?" I asked.

"This time, I confronted him." He shifted, leg rubbing mine, hard and assertive, echoing his words. "I told him what I thought and then . . ."

He paused, his leg shrinking back.

"And then?" I prompted.

"He promised to straighten it out . . . but he never did."

I resisted the urge to shake my head. Three months ago, Thomas would never have worked up the nerve to confront a coworker. At least we were making progress.

I waved my hand over the cards, eyes half closed, then snatched up the two I wanted.

"The Chalice card," I said. "That signifies a desire that will be fulfilled. However, coupled with the Key card it means that while you possess the means for fulfillment, you need to take action. The door will not open on its own. I see that your coworker has no intention of sharing the credit. I see you speaking to a woman, about fifty—"

"My boss."

"Perhaps."

Several months ago, he'd briefly mentioned his boss's birthday party. That was the secret to omniscience: forget nothing. Nonna taught me that.

I continued, "You speak to her. You don't blame your coworker. You suggest that he thought she understood you'd helped on the project . . ."

And so it went. My grandmother would flip in her grave if she saw what I was using my psychology degree for. When she died, she'd bequeathed her cards and—unwittingly—her legacy to me.

The cards weren't like any other I'd seen. Nonna used to say that they came from her great-great-grandmother, a Gypsy who'd been hanged when she accurately foretold the death of a nobleman's son. That the ancestor's spirit still inhabited the cards, helping her descendants foretell the future.

Bullshit, of course. Nonna had found them in an antiques store. She'd been right about one thing, though. This deck did have a resident spirit. Only it wasn't some Gypsy fortune-teller.

". . . then and only then will the promise of the Chalice card come true," I finished. "Now, another card . . ."

The roar of a motorcycle drowned me out. When I tried to continue, the engine revved. Thomas glared at the open window.

"Sorry," I murmured, getting to my feet. "The disadvantages of living next to the highway."

Thomas's gaze followed me as I crossed the room, sliding up my legs to the hem of my short peasant skirt. On Thomas's days, I took extra care with my appearance—leaving my dark curls out of their usual ponytail, wearing makeup, putting a little more swing in my step. Nothing overtly encouraging—just enough so he'd know his attention was flattering. His job wasn't the only area where Thomas needed a confidence boost.

I reached for the sash to pull the window down. A riderless motorcycle idled right below. As I cursed whichever tenant was responsible, a face popped up from under the window. It was a man in his midtwenties, with dark blond stubble and hair that flopped into his eyes. When he brushed the hair back and I saw bright green eyes, my surprise turned to a scowl.

Jack only grinned, then waved his hands over his outfit—leather jacket, tight jeans, tighter T-shirt showing off muscled pecs.

"Like it?" he mouthed.

I rolled my eyes and closed the window. As I returned to Thomas, the motorcycle revved, then faded, then pulled into the parking lot around the back, behind the kitchen.

I sat down. The kitchen door clicked open. It had been locked— it always was—and Jack didn't have a key, but that didn't matter.

I reached down automatically, unthinkingly, and almost flipped over the Death card. Damn Jack. I grabbed another one.

"Ah, the Queen. A sign of romantic success—"

And so it went. In high school I'd run a charity fortune-telling tent at the local fair. On the sign I'd written, in large letters: "For Entertainment Only." But no one listened. The clients still asked me to tell them whom to marry, which career to choose, whether to buy a house—decisions that should never be entrusted to a six-teen-year-old with a deck of old cards.

After a year spent working in real counseling, I realized that peo-ple paid more attention to my advice if I used my cards. And it was then, frustrated by those cases that no gentle prodding would fix, that I discovered the real power of the Death card.

"And that's it for this month," I said. "Remember—"

"Fate is what you make it," Thomas said with a small smile. He rose halfway, then stopped, fingers tapping the table. "Daniella . . ."

"Yes?"

"Some things you mentioned today—I've been thinking—" He took a deep breath. "This is going to sound crazy, but I've been try-ing to inject some spontaneity into my life, right?"

I smiled. "What's life without it?"

"Right. So . . ." Another deep breath. "My company's having a conference in Daytona Beach next weekend, and I wondered if you'd like to come along. Separate rooms, of course." His eyes met mine with a look that said he was serious about the separate rooms . . . though he really hoped I wouldn't hold him to it.

I looked out the window at the gray November day, dark clouds threatening the first snow of the season. "Daytona Beach . . ."

The kitchen door banged open. "Hey, babe. Where's the—"

Jack stopped in midstride and licked something off his fingertip. Then he tipped his head, letting his hair fall forward, his bright green eyes peering out through the blond curtain. He swept his hair back, flexing his muscles as he did, like he was posing for some damned romance novel cover.

"Uh, sorry," he said. "Didn't see you had a . . . client."

I shot him a lethal glare. Sadly, like all things lethal, it had no effect on Jack.

Ignoring Jack, I walked Thomas to the door. I was going to apologize—explain Jack away—but the look in Thomas's eyes said it was better if I didn't. He seemed almost relieved, as if he'd been expecting me to say no to Daytona, but that was okay, because he realized I had a reason.

I waited until he'd gone, then turned on Jack.

"You know the rules," I said. "You don't meet them until I give you the list."

"Is he on it?" he said, brows arching hopefully.

"We haven't reached that stage yet. And I don't think we'll need to."

Jack watched Thomas out the side window. "Oh, I don't know . . ."

"I do. Don't test me. You just cost me a weekend in Daytona."

He snorted. "Like you were considering it."

I headed for the dining room to clean up my cards. "Thomas has confidence problems with women, and you know how much I love to help."

Another disbelieving snort.

"You're right. A weekend in Daytona would be overkill. No need to go that far . . . when I could just take care of it right here. Sweep the cards off the table, lay him down, and—"

Jack cut me off with a growl. He grabbed me from behind, his hands shoving up my skirt, gripping me by the hips, and pushing me forward onto the table.

"Mmmm, this would work even better," I said. "Lean across the table in front of him, hoist my skirt, and say, 'Pretty please.' " I twisted from his grip and brushed my lips across his stubbled chin. "Thanks for the tip."

He followed me into the kitchen. "You won't. Know how I know?"

"Unearned confidence in your ability to keep a girl satisfied?"

"No. This." He swung past me and lifted a bowl from the counter. "You were making me brownies."

He dipped a finger in the batter and licked it off, eyes closed, a growling groan of pleasure rumbling from his chest. I shivered and fought the urge to slide over, lick the spattered bits from his chin. When he opened his eyes, they shimmered, rippling like stones thrown into still water, and I caught a glimpse of what lay behind them. I shivered again.

He took another finger of batter and held it to my lips. When I parted them, he slid his finger in, then out, so fast I barely got a taste. Then he licked the rest off himself.

"Tease."

"There's still a bit."

He held up his finger, but before I could get it, swiped it across my throat and lowered his mouth to the spot. He hoisted me onto the counter as he licked and kissed my throat, nipping the skin gently between his front teeth. His lips slid up to my ear, teeth scraping the lobe.

"Delicious," he murmured. "I could eat you up."

I chuckled. "From most guys, just a bad line. From you, though . . . I'm a little worried."

"I'd never hurt you. Too much to lose."

"Oh, I'm sure you could find someone else to take the cards, and cut you the same deal."

He pushed open my knees and slid his hands up my thighs. "Perhaps. But there's more to this than that. I don't think I'd ever find another fortune-teller who makes me"—his hand slid away, then returned with a finger of batter—"brownies."

I laughed. As my head tilted back, he dribbled more batter down my neck. I closed my eyes, reveling in his kisses and nips.

He tugged on my peasant blouse, sliding the loose sleeves down my shoulders and exposing the tops of my breasts, smearing trails of batter down them to just shy of my still-covered nipples. As he licked it off, he thrust against me and I wrapped my legs around him. One sharp tug on my blouse and my nipples popped out. I leaned back further, then jumped as the batter, still cool from the fridge, hit them. Jack chuckled and lowered his mouth, sucking one nipple in, teeth and tongue working—

A car door slammed behind the kitchen. From my parking space.

"My next client's here," I said.

"We'll be quiet and he'll go away."

"She. And I'm planning to give her the last place on the list."

I expected Jack to stop at that, or at least pause, but he kept suckling, lips tugging on my nipple, tongue flicking over it.

"If I don't, you'll have to wait," I said. "At least a week. Maybe more."

"Don't care."

I gave a soft laugh. "Really like that batter, don't you?"

"Love it." His hands slid up my thighs, thumbs going under my panties and parting me.

"Take a look out the window," I said. "See if that changes your mind."

I hopped from the counter, shrugging my blouse into place,

then steered him to the dining-room window. A young woman sauntered up the lane, hips swiveling. Straight blond hair fell to an ass covered by a too-tight skirt.

I stood on my tiptoes, lips going to Jack's ear. "See, now, if I wore a skirt that short, I wouldn't need to push it up to give Thomas an invitation. Just lean over the table. And you can bet your last cup of brownie batter there aren't any panties under that one."

Jack made a noise in his throat. His nostrils flared, as if picking up the woman's scent.

"Changing your mind?" I murmured.

He only growled.

"See how good I am to you?" I said. "You cost me a trip to Daytona Beach, and I still offer you that."

"Not the same. What I want from that? A very different thing."

As his gaze followed the girl, I lowered my hand to his crotch. His cock strained at the fly of his jeans, rock hard.

"Maybe not so different," I murmured. "So is that a yes?"

"As long as I can come back after," he said as I rubbed him. He paused, then glanced down at me. "You'll watch?"

I arched my brows.

His eyes glimmered with challenge. "Yes?"

"We'll see."

His lips took mine in a brief, hard kiss. "Go deal."

As I shuffled the cards, Kendra shifted in her seat, forearms plumping her breasts in her low-cut bodice. Jack had left the kitchen door open a crack, presumably to eavesdrop, but was he watching as well? Watching Kendra maneuver until crescent moons of dark aureole showed above her bodice's neckline?

I smiled as I dealt the cards, thinking of him behind the door, enjoying Kendra's display. With any other lover, amusement would hardly have been my reaction, but with Jack . . . Jack was different.

Kendra noticed my smile. Mistaking it for encouragement, teeth nibbling her lip, she tried to catch my eye. I just kept dealing the cards, knowing she wouldn't be terribly disappointed if I didn't respond. Women were a distant second choice for Kendra, something to be resorted to only when men were unavailable. Any port in a storm. Unfortunately, for Kendra, it was always stormy.

Nymphomania would likely be the clinical diagnosis, but I hate labels. For Kendra, sex meant attention, self-affirmation, and entertainment, and her life was so bereft of all three that a predilection for casual encounters had escalated into a dangerous obsession. After two failed therapists, she'd come to me. Unfortunately, I wasn't faring much better with her.

The solution was within Kendra's grasp—dump the dead-end job, finish her abandoned education, and get some self-respect. But every time I managed to nudge her in the right direction, she slipped back.

There was only one thing left to do.

I turned over the first card. "The Queen—"

"That's me, isn't it?" Kendra cut in.

I nodded. "In the past, the Queen has seemed to represent you, so the next card—"

"Is all about me."

I flipped over the Death card. The skeletal head grinned up at us.

"Does that mean—?" Kendra began, her smile gone. She blinked. "No, of course it doesn't. It's one of those symbolic things, right?"

"It—it could be. Sometimes . . . At least, in conjunction with the other cards—" I let my voice trail off and dropped my gaze, quickly gathering the cards, a slight tremor in my fingers. "It's probably a mistake."

"Better be," Kendra said, her smile as shaky as my hands. "It's bad business to predict people's deaths, Daniella, especially when they're behind on paying you."

I forced a tiny smile. "I know you're good for it."

"I *will* be once I get rid of this stupid job . . ."

And so, the specter of death was banished.

Nonna had sworn by the power of the Death card—flash it to someone, and they'd rethink their lives, forgetting their petty problems. But Nonna had been a traveling fortune-teller, rarely seeing the same person twice. When you worked with a steady clientele, as I did, you saw the limits of the Death card. Lives slammed back on track would veer back off course when the prophecy proved false.

By the time Kendra left, I doubt she even remembered the Death card. Or so her actions certainly suggested. Closing my front door, she walked around back to fetch her car, and found a leather-jacketed blond hunk tinkering with his motorcycle. As I watched from behind the curtain hanging on the kitchen door, Jack asked if she had a wrench. An unnecessary icebreaker. The moment she'd seen him, she'd slowed, waiting for him to notice her. Once he did, she was hooked.

No wrench? How about coffee? Good. Come on—he knew a shortcut.

And with that, a young woman who'd just been warned of impending death followed a stranger into an alley.

I caught up as they walked down an alley joining two others—a silent, empty tunnel with no street access. Kendra sashayed in front of Jack, oozing invitation with each step.

I waited around the corner. Two-thirds of the way down, Kendra let her keys drop to the pavement. She stopped short, bending to pick them up, skirt riding up her ass enough to show Jack—and me—that she was indeed wearing nothing underneath.

Jack bumped into her from behind, his hands clasping her thighs. "Whoops."

Her laugh rang down the alley. She wiggled her hips back against him. He grabbed her under the arms and swung her up, backing her into the wall. He pinned her there, then moved his hands down, under her skirt, spreading her legs and moving between them. She reached to undo his fly. He caught her hand.

"No need to rush," he murmured.

He lifted one hand to the side of her face, and she tilted her head back. His mouth lowered and she closed her eyes, lips parting expectantly, but he stopped before touching her, hovering there, lips over hers. Eyes still closed, she strained for his mouth. His lips parted and he moved until they were only a hairsbreadth from hers. Then he inhaled so sharply his body jerked.

Kendra gasped, eyes flying open. Jack straightened, hands kneading her bare ass, grinding her against his jeans-covered crotch. Kendra's eyes closed, relaxing. Again he lowered his mouth almost to hers. This time, he inhaled slowly and she moaned, arms going around his neck. When he pulled away, her moan turned to a whimper and she arched her whole body, legs tightening around his waist, pushing herself up, eyes still closed, lips open, seeking his.

Jack shuddered, the tip of his tongue appearing between his teeth. Then, as Kendra wriggled against him, hunting desperately for his kiss, his gaze swung my way. I slid a few inches from my hiding place. He saw me and nodded. Then he returned to Kendra, mouth going to hers.

She groaned, frantically pressing against him as if trying to dissolve into his kiss. After a moment, when he didn't break off, her groans took on a shrill note. Her eyes flew open. Her hands went to his shoulders, now pushing just as desperately as she'd tried to pull him to her before. He only kissed her harder, inhaling her life.

Then, as her struggles reached a frenzy, eyes rolling in terror, limbs flailing, he let out a snarl and yanked away so fast Kendra slid down the wall. Skirt tucked up around her waist, legs sprawled wide, her bare ass hit the ground. She sat there, fingers digging into the dirt, eyes closed again, body straining upward, quavering in orgasmic relief, too busy reveling in the sensation of breathing to notice Jack walking away.

I backed around the corner. Jack stopped a few feet from me. Sweat soaked his shirt and trickled down the side of his face. When I looked into his eyes, there were no whites, no pupils, just a bright green sea, roiling under the surface, as if seconds from hitting a boil.

He blinked, and his eyes went human, but only for a second before being sucked back into that maelstrom. A snarl and a sharp shake of his head, trying to yank the human facade back into place. Failing, he looked at me, and I knew this was why he'd asked me to follow, to watch, to see.

"Daniella." His voice had changed, too, filled with an odd reverberation.

Jack ran his tongue over his lips, shivering, sweating, as if brought to the brink and left there on the precipice. I reached for his hand. He hesitated a moment before letting me have it. His skin was so hot I almost let go. But I forced my fingers around his, turned, and led him back to my apartment.

Once inside the kitchen door, he stopped. His eyes were still turbulent. Every few seconds, he'd shudder, as if trying to throw something off.

He flinched as I reached for him, then let me ease his jacket off, dropping the heavy black leather to the floor. I touched my fingertips to his chest and slid them down his sweat-soaked shirt, down to his crotch, his cock still hard and straining, jumping at my touch.

"I don't think you should . . ." He licked his lips and let out a soft growl as I stroked him through his jeans.

"It's what you wanted, isn't it? For me to not just know what you are, but see it. And make up my mind." I moved closer and pushed onto my tiptoes, looking into his eyes. "I see."

I brought my lips to his, barely touching. Then I rubbed softly against them, parting them.

He let out a low groan, not pressing his lips together but not opening them either, just letting me coax them apart. His hands went to my thighs, sliding under my skirt and lifting me against him. Then he pulled back, eyes meeting mine, his still flashing between human and other. For a moment, he let the pretense slide and I saw nothing but depths of shimmering green.

"I'd never hurt you, Dani. I meant that. But seeing is one thing. This . . ."

He stopped as I flicked my tongue against his teeth.

"I've tasted it before," I whispered.

"Not like this."

I moved my lips closer, so close they brushed his.

"Let me in," I whispered.

His hands tightened, yanking me even tighter to him. His mouth covered mine, so strong I gasped, and a flood of heat rushed down my throat. It was like toppling into an inferno, the flames so bright and so hot they drew you in even when every fiber screamed for you to run, escape. The heat ebbed almost immediately, and I huddled against him, my mouth to his, shivering and straining for more.

He chuckled, the sound almost a growl as it reverberated up from his chest.

"More?"

I looked up into his eyes and smiled. "Pretty please."

His mouth dove to mine, one hand going to the back of my head, the other dropping to my rear, scooping me against him as his hips slammed into me. The first rush of heat matched the first hard thrust, and I gasped, hands going to his hips, pulling him closer. The heat ebbed and flowed, giving me a glimpse into the abyss, then pulling me back.

His breath came in short pants, each a fresh blast of heat against my tongue. He swung me up, never breaking the kiss, turning us so I was perched on the edge of the counter. Dimly, I felt him ripping at my panties, felt the cool air as they came off and he pushed me back on the counter, parting my legs. Another fumble, undoing his pants. Then he was in me. My hands clenched, fingernails digging into his back so hard I drew blood, even through the thin cotton of his shirt.

He only groaned, mouth stretching wider, tongue twining around mine, enticing me in farther. I didn't need enticement. I opened myself up to him, tasting death and knowing he could give it to me; trusting that he wouldn't, but laughing at the foolhardiness of that trust, knowing this was someone—some*thing*—I should never trust.

With each push, he let me in, let me start to fall over the edge, then snatched me back as he pulled out. I writhed against him, trying to get closer, whimpering each time he withdrew, the thrusts coming faster, harder. As the first wave of climax hit, I breathed his name.

He whispered something back. I couldn't make it out, wasn't even sure it was a word. Then, as he said it again, eyes rippling, full green now, I understood what it was. His name. His real name.

I said it, and his eyes rolled, body quivering. His lips went to mine, as hard and insistent as his thrusts, and I came, screaming his name into his mouth.

The afterglow drowsiness wrapped me so tightly I could barely stay conscious, as if he'd drained something from me. He carried me to my bed, then crawled in beside me, tracing his fingers over my skin as I faded in and out of sleep.

At the creak of the bedsprings, I lifted my head to watch him tucking in his T-shirt.

"The list is—" I began, struggling to speak through a yawn.

"I know." He reached for the bedside drawer.

"When you choose—"

He leaned over me, finger stilling my words, head shaking.

"I just wanted to say, there's one guy—"

His finger pressed harder, cutting me off. "No, Dani. I take the list; I make the decision. You play no part in it. You take no responsibility for my choice."

I hesitated, then nodded and let my head fall back to the pillow. Content, I was asleep before he even left the room.

Three days later, I went onto the front stoop to look for my paper. It wasn't there. I knew it wouldn't be, but I looked anyway. My newspapers always disappeared for several days after I gave Jack the list. He could have mystically whisked it away, but more likely, he just came by and took it. For an otherworldly being, Jack was surprisingly short on otherworldliness.

As for exactly what he was, his name might tell me, if I searched, but I didn't want to. Not yet. Like I hadn't questioned where he'd come from before, accepting his explanation, tossed off with a grin: "I come with the cards."

Maybe that was true. Nonna had certainly never seen him. As he said, he'd simply taken his tithe when the Death card was dealt, no one ever being the wiser. As for why he'd changed his method, maybe something lured him out or maybe he was just looking for a change, or maybe, as he claimed, he did it for the brownies.

One problem with our deal was that it wreaked havoc on my income, and a check of my books that morning told me I'd need more clients. Which meant I needed to place an ad. Which meant I needed a newspaper.

On the walk back from the corner store, I read the classified rates, checking for any changes as I mentally planned my submission. I hadn't advertised in almost a year, and I was down twenty clients from Jack's deal.

Twice a year, I gave him a list of ten names. Nine of those, like Kendra, would undergo a near-death experience. And they would be changed for it, no longer needing my nudges to restart their stalled lives. Sometimes they came back to me, but only sporadically, and only for fun.

That was my reward: the satisfaction of success, the knowledge that I'd truly helped. With Jack's help, I had a ninety percent success rate when I dealt the Death card, far better than anything I'd ever achieved with counseling alone.

As for that other ten percent . . . the tenth person on the list . . .

I stepped out onto the stoop and flipped to the obituaries. A hand reached over my shoulder and plucked the paper from my fingers. I wheeled. Behind me stood a dark-haired, fortyish man in a well-cut suit, his gold watch flashing as he whisked the paper behind his back. Green eyes met mine and the dark brows arched.

"You like?" he said, with a flourish at the latest body he'd borrowed from some hapless guy.

"Not bad. Definitely a change from the last one. Just remember—"

"When I'm done with it, put it back the way I found it."

"Exactly. Now, my paper, please. I need to place an ad."

Jack unfolded the newspaper, tore out the obituary pages, and handed back the rest. I nodded, letting him stuff the obituaries into his pocket.

This was how it had to be. I gave him the list. I made no recommendations, no suggestions. And I never found out which name he'd chosen. An imperfect system, but so far it had kept me sane.

Jack opened the door and ushered me inside. I took the newspaper to the table and composed the ad while he sat across from me, shuffling my cards. When I finished, he laid the deck down, walked behind me, and leaned over, hands on my shoulders, thumbs rubbing the back of my neck as he read it.

Lost in the forest of life? Looking for direction?
Call Daniella, seventh-generation fortune-teller.
Specializing in life-changing experiences.

The Capgras Delusion

John Barfoot

Stephen Wilson awoke one morning to find that his wife no longer recognized him. It was worse than that. She screamed when she saw his face.

That first sleep-fogged scream, and the other, more strident ones that followed as he tried to approach her, affected him like physical objects. They were stones or blades she was throwing at him, and when she gained control of herself and began to hit him, it felt no different. He raised his hands against her blows, but she drove him from the room and dragged furniture over to the door. Then she began crying.

When the ambulance men arrived he was standing in the bathroom. His bruised and scratched hands were wrist-deep in warm water and he was looking at himself in the mirror. The face in the glass was cautious, reserved, almost without expression, and he realized that he had no way of knowing whether it was his. It looked like photographs in which he appeared, but that meant nothing. Even if he was identical to the face his eyes looked out from, it could still be someone else's. His wife thought it was.

The photographs were enough to satisfy the ambulance men. They stood outside the bedroom, suspicious of him, protective of her, and turned the pages of the albums. Holidays, celebrations, end-of-roll snapshots. The two of them. Together. Arms around each other. Intimate. A unit.

They kept looking from the photographs to his face. Then they stopped doing that. Just turned the photographs over.

It was late afternoon before she was taken away. It was an unusual case. The doctor had never come across anything like it and the ambulance men had to satisfy him as to the validity of the situation. Parade Stephen before her like some sort of exhibit, nod grimly at the doctor as she shrank away. Her pleas for someone to get her husband were heartbreakingly convincing, and twice that day skeptical policemen took pains to fully confirm his identity. They had been called in to advise, as if this were some sort of domestic quarrel, but ended up feeling sorry for him. When she stopped her struggling and screaming for a moment at the front door and hissed "Who are you?" at him, one of them gripped his elbow and said, "Don't worry, mate. The doctors'll sort her out. You'll see." Then they dragged her out.

The house was filled with cruel afternoon sunlight, and dust seemed to be everywhere. It dulled the surfaces of tables and shelves, gathered in white fluffy balls in corners, drifted in the air about his head. By comparison, the bathroom was a haven of cleanliness. Blinds closed, lights on. White tiles shining softly. Chromework gleaming.

He stood before the mirror above the washbasin and carefully scrutinized the face that looked back at him. At first he concentrated on small areas, letting his gaze roam over nose, lips, ears. Then he pulled back for a wider view, allowing all of the features to work together. What had she seen—or not seen—that made him a stranger?

After a while, something happened. He began to feel that he was the object of scrutiny, rather than the scrutinizer. That the face in the mirror was looking at him. Eventually, he narrowed it down to the eyes. The face could be anybody's. It was the eyes behind it that conferred identity. The mirror was a viewing port from some hidden world. He was being observed by eyes that had chosen this face to look out from.

He turned to the long mirror by the door. The body seemed to confirm the face's artificiality, its masklike nature. It was as if the eyes were burning nails the whole thing hung from.

Bedroom, hall, kitchen. He hurried from room to room. The eyes were waiting for him in every place where mirrors made observation possible. There was a knife on the draining board. The eyes looked out from the clean part of its blade. The hidden world was everywhere. All it needed was a reflective surface.

He drew all the curtains. Turned all the mirrors facedown or covered them. Sat with the heels of his hands dug into his eyes. He thought he knew what his wife had seen. The eyes of a stranger in the face of her husband.

It was at that stage that Stephen confided in me.

I can't think of a time when we didn't know each other, and I even met Louise at the same time he did. In fact, if things had gone differently, it could have been me she married.

That sounds like a spurned lover with a long-held grievance, but it wasn't like that. He won her fair and square, and I was happy for him. At that time, he was what she wanted.

I listened patiently to his fears, to the nonsense about eyes, the babblings about the hidden world he thought he'd discovered. And then I gently reminded him of something he'd forgotten. Something that turned the spotlight away from him and his perceived inadequacies. Something that explained Louise's condition very elegantly without the need to drag in fantasy.

We were both devourers of lists, part-work magazines, illustrated encyclopedias, "Did you know?" articles, and the like, and the Capgras Delusion was something we'd come across in some populist psychology book. Stephen had marveled at it as a mere curiosity and promptly forgotten it, but I had been affected much more deeply. I had even made it the subject of an entry in my Common-place Book. Now I prodded his memory.

Sufferers from the Capgras Delusion were convinced that some loved one, often a husband or wife, had been replaced by an impostor. It didn't matter that the impostor could be shown to be an exact double of the "missing" person in every respect. They knew, usually beyond any possibility of persuasion, that this was not the lover, partner, companion who had so inexplicably been taken away. Stephen had accepted at face value the article's assumption that the sufferer was deluded, and that was what he recalled at my prompting. My interest had been deeper, more philosophical. What if the loved one *had* been replaced by an impostor? That was what fascinated me.

Stephen naturally accepts responsibility in any situation involving blame. It was gratifying to see his superficial understanding of Capgras bring hope to his eyes as he realized that the problem might lie with Louise this time. She was ill. Of course. She was ill, and that explained her behavior.

He couldn't remember what caused the Delusion and I had to remind him that, so far as was known, it had its genesis in the body. Not a mental state, but brain damage. Mere physical injury to a part of the biological organism.

But how? he kept asking. How can her brain have been damaged?

He often forgets his own strength. The depth of passion when he loses his temper. Conveniently, I often think—but then again, it's not something that happens every day. And when it does happen, he usually manages to keep it private. In fact, I'm probably the only one, apart from Louise, who knows him well enough to have any idea. About the violence, I mean. Seething behind that guile-less face. He thinks I'm violent, but I don't lie to myself. I know what I am and I handle it. I know all about control. It's the Stephens who're dangerous. They're unpredictable.

I suggested a course of action to him. I would act as his representative. I was as familiar to Louise as he was—or had been—and I could
visit her on his behalf and use my knowledge and love for both of them
to try and sort things out. Stephen knows I can be very sensitive, very
aware of unspoken feelings. The body is a voice, too, and he knows
I understand it, can make it talk. He agreed to my suggestion. He
had no other choice, I suppose. But his consent was important.

"Hello, Louise."

They've told her I'm her husband's brother. It's what Stephen
told them, in his letter requesting visiting arrangements. They have
no reason to doubt it. We've always looked pretty much alike on the
surface. They welcome me. They're happy I'm getting involved. It's
a step along the road toward recovery.

She sits primly upright in the hospital bed, lightly sedated for
this first meeting, and at first she looks at me boldly. There is, after
all, no reason for her to be frightened. Her shock at waking up
next to an apparent stranger is in the past. She has been assured
that she is in no danger from the man she believes has taken the
place of her husband. Indeed, this man, who believes equally
strongly that he really is her husband, is so concerned about her
feelings that he does not want to subject her to the uneasiness of
his own presence; has sent his representative instead. In addition,
we're chaperoned. A young doctor with a boyishly soft beard sits
in the center of the room with a clipboard on his knee.

So her first scrutiny of me is direct, confident. But her eyes
quickly begin to show doubt, puzzlement. This is what I have been
counting on. She is here because she doesn't recognize the man
everyone says is her husband, even though she accepts that the
impostor is identical to the real man she married. Now she's confronted with someone who could almost be a second double. I fill
up with excitement I'm careful not to show. My hope is that she will
begin to doubt her own perceptions.

Instead she says, very carefully, as if making a move in some game, "My husband doesn't have a brother."

I smile briefly at the doctor, who ducks his head and begins to scribble notes.

"All right, Louise," I say. "No problem. Can't we just talk anyway? Whoever I am, I know Stephen very well. He's anxious to sort this out and bring you home."

"Why can't I see him? Stephen? Why can't he come?"

I glance at the doctor again, taking care to close my eyes briefly as I do so to signal distress.

"He'd love to come, Louise. But that's the problem, isn't it? You won't accept him. You think Stephen's not Stephen."

"Not him. I mean Stephen. The real Stephen." Tears spill down her cheeks. "I want my husband. I want my husband back."

"And that's why I'm here, Louise. I'm going to help you get him back. He's suffering, too, you know."

The puzzled look comes into her eyes again.

"He asked me to remind you of something, Louise, before you got married. He says you called a halt. You were Romeo and Juliet—his words—and then you decided to cool things off."

She's curious, waiting for me to go on.

"You wanted to let things cool down a bit, take a break, think it through. You weren't sure, suddenly. Everything was happening so quickly. So Stephen says you called a halt; for the time being, you said. You wouldn't see him or talk to him for six weeks while you 'sorted yourself out.' "

I have her complete attention now.

"He says it all ended happily when he wrote a letter that reassured you"—I remembered that letter, the hours we agonized over its exact wording—"but the point is that that's how he feels now. Rejected. Unfairly. No explanation. He feels he's out in the cold again, just like then, when you had your doubts."

Pain flickers across her face. "It was all going so fast. I didn't know what I wanted. Stephen was so kind. Gentle. But it seemed as if something was missing somehow. He was so upset. I couldn't help it. It just didn't feel right."

She smiles tightly, almost secretly. "And then he wrote that letter. It was like a different Stephen, a side of him I'd never seen before. Determined. Firm. Taking control. It all seemed so clear the way he explained it. He won me back." Her smile widens shyly at the phrase. "It's a side he keeps hidden. I don't know why. It's what convinced me."

She looks at me, then at the doctor, with the end of his pencil buried in the sparse, silky hairs of his mustache, and says, "He must be so hurt." Then she begins to cry.

The boy doctor says he thinks it's going very well as he walks me back down the corridor. Better than he expected. I tell him that I see her recovery as a long, hard struggle. Regaining ground inch by inch. A reminiscence here, an anecdote there. Things only she and her husband could know. No big jumps, just a determined, patient progress. Slowly building back up in her head the picture of Stephen that has somehow become scrambled.

It's what he wants to hear. The head of psychiatry is interested in the case—it's why Louise is in a private room—but she's away on some lecture tour. It's clear from the way he speaks about her that he doesn't want to make any mistakes while she's gone. My manner, my words, reassure him. I am safe, no cause for concern.

I mention the Capgras Delusion hesitantly, making a deliberate layman's stumble and calling it a syndrome. He's never heard of it, is lightly dismissive of pop psychology. I apologize. He beams and shakes my hand. "It's understandable," he says. "People concerned over loved ones are always having their hopes raised by half-baked tabloid rubbish. Journalists. Irresponsible, most of them."

I imagine what it would be like to pull out his baby whiskers, one by one.

• • •

I tell Stephen I'm making progress. But not to build his hopes up. It's going to be a long job.

His stare is dull. The curtains are still drawn, the mirrors still covered. He's lost weight. Fine bones are starting to show in his face. The early hope I'd seen is fading. Blunted after a quick flirtation, like most things in his life.

Don't let yourself go, I say. Keep strong.

I'm worried about him.

You know it's her problem, don't you? She's the one who's deluded.

He doesn't say anything, but there is a glint of cynicism in his eyes. I wonder if he's gone back and reread the entry in my Commonplace Book, my analysis of the real significance of the Capgras Delusion, the philosophical questions it raises about identity.

It doesn't matter. If he has, he'll forget it soon enough. Ideas are like a wind that blows through him. Calm always returns.

Not like me.

I burn.

On my second visit I talk to Louise about their honeymoon.

Junior Doctor has been bleeped to an emergency and has reluctantly left us alone with the door open, and a nurse detailed to look in from time to time. After that first double-take at seeing the face that confused her, there was now cautious enthusiasm in Louise's manner. It was as if she had prepared for an important meeting, and now that I was here we could get down to work.

"Stephen's been dredging up some very private stuff. He feels he has to prove himself to you again if you're ever going to accept him."

"You mean him," she says. "The other one."

"I mean the man who thinks you're his wife."

That's a slant she hasn't thought of. I can see the little wheels in her head going ever so slightly out of phase.

"He's been thinking about your most intimate moments. That's where he thinks I can establish some common ground. But it's forced him to be very honest with himself. He feels everything has to be clear between you if you're going to start again."

"It's Stephen I feel for, not him!" Her eyes brim suddenly with tears. "Why doesn't Stephen come to see me?"

"Louise. If you're ever going to get out of here and be with your husband again you have to see things through everybody else's eyes, not your own. Whether you believe it or not, all anyone can see is one Stephen, one husband of Louise. Whoever you think he is, it's really just the two of you. You're the only players."

The tears have gone, but they're visible, dried, on her cheeks. Her jaw is set.

"And there's me. Your brother-in-law. The one you don't remember."

She won't look at me. I wait. Then I start.

"So anyway, this Italian bloke you fancied on your honeymoon."

She looks at me now, sharply, her brow creased.

"Stephen says he saw it right from the beginning. This man was also a guest at the hotel? Offered to translate for you to the receptionist? You wanted an iron or something. Remember?"

"Yes," she says. She's still guarded, but her cheeks are a faint pink.

"Well. Stephen wanted me to remind you of that. Something only you and he would know. But he also wanted me to tell you the truth."

"The truth?"

"You remember at the end of your first week, after this Tommaso had bought you both drinks and joined you at your table a couple of times? Stephen left you alone one whole afternoon?"

She flushed at the name, Tommaso. Now she looks puzzled

again. "He said he wanted to go for a long walk alone. I couldn't understand it. Not on our honeymoon."

"Well, the reason he went on the walk, and this is what he wanted me to tell you—the reason was so that you and Tommaso could be alone if you wanted to be."

Her face is blank. Then she squints her left eye slightly and shakes her head.

"What are you trying to say?"

"I'm not trying to say anything. It's what Stephen told me to say. He wanted you to know that he understood, even then, even on your honeymoon."

"Understood what?"

"That he's no great catch. That there must be many other men you'd find attractive if you met them. That he didn't regard it as unfaithfulness. Just experimentation."

"This is ridiculous! What does he think happened?"

I recall Stephen's fantasy vividly. It was crude. Wide open legs, pink gash. Pushed-up tits, big, hard nipples. Fingers—thick brown fingers, darker in the creases, tobacco-stained—*Italian* fingers, thrusting powerfully, withdrawing wet, thrusting again. Hands and knees, arse in air, gaping, offered. Hard hands on hips, hard breathing. Slap of flesh on flesh. Liquid sucking. Gasps. Screams. Animal sounds.

The stud dealing with his bitch.

Effective, certainly.

But ephemeral. Good for one quick, shuddering release.

I preferred something more subtle, longer-lasting. Something to linger and build.

Afternoon. Dim hotel room. Blazing line between hastily drawn curtains. Two red high-heeled shoes abandoned in the middle of the carpet, one upright, one fallen. Flimsy panties hanging over the edge of a stripped bed on which lies naked Louise. Naked except for her bra, that is. White cups against rosy skin, body flowing and opening brazenly below. She smiles as he admires her, opens her legs accommodatingly as his hand moves up her thigh. He is fully clothed. She unzips him, exposes him, fondles him—then begins to tug, firmly, insistently. He enters her, starts a slow, repeating rhythm. Pale legs close around him. Her hands are in his hair, fingers moving, kneading. Sweat collects in the hollow of her throat. There are shallow valleys in her shoulders, where the bra straps take her weight.

I lower my head, as if ashamed. "I imagine he thinks you and Tommaso made love."

She jumps out of bed, stalks to the window, stalks back again. It's a hospital nightdress, but the stiff material charts the high points of her shape. Breasts, hips. I glance quickly to one side, quickly enough to let her know what I'm averting my gaze from. She hurriedly grabs her hospital dressing gown and struggles into it, half shouting as she does so: "I don't believe this! I don't bloody believe it! He left me alone? Deliberately? Thinking I'd sneak off to some hotel room with someone I hardly knew? A bloody Italian I'd only just met? Are you sure about this?"

I'm watching what her body's saying. It's not angry. It's excited. Hardly able to contain the energy Stephen's revelation has sent coursing through her. The energy she's trying to pass off as indignation. She'll never let herself face that, but I'm sure. Sure enough to tell Stephen.

"I think he saw it as some kind of gift to you. A secret he was being honest about at last. I don't know."

She's walking backward and forward, with the gown held tightly closed over her chest. "A gift!" she shouts, incredulously. And again, softer, but more vehemently, "A gift!"

It takes me a while to persuade her back into bed. I don't want anyone to see her agitation. Fortunately, she's still on some kind of drugs regime, and all this drama is having its effect on her. By the time the nurse looks in she's quiet. When Junior Doctor returns, she's asleep.

On the way back down the corridor he complains about staff

shortages, his workload. Tells me he thinks it'll be okay if I'm put down as just an ordinary visitor. Mrs. Wilson doesn't seem to object to me. Maybe my regular presence will help her as much as any official course of treatment. At least until the head of psychiatry returns.

Maybe! I'm laughing at him. He doesn't have the faintest idea what he's dealing with. The paper his boss could put together out of this; the boost to her reputation.

He hasn't even noticed the tiny contusions I saw on Louise's skull when I was tucking her back into bed. Just behind the hairline. Delicate. Fading already. It's like I told Stephen. The Capgras Delusion is caused by brain damage.

Tomasso, he says. Yes, I remember the name now. I was ashamed. He made me feel jealous, even on my honeymoon.

He's even thinner. His eyes have started to glitter, not shine. He seems to be sinking in on himself. I, by contrast, have never felt better. My sense of well-being is increasing all the time.

It's working, I tell him. Just a matter of time. Louise wants her husband back, just as much as you want your wife. Even the people at the hospital think I'll be good for her.

I hope I can hang on, he says, and lowers his head between jagged knees. It's like watching some bony crane maneuver an awkward load into place.

Later, I realize he's rubbed lard over every shiny surface he can find. The house smells of fat.

Third visit. I check in at reception and they just tell me to go straight along to Louise's room. I can't believe it. I could be anybody.

Louise is asleep. Her face is tense, her color high. There's a thin line of moisture trapped under the corner of her left eyelid, bulging slightly between the lashes. Slapped, but still proud. That's the image that comes to me.

I feel privileged to be able to watch her while she's sleeping.

This is something Stephen's had for a long time. Did he value it as much as I do now? I don't think so.

When she wakes up I'm sitting in a chair way down at the foot of the bed, giving her plenty of space. For a second, when she catches sight of me, I think she's going to start screaming the way she did with Stephen. But she catches it and I see the complex moment when she sees *his* face but recognizes *me* and relaxes.

"I got Stephen to pack some of your stuff."

She sits up in bed, rummaging through the carrier bags. Seeing her hands in the froth of lace and satin is exciting. Under her touch the neatly folded layers I sifted through this morning have come alive. I anticipate her.

"If you want to change I can go to the dayroom."

She smiles. "Just five minutes." The door locks behind me.

It's unlocked when I return and she's sitting on top of the covers, propped up by a bank of pillows. She's almost a different woman. It's not just that her own nightdress and dressing gown are prettier than the hospital issue; it's the way they make her feel. She's almost vivacious, and noticeably warmer with me.

"Thank you," she says. "The nightie I had on when they brought me in was a mess. I'd almost forgotten what it was like to wear my own things."

Her feet are small and delicate, peeping out from the bottom of her long dressing gown. As I watch, she leans slightly to one side, draws her legs up, and the feet nestle gently against one another. The nails are painted. There are one or two fine black hairs on her big toe. The combination is unexpectedly erotic. Her body speaks for her, even when she's silent.

I begin. "Stephen was thinking last night about the time you went on the residential training course. Some management thing after you got that promotion?"

She's wary. She sits up straighter, as if to be ready for whatever I throw at her. Her feet disappear.

"He was wondering whether you realized how much it disturbed him, you going."

"Well," she says doubtfully, "I knew he was a bit upset. He went quiet. He always goes quiet when he's upset."

"Did you know that he followed you?"

"Followed me. What do you mean, followed me?"

"To the hotel. He followed you right to the hotel."

"He couldn't have," she says stupidly. "I had the car."

"He hired one. Took the week off work, hired a car, and got to the hotel halfway through your first afternoon session."

"What? You mean, he was there? In the same hotel?"

"Yes. He stayed there for the whole week. It's not something he's particularly proud of, but like I said yesterday, he wants to be honest about the past."

She's really struggling with this one, doesn't know where to start. "Time off work? I . . . But I would have seen him. What for, anyway?"

She's angry now. "Yesterday he's perfectly happy thinking I'm screwing some Italian on our honeymoon, now he's checking up on me because I have to go on a bloody course, for God's sake!"

Why should she link it with the honeymoon thing? That's what I ask myself. Nobody said anything about "checking up." She reveals herself with every word. It's my duty to tell Stephen.

"He says he did it because he just wanted to observe you. See what you were like when you were on your own. He felt it was a part of your life he was excluded from."

"And what did he see?" She's trying for a kind of tired disdain, but she overdoes the weary bit; keeps her eyes closed a beat too long.

"Mmm," I say. "It's odd. He said that he did watch you on the first night, but it wasn't very . . . satisfactory. He got this idea that even though you didn't know about it, the very act of him observing made you behave differently. So"—and here I shrug, as if to say,

Don't ask me!—"so he stayed in his room for the rest of the week. He thought the only way you'd act normally would be if he wasn't actually watching you."

She's blank. Thinks she's missed something. Just looks at me fixedly.

"I know," I say. "It doesn't make sense to me, either. But that's what he says he did. Lay on the bed in his room, watching TV all day. Packed up and left on the Friday morning, when you were in your final session."

I'm not convinced by her low, puzzled "Jesus!" It sounds more relieved than angry or disturbed.

What she says next underlines it for me. "So he traveled all that way and he didn't actually see anything?" Transparent.

I just shake my head, remembering my excitement over the discovery Stephen made during those long days in his hotel room. Intuitive Imagining. Its capacity to reveal the psychological truth behind mere seeing. Its ability to ignore the appearance of innocence and reveal the real situation. Its power to confirm suspicion. Oh, yes. Its power to simplify.

The pressure's off. The feet have come back out from under the dressing gown. "This is all so strange," she says. "Like someone I don't know. It's . . . sick." For the first time, she gives me full eye contact: open, curious, trusting. "Was he like this before I met him?"

I sidestep the question. "Don't forget," I say. "Stephen *wants* you to know this stuff. Whatever was hidden before, he's trying to bring into the open. I suppose you'd have to call it brave, at least."

She doesn't say anything, just lifts her left eyebrow very slightly. I can tell that brave isn't what she thinks of it.

Stephen's hand is a husk, something discarded in molting, as if merely walking past would send it fluttering into the air. His mind is drifting. It's difficult to keep him on the subject. He tries to give the impression that his memory of the course was dim, unimportant.

A minute earlier he'd said, "I felt abandoned," then just stared into space. Now he makes a noise in his throat like leaves in a light breeze. "I just stayed at home all that week when she was away. You were away, too. I was lonely."

"At home," I say heavily. "You stayed at home, did you?" He won't look up. There's no mistaking the cynicism in my voice.

Her feet are exquisite. Very small and delicate. They're in my lap and I'm holding the left one, firmly kneading the sole with my thumbs. I've been giving her foot massages for the last couple of visits. It relaxes her while we talk. I can't remember which visit this is. Eighth? Ninth? Something like that.

She trusts me now, looks forward to my arrival. Junior Doctor doesn't bother us at all. She says he pops in now and then to ask how she is, always with an air of stealing time from something very pressing, never really paying attention to her answer. As far as he's concerned, she's on the mend; no need to waste time trying to understand what happened to her.

I can feel stubble on my fingertips. She likes it when I move up past her ankles. I can tell. A little wave passes over her skin and she relaxes ever so slightly. Today I keep going, sliding my hands around to cup and squeeze her calves, pausing to cap her knees, finger the taut membrane of skin and cartilage spreading sail-like as she draws her legs up an inch or two. She pretends not to be aware of what is happening, needs me to distract her so that she can continue to allow my advances.

"He has his spy holes all over," I say. "He admits himself that he became obsessed with what you did when he wasn't there."

My hands are under the hem of the nightdress now. Her eyes are closed. I feel her legs open infinitesimally, and at the same time she speaks. She needs to disguise the movement, pass it off as involuntary. "So where are these spy holes?"

"The bedroom," I say. "Bathroom. Toilet. Everywhere." My

fingers are opening out over the spread of her thighs. I'm advancing and lingering, then retreating an inch or two, consolidating before advancing again. I'm gaining ground, slowly. I know what she wants. I'll make her wait.

"I thought you said he had this thing about not observing me in case I behaved differently." There's a catch in her voice, her breath not entirely under control.

"Oh, yes," I say. "As I understand it, he never actually used the holes after making them. But he needed them to create the potential for spying. Once he knew he could look at you wherever you were in the house . . . without you knowing . . . then he was content to *imagine* what you were doing."

I've tried to give her some real insight into Intuitive Imagining over the last few weeks, but she doesn't really understand. Just thinks it's weird. Now she ignores the last part of what I've just told her and goes straight for what she sees as the meat. "You mean that there was nowhere private in the house? He was watching me all the time, even when I thought I was on my own?"

Undertones of indignation, but there's fear in her voice as well. There's something shameful she thinks Stephen might have seen. I imagine a white towel, crisp and clean. It's twisted into a thick rope, pulled taut along the edge of the bath. Louise is sitting astride it, grinding herself into the rough cotton pile, riding it hard, her mouth pulling down, ugly, as her legs begin to tremble. She makes an involuntary sound, stops moving instantly. Can Stephen hear? Down below her, in his chair, watching television. Can he hear? Nothing. She waits a little longer, resumes her slow riding.

I gently squeeze the soft pillows of her thighs, remind her of here, now.

"Sort of," I say. "Stephen would probably say it wasn't as simple as that, but as far as I can see, he's been spying on you one way or another for a long time."

The first outposts of coarse, wiry hair are rolling under my fingertips. She closes her legs, tries to push my hands away, but I can tell her resistance is finely gauged. Stephen and I have read about this sort of thing. She doesn't want me to stop, but she doesn't want me to think she's easy. I persist, and to my surprise, her grip on my wrist tightens until it's almost painful. She's obviously not very good at this clumsy play-acting—I might easily have lost my desire. Fortunately, I've already felt telltale signs of wetness. Oh, yes, she wants me all right.

She wants me, but it's more complicated than I think. I could swear she's genuinely unwilling at first. If she is, there's a point when my ardor wins her over. I think it's when I finally work my thumb through the folds and complications and feel it slide suddenly in, sink deep, until the palm of my hand is beneath her, cupping her buttocks, squeezing and relaxing as I move in and out of her. Tears squeeze from under her eyelids, but there's no mistaking it—she's pressing down, starting a slow bump and grind, resigning herself as if to the inevitable. I like that hint of coercion, roughly pull the front of her nightdress down to expose her breasts. The nipples are rosy and firm. I encourage her to play with them. After a while she does: pinches, rubs, strokes herself, slides forward onto my working thumb. She becomes quite ardent. Doesn't even attempt to disguise it. For all his spy holes, I'm sure Stephen has never seen, or imagined, this side of her. When she comes there's no coercion, no humiliation. Instead I'm touched to see genuine relief as her eyes close and her face twists and she abandons herself to the long, prolonged, drawn-out moment, her whole body rocking on my rigid thumb.

Afterward, I return to her feet, holding and stroking, kneading and squeezing. I'm maintaining the sensual mood. Ensuring she knows my interest in her continues beyond mere gratification.

When I enter the house it's like walking through a fine veil, a cobweb curtain. There is resistance, tension, then sudden release. Dry strands trail across my face and there's a faint sound in my ear.

Stephen.

He has lost more and more weight as the days have worn on and his wife has not returned. Now he is little more than a gauzy blueprint, the faint remains of a rotted sack. All reflective surfaces in the house have been covered or dulled in some way, but they still exert a pull on him that is almost gravitational. He feels his substance billowing and tearing in a complex web of forces.

I try to tell him this is happening only because he is allowing it to. Imagining a hidden world does not mean that it exists. Eyes are merely sophisticated flesh, not beings looking out through human faces. I'm having great success with his wife. Louise is comfortable with me. The face he and I share no longer makes her scream.

But nothing gets through to him. It's as if he is turning into an abstraction, an idea, and the language of the real world is too crude to make sense. He tries continually to talk to me, but his voice is like fainter and fainter pencil strokes, never combining to form an image.

It occurs to me that my own rude health and no-nonsense attitude may seem like a constant rebuke to his own increasing incorporeality, that I may seem to have passed beyond caring for him. Nothing could be further from the truth, and as I work at cleaning the house up for when she comes home, feeling him flutter around me like a cloud of brittle ghost insects, hearing his voice like dry leaves on a dusty concrete floor, I tell him so. His condition, unfortunately, now seems irreversible. But he isn't to blame.

"I know who's responsible, Stephen," I say as I sweep and dust and polish. "I know who's done this to you. To us. I'm not saying you didn't miss a lot of opportunities, old son, because you did. No getting away from it. But that doesn't mean you deserve this. No way."

Leaves scrape quietly in my ear. I pretend to understand. "No, I'm sorry. There's nothing I can do for you now, mate. You're on your own. But I'll never forget you. And she won't either. I'll make sure of that."

I begin to clean the knives and polished surfaces Stephen has deliberately obscured. Husks and paper scraps spin and whisper.

"I'm sorry, Stephen. It's got to be done. The house has to be returned to normal."

The whispering rises to a dry rattling. I begin to uncover the mirrors.

It's my last visit and Louise's last day in the hospital. I'm taking her home.

Junior Doctor was worried at first. His boss wasn't back and the responsibility was all his. Louise might be fine with me, but what about her husband? How did we know her condition had genuinely cleared up?

The brain damage, you fool! That's what I felt like saying to him. *The brain damage was minor. It's cleared up. She's okay.*

But the Capgras Delusion remains tabloid nonsense to him. Although he has no idea why Louise behaved as she did, he still refuses to entertain suggestions coming from a layman.

In the end, though, he had no choice. He has no powers to detain. If Louise wants to go, he can't stop her.

And she does want to go. I've told her the whole story now. How Intuitive Imagining led inevitably to Physical Retribution. About the cumulative effects of Stephen's violence, especially the blows to her head. About his genuine next-morning contrition, his pleas that he was "someone else" last night, that kept her from leaving. About the final attack, the one that not only erased all memory of her earlier sufferings, but cut all the lines that connected him to her. Made him a stranger, an impostor in her husband's body.

And, most important, I've told her of my own part in all of this, my own feelings for her. She sees it in black-and-white terms. Good brother, evil brother. Now, almost like magic, she has what she wants. Same body, different inhabitant. Someone she can love. Someone who loves her.

She had some difficulty with it all at first, kept finding loose ends. But she knows, because Junior Doctor tells her, and the nurses tell her, and I tell her, that she's been very confused. And deep down, she wants it to be easy. Wants to simply draw a line and start again.

I'm her man. I can make that so.

She's standing against the door. On tiptoe. She's naked, vulnerable. I'm fully clothed, unzipped. I'm inside her, fucking her brutally—that's the word I choose to describe to myself what I'm doing. I need that extra level, that objective distance, otherwise it's just bodies. The way she's moving, impaled on me—it could be seen as ugly. It is ugly. But then, at this moment, she has only one purpose. She is this and nothing more: a receptacle for what I have to pump into her. There's nothing elegant about that.

Especially when she makes those grunting noises as she milks me.

Her body is thumping against the door, making it rattle. Out in the corridor there might be someone passing by, someone who wonders what the noise is, someone who might investigate. Under my tuition, she's developed a taste for this kind of risky semipublic sex over the last few weeks. She was reluctant at first. Now she doesn't even pretend. She's turned on by the possibility of a nurse, or even Junior Doctor himself, coming into the room unexpectedly; thinks I don't know that if that happened she'd pretend not to notice, would lose *all* of her inhibitions, would cast a triumphant glance at the onlooker just as she reached the height of her abandon.

It was there all along, this . . . coarseness. Stephen sensed it and punished it, but he never experienced it.

Stephen used to persuade himself he didn't like hurting her. Afterward. But it was the absence of self-control he was really ashamed of.

I'm always in control. I know how to take her to the outer edges of pain. Not so far that pleasure is left behind, just far enough to mingle the two. She likes it now. Likes me to hurt her just that little bit. She thinks I'll slacken off before she has to tell me to. She trusts me.

And now, we're back home. Even though I reassured her again and again in the taxi that Stephen was gone, that her flirtation with Capgras had been crucial for him, too, had sent him off on his own journey, she's still nervous, wondering what she's going to find.

But that fresh, newly cleaned smell hits her as soon as she steps through the front door. I see her start to relax. She's still hesitant, looking warily up the stairs, listening for noises. But when she sees the huge arrangement of flowers in the new crystal vase on the front-room table, she forgets her fear and runs forward to smell and touch the blooms. My note's hanging from a flower stem by a length of elastic silver thread. She reads it and turns to me.

"I love you," she says, and I murmur something coarse into the hollow of her neck. She turns to look at the flowers again, so I'll think she hasn't heard. Despite the reserves of . . . crudity that Stephen didn't know how to find, she's pretending coyness. I don't want to destroy her illusions about herself. Yet. And anyway, I can detect a genuine hesitation underneath. Perhaps some last vestige of feeling for Stephen.

But then she says she's going upstairs. Wants to "have a lie-down" in her own bed again. Yawns elaborately and smiles at me. She heard all right.

I hear her in the toilet. Then quietly checking the other rooms, just to make sure. Each one is scrupulously clean and I know that the gleaming woodwork, the sparkling windows, the freshly vacu-umed carpets will all be working to reassure her, make her relax. She'll be settling in between the new sheets about now, naked, spreading her limbs luxuriously, waiting for my footsteps on the stairs, perhaps even touching herself.

There are other things in those rooms she's just inspected. Things tucked away at the backs of drawers. Behind sideboards. On the high top shelves of wardrobes. Things that help with the complex business of mixing pain with pleasure. Things that focus attention when the balance tips.

Stephen knows where they are, what they're for. He watched while I wrapped and concealed them. Every time I caught a glimpse of myself in a mirror, in the silver back of a hairbrush, in the glass plate protecting the dressing-table top, he was there. Looking out at me from my own reflection. Remote, resigned, distant.

I feel his presence now. Inhabiting the house. Enclosing us. He knows what I'm going to do. There's a flame at the back of those cold eyes that tells me he approves.

He should. It's all for him.

Odor of Fate

Muthoni Garland

She was both the center of attraction and the orbit of disgrace. I was not the only man equally attracted and repelled by the giant woman, black as vinyl, dancing by herself under ultraviolet light in the infamous Bora Bora Discotheque. She was wild excess, writhing in mists of dry ice, a license for others to dance with greater wantonness. Her clothes, barely there, molded her body, not an uncommon sight in this den of prostitutes answering the mating call of British and American sailors on shore leave in the dirty, exotic town of Mombasa.

I did not mind them, the twilight girls and the soldiers of sexual fortune. In fact, I greatly enjoyed the buzz of their unfettered lifestyle, an enthusiasm so different from the restrained, prettified atmosphere of my world. It was my weekend escape, the bump slowing the journey to premature aging, and refuge from a conventional wife who loved my diplomatic wallet but hated the country that stuffed it. Our two teenage children in England provided an excuse for her to stay away for months at a time, even though they were in expensive boarding schools. It left me at liberty to enjoy the freedom of local friendships.

Of course, I had to be careful. An accidental meeting with United Nations paper shufflers, expatriate bosses, or fellow diplomats would severely dent my image. And Kenya is an AIDS hot spot. So I carefully planned how to avoid the penalties for my immoral fun. I cultivated hideaways, tested disguises, and practiced lines to use if I got caught. And I bought reinforced Dutch condoms.

But the simplest strategy proved the most successful. White executives working on contract in black countries don't go to black places, and they certainly don't go anywhere low class. They write proposals for poverty eradication and recommendations for development projects from the comfort of leafy, suburban neighborhoods. Only the odd one, perhaps, consults with an upper-class black person.

I could not care less for race and racial problems. The more they are given time to breathe, the more oxygen they suck. But this simple delineation of race and class made it possible for me to dip back and forth, frolicking with the hares and drinking with the hounds.

My gaze, like the purple light above, trailed the writhing figure. She moved as though her body were anchored on two different axes. Her generous breasts vibrated while she gyrated her sumptuous bottom in a fast, continuous motion. Just when I was sure that something would break, or that centrifugal force would fling her up and out the glass-domed roof, she changed direction. She rotated her top end, swaying arms to the sky and then with legs apart dipped almost to the floor, vibrated up again, exhibiting restraint and abandon in equal measure.

My mind filled with images of earthquakes. They come with a bang, crack open our fault lines, and can even swallow us whole. Our hope lies in the fact that their violence is soon spent, leaving us to grapple with consequences.

Other revelers moved away from her and crowded me to the fringes of the dance floor. I had to cut loose from a Pretty Hopeful to force my way to the inner circle. I soon realized they had melted away not only to get a clearer view of her ecstatic show, but also to escape her odor—a heady texture that brought to mind autumn leaves composting, yeasty underwear, overripe fruit, black cotton soil steaming after a downpour, full-bodied red wine, gorgonzola cheese, and, yes, unrefrigerated meat. All overlaid with a stinging Oriental perfume.

Draughts of this odor drifted toward me, bit my nose, lingered in my mouth, and had so much character that I had to leave her altar for a moment to find a drink with which to wash it down.

Confronted with the seductive whispers of my dangerous long-ing, I gulped the gin and lemon and moved in, ever closer. She was now within reach, but I did not attempt to touch her. Instead I moved my body to the frenetic *lingala* beat, and chased away the notion that I probably looked an absolute fool.

Sweat gathered under the silk shirt that clung to my armpits and love handles. My heart thumped in tune with the music. I snapped my fingers in the air while my feet jerked about, released of all inhi-bition. The beginnings of an erection tingled pleasurably. My mind floated on a cloud of heat and vapor. I throbbed with my giantess and her music, bestirred and becalmed.

I cannot recall the exact moment I became part of her rapture. It was as smooth as the way the music changed to the deep gravel tones of Barry White. As uncomplicated as the way her long arms reached around my waist, and as natural as the way I eased my head onto her heaving bosom and let her overwhelming redolence imprison me.

Smoother yet was the path, cleared as if by magic, through other dancers into humid night. The taxi could have been old, held together with safety pins; the ride to my room in a cheap hotel probably bumped bumpety-bump over potholed roads; it could have cost more than the Concorde flight from London to New York. I did not register any of that.

Up close, the citrus notes in her Oriental perfume stung like a nest of angry wasps, overriding the fetid muskiness of her unwashed body, and yet, every now and then, a waft of that something unsa-vory made me cringe.

Still, I fucked her and fucked her and fucked her.

She was the burning center of the volcano, the voracious black hole, the source of evil and ecstasy. She swallowed me, agitated and regurgitated me, extracted the essence of my very being before disgorging me, a limp rag hung out to dry.

On the equator everything dries quickly, but it surprised me how soon I hungered for her again. I fed the hunger that day and the next and the next. I tore through the condoms and eventually threw them away. In mindless frenzy, I spanked, sodomized, and came all over her. I licked every drop of heady sweat on her body and then created more. I experimented as I pleased, doing unspeakable things, groaning in a way that would have had me arrested on suspicion of murder in Queen Elizabeth's old Blighty.

She was obliging, moved her body this way and that, letting me dictate method, pitch, and frequency.

Three delirious days passed before I remembered to call the embassy. I lied to the receptionist that I had to fly out on a personal emergency and hung up before she could summon a superior to take responsibility for my strange message. On the wings of lust all other obligations flew from my head.

Her name, when I finally asked, was Anastasia.

Her face was not conventionally attractive, although individual features had their own charm—milk-white teeth, unblemished skin, and a flaring nose. Her figure, though, was cartoon-like in its disproportion. Slim shoulders rested on a mighty bust hinged on a tiny waist that in turn swiveled on a bottom that was a firm bench on which you could rest the *Unabridged Oxford Dictionary*. And her slim, well-muscled legs went from Cape to Cairo and right back again, all the way up to her magnificent buttocks.

She spoke in a discordant voice with an accent that told me she had learned her English at a late age from American customers. It was a strange ratatouille of Bantu, American slang, and bits of

English, so that when you finally heard a word you recognized, you said "Aaah!" It was just as well that her gestures were so illustrative, you rarely needed to understand her speech.

Her laugh, though, was an encouraging rumble like a tractor accelerating uphill. And even in repose her dark face rippled with a quiet amusement that indicated she had experienced the depths of the ocean, come up surfing, and was now unable to take the floating world too seriously. It made me want to prove that I had to be taken seriously.

So I fucked her.

Her appetites were all healthy. She consumed snacks, fruit, tea, drinks, and her meals as well as half of mine. At first, I had them delivered on a tray or we ate downstairs in the small dining room. As the month wore on and my body screamed for pause, I took her to Swahili and Indian restaurants where she mopped up fish sauces with balls of cornmeal rolled in her hand, or gulped lamb koftas with rice biryani.

And she attracted attention without inviting it in any way that I could see. The attention awakened Mr. Jealousy, who stimulated the need, so I took her to our room and fucked her.

I was generous, gave her money, and complimented her as extravagantly as a teenager in the grips of hormonal rage. She smiled and said something that I took to mean thank you. We went shopping and I bought her voluminous *kanzus*. It was in a vain bid to cover her voluptuousness from the eyes that followed her, as though she were a glow worm in the dark, a sumo wrestler in pink lingerie, or even a caged gorilla with an erection.

Those lustful looks made me behave more outrageously. I dipped a hand inside her cleavage to massage her bosom. I turned her chair to face mine so she could extend a leg for me to suck her long toes. I slipped my finger into her cunt, and then licked it in full sight of scandalized men and women.

Unappeased, I took her back to our room and fucked her.

She expressed no curiosity about me or anything else, asked no questions, offered no insights. But she answered every question put to her, so I gleaned the bare, ugly facts of her life. She had grown up in the slums of Nairobi, born of parents too poor to keep their children in school. Her own children were burned in a fire set by a jealous lover, and her family disowned her for turning to prostitution.

A lust-struck Italian took her to his country, where he was ostracized by his community and soon committed suicide. She came back to Kenya on the arms of another, older, Italian and landed in play-town Mombasa. The romance was short-lived when he, too, died, of a heart attack. It barely created a ripple in her life, although she confessed that she would rather not be with an Italian, given a choice, as they were so prone to dying on her. Strangely, this Italian oddity weighed more on my enraptured mind than the incredible burdens of her past.

She acquiesced to everything with a beatific peace, be it her lifestyle, copulation, lustful looks, food, clothes, money, compliments, suicide, customers, me. She asked for nothing and accepted all that happened.

Maybe that's why the dissatisfaction began, a gnawing at the edges of my obsession—a growing suspicion that I could never give enough or get enough to make a significant difference. Or maybe it was because I had also begun to wear *kanzus*, eat with my hands, and happily fart in public.

Was I facing a midlife crisis and these were the symptoms? Me, a healthy, civilized man of fifty-four, with husbandly, fatherly, and professional responsibilities, which, for now, could go chew curd or bay at the moon for all the attention I spared them?

I was falling out of control, flirting with insanity while a storm whistled overhead. I had to repair breaches, shore up my defenses, and batten down the hatches before my world crumbled.

So I tried to rein in the sex, ration it, tether it as far away as possible from whatever sticky patch of sanity remained. I rented an adjacent room, locked her door and mine, and fell asleep watching soccer on a little black-and-white television. By 3 A.M. I awoke with such an insistent erection that I forgot I had the keys and broke down the doors in my haste to fuck her.

Then I tried to tire myself with masturbation, three to five times a day, until I proved the theory that it will drive you mad by fucking her.

It was her odor to blame, baiting me and groping everywhere, ignoring all obstacles, even doors. It seemed a separate living thing, bent on provoking my need and stifling my dreams. And, uninvited, this malodorous quiddity finally invaded and lodged in my body.

A few times I caught its waft on myself and dismissed it as arising from her proximity. But on the day I left her in the room to walk to the bank, even people across the street wrinkled their noses and looked in my direction, puzzled. At the bank, queues mysteriously dwindled. I took a taxi back, and the driver insisted that the windows stay open.

I took to calling it The Odor. It was strange indeed. When I was by myself, The Odor disgusted me, and all those around. But when I was with her, it acted like a fertilizer, a catalyst, and an integral part of our desires. It fomented, agitated, and copulated along with us like the pressure that pushes the pistons in an engine. And the stronger it was, the greater my need for her. And the more I fucked her the stronger it became. I was held fast in its grips, sucked into its raging whirlpool.

I became convinced that if I could get rid of The Odor I would be free of this obsession.

Ours was not the type of hotel to have running hot water, but twice, thrice, and even four times a day, I had the claw-foot bathtub filled with hot water brought to the room in plastic buckets by two teenage boys. They shyly glimpsed sideways at her lying on the bed, so I stroked her breast or fondled her stomach or just stood between them and her, glowering with a dangerous jealousy.

She accepted it all without comment and gave no sign that she was aware of the turbulence in my heart.

I washed her with scented soaps and scrubbed her raw with a loofah. I buffed her with mentholated toothpaste. I used a machine-wash detergent that contained "powerfoam bio-enzymes guaranteed to eliminate all odors." I soaked her for hours in bubble baths, shampoos, and foaming gels. Once I poured in a bottle of olive oil, which had us slithering around like baby snakes. On another occasion, I abraded her with ash, collected from charcoal *jikos* in the kitchen, which turned everything in the bathroom black.

And everything I tried on her, I used on myself with exactly the same result. No change. If anything, The Odor raged with greater potency, as though recognizing a worthy foe.

So I experimented with various potions and lotions recommended by Indian chemists, but to no avail. I went to see a local doctor who bent toward me and asked me to open my mouth wide and say "Aaah."

He fainted.

When he roused, gagging, he asked me to sit outside while he wrote the prescription. It was for drugs that added another layer, a medicinal coat, to The Odor rather than eliminate an iota of its punch.

I consulted a famous healer, a witch doctor. He fed me bark broth, sprinkled me with chicken feathers, and made incantations. When this didn't work, he ushered me out with two proverbs, "A poisoner cannot stop the effect of poison" and "He who is the cause of his own troubles never gets to the end of them."

I was clearly getting nowhere near the end of The Odor.

Finally, I tested masking smells. Her Oriental perfume was the most successful when compared to baby powder, antiseptic, mentholated spirit, VapoRub, and several designer colognes, all of which made us gag or itch or break out in a rash, or all three at once.

I lifted an old Bible from the drawer in the room and read long passages, but they revealed no epiphanies for my salvation.

In a hired car, I drove to the Shimba Hills wildlife reserve for long periods of contemplation. I saw crocodiles tear zebras apart, hyenas fight over carcasses, lions mate for hours, and elephants trample down fever trees. Even though I parked the car to take forbidden walks in that dangerous territory, none of these beasts exhibited the slightest inclination to approach me.

Quite the reverse, they shied away in droves.

Each time I left her in the room. I always found her there on my return, but she never asked where I had been.

So I fucked her. And fucked her. And fucked her.

The Odor's gravity had stripped away my armor and dragged me down to the level of beast, my mind reduced to basic Pavlovian responses, my body held captive on the lowest rung of Maslow's hierarchy of needs.

Was this how I was doomed to live the rest of my life—yet another foreigner fucking pliant Africa? Or would my days be prematurely shortened by these endless exertions? Surely it could not be my fate to forever wallow in a malodorous miasma!

But how was I to rid myself of this obsession? My pathetic attempts to ignore, deflect, medicate, or camouflage The Odor had only fed its potency. Immune to appeasement, half measures, and gray morality, *The Odor* demanded the clarity of extremes.

Pebbles be damned, I needed balls of might. I had to think on a grand scale, rise above the quaking ground, and become God of my fate.

Freed of limitations, my thoughts plunged the depths and scanned the ages. Like lightning, wisdom blinded me.

Healing necessitated destruction!

Of course, I had to kill the source. It was the only guaranteed method to rid myself of The Odor. Yes, I had to murder my Anastasia. It was a black-and-white decision.

I had no doubt that she would accept it just as she accepted everything else that life dealt her. I had no doubt that I could do it. And get away with it. But I could not bear the thought of leaving no monument to honor her potency, no Mecca to go on pilgrimage to flay the devils that so often beset me, and no confessional in which to seek absolution and forgiveness. She was to be, after all, just a sacrifice for my sanity.

So I bought a plot in a cemetery in the leafy Nyali suburb of Mombasa, and hired artisans to build a fine tomb—an underground tomb with steps leading to a heavy door made of *mvuli*, a rare and deeply whorled hardwood illegally imported from the Congo Equatorial Basin. Embedded with spikes of iron and decorated with shards of mirror and ceramic in Arabic-influenced Lamu style, it was guaranteed to last the ages. I had carved on it, in Swahili, italicized inscriptions of everything I knew about Anastasia's life. Inside was a pink-and-white soapstone sarcophagus, raised on a hollow platform, to encase her coffin.

I hid the knife under the pillow, maneuvered her onto her hands and knees, and executed the ultimate fuck, which almost killed me before I could finish the job on her.

I raised the knife. She jerked, craned her neck toward me. I thrust at her kidneys.

"Eeewwwooohhh" she snarled, a wildcat, as the crunch of steel on hipbone rocked the room.

Blood spurted. Blood pounded in my head. She reached back and gripped my wrist.

I pressed her down, my weight on her back as she tried to twist around. The bed scraped the floor. Her hand tightened on my wrist like a steel cuff. Slithery with blood and sweat, we wrestled, naked, hot, stinking.

A pierced volcano could spill in any direction. I struggled to free the knife and wrest back control. I struck her with left-handed blows, and bit her, kneed her, clawed. But she hissed and grunted as though in labor, and refused to break.

Then her head slammed against the wall. Her body juddered as though in epileptic seizure.

Victory! A perverse cacophony of Handel's "Hallelujah Chorus" rose and merged with The Odor. Vomit burned my throat.

How easy to underestimate a woman you fuck. How seductive to think there are depths from which a person might never surface! I had paused my hand, had prematurely ceded to the high-strung twins of horror and exhilaration.

I heard my wrist crack as she wrenched herself free and flung off my weight like yesteryear's garbage. A phoenix risen, she towered over me, laughing like a banshee, once again the possessed giantess I had met that fateful night.

But the knife was still in my hand. I lunged, all body and movement. Her grip on my broken wrist made it seem as though she were stabbing at herself.

Eyes blazing with recognition, she danced around my knife, baptizing me in blood. Her laughter shook the foundations of the earth when she turned the knife on me.

The Odor burgeoned, poked its ghostly fingers into my every crevice. Despite the pain, I felt my Judas body stir.

I choked on self-revulsion as The Odor consumed me.

When I came to, Anastasia was gone.

Recriminations followed thick and deep, but I could not return to my other life of delusions. I severed the umbilical cord to my diplomatic, husbandly, and fatherly past, or perhaps it would be more accurate to say it was shorn from me.

• • •

My volcano is not dormant, just temporarily spent. In between its distant rumblings, I wander the streets of Mombasa in search of Anastasia. A voluminous *kanzu* shrouds my wounds—the pockmarks on the crater. Disgust, bemusement, or pity cloud the averted faces of those who behold me sniffing the air, following an invisible trail. Maybe you are one of them.

Even though they avoid all questions to do with Anastasia, twilight girls are my only friends. They assure me that when lava cools, it becomes fertile ground on which to plant different dreams. This may be true, but they cannot satisfy my bouts of odorous craving.

A volcano is more than a seething boil on Earth's face. It is an outward manifestation of Earth's core, that elementary burn of planetary star is the prophet who reminds us of our fiery roots and foretells our dust-to-dust ending.

Whenever The Odor rages, I drag my broken body to Anastasia's tomb. In this sanctuary, The Odor mysteriously dissipates—a temporary reprieve.

My rituals are simple. I lie on top of her tomb, on its pruned carpet of grass, and shout sacrilegious nonsense at the stars. It seems appropriate that they are not moved. When my throat seizes, I write this testament over the thin pages of that old Bible. Then I climb down the narrow staircase, and open the *mvuli* doors. I creep under the platform of her sarcophagus with its empty coffin.

I sleep, hoping never to wake, but I always do.

Yet I sleep an odorless sleep of peace.

"It's All Right, Ma (I'm Only Bleeding)"

Mitzi Szereto

"Lay, lady, lay . . ."

Oh, God, not again! That horrible nasal whine. Sounds like the man should blow his nose.

"Lay across my . . ."

I'll give you brass beds. Maybe a nice brass bedpost to smash your head in with. Oh, silence. Oh, bliss.

"*Hon*-ey, did you pick up my blue suit from the cleaner's yet?"

She sighs. Yet another thing she's forgotten. Like the Kellogg's Frosted Flakes for the kids. She'll catch hell tomorrow morning at breakfast. She can see their matching blue eyes, glaring at her in accusation. *"M-a-a-a-h-h!"*

A lawn mower starts up next door. Christ, it's not even 8 A.M. Well, at least it helps drown out those Bob Dylan CDs Richard puts on every morning while he's getting ready for work. Not to mention every night before going to bed. CD player in the living room. CD player in the bedroom. CD player in the bathroom. She can hardly wait for him to get out of the house so she can have some quiet. She wishes they had CDs with silence on them.

Her dumb luck his office moved into the suburbs. His early-morning train to the city has now been replaced by a quick ten-minute drive to the industrial park at the edge of town. Richard couldn't have been happier. It meant he could get in a quickie before work. That, and playing his goddamned Dylan. A yawn, a poke, a fart—then off to the shower. Not the sort of sex she reads about in *Cosmo*. But maybe *Cosmo* girls aren't married to Richard. Could be she's too old for *Cosmo* these days anyway. Might be time for *Reader's Digest*.

Middle-aged. Okay, *late*-middle-aged, if you want to get technical. When will her husband realize it's time to put away the love beads, the antiwar slogans? He can't seem to disconnect his late-middle-age self from his hippie teenage self. Well, pseudo-hippie. They were both raised in Hartsdale, New York, not exactly a bastion of poverty and underprivilege. So they both ran away to Woodstock in high school. Big deal. That didn't qualify them as hippies. Hell, they couldn't even get near a stage to see the performers. Hendrix was in a purple haze, all right. It was just a sea of mud, people OD-ing, backed-up Porta Potties. But talk to Richard and he'll go on and on about how great it was, like the Second Coming. She came home with tetanus. You call that great?

It wasn't so bad before, but something seems to have gone off in his head—a time bomb that's driving him to regain his lost youth. It started with the Grecian Formula. So what's wrong with a few gray hairs? She's got some herself. Yet every time she says they make him look distinguished, he drives off in a huff to the Costco to pick up a supersized bottle of the stuff. Why doesn't he do something about his spreading gut? After all, he's not exactly Richard Gere in the buff. Not that she's ever actually *seen* Richard Gere in the buff, but she can draw a good enough picture from his movies. Next was the new car. Here she's stuck driving their wheezing ten-year-old Chevy with its seats sticky with melted candy and old chewing gum, and Richard's flitting around in a shiny red Japanese model with a spoiler on the back. "I need it for work," he says. Work? It sits in the parking lot all day! Then came the prescription for Viagra. "But honey, isn't that for old men suffering from impotence?" she asked, later thinking it might've been more PC to use the term "erectile dysfunction." After all, Bob Dole didn't mind letting the entire country know he couldn't get his pecker up. Well, Richard set her straight on that one. She still wonders whether the kids heard them in the bedroom, what with the headboard slamming against the wall and Richard's Tarzan yodels. They did look at her with more contempt than usual the next morning at breakfast. Okay, so she might manage to put up with a few annoyances when it came to her husband. But now, to top it off, they have the resurrection of Bob Dylan. Christ, it's like he's in bed with them! It might work as an aphrodisiac for Richard, but not for her. Give her soft music, some candles. . . . She can dream, can't she?

Maybe she should get one of those vibrator things. There was an article about them in last month's *Cosmo*. (Not that she ever has the nerve to buy a copy; she reads them at the library, always tucked discreetly inside a copy of *Good Housekeeping*. After all, you never know who you might run into.) They actually have the kind of vibrator you can carry with you in your handbag. She can see it now: get all hot and bothered over the zucchini at the supermarket and off you buzz! Obviously if she bought one, she wouldn't be able to tell Richard. She knows how he'll react—all hurt and offended. "But I'm your husband. *I* should be pleasing you, not some inanimate piece of plastic." Yes, dear, but that inanimate piece of plastic has three speeds! Oh, what's the use? She'll never get one. Looks like it'll be Richard's inept fumbling to the nasal warbling of Mr. Dylan till they draw their last dying breath. With any luck, maybe Richard'll kick off first. Statistically, men do die before their wives.

Oh, what's she saying? She loves Richard. They've been married nearly fifteen years. Of course they lived together for eons before that. When they first met, *no one* got married. It was too old-fashioned. Not the thing to do. But years later, when she got pregnant with Sammy (who absolutely *hates* being called Samantha), the

parental pressure to make it legal became too much and they finally took the plunge. Good thing, too, since Tyler (who prefers to be
known as T) came along a year later. God, what a terror he was. *Is*.
Those horrible baggy jeans he wears. How he can walk in them is
beyond her. They hang so low the waistband of his Fruit Of The
Looms sticks out a good four inches. And the way he speaks—she
can't understand a word he says anymore. Plus he's always making
these jerky hand gestures like some kid from the ghetto. Not that
she's ever actually *been* to the ghetto, but she does watch television.
Unfortunately, Sammy's no better. Barely fourteen and she's wearing black lipstick and drawing weird symbols on her arm with a ball-
point pen, since they told her she's way too young to get a tattoo.
She was such a pretty little girl. Always Daddy's girl. These days
Richard can hardly stand to look at her.

The thing is, she really does love Richard. He's a good husband,
a good provider. Their little family never lacks for anything. The
kids go to camp every summer, she and Richard always take a nice
vacation when he gets his requisite two weeks off work. Last year
they even made it to Europe. London, Paris, Rome. The weather
was sweltering and it rained a lot, but who cared? They were in
Europe! She's never had to work. It was her choice. Just as it was
her choice to stay at home with the kids. She happily gave up her
career in pharmaceutical sales to be a stay-at-home mom. It felt like
the right thing to do at the time, and, no, she's never regretted it.
Of course now that the kids are older there's the question of what
she'll do with the rest of her life. No more kids, that's for sure! The
hot flashes have already started to kick in; she's going to have to get
one of those HRT patches soon, before she goes nuts. Besides
which, the risk for Down syndrome is so much higher at her age. It
was risky enough when she got pregnant with Tyler. Sorry. T. Thirty-
five's the cutoff year, according to the articles. Which means she was
playing Russian roulette with both Sammy *and* T. On the one hand,
they tell women to have careers. Then, when you do and wait till

you're older to have kids, they go and tell you you're risking giving birth to a Mongoloid. Horrible word. Her mother always used it whenever she saw a child with Down syndrome. Always an embarrassment, her mother.

She's been thinking of going back to school for a master's degree in business management. The university has it where you can attend classes at night. That would be perfect. She could still be there when the kids come home from school and Richard from work. They could still eat dinner together as a family, though it would need to be just a little bit earlier than usual for her to make a 7 P.M. class. She thought Richard would be thrilled for her. The night she finally made up her mind to do her master's she had the brochure from the university all ready for him to look at. They were lying in bed, watching Jay Leno on television and listening to Dylan, when she reached into the bedside drawer and pulled out the color brochure. The cover had all these happy, smiling faces of men and women, black, white, Hispanic, Asian, many of them her age. She felt certain she was making the right decision. She set it on Richard's lap like a prize.

Silence.

"Wel-l-l? What do you think?" she asked.

Richard cleared his throat. It sounded like something had gotten stuck in it. She hoped it wasn't those expensive lamb chops from New Zealand she cooked for dinner. She knew she should have bought another bottle of mint sauce to go along with it. The kids used up the whole thing, then didn't even bother to eat it, just let the pink juice from the meat leach into the jellified green, turning it a bloody purple. God, how they waste food. Finally her husband spoke. "You know, there are plenty of women out there who find me attractive. *Young* women."

Before she could grasp the meaning behind his words, Dylan was knocking on heaven's door, and Richard was doing likewise in a Viagra-induced frenzy.

She was sore for a week.

It took her another week to get up the nerve to ask him what he'd meant by his "women" comment. "I was just saying, that's all."

"Richard, are you seeing another woman?"

"No, I'm not seeing another woman. Don't be ridiculous! I love you. I love the kids. Why would I do anything to jeopardize that?"

That night a hard rain fell. At this rate she was going to have to get over to the Costco to pick up a supersized tube of K-Y.

Cosmo doesn't have articles about women whose husbands are experiencing what Richard seems to be experiencing. Sure, there's plenty of those "how to get a man" things, all of which pertain to sex. Oral sex. Anal sex. You have to do both these days in order to be competitive. Yikes! Just the thought of Richard putting his what-sit up her whatsit—it doesn't bear thinking about! Some things are best left for what God intended them for. Where do people come up with such crazy ideas? Aren't vaginas fashionable anymore? Maybe Dylan really was a prophet. *"For the times they are achangin'..."*

Because it was only a matter of time before Richard caught on to the latest fad. "Let's do it the other way," he cooed one night, Leno flickering on the TV screen, Dylan wheezing and whining in the background. *"Something's burning, baby."* She grimaced. By then she'd already bought the supersized tube of K-Y, and he discovered it in the bedside drawer along with her forgotten brochure from the university. Before she could stop him, he'd flipped her onto her belly, stuffed a pillow under her pelvis, and taken off at a gallop. By the time he rolled off her, Dylan was nasal-warbling, *"It's all over now, baby blue."* She noticed the bottle of Viagra lying on the carpet beside the bed. It was empty.

"C'mon, hon, it's no more painful than taking a shit," Richard told her the next morning when he wanted to go at it again before work.

"Ragged and Dirty" was playing on the CD player. That's pretty much how she felt.

And angry. *Really* angry.

Later that morning she went down to the university to speak to a postgraduate adviser.

That evening dinner consisted of KFC. There would be no more lamb chops, no more mint sauce. The days of the perfect wife were over.

So now she's in her first semester as a graduate student. She thought she wouldn't fit in, but it's been no problem. There are plenty of people her age, including one man—a funny little fellow—with an eastern European accent and a mustache. He always smells of pickles. She probably shouldn't say anything, but he's sort of been coming on to her. Not that she takes it seriously. Just a little flattery. She knows she's no hot potato. Not that she ever *was* a hot potato. Of course she's still a woman. It's nice to be made to feel attractive, even if you're not. She can't remember the last time Richard gave her a compliment, though he did bring her some ragged-looking red roses on her birthday. For some reason she thought he'd recycled them from work, some discarded gift to one of the office girls for Secretaries' Day. They did smell of coffee grounds, as if he'd taken them out of the trash.

Ever since she started school, Richard has developed a hostility toward her. Okay, so she never made good on her pledge to step down from Perfect Wife status. She still keeps up with the nice meals, the clean house. And, yes, she still keeps up with—or should she say puts up with—the Dylan. But the other stuff, that's got to stop, already. Richard has to realize she's not some piece of meat to be used and abused, some porn image come to life for him to act out his twisted fantasies on. Oh, yeah, did she mention about the porn? Now Richard's into that, too. She found out by accident when she was doing some research on the Web. She needed to find a home page she'd visited a few days before, so she checked for it in the "history" folder. Well, it was there, all right. And so were a lot of other

175

home pages. At first she suspected Tyler. You know teenage boys and their hormones! Of course it was disconcerting to think that her sweet little boy would be viewing such disgusting smut. The things that were there—she never would have imagined women allowing themselves to be used like that. Why, they didn't even look like human beings anymore. It was just so heartbreaking that her young son's budding sexuality should be developing in this way. She was so upset she decided to discuss it with Richard. After all, it's a father's responsibility to discuss sex with his son, not a mother's. Well, did she ever get a surprise when Richard broke into laughter, admitting he was the one who was the consumer of extreme Internet porn. She couldn't decide whether she was relieved or horrified that it was her husband, not her son, who turned out to be the sicko.

She probably shouldn't have been surprised when one evening Richard came home from work with a camcorder. "I thought it'd be kinda fun to film ourselves while we're doing it," he said, setting the thing up on a tripod. Christ, she didn't even know they owned a tripod. "Lots of couples do it," he added by way of comfort.

That's when the proverbial penny dropped. She remembered one of the Web sites—it featured real couples having sex, particularly kinky sex. Was this what he had in mind? To broadcast their crude couplings to the entire world? And to the nasal sound track of Bob Dylan? What if someone they knew actually saw it? Not that she could imagine anyone in their social circle visiting such a Web site. Then again, Richard probably came across as pretty innocuous to friends and colleagues. Guess you can never tell about people.

Richard was determined to go through with it. She was determined not to.

He had it all planned, even marking it on the calendar by circling the date in red. A Saturday night. The kids would be weekending with friends. It would be just the two of them, a bottle of Viagra, and Dylan.

Oh, and the new camcorder.

• • •

D-Day arrives. The day she's been dreading.

Richard announces that he's going to take a bath for the event. How mighty big of him, she thinks, hoping he runs out of hot water. No sooner does he turn on the taps than the CD player in the bathroom begins wheezing and warbling with Dylan. "It's all right, Ma . . ."

She goes into the kitchen to get a stiff drink. She never drinks. Well, maybe the occasional glass of white wine with dinner, but not the hard stuff. But tonight she chugs down three shots of J&B as if they're Coke. Her stomach roils as she hears her husband singing along with Dylan. She can't decide which of them sounds worse.

All day Richard's been leering at her. It makes her flesh crawl. She never understood what that meant before, but she can feel her skin writhing over her bones in some Edgar Allan Poe-esque frenzy. She catches her reflection in the kitchen window. It looks reptilian.

Splash. She can see him soaping his genitals with the bath-sized bar of Ivory soap. Not a pretty sight as she envisions his shrunken penis and furry balls bobbing and billowing in the sudsy water. "Hon?" he shouts from upstairs. "You about ready?"

She swallows one more shot of scotch, feeling the burn going down, way down. It matches the burn she's been experiencing in her hind end courtesy of her loving husband. Isn't there some kind of law against what he's been doing to her? She knows some states still have antisodomy laws in their books, although they are generally aimed toward homosexuals. How do they do it? she wonders, setting down her glass. How do they take it up the ass all the time?

Ever so slowly she mounts the Berber-carpeted stairs, Dylan's voice growing louder with each footfall, his every nasal whine mounting in intensity. The splashing sounds are becoming more furious. What the hell's Richard doing in there, jerking off? Then suddenly she realizes this is exactly what he must be doing. If he comes now, he'll last longer for when he's got the camera trained on them. Christ, it's gonna be a long night.

She reaches the bathroom. The door's wide open, and she can see Richard's right arm moving frantically in the tub. She steps all the way inside, receiving a big smile for her efforts. Dylan's voice is in full nasal throttle now; it's like being locked inside a bomb shelter with Felix Unger from *The Odd Couple*.

"Hey! 'Bout time," Richard scolds good-naturedly, grabbing his erect penis and waving it at her, as if this is sufficient to inflame her passion. "Hand me that towel, will you? *Or* would you like to get in here with me?"

Her eyes drift to the CD player. It rests on a wicker shelf beside the tub, the electrical cord plugging into the socket directly behind it. They're lucky to have so many outlets in the bathroom; there's another one by the sink, where Richard can plug in his electric razor and she her hair dryer.

"So Miss Roberts, are you ready for your film debut?"

Miss Roberts. By that he means Julia Roberts. She's his favorite. It's her large mouth, you see. Richard has fantasies of—well, never mind. You can probably guess.

She moves nearer. Richard's penis bulges obscenely in his fist. It looks as if it's being strangled.

"Hon, have you been drinking? I swear I can smell booze on you."

"Just a little scotch."

"Scotch? But you hate scotch!"

She shrugs. She doesn't hate it anymore. She likes the numbness it gives her. Maybe she should've taken it up earlier. Guess it's never too late to make new friends.

Richard slides downward in the bath, his freckled shoulders disappearing as his knobbly knees crook up. "Did you shave?"

"Huh?"

"*You* know. *Shave.*"

Oh, yeah. He's asked her to shave her whatsit so she'll be more exposed for the camera. She forgot all about it.

"You forgot, didn't you?" *Splish-splash.* "Want me to do it for you?"

Dylan's whine is unbearable now. It's as if someone's turned up the volume to full blast. She stares hatefully at the CD player, willing it to be quiet. The J&B has given her a headache. Or perhaps it's Dylan.

"C'mon, jump in. I'll take care of business." Richard holds up the pink razor she uses for her legs and underarms, his smile broadening. What an idiotic expression he has. It reminds her of President Bush. She feels an overwhelming desire to tell him this, knowing it would be the ultimate insult.

Her head's really beginning to pound now. It's like all the air's being sucked out of the small room. The steam from the bathwater has fallen over her eyes, clouding her vision. Richard's goony expression has gone hazy, as if she's viewing him through a Vaseline-smeared lens. His lips are moving, but she can't hear anything coming out. All she can hear is the Dylan.

"I'm only bleeding . . ."

Her hands grab hold of both sides of the CD player. It's lighter than it looks, she thinks, as she drops it into the bathtub.

Richard's lips stop moving.

The bathroom light flickers.

Silence.

His Last Duchess

Lauren Henderson

I watched him from the bow window on the staircase as he loaded his things into the Range Rover and climbed up into the driver's seat. We had only been married a few weeks and there was still a secret, furtive thrill at the sight of him like this, unaware that I was looking at him, seemingly free. But he wasn't; he was mine. I twisted the ring on my finger automatically. With other men the thrill had always dissipated after a while; sooner or later I would see them coming up the steps from the tube station, or doing something equally mundane, and no matter how handsome or endearing they looked, suddenly a wash of familiarity would surge through my veins like a tranquilizer dart and I would want to yawn so hard it felt like the corners of my mouth would split apart with the effort. Yawning, a boyfriend told me once, is simply the body's way of getting extra oxygen. He said that to reassure me, because I was yawning so much that evening. It's okay, I'm not offended, he was saying. And I stared at him in disbelief. What could be more offensive than someone who needed repeated blasts of oxygen to get through an evening with you?

He didn't last. None of them did. And yet I had married my husband after having known him for barely a fortnight. Clearly I did not anticipate being easily bored by him.

I turned the bunch of keys over in my hand.

"Explore the house," he had said. "That should keep you amused in my absence. Put that degree of yours to good use."

"Shall I write you a thesis?" I said. I was always casting him as my professor.

"Oh, it's scarcely coherent enough for that. Take one of those rambling travel books written by eighteenth-century travelers as your model. 'Sundry Observations on a Journey Through Herr Brinkmeyer's Scottish Mansion.' That sort of thing."

"Why don't you give me an oral?" I suggested.

He leaned forward and kissed my mouth. The texture of his beard was still shocking, silky and bristling, almost obscene. His breath was hot, his tongue pointed and wet. I hardly moved, letting him kiss me, closing my eyes to savor it even better. Finally he withdrew his hand from between my legs and stood back.

"You can use all the keys but the smallest," he said. "It's the one for my darkroom."

He smiled at me, his dark pink lips moist with my saliva.

"I keep my failures there, to remind me to do better next time. I can't have anyone but myself seeing them."

I nodded. The keys were heavy in my palm.

"I'm the chatelaine," I said, lifting them by the central ring. It was iron, waxy in texture, almost big enough to fit over my wrist, and the keys hung from it in an extraordinary jumble: gigantic old-fashioned ones crowned with elaborate swirls of iron, like something from a fairy tale, dwarfing the shiny modern Chubbs and Ingersolls with their miniature scratchings of teeth.

"I'll be back tomorrow," he said.

He would often visit the hut for a few hours, but this was the first time he had stayed there overnight. It was on the tip of the island, a high ridged promontory cutting out into the sea like the prow of a racing yacht. When I first came here he told me that occasionally he would spend the night there and asked whether it would bother me to be alone in the house. No, I said, I would be fine.

What would he have done if I had said yes? Got straight back in the launch and taken me back to the mainland? Probably. But then I was only a secretary. Simple enough to advertise for another one. A wife was not so easy to replace.

As the front door closed behind him I went straight up the nearer wing of the staircase to watch him go. The wind caught his hair, and the sunlight turned it the blue-black of sables and ravens. My gothic husband. His skin was dead white, thick and matte like heavy paint, his lips rose madder. Snow White's grown-up son.

He went down the wide stone steps as lightly as if he were unencumbered by the cameras slung over his shoulder, the pockets of his Barbour bulky with film and lens caps. I thought of the way he was always surprising me in the house, coming up on me as silently as if his shoes were soled in velvet. For a big man, he could seem weightless. (That made me think of bed, his body on mine, and I flushed with remembered excitement.) The door of the Range Rover banged shut. How final that sounded, the heavy slab of metal swinging into place. As the jeep crunched and ground the gravel of the drive, rounding the far corner to disappear down the oak-lined avenue, I realized that I felt bereft.

My first instinct was to reach out for someone else to fill the hole of his absence. It was lucky that there was no phone in the house; it would only have reminded me that I had nobody to ring. That may sound maudlin, but it wasn't. I simply had no family, or none that I ever would choose to speak to again. And this deliberate isolation from my relatives had kept my friendships few and shallow, too; I had learned no other way. There were ex-flatmates, old students from college, but no one whom I would ring now, with my monumental news. It was too big a conversation to have with someone I knew only casually. And how could I have anything less?

I looked around me, taking stock of the house. This was mine, too; well, ours. But his leaving me alone like this, with the keys in my hand—for a moment it seemed all mine, to do with what I liked. I put the keys down on the padded velvet of the window seat and sorted through them. None were labeled. He knew them so well he reached for the right one automatically. When the cleaning people came—a boatload from the mainland, once a fortnight—he would open all the doors necessary and we would leave the house for the day. Once, the weather was perfect, and we hiked around the island, climbed down to the little beach, took a picnic, and sat with our backs against the rock, listening to the white waves tear along the shingle. The other time we crossed to the mainland. But that wasn't exactly routine. That was the day we got married.

The advertisement had been simple: secretary wanted for photographer on his Scottish island. House beautiful but remote. Must be able to work in solitude.

"Must be able to work in solitude," I said aloud, my voice echoing in the vault of the mahogany staircase. The cleaning team had come a couple of days ago and on either side of the crimson carpet the treads were dark mahogany mirrors, the two wings of the stairs reaching down on either side of me like great outstretched arms.

I had never been good with people. The idea of being marooned on an island was almost perfect. Why hadn't I thought of that before? The only catch was the personality of my prospective employer. If he were a chatterbox, a lonely man buying company under the guise of a paid assistant, the house would be a cage, not a liberation from society. He rang me to say that he had paid my fare to Edinburgh, where he would come to interview me, so he must have liked my letter. When I got out of the taxi he had sent I believed that at the imminent meeting the advantage was mine.

Well, that changed as soon as I laid eyes on him.

His money for the airplane ticket, his private taxi to collect me, his hotel suite, and his presence, his restraint, only emphasized his power. I felt bought by him the moment I stepped into the room, like something he had taken on approval which he could return to the shop whenever he wanted. And I liked the part about being bought. Free, unfettered, equal-rights me; I liked it. It was liberatingly simple. I just didn't want to be sent back.

I picked up the key ring and went slowly upstairs. It was so heavy I felt I should have it hanging from my belt, like Mrs. Danvers. Only I was in jeans, and on me the effect would be more handyman than ancestral housekeeper. Maybe on another woman it would have been different, but I had an irredeemably practical face and body. Straight mousy-brown hair, features that didn't suit makeup—it always made me feel like I was in drag—a bottom as flat as a teenage boy's and a chest hardly more developed. I didn't care much about clothes. My jeans were paint-blotched and my layers of sweatshirts were old and familiar, softened over the years till they felt like second skins, as cave people must have felt in their furs. My fingernails were always chipped and stained with caulk or wood sealant. I did most of the repairs around the house.

Along the upper corridor hung a whole series of his photographs; his last wife, the beautiful Brazilian who had lasted precisely two weeks on the island before returning precipitately to São Paulo. His last wife. I almost giggled at the gothic resonances; it was Rebecca again, the gorgeous ghost tormenting the new, obstinately plain woman trying ineffectually to take her place. Only Ana wasn't dead, and I had never been the jealous type.

Ana stared over her shoulder rather sulkily. She had a bottom I could have built a shelf on, defying gravity with its upward tilt. With a woman that beautiful it was hard to tell what she was feeling; she looked bored, though, which might have been a pose, but could also have reflected her first inklings that life on the island was a catastrophic mistake for her. I saw myself reflected in the glass, and I grinned; how different we were. He had been married before Ana, but so far I hadn't seen the photographs of the others, though they must exist. I wondered whether he went from one type to another, disliking to repeat himself, and I liked this idea, having done the same myself. Always a fresh start.

Imagining him putting up photographs of me beside Ana. I laughed out loud. Me in my workshop, planing down a piece of wood, or on my knees in front of the library door, replacing the screws on the doorknob so that it didn't wobble annoyingly. What a contrast that would make.

He had taken a couple of rolls a few days ago, and said they were the best of me so far.

"You concentrate on your repair jobs with the same absorption with which my second wife put on her makeup," he had said, amused. "How the modern woman is changing. I'm going to pull out some old shots I did of her to show you what I mean."

He knew the contrast wouldn't worry me. That was the great thing about this marriage. We had known a few central things about each other instantly, and all the rest was there for us to discover. Layers upon layers. I wasn't in a hurry, or I hadn't thought I was. But I found myself going up the farther flight of stairs, uncarpeted wood, that led to his studio. Maybe the photos of me would be developed. I was curious, yes. All women are, he often said. Well, we had that in common with the rest of the animal kingdom, I said. Without curiosity we would be stuck in ruts, moldering away. You mean dead, in other words? he said. I nodded. Or as good as. He smiled and changed the subject.

I pushed open the door to his studio. It was always closed but was locked only when he was working on something and was not to be disturbed. The photographs of me were everywhere. I didn't realize that he had taken so many. They were all in color, which seemed appropriate. I didn't have the mythic black-and-white, film-still beauty of Ana or of his second wife, the opera singer whose name I could never remember. There was a detail to the photographs which astounded me; somehow he had captured all the minutiae of whatever task I was busy on. And I was always busy, my expression always concentrated, focused: squatting, a heap of tiny screws spread out on the floor in front of me, or with a drill in my hand and splinters flying up into the air like sparks from a fire. My eyes never met the camera lens. How competent I looked, and, yes, how absorbed, as if I were in a world of my own which no one could touch. Was that how he saw me?

This was what I had been curious about: his image of me. And here I had it, along with further proof of my difference from Ana— who, bored though she might be, was always acutely aware of the eyes on her, of her audience of one—or the opera singer, who in the single photograph I had seen was neither bored nor distant but nakedly engaged with the man behind the camera, her great eyes wide, almost pleading, as if no amount of his attention would ever be enough.

I wondered if he had found the shots of her he had mentioned just now. They weren't here, or at least not on view; every single image was of me, a collage on every surface, as if he were trying to fix me in his brain for all time. As if I had gone, and he was trying to remember every detail of how I had been. Well, I wasn't planning to head off to São Paulo anytime soon. He would just have to get used to the flesh-and-blood version.

My fingers ran over the keys, feeling automatically for the smallest one of all. I knew he had said not to enter the darkroom, but the red light was off over the door; it wouldn't damage anything. Besides, he would never know. A quick glance, just for a moment— how irresistible it was to do what you knew you shouldn't.

I found the key. As I took it between index finger and thumb, the others fell back from it so heavily that I nearly dropped the iron ring. The weight would unbalance the key in the lock; eventually the teeth would begin to bend out of shape. What was he thinking of? I untwisted it from the ring, making a careful note of its position among the others. Then I crossed the room to the darkroom door and slid the key into the lock.

They were all there. In the dim red light, as soft and flattering as pink-shaded lamps in a plush crimson velvet restaurant, their faces gazed back at me, their expressions calm, their eyes wide. I had known he had been married four times before; he had made a joke of it. But somehow seeing all his ex-wives, one after the other, so much larger than life, ranked in what I assumed was chronological order, a series of beautiful black-and-white photographs running down the left-hand wall of the darkroom—I took a deep breath. I was unable to decide whether I was more confused by the knowledge that he worked like this, under the constant, unwavering gazes of those four women, or the fact that there was so much empty space still left. Instead of widening out the frames to fit evenly along the wall, he had hung them close together, almost touching. There was room for at least another four, maybe five. The blank red-lit plaster seemed to be staring at me even more than my predecessors did: look, it said, look where your image will hang, and the one after you, and the one after her. . . .

Oddly enough, I took it as a challenge. So he's not sure this marriage will last? Well, I thought, I couldn't blame him. There was the evidence of divorce on the wall in front of me, in black and white, unignorable. Perhaps he kept them there to remind him of his past mistakes. My shoulders straightened and for some reason I looked down at my hands, my rather large, blistered hands with their stubby, cracked fingers and short, ragged nails. They reassured me more than anything else could have done; more than his arms around me, his comforting words. My hands were brutally practical, like me, and they said that there was no point worrying about the past, that I was the present, and the present was all there was. I turned the key over absently, its cold, unyielding metal shape solid in a sudden drift of uncertainties. I always came back to objects in the end. You knew exactly where you were with them.

Across the darkroom was a door, half ajar. A ghostly white light filtered around the jamb, like dry ice melting into the red glow. When I had come in I had flicked the main switch; it must have turned on the light in the far room as well. I crossed the studio and pulled the door fully open.

They were all there. It took me a long, long moment to work out what I was seeing, doubtless because I was resisting with all my will. Again, they were lined up chronologically, their glass coffins propped at a slight angle against the left-hand wall. Whatever system of tubes and pipes he had installed to preserve their bodies emitted an odd greenish light, which cast an eerie glow over their faces. Perhaps that was what initially had made the scene before me look so unreal. I thought of an art exhibit, of dead animals fastidiously preserved in formaldehyde, floating hacked-apart in a pale bluish liquid that echoed amniotic fluid. No such comfort here, no substitute womb.

The coffins must be fiberglass. And the apparatus was there to drain off the gases produced by decaying bodies, avoiding any stench or increasing pressure that might cause the coffins to explode. The wounds on their bodies were all different but all equally unmistakable. A ligature mark as thick and deep as a man's thumb, blackened as if scorched in. A single stab wound, slicing up through the ribs, glaring open like a mouth. The opera singer's head lolling, oddly relaxed, at an inhuman angle. Ana, a hole in her chest big enough to put a fist into, singe marks around it showing how closely the shotgun had been held to her body.

The gun room downstairs was full of them, always cleaned and broken after a day's shooting. I would never know which one he had used.

The key fell from my hand. Oddly enough, the flat metal noise as it hit the concrete floor was reassuring. My universe might have suddenly turned upside down, but things still fell down, rather than up, and sounded just the same when they did. I didn't pick it up straightaway. I was staring at the rotting flesh of my husband's first wife, observing how her wound seemed larger than it must have been when he first stabbed her, because the skin was decaying, falling away from the gaping crack, pulling it wider and wider as time passed, until just the bones would remain, only some cuts on her ribs to show how she had been killed.

What did he have in mind for me? He seemed to have covered most of the conventional bases already. At this thought a spasm gripped my ribs, almost like laughter. I bit my lip hard to steady myself and bent down to retrieve the key. It was so white in here my eyes were dazzled by it. The walls were blurring into each other. I felt as if I had been in this room for hours, days, and understood the full force of sensory deprivation, how disorienting it could be. It was a struggle for me to find the door. The white light blotted out everything else. I groped around in a controlled frenzy and only stumbled into the open door by chance. The doorknob under my hand steadied me more than I could have imagined. The metal was cool in my palm, round and solid, reassuringly real. If it broke I would know how to fix it.

I set the door at the same angle, more or less, that I remembered its standing before. I don't remember picking up the bunch of keys or leaving the darkroom; I don't even remember locking the door, though I know I did, because I went up those stairs later and tried it, to be sure. The first thing I remembered was finding the place on the ring to put the darkroom key, separating the others with my fingers and pulling the key out of the lock, turning it around to start sliding it around the ring. And noticing the red stain on its teeth, bright as fresh blood and equally impossible to overlook.

While the key was soaking in a concentrated solution of Stain Devil and bleach, I took stock of the situation. Every few minutes I would scrub the key briskly with a nail brush—a wire wool pad would have left telltale scratches—and then let it fall back again to the bottom of the sink. That no tinge of red was beginning to infuse the thick white liquid I didn't take as a sign to panic. I had never understood how these stain removers could absorb blood into themselves. The water merely turned slightly dirty, slush rather than snow.

The fortnightly cleaning and maintenance team would have done all our laundry, down to the occasional touch of monthly blood on my underwear, without batting an eyelid. They were paid a fortune to do everything that needed doing without being asked, and to keep their mouths firmly shut. He had chosen them well. A grimmer, more dour bunch of people I had never seen, so disinclined to gossip that they much preferred all current occupants of the house to be off the premises when they went about their work. But it would never have occurred to me to let someone else wash my dirty underwear. I did that all myself. Which was why I was probably the first wife of his practical enough to look at a blood-stained key, think, "It'll be much easier to get that out straightaway, while it's fresh," and trot immediately down to the laundry room to get the small magic bottle of Stain Devil (blood, red wine, and fruit juice).

I lifted the key once more and glanced at it. The stain was almost gone. I let it drop without even bothering to give it a scrub. It tinkled to the base of the sink, a few bubbles rising briefly in its wake, and disappeared. The bloodstain itself was a mystery to me. I couldn't believe there had been blood on the floor of that room; surely I would have noticed it, even as distracted as I was. And even if there had been fresh blood on the floor, how could it possibly have flowed from those poor desiccated bodies? At the memory of them I felt myself shiver, and as if from a long distance away I observed myself, surprised to realize that the shiver was not entirely one of revulsion. I felt oddly excited. My heart was pounding, my pulse racing, no matter how calm and automatic my movements were.

Adrenaline, obviously. I was in a serious situation. The cleaning team had just been a few days ago; it would be well over a week until they returned. And even then I half doubted that they would let me travel back with them. He paid them munificently for their discretion; now I wondered how far that ran. Did they know, or suspect, that his previous wives had never left the island? He had his own motor launch, his own private landing stage on the mainland with another Range Rover waiting. There would be no way to tell for sure who had come and gone. Yet I thought they might suspect something, if not the whole. Now that I looked back on it, there had been a change in their attitude to me when he told them about our marriage, and it was not just the extra deference to the lady of the house. Was I imagining it, or had there been something assessing, calculating in their narrow stares, as they wondered how long I would last—or how long it would be till he set the trap, his overnight absence at the hut, the bunch of keys with the prohibition on using one of them, even his previous allusion to the photographs he had done of me, an extra bait?

The key was clean, but smelling slightly of bleach. I rinsed it in soapy water till the ammoniac smell had gone, dried it off with a cloth that wouldn't leave traces, and put it back on the ring.

After that I was free.

I could have shot him as soon as he walked in the door. The evidence upstairs would acquit me of anything; they wouldn't even press charges. But I didn't even bother to check the gun room. He knew me, or at least that side of me, knew how practical I was. The first thing he would have done before leaving would have been to make sure that none of the guns was usable. He had probably taken all the ammunition away with him in the Jeep.

I jingled the keys in my hand, absently, thinking things through. The keys—the prohibition—the blood—even the deliberate mention of his darkroom and his failures, just before he left. It was all a trap. And it had the air of being strictly regulated, a kind of macabre game whose rules were always the same. So what if I didn't spring the trap? What if I handed the keys back to him, clean as they had been when he left? What would he do if I sprang the trap on him instead?

I had never seen my husband speechless before. It was a heady sensation. I watched him stammer, unable to form the words, genuinely, completely, taken aback, and I could have hugged myself with excitement.

"So what have you been doing to amuse yourself while I've been gone?" he asked affably, taking off his Barbour. "I do hope you haven't been too bored."

"Oh, no," I assured him. "I listened to the football on the radio last night. And I've been messing around with that driftwood I've been collecting. I thought I might try to make a frame with it. Something simple, to start with."

"Good . . . good," he said. I thought he sounded surprised at the easiness of my manner: well, so was I. I never realized I had that much potential for dissimulation.

"Do you have my keys?" he said so casually that I knew at once that this was just the way he had pronounced this sentence four times before.

"Yup—they're here, somewhere . . ." I had thought it would look too suspicious to produce them patly. I scrabbled around on the hall table for them. "Here you go."

"You'll have to forgive me," he said, counting through them. "An old habit of mine when I've been away, even for short periods—I like to check everything. . . ."

A long moment later, after a pause filled only by the chink of key against key, he looked up. His face was wiped blank, his lips parted as if to ask a question his brain would not allow him to make. Speechless, as I said. It was perfect. Had he expected the key to be missing? Or had he actually thought I would have left it there with the stain still on it?

I had a sudden rush of impulse. His mouth, his moist lips framed by his dark beard . . . I leaned forward and kissed him, not the swift brush of greeting but a deeper, proper kiss, my tongue slipping into his mouth, my hand sliding around his neck to hold him to me. I felt him stir against me; he was already hard. The anticipation of catching me out, perhaps; had he already decided how he would kill me? I moved against him, grinding my hips against his. I am tall for a woman, and our heads were nearly on a level. I reached down and started to unbutton his trousers.

"I've missed you," I whispered into his mouth. "I missed you a lot."

My hand slid through the slit on his boxers and caught hold of him. I realized that I had never been like this with my husband before. I had always let him make the initial approach. In awe of him, maybe, feeling that the rules were his. He was the vastly experienced older man with houses in three countries and four ex-wives; I was just the secretary with a nice plain face and a gift for carpentry. But now the rules were changing. Everything was blurred. I was free to do what I wanted. I sank down and took him in my mouth, and when he was groaning I pulled him down to the floor and straddled him. The noise we made echoed through the rafters of the hall. Afterward, as I collapsed on top of him, he looked at me as if he had never seen me before.

I knew that he would go away again, for longer periods, and he would press the keys on me, urgently imploring me not to go into his darkroom, dropping all the hints he could until he practically hung a sign on the door. But I wouldn't go in. Once had been enough. I would like to; I would like to look at them again. Still, my practical nature told me that he might lay other traps. Why run the risk? He belonged to me now. I had broken the pattern, and now it was mine to make. My husband lay beneath me, arms outflung, limbs loose, as if I had just thrown him from the balcony above. He was panting as if he had just run a race. I closed my eyes, nuzzled my head into his shoulder, and smiled.

Hate Mate Awaits Fate

Jan Wildt

Mike Stotlund, a carpenter between jobs, was clearing his head with a 6 A.M. walk along the beach in Venice when he saw a man stagger in from the surf and collapse on the sand. The man might have drifted in from Hawaii. He clung to an antique-looking longboard.

The board looked interesting. Stotlund went over. "You all right, bud?"

The man tried to roll over. He was an old guy—fifty, sixty, maybe more—and Asian or something. He looked cold.

"A doc," the man whispered.

"Sure," said Stotlund. "My car's around here." He bent to pick the man up, then stopped and took the board instead.

"Sorry, man," he explained. "If I take you first, that stick is gone."

He carried it to his car, leaving it poking out a window, and drove back to the man. He took him in his arms.

"You hurt?" Stotlund said.

"Tired," the man said, but it looked worse.

They went to an ER some miles down the highway. Neither spoke until the man was on a gurney; then he grasped Stotlund's fingers in a weird handshake. "Thanks, brah."

"How about your board?"

"Take care of it good. No one else. You."

Stotlund, studying him, said, "You, uh, might not come back."

"Nope," the man said.

Stotlund watched the receding gurney and said, "I don't even surf."

He drove to a breakfast joint, the board still protruding from his back window. He ordered *huevos rancheros* and sat where he could keep an eye on things.

He soon saw he was being appraised by a fellow diner: a slight, expensively bespectacled guy about his age, twenty-five or so, turned out in Euro-weenie casual, working on a yogurt fruit plate and pretending to read *Variety.*

Stotlund paid and left and was outside digging for his keys when the weenie approached. He readied himself for a tedious faggot punch-out.

"Nice board," the weenie said.

"You say that to all the fellas."

He backed off. "Easy, dude. This is one proposition you might want to hear."

"Fuck off," Stotlund said, getting in the car.

"I'm Alex Murkin. Personal assistant to Her Highness. That trip your trigger?"

Stotlund knew who he meant—anybody would. Her Highness was front woman for the Dancing Wu Li Masters, an abrasive noise band targeting a pallid, pierced slice of the fourteen-to-twenty-year-old-male demographic. A mainstay of their show was an exhibitionistic number called "Queen Hate" ("I'm all that I need/I'm in love with me/I hate you all," and so on), during which she received the simulated simultaneous romantic attentions of eight or ten onstage courtiers. But this had soon evolved into a new take on crowd surfing. You hadn't really been to a Masters show unless you had laid a hickie on or copped a serious feel off Her Highness during

"Queen Hate." She enjoyed being the center of a seething vortex of cretins. The requisite legal and security contrivances (including an industrial-strength chastity belt) were a small price for the Masters to pay for having distinguished themselves from thousands of other artists who otherwise exceeded them in talent and vision.

"And I'm Lady Di," Stotlund said. "See ya."

"You *do* know who I mean?"

"Sure," Stotlund said. "She's with some band that nobody gives a shit about because they're all too busy watching her fucking and sucking onstage. And off. She's like this colossal slut."

"Don't mince words," said Murkin. "I want your honest thoughts."

"I think her flunkie wouldn't look like you," Stotlund said.

Murkin drew in his breath. "Putz, I could care less about convincing you. But you happen to be her type."

"That's anything with a dick."

"No, really. You interest her. Take it from me." Murkin put his palm to his heart. "I'm her eyes and ears."

"Eyes and ears, huh," said Stotlund. "You could have done worse."

"One last time, beach boy. *Her Highness is looking for a few good men.* Know what I'm saying?"

Murkin watched it sink in.

After a reflective interval Stotlund said, "You shit me."

"Let's get it straight. You do as you're told. You don't talk. You don't get paid, you don't get off, you don't get famous. Your reward begins and ends with the knowledge that you have briefly touched and served, in an intimate way, the hardest-working sex goddess in showbiz."

"I can visualize that."

"Come by my office. How's ten-thirty?" Murkin handed him a card.

"She gonna be there?"

"No. And shower first."

"Okay, Murkin," Stotlund said. "Why me?"

"She's into beach bums this week," Murkin said. "Fuck if I know."

Stotlund had seen on MTV how some roadie had wanted $100,000 from the *National Enquirer* for a firsthand account of secret post-concert orgies Her Highness was said to have been staging for her own delectation—as opposed to the onstage activity, which was her selfless gift to mankind.

The *Enquirer* had declined.

They had declined because Her Highness's own people had just been there, talking about it for nothing. A documentary was in the works.

Stotlund took a seat. Across the desk, Murkin consulted a printed list.

"Okay, dude, some personal questions. Married?"

"No," Stotlund said.

"Lady friend?"

"We sometimes think so."

"It's a—sexual relationship?"

"While we're fucking."

"Humorous," Murkin said. "Dating other women?"

"Till their ears bleed."

"And we already know your feelings about guys." Murkin looked up. "Sexually transmitted diseases?"

"Nope."

"History thereof?"

"Pure as the driven snow."

"Hmf," said Murkin. "All right. Scott, do you consider a woman's breasts to be an erogenous zone?"

"They're erogenous to me," said Stotlund. "And my name ain't Scott."

"Do you find that stimulating a woman's breasts can give her pleasure?"

"Well, sure. You know."

"We're interested in what *you* know, Scott."

"Okay," Stotlund said, "frankly, some women are ice-cold about it. But some of 'em love it. A few even come that way."

"Ah. And how exactly do you accomplish that?"

"Murkin, you playing pocket pool? Hands on the table, please."

"Allow me to review, wise-ass. Her Highness has *asked me* to *ask you* what *you* do to bring a *woman* to *climax* by breast stimulation alone."

"What is this, research? I'll need a consulting fee. This is expert advice, heh heh," Stotlund said. "Or tell her to come here. I'll show her for nothing."

"You will?" Murkin said.

He opened a desk drawer and took out a small black plastic bag closed with a twist-tie. He tossed it across. Its weight and density caught Stotlund off guard.

"It's a scaled-down Hefty lawn sac," Murkin said.

"What's in it?" said Stotlund.

"Pillsbury Poppin' Fresh Dough. That's right, take a look. I wouldn't want you to trust me. Now close it back up and show me your stuff."

"Huh?"

"Pretend this part's the nipple."

Stotlund studied the bag in his hand. He looked at Murkin. Then he looked back at the bag.

" 'Alas, poor Yorick,' " Murkin prompted. "You're blowing your audition. *Suck.*"

Warily Stotlund raised the bag to his face. He put his lips to it, flicked it with his tongue a few times.

Murkin twirled his pencil. "She's considering getting excited."

Stotlund took more of it into his mouth, nudged it around.

"Oh, wow." Murkin yawned. "She's *really* taking it under advisement now."

Stotlund swirled his tongue around and around, flailing his head for added effect.

"Look, let's just say she's almost there. She's almost there, for God's sake!"

He heaved the bag into his mouth with a suck that came from his tonsils, tongue bucking like a hooked marlin. The bag ruptured. A tsunami of dough bounced off the back of Stotlund's throat.

He bent forward, hacking beige gouts onto the floor.

"That'll work," Murkin said.

Murkin stood, buzzed the receptionist to clean up, and left. In the restroom, he took a pee, then checked his grooming in the mirror. He told his reflection, "This fucking job."

"They open the cabana locker room at eleven P.M.," the receptionist told Stotlund. "If you get there at eleven-thirty you have plenty of time, but be there at eleven sharp this time, because Alex wants to orient you."

"What exactly does that mean?" said Stotlund.

"Bring your own lock, please. You're expected to shower, wash, and at least towel-dry your hair, use perhaps a *light* application of an unobtrusive men's fragrance, and antiperspirant if you would please, not just deodorant. Brush your teeth. Use mouthwash."

"My dental floss is unwaxed," said Stotlund. "That okay?"

"If you ask me, the mouthwash seems a little much. She never kisses anyone. But what do I know?"

"Are you involved?" said Stotlund.

She giggled. "No. Oh, and your assignment is right breast. Have fun!"

• • •

Stotlund showed at 11:05 P.M. Murkin had a video ready to roll. A nice setup for a film shoot. "We don't tape anymore, but I keep a few for reference. See how everybody's arranged here."

It was an aerial shot, a bird's-eye view. "Decent angle," Stotlund said.

"You like that? We brought a freakin' dolly in there. Me hanging over the side. I thought, 'Mrs. Murkin, if you could see your boy now.' "

A symmetrical cluster, some deep-sea organism, was arrayed on a white expanse of bed. Her Highness was in there somewhere on all fours. An athletic, brown-complected individual was at her from the rear.

"That's Nacho in the driver's seat," said Murkin.

"Nacho?"

"Ignacio. Her trainer. Nacho's *always* in the driver's seat."

Two guys were crouched at her ears, nuzzling. The breast guys were supine, heads out of view, bodies diagonal to either side of her spine. Wedged in between them and Nacho were two masseurs, working on her buttocks, thighs, and back.

"They're all naked." Stotlund stated the obvious. One of the breast guys had an erection; the other didn't.

"For a while it was casual clothing. Lately this is what she's wanted. As you might guess, there's a tendency for attendants to get, um, wound up. You can't expect to be indulged, of course."

"It goes without saying," Stotlund said.

Nacho's right hand moved off her buttock and reached around her flank to plumb her nether regions. It was like dropping a hot dog on an anthill: everything went frantic, signal sweeping through system. She raised her head and Stotlund saw the midline part in her hair. Each participant bore down afresh on his task and strove to make his mark amid the tumult.

"The reach-around," said Murkin, "always interferes with that side's breast *and* masseur. It's an unsolved problem in topology. So Nacho always uses his right hand. Because her left breast is more sensitive. Her left is like a direct pipeline to Down There."

"She always take it like a doggy?"

"The missionary position's too crowded."

"She could cowgirl it."

Murkin considered this and said, "You'll go far."

"So how does Nacho rate?" Stotlund said.

"Scheming on his slot already? Forget it. They go way back."

"What is he, hung like a horse?" Stotlund squinted. "Can't really tell."

"No, just like you and me. You'd think with all this other stuff she'd want some high-tech G-spot megadildo, too. But no, she likes a human with a conventional dick. And she does *not* want a condom or a diaphragm. She's on The Pill, as far as that goes. She likes the feel of a big wad squirting in there."

"How would *you* know, Murkin?"

A couple of guys walked past and waved on their way into the locker room. Murkin barely acknowledged them, but said to Stotlund, "Seen them? A not-so-well-known comedy duo."

Onscreen, things were slackening.

Making for the locker room, Stotlund felt Murkin's hand on his shoulder. "Scott, please don't get the idea that you're entering a lasting arrangement. Nacho is the only constant. She likes variety. Okay, Jackie and Gene there are setting a kind of record: three times in a row. But anyone can lick a tit. You can't expect to have the indispensability of, say, me."

"Of course," said Stotlund. "You run the projector."

"Ass-wipe, the difference between you and a cocksucking whore is, *you* don't get paid. Dipshit. Go break a fucking leg."

• • •

Stotlund went into the locker room and disrobed. The two guys ahead of him were already gone.

He showered and shaved with a brand-new blade. He sprayed on some Right Guard Sport Fragrance. He donned an unassuming but streetwise taupe terry-cloth robe styled like a fighter's warm-up outfit. He was getting into this. He brushed his teeth. He used his mouthwash.

Stotlund came out of the locker room. Murkin was there. He scooped a palmful of air from Stotlund's personal space and sniffed.

"Okay," Murkin said.

Stotlund considered saying, "Check my mouthwash, honey," but didn't.

He continued to an anteroom, where the other two guys were watching NFL highlights on ESPN.

"I'm Jackie," one said. "This is Gene. We're the ears."

"Scott," Stotlund said. "Right breast."

"New and untested," Jackie said. "Remember in Little League? They'd put you in right field."

"I thought we took our clothes off," Stotlund said.

"In there," Jackie said. "She and her boyfriend go in alone at first and get warmed up. Sooner or later that little bell goes *ding*. Murkin rings it. You're the first one in. Just go in, close the door, contemplate the tableau before you according to your own fashion. They'll be officially at it by then. Smile hello. Let your robe slip and amble on over like Johnny Wadd. *Sang-froid. Sans souci.*"

"Huh?"

"You don't know this? Murk's not doing his job. There'll be a pillow under your chest—she wants you comfortable. You've seen how to lie diagonal so you're out of our way. Then do your thing. Pace: strictly up to you. Slow buildup or full-bore."

"Not like she wants a routine or anything," Stotlund said.

"Pretend she's feeding you a peeled cantaloupe," Gene said.

"Have you done it?" Stotlund said.

"We wish," Gene said. "Who do *you* know?"

"Swift, massive tongue thrusts are the key," Jackie said. "Glom maximally, suck big, and sock it like a punching bag."

"You'll be working left breast in no time," Gene said.

"But not with warning-track power," Jackie said. "I'm telling you, she likes it huge."

"I hear you guys are old-timers," Stotlund said.

"We've had a run," Jackie said. "But we're all dispensable. Except the point man, the coital partner: always Nacho. Could this be some quaint vestigial notion of fidelity? Or is it hard-headed pragmatism in the face of infectious risk?"

"Maybe they're the same thing," Stotlund said.

"A thinker," said Gene.

"She got implants?" Stotlund said.

"No," Jackie said. "They've got heft, though. Definitely pendulous."

"I copped a feel once," Gene said. "In all the commotion."

"Yeah, right," Jackie said to Gene. "We'd've scraped you off the wall. Homie don't play dat."

"Why should Nacho care?" Stotlund said. "She only gets gang-mauled in public every night."

"That's business," Jackie said. "This is personal."

"She calls him Iggy," Gene said.

"We don't."

Another guy came in. Jackie introduced him as Left Masseur. Right Masseur fell in close behind.

"So what's your earlobe technique?" Stotlund asked Jackie.

"Keep to your own bailiwick."

"You guys were on Letterman, weren't you. Funny guys."

"Not as funny as we thought," Gene said.

It was eleven forty-five. There followed a full fifteen minutes of Jackie-and-Gene interlarded with football commentary before Left Breast straggled in. Jackie commented obliquely that Murkin had a punctuality disorder and Gene glossed this as you could stick a fork in Left Breast, he's done, toast. Left Breast told Gene to blow it out his ass sideways.

A door slammed somewhere: Nacho and Her entering the arena.

Nobody went to the window to watch.

The little bell went *ding*.

Stotlund stepped through the door. On the gigantic bed, facing away from him, she was doing a slow grind onto Nacho, in the driver's seat. Stotlund noted that by coming in behind them he would be taking his place without Her Highness ever having to look at him.

Macho Nacho wasn't working too hard. His buttocks were clenched. Mellow space music was playing from somewhere, very un–Wu Li Masters, the kind of stuff Stotlund's lame-o brother-in-law had played while his sister was in labor.

A wave of absurdity came and went. It struck him that maybe Nacho felt like an idiot, that Nacho was only doing this because it was, well, what was done.

He shed his robe and his attitude and walked on over. He'd expected butterflies, but there weren't any. He lay down on the pillow and placed his lips upon Her Highness's hanging right nipple. He would give his all for the Queen.

She may not have looked at Stotlund, but she let him know that she liked what he was doing, whoever he was. Her nonverbal critique was definitely stepped up a notch from Nacho.

He was congratulating himself on this when Left Breast came in and affixed himself, rubbing temples with Stotlund. Her Highness stepped it up *way* higher. Stotlund was irked at losing his exclusive feedback channel. And Left Breast's mouthwash wasn't working too good.

But he continued in a workmanlike manner. The enterprise was coalescing around a rhythm. Rowers in a slave galley. Gene came in and hunkered down to her right ear and gave a collegial nod to Stotlund, who for the first time felt kind of dumb as he threw back a savvy eyebrow gesture with his mouth full of tit.

Gene made with some ear-breathing, which turned into slurping and God knew what else. Jackie came in and took the other ear. Gene whispered some remark to Jackie, and necessarily Her Highness, but she didn't show it. Right Masseur came in, and then his counterpart. Stotlund considered that he might have put them earlier in the routine, maybe before the breasts even.

He was getting to feel at home with his head in this little pup tent formed by the thighs, arms, and torso of Her Highness. They had not exchanged a word or even a glance, but he played with the notion of a special relationship with her. Out there was the sweating, slurping, smacking hurly-burly of the world; in here, she was providing him shelter from that world, doing so with her most intimate aspect, and in return she asked only that he nurse at her breast like a babe.

A muscular brown arm interrupted this reverie by inserting itself alongside Stotlund's neck: Nacho coming in for digital clitoral stimulation. The arm fumbled and worked its way past, and Stotlund took an elbow in the face; then the arm pried up against Stotlund's jaw. He heard Nacho say, "Sorry, man"—not trying to offend; just a klutz. The ride started getting wild. It was no longer a bucolic idyll. The occasion seemed to demand that Her attendants grunt and moan in sympathy, and now he was some gasket or gear embedded in a cranking machine of buffed limbs and torsos, a muggy miasma of perfume and sweat and breath.

Her Highness's face, like all faces, had a vaguely canine appearance. This was accentuated during transports of physical ecstasy. In the doggy-style position with this week's golden-and-chestnut tresses squiggling down her back and her head flung back as though baying (but in fact only faintly vocalizing), her vaguely snoutlike lower face did somehow become more protuberant. As the vulva effloresces in readiness for pleasure, so did her facial lips part and retract, exposing zones of gum not seen in her casual smile, and the long teeth, the incisors and canines, almost seemed to tilt slightly outward toward each other, framing her quivering tongue tip. She was lost now. This, and only secondarily the present orgasm, was what she was after. She was immersed in others gathered there on the half-acre bed to deliver to her these few seconds of loss. The room was warm, the air fragrant. The Valium of the mealy-minded New Age sound track contrasted almost sardonically with the bed's amphetamine maelstrom.

As the machine wound down, a wet sheen erupted on everyone in the room—a neck and chest flush on Her—and, despite the climate control, the room was abruptly as humid as a shower, as though the atmospheric pressure had halved, unloading pent-up sweat into vapor.

Following the others, Stotlund disengaged with what he styled a reluctant tenderness, stood, and picked up his robe. Instructions were to leave the room in silence while Nacho remained at his post, that the two of them might uncouple in private, like Ozzie from Harriet.

Stotlund cast a glance back and saw them: Nacho kneeling and staring dumbly into the middle distance; Her Highness, head bowed, contemplating the bedspread's dobby weave.

As the attendants filed out, she made intelligible speech for the first time.

"Thank you," Her Highness murmured, to no one in particular.

In this Nacho heard: exhaustion.

Gene heard: staged humility.

Jackie heard: *faux* unobtrusiveness.
Stotlund heard: regret.

The offstage clatter of the locker room subsided. Even Nacho had repaired to his personal grooming quarters. Her Highness had the bedroom to herself. She had on a plush white robe and was sitting on the floor, hugging her drawn-up legs and staring at the smoke from a stick of sage incense. She looked small.

She stood up when Murkin came in. He seemed about to hug her, but didn't.

"How was that, babe?" Murkin said.

She smiled. She reached up inside, pulled out her hand, and slid two fingers diagonally across Murkin's receiving face. He closed his eyes and drew spent lust into his lungs. The two wet stripes looked like an insignia of some humble rank.

"Good one, babe," Her Highness said.

The next day Stotlund returned from In-N-Out Burger to find a message on his answering machine: "Murkin, checking in. I'll call you back at one."

The phone rang right at one o'clock.

"Pillsbury Doughboy," Stotlund said.

"Your take on last night?"

"Boring."

"But you'd do it again."

"A bit specialized for my taste, really."

"You'd do it again."

"Sure."

"Remember, Scott: it ain't a long-term gig, but this is your lucky day. You're being asked back. Next Saturday night. Interested?"

"Sure. Beneath the coy facade I knew she really cared."

Saturday found Stotlund back in the locker room, again with the toiletries. He now had a bottle of Paco Rabanne that, bless him, he'd gone out and bought for the occasion, more to override Left Breast's funky halitosis than anything else. He dribbled some Paco on his left index finger and touched it to his neck and chest. He put on his robe and entered the staging area.

Murkin was there, consulting a clipboard.

"Put me in, coach," Stotlund said.

"You're left breast tonight," Murkin said without looking up.

"Gee," Stotlund said. "I'm not sure I know how."

"Left breast, that's what it says here. She must like you."

"Left breast?" Gene said. "How'd you manage that?"

"That's like the Gold Glove," said Jackie.

"Shoulda told 'em you wanted to take the mound."

"*I* wouldn't balk at it."

"Suicide squeeze at the hot box. On deck in the hole."

"What happened to the old Left Breast?" Stotlund said.

"Kept his day job," Gene said.

"I happen to know," Jackie said to Gene, "she's had her eye on this ex-Olympic water polo paralegal in Joel's office. Fifty gets you a hundred he turns up at right breast tonight."

"What I want to know," Stotlund said, "is how did Murkin get this gig?"

Jackie looked at Gene. Gene looked at Jackie.

"In the old days Murkin and Her were an item for about five minutes," Gene said. "He's, you know. Pure linoleum."

Stotlund didn't.

"Lay it right once and you can walk on it for years," Jackie said.

The others were showing up. "Here's one for *you*, bud," Jackie said to Stotlund. "Why does she do this?"

"You mean us?"

"Yeah. Why does she put together these little tête-à-têtes?"

"She's rich and famous," Stotlund said.

"Wrong," Jackie said. "She doesn't fancy-fuck *because* she's famous. She fancy-fucks to *get* famous. This is great ink. You think half of this industry—the half that matters—hasn't heard about this?"

"I see the headlines," Gene said. " 'Eight slate Hate date.' It only rhymes if you count Murkin."

"Look at middle-period Madonna," said Jackie. "You think she diddled herself with a bottle onstage because it *felt* good? Look at Sharon Stone flashing her crotch."

"I know I do," Gene said.

"It's her job, Scott."

"I don't know," said Stotlund. "I think she's different. This is where it's at for her. Fame buys her a certain type of fucking."

"Impressive," said Jackie. He drew a stertorous breath, like Darth Vader. "Most impressive. But you are not a Jedi yet."

"The lust for fame is part of that woman's molecular structure," Gene said. "It's in her like a freaking virus."

The little bell dinged.

"The virus of fame," Jackie mused. "Well, it ain't transmissible by earwax."

It didn't go well this time.

Deployment: according to plan. Nacho as usual, then the new guy, Todd (indeed a water polo player), at right breast, then Stotlund at left, and so on. After a decent interval, Nacho reached around, and it was Stotlund's privilege to watch Mr. Water Polo deal with the intruding arm.

Then, inexplicably, the arm slithered back out—with Her Highness clearly unfinished.

He took a sidelong look. A masseur was proffering a jar of goop, Liquid Silk, and Nacho was dipping a finger into it. *She needs a lubricant?* Stotlund wondered. *Come on, we're not that bad* . . . And he reached over and checked Her himself, using, incidentally, the finger with Paco Rabanne on it, and she sure as hell didn't need

Liquid Silk or anything like it, which got Stotlund wondering exactly what kind of clown Nacho was, or maybe this was some weird protocol of Hers, but in any case the train was again cranking full steam ahead with Stotlund now manning the throttle, and Nacho, who misread this surge as something innovative from Left Breast per se, innocently worked his gooped-up finger down past Todd again, slopping some of it on Todd's shoulder and even Stotlund's (Jesus!), and found his place again, and came to rest on what Nacho first took to be the object of interest, but which he almost immediately appreciated had a fingernail of its own and was in fact *another finger*, not his own, rolling left-right-left over said object, merrily merrily merrily merrily, life is but a dream.

And just like that the organism broke into eight separate people.

And Nacho stood.

And Nacho roared, *"MotherFOCKer!"*

He might have been Job, naked, palms outward in supplication, apostrophizing the merciless skies—"This is *bullshit*!"—were it not for the unholy tableau before him, and of course his half-hard whanger, pointing and nodding at the site of the indiscretion.

Sure enough, some tinny loudspeaker—hitherto unnoticed—crackled on and issued the commands of Murkin, an old and weary Jehovah: "Keep it going, people . . . We'll resolve this later . . . GO *ahead*, Nacho . . . Scott, *hands off*, please . . . Everybody just pick up where you left off . . ."

Consummate paraprofessionals to a man, everyone did creditably pick back up where he left off—except Nacho, who was having a little trouble picking up just now.

"Just wait a sec!" pleaded Nacho, and God cut in again: "Aw, fuck me . . . Get the dildo . . . *today* . . ." And Right Masseur handed the dildo to Nacho, and, oh, you know.

The rule of silence having already been broken, no one felt particularly obliged to observe it during the withdrawal phase.

"Sorry, man," Stotlund said to Nacho—not at all apologetically.

Nacho hurled the dildo at the observation window and stomped off to his room.

Jackie made a crack about a Cuban missile crisis.

Murkin came in and shooed everyone out: "Thank you, gentlemen, don't call us, we'll call you. And *you*"—he motioned to Stotlund—"get the fuck *out*, I never wanna *see* you again!"

Stotlund exited laughing, expecting to rumble with Nacho on the way out, but it didn't happen.

Only Murkin and Her Highness remained. As was Her custom, she had not watched the others go, silent in a fetal version of all fours.

Murkin couldn't read her mood. He draped a kimono over her, laid a hand on her back. "You all right, babe?"

"Who's Scott?" Her Highness said.

"It would appear," said Murkin from across his desk, "that I am going to apologize."

"Who am I to judge?" Stotlund said.

"You understand why I was angry. I try to run a tight ship here."

"I closed my eyes and thought of my homeland," Stotlund said.

"Because we've had problems with—uh, improvisation before," said Murkin.

"But not this time," said a mousy little thing next to Murkin, reaching across to squeeze Stotlund's wrist.

She had on a plain gray sweatshirt; the only black was spandex bike shorts. She looked like an off-duty bank teller. There was none of Her Highness's weird makeup or body accessories or tattoos, and, primly coiffed, she lacked even the trademark wild hair. "Scott, right?" she said.

"Call me Paco."

"Paco, I love that," Her Highness said. A quizzical plosive from Murkin hung in midair; Stotlund cut him off with "How's Nacho?"

"Funny you should ask," said Murkin.

"I told Iggy not to worry about the finger work next week," said Her Highness. "I want you to do it."

"Cruel town," Stotlund said.

"He didn't like that," she said. "He said it was all or nothing. And I said fine."

"He's gone, Scott," Murkin said.

"He's gone?" Stotlund said. "He was your trainer."

"*He* was *my* trainer? Ha."

"Nacho was on his way out anyway," said Murkin, looking at Her. "I think it's fair to say that."

"I get it," said Stotlund. "You hit the big time. He stayed small-time."

"So, Scott," Murkin said, "it appears we have an—well, put it this way. To go further, you need to consent to some blood tests."

"We getting married?" Stotlund said.

"No, silly," Her Highness said. "We just need to know you're clean. A girl can't be too careful, right?"

"Her Highness is rather fastidious about this," said Murkin. "You could say obsessed."

"Right," Stotlund said. "Absolutely."

"Good," said Murkin. "Sign here. It's just the routine bad shit, see—AIDS, hepatitis, syphilis, herpes—"

"How about you?" said Stotlund.

She stopped smiling.

"What?"

"Well, with all due respect, Your Highness," Stotlund said, "I need to be careful myself."

"Are you hearing this, Alex?"

"Scott, believe me—"

"No test, no deal," Stotlund said. "My cousin's fucking dead of that shit."

"Ungrateful putz," Murkin said. "You scumbag."

"Come on, Murk. She's made a career out of getting hosed! Wouldn't *you* be careful?"

Murkin pointed. "Go away."

"Fine." Stotlund stood up. He looked at Her Highness. "Um, thanks for the mammaries."

Murkin watched him leave. When was the last time she'd looked this upset? A long, long time ago.

Stotlund got a call that night.

"Yuh."

"You honestly think I got where I am by *getting hosed*?"

"Not really. You can only fuck your way to the middle."

"I will have you know there has been only one serious love in my entire life and I can be very faithful."

"Hey, what do you care what I think? You're *supposed* to be a slut, remember? Queen Hate? What, do you get up there and say, 'Hey, everybody, I'm not really a sperm-spittoon'?"

"Paco, something special passed between us. You're not in the audience anymore."

"Let's see. I push your button, pass a blood test, and I'm what, Lover Number Two. How 'faithful' is that? Shit-can your boyfriend soon as someone lays a finger—"

A long pause on the line. Stotlund actually thought she'd hung up.

"Paco, don't you get it?" she finally said. "Iggy was no boyfriend. Boy *toy*, maybe. A six-foot inflatable. What did you think?"

"Well, pretty much like that, except . . . Nacho wasn't your boyfriend?"

"That isn't love, Paco. Don't you know?"

I'm being lectured on love by Queen Hate, Stotlund thought.

"Surfing aliens. Looking for kicks," Murkin said in his office. "Tossing asteroids into the Pacific. Raising—and riding—mile-high tidal waves. Vegas is *beachfront*. They're on these ion-powered—"

"Murk," said Stotlund. "What the fuck is this?"

"Just idle conversation—would you see this picture? Because this is Her big break into film. This is *Nectar*. Directed by none other than Jerry 'Bug People' Nauman. Starts shooting next week."

"I'm stoked. Fuck a bunch of surfing aliens. I thought we were gonna talk tests."

"Her Highness is not taking any tests. She was deeply distressed at your lack of trust, by the way."

"So who's batting cleanup?"

"Well, we don't have Nacho, and we don't have you, and contrary to your cynical belief system, she won't have just anybody. So Saturday night is off."

"Why don't *you* do it, Murk?" Stotlund said. "Be good for ya."

"Like I said." Murkin showed a trace of petulance. "She won't have just anybody."

"Or you just like to watch."

"Hey. As Her Highness's personal assistant, I am selflessly dedicated to the advancement of her career."

"And the pimping of her evening entertainment."

"And *Nectar* is going to be a huge step for her. Wait and see."

"I hear you and Her are old buds," Stotlund said.

"Says who?"

"Whoever it was, he whispered it in my left ear and then licked it."

"If you want the truth," Murkin said demurely, "we *were* high school sweethearts."

"You wanna know how it looks to me?" said Stotlund.

"No."

"Just man to man? Let it go. She's steppin' all over you."

"Fuck you for sharing."

"And maybe she doesn't test because she doesn't wanna know. Maybe she *already* knows. You, too. You might be tryin' to kill me, you puke."

"Scott. You may have a hard time understanding this, but I bear you no ill will for those obtuse remarks or anything else you have said or done. I actually wish you well. Why? Because Her Highness does. Which reminds me. She seems to think Jerry Nauman would want to meet *you*."

Two years later.

The wave of derivative surf flicks rolls on, and none can duplicate the franchise fizz of space, sex, and shreddin' concocted by genre pioneer **Jerry Nauman** in his twin smashes *Nectar* and *Sweeter Than Nectar*. Now Nauman's thrill-seeking aliens return to smack down the imitators with a third installment. **Paco Scott**'s Warp and his crew, decimated by a dandruff-causing fungus at the close of *Sweeter*, come back to revenge themselves and reindulge their penchant for lobbing large objects Earthward in *Nectar 3: Moon over Miami*, out next month. (*Vanity Fair*, "Fanfair," p. 90.)

Paco Scott and Her Highness: Poster kids for celebrity conjugal bliss.

We sometimes forget: they owe their reign to the unlikely conjunction of a dolly, a catering wagon, and Link Hanscom. Hanscom's freak accident on the original *Nectar* set—on day one of shooting—left uncast the role of Warp, the suave Arcturan surf maniac who now *is* Socko Paco. (On a hunch, mercurial Jerry Nauman literally pull the unknown Scott—then Michael Scotland—in off the street.)

Talk about meeting cute: HH and Paco first shook hands at nude rehearsals for *Nectar*'s sizzling interspecies love scenes—then kept up the serious ad-libbing long after steaming up the optics. A torrid off-screen fling between romantic leads never hurts at the box office, but these two lovebirds confounded cynics by tying the knot last year and nesting in their Coldwater Canyon aerie. (Not that *Nectar* needed help, anyway. The pic sprouted legs with the serendipitous discovery, three weeks into the run, of intelligent life on Venus.)

Her Highness has since drawn a Best Actress nomination for her Ophelia in **Kenneth Branagh**'s *I'm Not Rosencrantz*, and is **Steven Spielberg**'s choice for the lead in *The Crying of Lot 49*, now lensing. Paco, for his part, remains happily typecast as a tubular dude. As for the canard that Paco doesn't even surf, he retorts, "Hey, before I could *walk*, I was surfing." "Channels," puts in HH. (*Vanity Fair*, "A Hollywood Gallery," p. 317.)

Sighted just before their presentation of the Best Visual Effects award: **Her Highness** in the wings *weeping in hubby* **Paco Scott**'s *arms*—wiping away the last tear just seconds before going on. Stage fright? Hardly. Sweating out the Best Actress award? Perhaps—who knew it would go to dark horse Johnny Depp? But if anything's certain in this town, it *wasn't* a spat. Close friends say these two are as smitten as the day they met . . . (*Vanity Fair*, "Backstage at the Oscars!" p. 254.)

Murkin lay peacefully, zoned out on intravenous Ativan and morphine so he'd tolerate the ventilator. His eyes were closed. The left corner of his mouth was pulled to one side by a plastic tube through which the machine breathed for him.

His medical portrait hung on the X-ray box: a pair of lungs filled with fluff in place of air, the classic picture of *Pneumocystis carinii* pneumonia—a standard mode of exit for AIDS patients.

His nurse, Clenette, disconnected the vent long enough to thread a flexible catheter down the breathing tube. She sucked out a gob of mucus. Murkin coughed violently.

Dr. Lampley entered the room. Clenette tsk-tsked and said,

"It's pitiful, Doctor. How much longer has this poor man gotta suffer?"

"Waiting to talk to the missus. She ever come in?"

"She never comes in. The only visitor is his famous, um, boss. Her High Almighty you-know-who."

"Well, she doesn't count. And I finally got a message from his wife. Wants me to call her," he said, dialing a number.

"Beginning to think she didn't care."

"Me, too," said Dr. Lampley. "But then, I wouldn't want to hear this either. Mrs. Murkin? Dr. Lampley here."

"Doctor!" The lady was already hysterical. *"How is he?"*

"Sounds like you're at a convention or something. You have time to talk?"

"N—not really, but I need to know! How is he, please?"

"He is . . . worse. And you and I need to discuss this. The bottom line is, it's quite likely he will not be coming off the machine, understand? And it could be days. It might even be hours."

Mrs. Murkin wept. Dr. Lampley envisioned her already in mourning: blonde no doubt, trim in fashionable black, sobbing into a hankie beneath a pillbox hat and veil.

"I'm sorry to do this over the phone, but I've had trouble finding you and think it best to lay the cards on the table. I really am sorry. I hope you can call my office when you have more time. But soon. Okay?"

More sobs. "Yes, Doctor, thank you. Good-bye."

She hung up. She buried her face in Stotlund's chest, clutching and pounding. "Oh, Paco, he's dying!"

"C'mon, get off me," said Stotlund. "Your makeup, my tux."

"Paco, I can't go out there. I can't. Go alone. Please."

"Ninety seconds, Paco, Your Highness," someone said.

"And I'm the—*I killed him*!" Her Highness said. "God*dam*mit—" She pressed against him, blubbering.

"You?" Stotlund said.

Her hot breath rose up to him, bearing, it seemed, moisture from her tears.

"*You* gave Murkin AIDS? I fucking knew it. I *knew* you were positive. And I was next, right? Thank *God* we've never made it. You—"

"Sixty seconds!"

An aide rushed to fix Her Highness's makeup. "I need another fucking coat," said Stotlund. "Move!"

Her Highness went somewhere deep within, self-composing. Paco suffered the attentions of the gofer wiping his coat and shirt, barely containing his rage. "Fucking bitch . . ."

"Thirty seconds. Come on, you two, *ready!*"

"No, I am not positive," said Her Highness quietly. "We were just driving. Young and crazy and partying down in Mexico. We were gonna take over the world. Both a little stoned, you know? We went off the road while I was—pleasuring him. He was laid up for months."

Stotlund murmured, "You love Murkin."

"He got this bad blood transfusion. Seven years ago. On our *honeymoon!*—"

People were shouting now, ushering them onstage. Someone shoved an antique-looking longboard at them. "Hey, Paco, don't forget this!"

"He's my husband, Paco. The whole time."

"Huh." Stotlund hefted the board. "In all ways but one."

"So what? Paco. That's not love. You don't know shit about love."

The orchestra struck up. An announcer's voice intoned: "Presenting the award for Best Visual Effects, here are Paco Scott and *Her Highness.*"

(Theme music; applause)

Paco: Riding a three-hundred-foot wave or levitating a building are not things we try at home. This award honors those wizards who make it look so easy.

Her Highness: Without the extraordinary abilities of these unique artists, *2001* would have just been *1968*, and (*to Paco*) *Nectar* would have looked a lot more like *Beach Blanket Bingo*.

Paco: Now, baby, we've been over this before. They're never gonna mistake you for Annette Funicello. (*Laughter.*) For Best Visual Effects, the nominees are . . .

Her Highness: Laszlo Cram Associates, *The Swap*.

Paco: Charles U. Farley, *Killbilly 6: Kissin' Cousins.*

Her Highness: The design firm of Finetti, Fine, Fung, and Fu, *Word and Object: The Life and Work of W. V. Quine.*

Paco: Industrial Light and Magic, *The Checkered Demon Meets the Hog-Ridin' Fools.*

Her Highness: Survival Research Laboratories, *Splatterday.* (*She hands him the envelope. He drops it, mock-accidentally. He sets down his board, stoops for the envelope, and makes a show of dusting it off and handing it back.*)

Paco: Um, you read it. I guess I'm kinda flustered—standing here with the hardest-working sex goddess in showbiz.

Her Highness: Aw, Paco, that's the nicest thing you've ever said to me.

Paco: It's like the only thing I've ever said to you.

Her Highness: (*All business now.*) And the winner is . . .

Devoured

Edward Picot

When Joy first met Peter at Cambridge in 1980, she was an art history student: tall and striking, with long black hair and large breasts, always a little plump, but never worried about her weight, because she never found it difficult to attract men. She thought of herself as Rubensesque.

She intended to have lots of children. Perhaps some of them would be illegitimate, because although she was still a virgin when she came up, she quickly had a number of love affairs, one of them with a fellow of St. Cats, as St. Catherine's College was called, and she was inclined to be careless about her contraception. Secretly, she was half hoping something would happen. The scandal would have suited her.

Then she met Peter. He was thin, dark, and introverted, a mathematics student, completely inexperienced with women. He was pointed out to her at a party: somebody told her he was a genius, but terribly antisocial. He was dressed in fantastically scruffy jeans, smeared with oil and paint, and a brown pullover with holes in the elbows. His hair was severely short, his ears stuck out, he wore circular steel-rimmed glasses, and he was smoking hand-rolled cigarettes. Somehow or other, he didn't look like a nerd.

Later, she noticed him in the kitchen by himself, apparently staring at the cold tap on the sink. She went and spoke to him.

"Hi," she said. "I'm Joy."

"Hello. I'm Peter."

There was an awkward silence, during which she smiled at him encouragingly.

"Why were you staring at that tap?" she asked eventually.

"It's dripping."

"Oh. Haven't you ever seen a dripping tap before?"

"Of course I have," said Peter, not realizing he was being teased. "I'm reading a book about chaos theory. There's a man called Robert Shaw who did a mathematical analysis of a dripping tap. It's quite interesting."

"I've got a dripping tap in my room," volunteered Joy. "I've asked them to fix it, but they haven't done anything yet."

"I could probably fix it for you. I know all about plumbing. It's quite a fascinating subject. When Victorian plumbing came in it was an environmental breakthrough, whereas now it's a catastrophe. Wittgenstein was very interested in plumbing, too."

"Do you model yourself on Wittgenstein?"

"Not at all. What a stupid thing to say. I don't even understand him properly."

"Why don't you come and mend my tap for me?" said Joy, not at all abashed to be called stupid. "You could tell me all about Wittgenstein and plumbing."

"You wouldn't enjoy it. I'd bore you."

"But at least I'd get my tap mended."

He turned up at half past eight one Saturday morning, when she was still asleep, with the result that she opened the door in her nightdress, with her face flushed and her hair tousled. He was obviously confused by her state of undress, and she played on his feelings instinctively, yawning and stretching, sitting him on the bed, then bending provocatively to plug in the kettle, and finally announcing that she was going to get changed.

"You'd better close your eyes, if you don't want to see my naked body."

"What if I do want to see it?"

"Then you'd better keep them open."

She pulled off her nightdress while he sat on the bed and stared at her. Then she came and sat beside him. "It's too early to be up," she announced, putting her hand on his thigh. "Why don't you take off your things and get in here with me?"

Looking back on their first two or three terms together, neither of them could remember, afterward, how they managed to get any work done. In retrospect there seemed to have been a complete suspension of their studies. They couldn't remember attending any supervisions or lectures, writing any essays or reading any books. They could hardly remember speaking to anyone else, going home for the holidays, or venturing out of their rooms, except for long hand-holding trips to the Fitzwilliam Museum, Kettle's Yard, Heffers, or the Arts Cinema. They seemed to spend almost all their time naked, sharing a single bed. Occasionally they would eat, ravenously, bowls of cornflakes or slices of toast first thing in the morning, bizarre cooked lunches such as pasta with fried carrots, hastily prepared in their rooms from whatever ingredients happened to be on hand, or takeaways they rushed out to buy late in the evenings. Peter never had such an appetite again. Joy never again went for such long periods without food.

Twenty years later they were still together—but everything else had changed. They never made love anymore.

They lived in a converted lighthouse on the edge of a white cliff, overlooking the English Channel. Civilization was near at hand—there was a dual carriageway within a couple of hundred yards—but they never had any visitors. They went shopping once a week. Other than that, they scarcely spoke to another soul. They didn't even possess a television. Joy had her radio, and Peter his computer. Joy was now obesely fat, while Peter was unpleasantly scrawny. He was almost completely bald, and as if to compensate, he had grown a goatee, which she secretly hated. He went running along the cliff tops every day to keep himself fit. She thought it ridiculous of him. When he came back, scarlet in the face and pop-eyed, breathing in whooshes and glistening with sweat, she could scarcely bear to look at him. She disliked the little pool of moisture that collected in the hollow at the base of his throat. She didn't like the smell of his hot body, either.

Joy never took exercise of any description. She never even climbed to the top of the tower. When they first arrived she had tried to start a garden, but the constant buffeting wind, loaded with sea spray, killed everything she planted, so she gave up.

Apart from his daily run and his meals, Peter spent all his time alone on the top floor, in a bare octagonal room sided with glass, where the lights and reflectors had once been housed. Now it was equipped with a computer and a telescope.

He made his money from investments, which he handled via the Internet. This only took him four or five hours per day. Originally, his plan had been to work on his investments in the morning, and his math in the afternoon. He had been struggling to perfect a theorem of his own ever since he graduated: something to do with the effects of human observation on probability. But then he lost interest in the problem. His computer, and the views from his windows, began to distract him. He was an environmentalist, and he began to scrutinize the outside world through his telescope, or trawl the Internet, for evidence of environmental decay. Soon he could recognize detritus and filth wherever he looked. He gave up his mathematical researches entirely. They no longer seemed important.

From his vantage point at the top of the tower, Peter could observe a great sweep of the sea. There was never a moment during the day when less than three boats were in sight. Roll-on roll-off ferries and hovercraft came and went from the nearby port. Huge rusty-looking oil tankers crawled along the horizon. And the lighthouse was under a flight path, too, which meant that on cloudless days there were always a couple of planes to be seen, glittering in the air.

Inland, the landscape was badly scarred by the dual carriageway, which had been a simple main road when he and Joy first arrived. There was a roundabout, and alongside the roundabout had materialized first a garage, then an out-of-town superstore, then a huge red do-it-yourself emporium, then a bedding center, and eventually a whole conglomeration of chain stores.

The rest of the landscape was still mostly fields; but in the last fifteen years most of the hedgerows had vanished. Small fields had been merged into larger ones. Livestock had disappeared from the open air into huge concrete and steel barns. Even the crops had changed: the early summer months were now dominated by blazing yellow fields of rape. Peter viewed all these changes with deepening gloom. In his mind he pictured the whole planet as an expanded version of what he could see from his windows: a natural landscape defaced by the works of man.

At first they intended to have children as soon as possible, but nothing materialized in the first couple of years, so they started to tell people they were holding on till they were more financially settled. After another three years they both began to think there must be a problem. Then Joy finally did become pregnant, only to have a mis carriage, followed a year and a half later by an ectopic pregnancy.

"Oh, well," said Peter, as a way of comforting her. "It's a shitty old world anyway. Who wants to bring children into a shitty old world like this?"

He seemed to have lost interest, not only in starting a family, but in sex, too. That was when Joy really started to put on weight. Eventually she got up to two hundred fifty pounds. She ate three square meals a day, plus a dessert with her lunch, and in between times she snacked on chocolates or sweet biscuits. Every evening she opened a bottle of wine to share with her husband, drank most of it herself, and went to bed with a nightcap of Courvoisier or Tia Maria.

It wasn't that she and Peter weren't close. He spent a lot of time at the top of the tower, but he came down for his meals, and by eight o'clock he was finished. She saw more of him than she would have done if he'd worked in the city, for example. And he talked to her. Most of her news of the outside world came through him. She never paid attention to the news on her radio; she was only interested in the music; but Peter, when he came down, would tell her what he had seen from his windows or discovered via the Internet. Tales of environmental destruction. Her vision darkened in accordance with his.

At night he always turned his back on her to go to sleep. She slept on the left side of the bed, and he was most comfortable curled up on his right. On moonlit nights, because he was so thin, she could see the knobs of his vertebrae sticking out. He always fell asleep immediately, while she sometimes lay awake for hours. And he never dreamed, whereas she had vivid dreams almost every night. She dreamed she was pregnant, or else they already had a child. Sometimes the child was lost, and she was searching for it along the edge of the cliff, while Peter sat upstairs with his computer and his telescope, not caring. Sometimes the cliff was crumbling and the tower was toppling into the dirty gray waves below.

If she couldn't sleep, or if her dreams woke her, she would get up in the middle of the night and go to the kitchen for a slice of cake, or another nightcap. Peter never stirred. It was no good trying to wake him up for the sake of conversation, either. She would have had to shake him and poke him for ages. He could sleep through thunderstorms or anything. It was almost like a coma.

One week the car broke down on the day they were due to go

shopping. That night there was only enough food for a plain evening meal of pasta and sauce, with no dessert to follow and nothing to snack on afterward. The freezer in the basement was completely empty except for a few frozen vegetables. There was no bottle of wine, either. Joy was ravenous.

She managed to find an old box of milkshake mix at the back of the cupboard, so she used up the last of the milk on that. She took the drink to bed with her and drank it through a glass straw, followed by the last of the brandy. But she couldn't sleep. She got up after an hour and polished off the last of the Tia Maria, but she still couldn't sleep.

Without sufficient food or alcohol, she became oppressed by thoughts she normally managed to keep at bay. It was a bright warm night, and Peter had pushed the duvet almost down to his waist. All the knobs of his backbone were plainly visible in the moonlight. The sight of them repelled and fascinated her. She began to think about sex, partly as a means of distracting herself. She remembered the sight of his large penis becoming erect, grotesquely thick and long in the middle of his scrawny body.

The empty tumbler which had held her milkshake was still sitting on her bedside cabinet, with the glass straw in it. Impulsively she took the glass straw and plunged it into her husband's back, right into the spine, between two of the vertebrae. To her surprise it went in easily. He didn't even wake. He gave a soft grunt, and his left hand, which lay on the pillow in front of his face, clenched convulsively.

She put her lips to the straw and sucked. Immediately, a thin jet of life force squirted into her mouth, sweeter than chocolate and fiercer than brandy. Peter gave a sigh. She took a long drink. Her ill feeling vanished. Eventually she withdrew the straw and replaced it in the tumbler. She could see the dark puncture between two of the knobs in her husband's back, just below his neck, but otherwise there was no evidence of what she had done. He slept on, breathing deeply and evenly. Within a few seconds she was asleep, too, deliciously asleep, and for once there were no dreams.

Next morning she was awake early and out of bed before Peter, which was unheard of. She wanted to get the straw washed before he could see it. As it turned out there was only a little blood on it, but it might have been enough to make him suspicious. He slept an hour longer than usual, however.

When he came down he looked pale and tired. There were dark smudges under his eyes, and he kept rubbing his shoulders and the back of his neck. But he was unusually affectionate. He kissed her on the lips and gave her shoulder a warm squeeze before he sat down.

There was nothing for breakfast except a cup of tea. "I'll walk into town and get you something to eat," said Peter. "We can sort the car out afterward."

"No hurry."

"I thought you'd be starving by now."

"No, I feel fine." To her own surprise, it was true. "Aren't you going out for your run?"

"I don't think I'm up to a run this morning. I don't seem to have any energy. Perhaps I'm getting a virus."

He kissed her again as he left, and smiled tenderly into her eyes, seeming more affectionate than he had been for years. But when he came back three hours later, he was in a bad mood. He complained about the traffic, noise, and exhaust fumes in the middle of town. And although much of his walk had been along a cliff-top path, through comparatively unspoiled country, the path was strewn with litter, and he couldn't help noticing how sparse the local populations of birds and butterflies seemed, compared with ten or fifteen years ago. He also objected to the weather, which was unseasonably bright and warm for the time of year—it was March. A sign of global warming, he declared grimly.

"What a shitty old world this is," he said.

But Joy was impervious to his ill temper. All morning she had been thinking about the previous night, and every time she thought about it her heart beat faster with excitement.

"Did you get any more of that milkshake mix?"

"No—why? I didn't know you were using it."

She blushed. "I drank some last night. It was nice. I might make a habit of it, instead of a nightcap."

"I'll get you some next time I go out," said Peter, observing her blushes. They made her look girlish and pretty. It never occurred to him to wonder what she was blushing about.

He was in a bad mood again by the time he came downstairs that evening—having been observing the world from his windows, and gathering information from the Internet, in his usual jaundiced fashion—but he found Joy looking even prettier and younger than before, and he noticed at suppertime that she took only a modest helping of the main course, with no dessert.

"Are you on a diet, Joy?"

"No, not really. I'm just not very hungry."

"How come?"

"I don't know. I can't really explain it. I feel a bit—sort of—excited and flustered, but I—I don't know what the reason is."

That night she repeated the experiment. She had been thinking about it all day, at one moment telling herself she'd better not do it again, at another making up her mind equally firmly to give it another try—but always with a beating heart and a dry mouth.

When they went upstairs, she took a glass of cold milk with her, complete with glass straw, reasoning that just because she had the glass straw with her, that didn't mean she had to do anything with it. She sat up in bed and drank the cold milk with her heart pounding. She drank it in the dark, in small sips, and by the time she got to the end Peter was asleep as usual, rolled over on his side with his back toward her, the knobs of his spine showing above the duvet.

She could see the black puncture mark just below the nape of his neck. It didn't seem to have healed, or even formed a scab. From what she could see in the gloom, it was just a small round hole. It looked as if she could slip the glass straw into it without even having to push.

She took the glass straw and inserted it. Sure enough, it slid into place without any resistance. Peter gave a slight moan, as he had done the previous night, and once again his hand clenched on the pillow in front of his face. She leaned forward and sucked. The life force gushed into her mouth, warm and delicious. Peter gave a sigh.

After that she did the same thing every night. Sometimes she tried to convince herself that she should leave it for a night or two, if only to give Peter a chance to recover, or to reassure herself that she wasn't completely addicted. But she was. When the night came, and they went to bed, she couldn't help it. She tried leaving the tumbler and straw downstairs, but then she only had to go and fetch them.

The effect on Peter, physically, was frightening. He was wasting away before her eyes. He no longer went out running. He didn't seem to be in any discomfort, but his movements were slow and feeble. Once he fell asleep on the toilet. His face became more and more haggard, his eyes sunken and ringed with black. His body had always been thin, but now it was emaciated. All the muscle tone was gone. His ears seemed to be getting larger. They stuck out grotesquely. Eventually, he even stopped going to the top of the tower.

"I can't be bothered anymore," he said. "What's the point? It only makes me depressed." Psychologically, he was undergoing a change of a different kind. Instead of expending all his mental energy on the state of the environment, he was refocusing his attention on Joy.

"You're getting more beautiful every day," he said.

And it was true. Her excess weight had melted away. Her body had attained a chubby, voluptuous firmness, all rich curves, her skin glowing and her hair shining with health. Her breasts were larger than before, and her nipples were darker, as if she were getting ready to breast feed. Her senses were heightened too. She could smell things and hear things with exceptional acuteness. As spring turned to summer and the weather got warmer, she took to sleeping naked, and the feel of the sheets against her bare skin filled her with shivers of excitement.

That was why it was so difficult to contemplate giving up the glass straw and her nightly drinks of life force. She hated the thought of her old life—or, rather, her old lifelessness, buried in a sad mountain of desensitized flesh.

Then one night, when Joy inserted the straw and took her first sip, Peter failed to respond with his customary moan and sigh. The hand on his pillow remained unclenched.

She straightened and touched him on the shoulder. He felt cold. He didn't seem to be breathing. Horrified, she pulled out the straw. "Peter!" she cried, shaking him. "Peter!"

Eventually he groaned and rolled over. "What's the matter?"

"God, Peter, don't do that to me! I thought—you didn't seem to be breathing. For a minute I thought—" She put her hand on her breastbone and laughed with relief.

But Peter gazed at her in silence. His eyes were enormous and dark in the gloom, like two bruises in the vague pallor of his face. "Don't stop what you were doing," he whispered eventually.

Her heart gave a guilty lurch. "What?" she said loudly, then cleared her throat and added in a more normal voice, "What do you mean?"

"You know what I mean. I don't want you to stop. I want you to go on."

She couldn't bring herself to reply.

"I want you to go on," he repeated.

"I can't, Peter. I don't want to stop, but I've got to. I thought you were dead just now."

"I don't care," he whispered, still gazing at her. "I'm not bothered about that. Who wants to stay in this shitty old world anyway?"

"Don't say that."

He reached out under the duvet and touched her hip. His fingers were as cold as ice. "It's all I've ever wanted," he said. "To be inside you."

Then he rolled over until his back was toward her again, the same as usual: the bumpy ridge of his spine arching away, with the little black hole just below the nape of his neck. She put the straw back in the glass, but then leaned over to kiss him on the wound, a light kiss, as if to say good night. A little of the life force leaked onto her lips. She tasted it with the tip of her tongue, then kissed him again, this time with her mouth open, her tongue lapping the wound. Her head swam with the sweetness of it. She clamped her lips onto the place and sucked with her eyes closed, forgetting everything. For a moment there was a sense of obstruction, then Peter gave a loud gasp and threw himself backward against her, legs stiffening. She felt his soul thump into her throat, like a bolus of fire. Before she could stop herself she had swallowed it. She felt it burning painfully inside her chest as it went down.

She sat up in bed, shakily wiping her mouth with the back of her hand, and switched on the bedside lamp. Beside her lay Peter's corpse, still curled on its side, but shrunken and pale, reduced to a mere husk. She got out of bed and went around to the other side, to see if she could lift it. It weighed no more than a figure stuffed with newspaper. She dragged it out without much effort and down the stairs to the basement.

In the basement was the big chest freezer, stuffed with all the food she no longer ate: legs of lamb, beefsteaks, chickens, packs of bacon, burgers, frozen vegetables, and at least a dozen tubs of ice cream in a variety of flavors. She unpacked all the food onto the floor as quickly as she could. She had to chip out some of the lower packages, which were locked into the ice.

By the time she was finished it was five in the morning, and her hands were numb with the cold. She heaved the corpse into the freezer and slammed the lid shut.

Her abdomen felt swollen and uncomfortable.

She climbed up the stairs from the basement, and instead of stopping when she reached the lower floors she kept going, climbing upward. She hadn't been right to the top for years, partly because of her weight and partly because Peter didn't like to be disturbed. But now she had the whole tower to herself. She felt a sense of transgression and compulsion, the same mixture of emotions that had driven her to plunge the glass straw into her husband's spine in the first place.

She reached the top. It was early morning, and the blueness overwhelmed her. She had been expecting to see Peter's version of the world, dirty and overcrowded. Instead, she found herself in the middle of a huge blue empty space, vertiginous. Beneath her were the wrinkled sea, the white cliffs, the green landscape. Yes, there were glittering planes in the air; yes, there was a ferry on the sea, plus a tanker on the horizon; and yes, there was the road, thick with traffic even at this hour. But all the same . . . It was so much bigger and brighter than he had led her to believe.

It was warm, too, with the early sunshine pouring through the plate glass. She suddenly realized that she was immensely tired. She lay down flat on her back on the floor and fell asleep.

She woke a couple of hours later. By this time it was getting hot, and her mouth was as dry as dust. The distension and discomfort in her abdomen were intensifying, too: in fact as she rose from the floor she experienced a spasm of cramp, followed by a wave of nausea. She opened one of the windows, to get a breath of fresh air. She heard the dull roaring noise of traffic from the dual carriageway, pierced by the scribbling song of a skylark somewhere nearby.

Another spasm of cramp, and another wave of nausea. This time she really thought she was going to throw up. She hurried to the top of the stairs, pressing one hand to her mouth, and stumbled down the metal treads as quickly as she could, till she came to the bathroom.

By the time she got there, the nausea seemed insignificant by comparison with the pains in her abdomen. Something was trying to force its way out of her. She squatted over the toilet, almost fainting with agony. In the confusion of her senses, she didn't know if she was passing a clot of blood from her womb or opening her bowels. She felt something big come out of her, and heard it fall into the water with a splash.

When she stood up and looked down, she saw that the bowl of the toilet was streaked with blood, and at the bottom there was a dark obstruction. After a moment she recognized it. It was Peter's face, shrunken to the size of a doll's, but at the same time swollen and vile, grimacing like a gargoyle. She pulled the chain. Clean water gushed into the bowl, but instead of whirling and draining away, it slowed dreamily and rose up, right up to the rim, as if it were going to spill out onto the floor. Peter's face came floating toward her, and she saw the eyes move. She stepped back with an exclamation of disgust. Then the water sank, and gurgled away around the U-bend.

She flushed the toilet again. The gore and muck disappeared. Peter was gone. The water ran clean.

Later, she went down to the basement. The floor was puddled with melted ice cream, which had seeped out of the cartons after she threw them down. The meat had begun to thaw, too. She smelled the rank smell of blood mingled with the sickly sweet odors of vanilla, strawberry, and chocolate. She picked her way through the mess and opened the lid of the freezer. It was empty.

Shortly after the loss of her husband, Joy experienced symptoms of the menopause, and soon she began the second stage of her womanhood. She put some of her weight back on, but only some. She ate freely, but no longer felt the need to fill an emotional void. As for Peter, she almost forgot him. Sometimes she caught herself wondering if he had ever really existed.

She began to spend more and more of her time out of doors. She planted a hedge of hawthorn and blackthorn all around the perimeter of the lighthouse garden, to get some protection from the sea breezes; and once this had established itself, her efforts as a gardener began to meet with success. She learned to grow plants that were suited to her environment—small, tough, some of them not far removed from weeds.

Every day she climbed to the top of the tower. She never looked at the computer, but walked all around the windows, gazing at the sky, the sea, the land, all the moods of the weather, and the various types of traffic coming and going. She never ceased to be surprised and refreshed by the size of the outside world, now that she was seeing it for herself.

Outpatient

Laurent Boulanger

"What happened?" I asked.

"You had an accident," he said. His voice was musical and soothing. It pinched a nerve somewhere at the back of my mind.

I didn't see him immediately, but I heard him sigh and smelled the muskiness of his groin. I thought at first that it might have been another machine, but then I saw the overalls and knew he was a technician—midtwenties and handsome with dimples and flamed hair. His white uniform hugged his figure like a stocking, accentuating the contour of his hips and the firmness of his chest—he wasn't wearing an undershirt, and the shape of his nipples stared at me like a second pair of eyes. His lips were chunky, like ripe strawberries ready to be enjoyed.

"You're lucky to be alive," he added.

Images came back flashing. I never saw the K-72P hurling toward me. And even if I had, it would have been during the last millisecond before impact, and by then, much too late.

I tried to sit up but I was too weak. Tubes were running from my forearms and breasts. An aqua liquid was being pumped in and black plasma being drained out. The air smelled of metal and oil and was chilled like the inside of an icebox. I was overdue for a full service by two months. Financially, I hadn't been able to afford it, but now with the accident, MU1 had no choice but to give me a total overhaul.

I tried to remember more, but the accident felt as if it had happened such a long time ago.

"How long have I been out?" I asked.

He looked at me and smiled.

Right at that moment, I could have ripped off his uniform and been totally consumed by the hardness of his leathery flesh. I wanted to show him a love he probably had never experienced.

He said, "Twenty-three hours. There were only minor damages, nothing that couldn't be replaced."

Twenty-three hours? I felt as if I'd just come back from a coma that had lasted light-years.

"Are you sure?" I asked.

"Positive. We've recovered the revlis box, and the information is all in there. We've contacted Klarch-21."

That was standard procedure—to contact one's maker. Makers know more about their machines than maintenance unit technicians, but I didn't want to go back home and be subjected to all types of diagnostic tests just to figure out what went wrong. I was an autonomous model and had the choice to refuse to meet with Klarch-21. She would probably keep me in some depressing convalesce storage unit with other machines. I was antisocial toward replicates, even though I had been programmed not to be. Personality and attitude were still wild cards, and the only two attributes we possessed that made us so humanly pragmatic.

Soon I would be back on my feet, and in a matter of days would return to the old routine. Years from now, the accident would remain nothing more than a fleeting memory—a cosmic dust in the infinity of my motherboard.

The driver of the K-72P pulverized on impact. The spaceship was a discontinued model, one that shouldn't have been on the lightway. It didn't even have an L-tag and was traveling illegally.

The technician reassured me that it wasn't my fault—and that whatever guilt I was experiencing, I should deprogram it immediately.

"Who was driving the K-72P?" I asked.

"Some insurance man from Tunnep."

"That explains."

He smiled again and bit his lower lip. I could have sworn he wasn't wearing any underwear because of the bulging and the dark patch that was showing so evidently through the white material of his uniform. He must have known because humans don't forget to put on underwear when they get dressed. I wanted to consume him, to explore every inch of his masculinity, to feel the texture of his pubic hair against my own skin, to be entered by his innermost being. I wanted him badly even though it was wrong for me to even think about it. Humans don't know how much machines long for the flesh.

That's another thing that isn't configured at the factory.

Lust has a life of its own.

By late afternoon, I felt much better. At least I didn't feel guilty that I had destroyed another life because of my own carelessness. The sexy flamed-haired technician showed me the printout that confirmed that it was the driver of the K-72P that was at fault, and that there was nothing I could have done.

He came in and out of my room all afternoon to monitor the fluid change. Every time he worked on my body, I was mesmerized by the way the firmness of his back muscles arched so gently when he moved. His skin was crying to be touched, to be caressed and abused by the love I held so deep inside me.

He must have sensed my desire because he looked at me strangely, as if I were some space debris that had fallen from the sky. I knew I wasn't debris. At least my random-access memory hadn't been affected—five hundred million zigabytes, factory presets, and all of them accounted for. I knew my name was Dorothy Pickard (they always give human names to androids), and I worked as an iso-emulator repairer. I was single and my ambition was to win the top prize at the annual Cisrofne Intergalactic Iso Expo.

"I'm not a nobody, you know," I finally said, tired of being looked down at as if I were only a generation away from a plasma laptop.

"I know who you are." When he said that, he caressed his right thigh, and I got a full view of the shape of his erection hiding under his white uniform. Was he purposely trying to arouse me? He rubbed his thigh gently, his fingers pointing in the direction of his groin. When I looked up, he was smiling. "In fact, I probably know more about you than you know about yourself."

That wouldn't be too hard, since I had three USB78.5 coaxial cables running from the nape of my neck to a virtual Apple ZigaMac mainframe with interactive monitoring and a real-time graphic user interface generator—which basically meant that he could stream through my three levels of consciousness without touching a keyboard.

I had Klarch-21 on the e-phone and told her that there would be no point in coming to see me or having me sent back home.

"I'm fine," I said. "Just the opti viper lens in my right eye had to be replaced; other than that it's just routine maintenance. Oh, and they also had to reset my vaginal chips—during the accident, the physical expansion and contractions from the heat caused the components plugged into my sockets to gradually work their way out."

She didn't insist because shipping me over would have meant more data processing and more expense. I came with a lifetime warranty, and since I was fully self-owned, it wasn't a bad position to be in.

My handsome technician served me dinner on a yellow plastic tray—steak, three baked potatoes, pumpkin, and snow peas—but I wasn't hungry. If technicians were serious about humanizing the maintenance units, then why were they still serving us synthetic trash disguised as organic food?

After dinner, I watched some program on cyberculture and whether its dominance would eventually force into extinction the half billion humans left in the universe—an aggressively prejudicial documentary that people would be laughing at five years from now.

I was about to shut down for the night, but I noticed a leak in my vagina. The technician came quickly and told me to spread my legs. With gloves on, he probed with his fingers, almost short-circuiting the wiring that connected my pubic region to my motherboard. He told me not to worry and applied pressure with his right thumb.

"It's just a clitoris displacement," he said. "We have an expert coming first thing tomorrow morning. If you feel a little rusty, just use the bottle next to your bed, and don't take more than you need, or you're going to stain the tray under the bed."

"Thanks, but I know how to take care of myself—I'm not an oiloholic."

"Just doing my job."

I smiled and chose to avoid confrontation. I was programmed to respect humans, even though the male variety needed more than just respect—they deserved my full attention.

"So what's your name?" I asked.

"Jeffrey."

"That's a good name for a human."

He looked at me as if my hydraulic ovaries needed replacement.

"I didn't mean it that way," I said.

"That's okay, androids are not known for their decorum."

"Really, I didn't mean to be insulting—I'm really not racist. I think humans are making a great contribution to our world."

He thought for a few seconds. "Then why are we always stuck with the crappy jobs? I mean, I've never heard of a human being made CEO—have you? When was the last time a human was president of the United Planets Consortium? Twelve thousand years ago?"

"Well—"

"Exactly my point."

I swallowed for effect and felt almost ashamed of my existence. It was my forefathers who had taken over the universe, so was it fair to blame our generation for everything? I mean, really, we had gone too far now, so it wasn't like we could just give it back to the humans. They wouldn't be able to handle the responsibility, and it would be like going back to the twenty-third century—pre-androidal times, heaven forbid. The last time they were in control, they messed up everything.

"Try to shut down completely tonight," he said.

"What do you mean?"

"Last night you started beeping in your sleep—you're sure you weren't on standby?"

That was news to me. No one had ever told me that I beeped in my sleep. Beeping usually means processing of information, but I couldn't remember anything. Maybe the motherboard got damaged during the accident, and I unknowingly suffered from electrostatic discharge. The technician would have been able to read the data processing on the Apple ZigaMac.

"I'm pretty sure I shut down," I said.

"Well, double-check because I need to get some sleep. I'm not a machine—if I don't sleep, I die."

"Did you check my high-memory area?"

"Yes."

"What did it read?"

He smiled. "You don't want to know."

And then he left the room, his scent trailing behind like bait.

It took me ages to shut down after that. I worried that the beeping would start again, and then he would think that there was something seriously wrong with me and report it to Klarch-21. I hadn't beeped after shutdown since I'd been certified independent; beeping after shutdown was as embarrassing as a grown human wetting her bed.

"It smells like crank oil in here," Jeffrey said and pulled the galvanized tray from under the bed. I had a wet dream and let the oil drip in the tray below. I knew that human females didn't have wet dreams, certainly not in the way human males did, but there was no differentiating between the wet dreams of a male or a female android—on the outside we looked different, but on the inside we were all the same constructions of metal, circuits, and microchips.

I could feel myself overloading. His groin seemed bigger than yesterday, almost bursting out of his white uniform. "When can I get out of this place?"

"This afternoon, if we can confirm that your zero insertion force is optimum. Otherwise we might have to keep you for a few more days."

"Great."

He bent over and emptied the oil from the tray into a yellow, androi-hazard container, while the smooth and perfect shape of his buttocks stared right back at me.

"Are you married?" I asked.

"That's really none of your business."

"I'm just asking, that's all—I mean, it's not like I'm going to ask you out, I'm a machine, for goodness sake."

"No, I'm not married."

"Do you have a girlfriend?"

"Yes, I do—anything else you want to ask me before your tune-up?"

He stood up.

I glanced between his thighs. The lure was strong and inviting. "Is it true that technicians don't wear underclothes beneath their overalls?"

He blushed and said, "That's an android fantasy, and it shall remain nothing more than a fantasy."

"Why can't you see it as a compliment—not all androids are perverts."

"Well, according to the data I recovered from your damaged cylinders—"

"What?"

"You seem to be spending a lot of time thinking about Jack."

"Who the hell is Jack?"

"You tell me—but he wouldn't be impressed if he saw you trying to seduce another human the way you are."

He took the tray outside the room, his hips swinging, his perfectly shaped arse confronting my desire to be one with its firmness.

He left me alone worrying. I searched my memory map and all revision codes, and the name Jack did come up, but from such a long time ago, it didn't make any sense. Jack was the first human I had lusted for—he had been one of my service technicians six months after I came out of factory. It was normal for androids to develop a crush on their first service technician straight after manufacturing, but it was a stage that mature androids grew out of—those who didn't had to be completely reformatted and reprogrammed. Jack and I had known that it was forbidden for androids and humans to have relationships, but we played the game anyway. I spent endless hours reprogramming my higher memory and enjoying a virtual-reality fantasy of the forbidden pleasure of his body, biting at his nipples, covering his groin with kisses, forcing his hard member into my cold, galvanized orifice.

When people saw us together, we told them we were engaged, and everyone thought we were both humans. For a while it was fun, but eventually I grew tired of pretending that we were an ordinary couple and that the love I was making was real. Fantasy can only satisfy you for so long. So I told him that I wanted something more. I said that it was time to bring our relationship to the next level—

what about lovemaking? He was mortified. He told me that it would be like making out with a washing machine. And then he asked his supervisor to be transferred from the Service Unit. I never saw Jack again. It happened 252 years ago, so it wasn't as if we would ever get back together one day—he had been dead now for a long time.

Still, the problem wasn't Jack, but the fact that I had fallen in lust with many more humans throughout my existence. If every data sector of human envy I had experienced were still encrypted somewhere in my damaged cylinders—chests, buttocks, penises, underarms, thighs, lips, eyes, flesh—then it would only be a matter of time before a technician would figure out the configuration code and access the data. And then Klarch-21 would request total reformatting of my hard disk, and everything I knew would come to pass.

First thing in the morning, I had to erase all evidence of my dubious past. Maybe I could ask Jeffrey to help me, but he was human, so he might not understand. I would have to convince him that really I wasn't a bad person, and that all this data about Jack was lust from the past—that I was over it now, and that there would be no point in reporting me to the authorities. I was a changed and responsible android, and I would never do something to hurt anyone.

I decided not to shut down that night, just in case the beeping occurred again. If someone evaluated the central system of my root directory and file-allocation tables, he or she might unwittingly download more information that might be used against me.

"You're ready to go," Jeffrey said.

"But I haven't even had the chance to thank you for everything you've done for me," I said.

"Don't mention it. The damaged cylinders have been fixed and reformatted. There's no evidence about Jack or anyone else from your past."

He moved close to my side of the bed and placed something in my hand. I smelled the sweetness of his breath and thought for a split second that I wouldn't be able to control myself. In my hand was a Tada 412 chip the size of a human fingernail and capable of storing 2 zigabytes of data (1 zigabyte = 100 million gigabytes). Technology never ceased to amaze me, even though I was a direct result of its innovation.

"What's in there?" I asked.

"All the erotic fantasies you consciously chose to erase from your high memory but were still accessible from your cache. I certainly would have appreciated it if someone had done the same for me." He smiled. "You androids are lucky—with humans, once the memory is gone, it's gone forever."

Clearly, not all humans were selfish, insensitive, and preoccupied with their own existence. Jeffrey had done something for a machine he'd only just met, even though he knew he would get nothing in return.

If only he knew what he had given me.

It is good to be home at last. I pour myself a long drink and sit naked in my favorite chair, overlooking the thirteenth moon of Oedvi—crystal blue with speckles of gold set against a backdrop of shimmering galaxies.

I insert the Tada 412 chip into the Com-21 socket under my right breast and log into the access area of my high memory. Everything comes back to mind in 2.3454 of a second. Jack, Paul, Robert, Alan, Philip, Michael, Peter, Frank, John, Steve—a total of 2,673 human males I had been lusting after—chests, buttocks, penises, underarms, thighs, lips, eyes, nipples, pubic hair, all shapes and sizes, all coming at once and reloading into my higher consciousness.

Lust has a life of its own.

The last entry is Jeffrey—my sweet, flamed-haired Jeffrey, who has taken such good care of me. I scan through all the times we spent together over the last few days. With the help of real-mode digital rendering, I undress him, even though he has never undressed before my lenses in real life. He stands naked—his penis strong and straight like I dreamed it would be—and I beep in climaxing pleasure. One hand explores the texture of his skin, massaging the solid muscles of his back, his spine hard and upright, while the other plays with the smoothness of his erection. I taste the strawberry lips and bite into them as if they are real.

>**Are you sure you want to reformat?**

What? A command stream is attached at the end of my memory patch. But it wasn't there before. How did it get into the high-memory area?

Frantically I choose the "No" option, but someone has permanently disabled the command.

>**Reformatting this disc will result in loss of all information. Are you sure you want to proceed?**

No, no, no, no! With both hands I grasp at Jeffrey's arms, trying in vain to hold on to something meaningful.

>**Reformatting in progress. Press the DEL command to abort.**

There's a vacuum inside me sweeping through every cylinder. I select the DEL command, but it, too, has been disabled.

>**Warning: 34.5 percent of formatting completed.**

I pull the 412 chip out of the Com-21 socket, but the formatting command is now locked into my high memory permanently.

Why would he do that? I love him so much—all I wanted was to be one with him. Why?

>**Warning: 62.3 percent of formatting completed.**

I try in vain to hold on to at least one bit of information—Jeffrey's strong, smooth erection.

>**Warning: 93.6 percent of formatting completed.**

I feel as if I'm regressing back into birth.

> **Warning: 100 percent of formatting completed.**
Formatting successfully completed.
Virus Lust #78678 successfully terminated.

> **Please enter new data.**
C:\> . . .

Underneath

Marcelle Perks and Kevin Mullins

They coughed between kisses, sucking in mold-ridden air as sex-lust quickened their needs. The man leaned down to enter her mouth, his body mimicking the curve of the ceiling. His hand pushed and slid to part her as the metal gods roared their approval. In, tight and holding, both thrilled further by the vibrations of the tunnels around them. The searing singing! Ah, so good! Just a wall beyond there were people chatting about West End shows, something about Britney Spears. They were going home, easing the day away. But the real underground was here, where life was deadened. It was sealed disharmony, a jerking cock-in-the-mouth, a secret world where fugitives took a mystery trip to the unconscious.

Chris thinks he looks dead ordinary in his London Transport oranges. Sometimes, when he dons the illuminated vest, punters ask him about trains and tickets. As if! But he's meant to blend in, don't want nobody to know. See, it's been happening a bit too often. They keep jumping, don't they? Two a week or more, no letup. Sometimes they're lucky and they get pushed into suicide pits, hollow ovals designed to displace a man made corpse from the thrust of the engine wall, but there's always the blade's breath of the rails and the resulting severed limbs; artery overload with its blood spill; bone dropout, giant skin tags. If he's unlucky the body gets drag-pushed the entire run to the mouth of the tunnel, greasing and falling out the whole stretch. Although it's filthy down there anyway and rats will pick-eat the carnage, the carriage has to be uncoupled, everything taken out of service. The whole thing pulled out to a lone siding, rubbed down, strip-searched. He collects all the evidence: bones, earrings, jewelry, teeth, scalp fragments. Often a photo from the morgue is sent to him, so he can fill in the gaps. His official title is Search and Recovery. You wouldn't believe how far a pinky finger can fly! Scrape and wipe, that's his job description, a position they could never advertise. And it's demanding, takes a genius to work out where everything is, the possibilities for fallout, the angle of the blood. A hard job, but someone's got to do it. Gossamer webbing forms between his gloved fingers as he delicately fingers stumps and seared flesh.

Rhonda gasped at the chill of the wall on her back. The rounded gloom looked congenial, but moist speckles drizzled onto her hair. It was damp down here. She'd chosen him for his perfectly spaced, open blue eyes. There had been a spark between them, a subtle movement of breath. And now that they were here there was less need for talk, far easier to just feel and press his penis. He had a nice hefty cock that felt heavier the more she sucked on it. Good energy, pulsating all the way down to the base. It was sexier in the dark. They were like mime figures in ancient Greece, shuddering shapes moaning in darkness. Down here her senses were heightened, her nipples never harder, insides leaking out with longing; all the pink skin screaming out for flesh, a good, hard shaft. It was so unreal, it almost didn't count, this milking of men in forgotten shadows. And this one, too, already she could taste the pre-come droplets on her tongue, imagine this stranger's entire body cued up to deliver a last extra-hardened jerk of orgasm. It would come like a wave of electricity, pulsating all over her. Vital, alive. This one she would engulf

raw, until every bit of him had fizzled inside her. Here, their heart-
beats were magnified, body movements in extreme close-up and
heat. His hand pushed into her slippery slit, the finger tickling the
edges of her labia, the panty edge useless, now being breached.
Look how the bitch wants it! They could smell each other over
everything else, the scent enflaming them. Kissing like pigs, nonsense noises loud now. Sitting on it, riding it, deep, deep into the
spot! Hah! Agggh!

Sliding underneath now. Have to get the body out first before they
can do anything. And this one was a splatterer. Fat ones were always
the worst, some of the shits that came out of them! And their body
fat, even uglier unpeeled, its consistency of chip fat and liver nearly
gagging him every time. The workload here is overwhelming, all
chore. He's now tired of this. Needs something else to keep him busy.
Maybe the latest closed-circuit video passed around among the crew.

Inside her, the chemical reaction. Millions of live sperm cells in
chase, needling and reacting to her. He was still shuddering, penis
limping down now. She'd be bumping and jerking off for hours.
Probably get Chris to milk her velvet insides, too, even if he's not
that fertile, at least his lovable cock could push this sperm around
her even deeper in. Manual insemination. What he didn't know
couldn't hurt him, not when he was being hurt by his failure
already. Her legs were damp like the weeping walls. She felt mal-
leable, but the station would be a hive of activity after the last train
had gone and they had to go awhile before they reached the abandoned interchange to the other line. She reached down to pick up
her keys. He stammered something, but she only put a finger to her
lips, gently pushed his chest, easing him toward the concealed exit.
It was powerful, this primal guiding instinct. A fantasy woman had
snatched him and fucked him underground. There was only the
moment. For her two fertile days she had to work fast.

Chris was used to death, to scraping it matter-of-factly off rails and trains. What he had problems with was life, creating it. Since the clinic had told him he had a low sperm count, it was like his penis had died. When she looked to it for sex, he pushed her away and she had to dry-hump his leg to get off. (Funny, he thought, that she now got off with him on one of the parts that was routinely cut off on the lines.) It was cool that he was kinky (they'd found each other at the Scala Cinema screening of *Nekromantik*) but not enough. Twisted things gave her pussy-ache, but sometimes a hard cock and a soft cunt were the only language she needed.

"The smell is stronger tonight," she said, ruffling his dark, almost black hair. Repeated exposure to death permeates; you can't simply wash it away. Aggressively, she pressed her semen-imprinted body in front of his. Nothing. He didn't resist, just started whining.

"Another fat guy, you know how they stink. Make more mess. Overtime for a week long, though." He looked tired, his hands were shaking. He saw her looking at his faded eyes.

"Why can't it be the cool goth chicks that jump the trains?" he joked feebly. He was still exhausted, head down.

She smiled, kissing him, knowing already that female bones are less likely to fragment, and thinner mortals stay more intact, are easier to dispose of. Tonight, he was tired. Let him watch fucking TV then. Like there was nothing else going on. He still didn't want to talk about it. She hid the pregnancy testing kit she'd bought safely in a drawer. If he couldn't guess the date, then fuck him. When it was positive she'd show him. Low didn't mean zero.

Underneath the very streets everyone walked on was something old and sacred, scarred into the city's shape, listless but fertile in the dusky dirt. London breathes resonance that tugs at the subconscious. Is it the pagan gods, or the Greek ones, or the apostles of Lucifer that haunt its medieval-formed alleyways? She could imagine her forefathers worshipping in dank caves, pushing out winter, hunger, unmedicated pain. The chanting faces mixed with hope and sorrow. Oh yes, *then*.

Now the awe had left the people. Everybody was the same and nothing. London on the surface was a bubble palace, all flash lights and gab. A sprawl of unmatched buildings, most of it old and shady. Everybody rich-poor and raging. But underneath, there were oh so many undercuts and passageways, in this most undermined city in the world. And all along the stretches and sprawls of commerce and laid back-to-back housing, the arteries of the city flexed their nerves. Hundreds of trains teemed in, out, and around the tunnels, feeding ever more strangers all the way, forcing them into darkness and decay. But under the neon lights, if you looked them carefully in the eye, you could see a tremor of hesitation; on dark nights it looked like fear.

Maps didn't really help. The old stuff wasn't built logically. The plans were still secret, Freemasons' mischief, whiffs of occult "magick." There were platforms that joined in the shape of a figure 8, a double track constructed that was never used, the abandoned stations left whole and rotting to slug up the city's heartbeat. And this was Chris's world, the dungeon behind the tiled façade.

The first time he'd taken her to an abandoned tube station she'd nearly pissed her pants. It was that scary, all the fear that she'd ever felt before was like nothing in front of it. He showed her the key, made her lick it before they scurried through the discreet door. Then down a decrepit, still-dirty staircase to the now-disused platform. Just yards from the hub of the main station, but here, deserted fading posters still hung on the walls. He leaned her against the hush and eased down her panties as images of mummified corpses flashed on the wall behind them. A surprise film show for her, something his bosses were trying to sell as a concept. Somebody laughed, a horrid cackle in the background. There were a few workmen in the tunnel, enjoying the show, the screen crackling as they watched. Each image had a shadow cloud of filth as the moving dust spots squeezed the dead station into life. That was good, the first time he touched her inside, the hesitating but unstoppable fingers. Her skirt, as always, was short and provoking. She looked past her lust at the flickers of the moving screen. It was uncensored footage from the Bodyworlds exhibition, real corpses plasticined and exhibited for the public. It was bizarre. At one point they stepped in front of the projector and the footage played on their frantic bodies. It was an experiment; maybe they would use the disused Aldwych to pander to film premieres. The Underground was a treasure trove of such decay. A stripped-away horseman onscreen grinned at her thrashing pleasure. And passion swept over all like a blackout. A lust that tunneled her into nothing.

It seemed to take ages for them to get to have sex. Oddly, he was old-fashioned, sometimes unbearably courteous. But after their first time, a heavy blanket of lust dropped over them. They couldn't seem to stop, yet had little lasting satisfaction. Nightly they made love, all the positions, mutual masturbation, all to heat and exhaustion. Sometimes it was 4 A.M. when the bed stopped heaving. And even after they had come the fourth, fifth time, it was never enough. Even after they were married. For all their sex, still nothing happened. The stirring of life they planned, failed to bud. Then came the consultations with doctors, strange pills that made them feel listless. The encroaching silences. She became desperate to revive her dark prince. And where better than in his kingdom, the womb-like tunnels of his private Underground—the forgotten stations—to court and milk her donors? What happened there wasn't real. It was passion and adventure, secrets and darkness. And the Underground was so much a part of Chris anyway, like the caverns behind his eyes. She took copies of his keys and found the best locations. Cruised from work's end when she was hot and ticking. There were risks, of course, but she targeted the one-time thrill seekers, hunted for the surprised look. She wanted a result. In the midst of life we are in the midst of death. And Chris was so down, he needed it.

After four weeks of cruising, she felt a flush of expectancy. Her eyes shone brighter, breasts pointed higher north. Something was in the air. At the same time, she was seeing even less of Chris, who had dealt with nine deaths below: an unusually high number—56 percent of attempts were unsuccessful. They were like Hades and Persephone, he to quench life, she to bring it forth. She thought of this as they curled up on quiet evenings. But something was stretching out, far and away. They were drifting apart, long tunnels separated by empty static. They sat in the evenings caught in the TV's glow, a still life of sadness.

The walls were stark, meant to be white. But it was impossible to judge color down here. The grain of the cinder block chewed into her hands as the man whom she often saw at Holborn thrust into her from behind. Funny, although he looked a capable guy, he had the angle all wrong, and it was hurting a little too much on the left side. She tried to maneuver, but ooh, everything goddamned scraped the skin here. The entrance this time had been a bugger to find. Odd that people had actually lived here once. Yeah, darling, come over from Jamaica and get a nice job with London Transport with free flat. Well, a code-named disaster known as The Hostel; it had been a revamped bomb shelter from the Second World War. Must have seemed like they'd left the sunshine and gone to hell. Roll fifty years, still she's keeping up the fucking spirit on platform 6. I bet those guys (usually they were guys) brought some gals down here. Yeah, just like she was giving this some fizz. He couldn't get a full rhythm going because the corridor was too narrow. But his cock was hard and it was inside her. The usual mashing rhythm. She let go, fell forward, her breasts scraping against the rough painted surface. If she closed her eyes she could be getting pressed against the roughness of a cave or tree. He was mauling her with his greedy hands everywhere. She decided to moan, give him some satisfaction. Aggh. His finger pushed hard up her anus. Unexpected. Extra kinky! Her stomach tightened.

"Harder!" she gasped. She could feel the poke of his finger span deepen. Yeah, come darling, before I leave you here to wank by yourself. She'd thought an older guy, one with silver streaks in his hair, might at least be proficient. Up for it. Maybe she wouldn't let this one come inside her. His sperm wasn't good enough for Chris!

She stood proudly looking at herself in the mirror. She looked back at her shining eyes and lustrous hair; something was up. Why didn't he notice the change in her? He was bathing again with the door shut. They always used to do it together, drinking lashings of wine with the water. Should she pop into the bathroom, show him her breasts? No, his bag was here. She just had time to steal a cigarette. Her hand reached down right between a file. Shit, it was photos, perhaps she'd creased one. Quickly, she pulled the file out. He was bringing his work home again. Photographs dotted with unique codes. All corpses vaguely swollen or mangled, rendered fantastic through the extent of their injuries. It was their vagueness that got her in the throat.

"AA456G T. 17 pieces + fluids. 8 Stone." The picture was of a teenage girl without clothes. Both her arms had been crudely severed. The pressure in Rhonda's head tightened; a flash headache was forming at the base of her neck. Still, she was somehow unable to draw her eyes away. More of them, too many. A fat woman in a flowery dress, the cloth surprisingly more intact than her body; a punk rocker whose head had been badly mangled. Was it really human? The gent with the snarled body, as if a dragon had breathed fire and cut him to pieces. His silver hair, all that was normal. The curious way after everything it still looked so neat and dapper. Her fingers throbbed just looking at it. It could have been that guy from the other night, the one who didn't know where her vagina was positioned and made her sore. She pushed the photos back into the file. She couldn't face this shit now.

The man wiped his hand with a neatly folded white handkerchief. Another stranger. Underneath he looked gnomelike, pig-ugly. He looked ruefully at her panting, now-aching form. Sometimes she got carried away. She inspected the scratches on her breasts and stomach, thinking ahead to how she could conceal them. Sometimes she felt weary doing it; it was just like another job. It took minutes of silent readjustment before they were ready to reenter normal life. From the open platform side the doorway looked like a storage cupboard, so it was difficult to go in or come out without its looking odd. Timing was everything. She listened for a long time while her donor shuffled impatiently behind her. When the coast seemed clear she edged open the door, checked that there was no one visible, and swung through. The man bundled after her. A moment after she'd looked up, a thin-faced black woman in London Transport uniform turned the corner and faced them. She seemed horribly familiar, somehow. The woman gave them a quick, hard glance, then turned away. Perhaps the security cameras had picked something up. Normally she got the man to take the first train, but they were both too eager to escape for that protocol to be even suggested. They separated with an awkward touch two stops down. She felt she could feel the ticking of her body as she eventually climbed a thousand steps onto a train. "Yes! Surely this was it!" How then to break it to Chris?

When she said she wanted to do something special, she'd meant dinner, candles. The local Italian around the corner, maybe. But tonight he was the old Chris again, dressed in gothic clothes he hadn't worn in two years, a daub of kohl around his eyes.

"Hey, babe." He reached for her and pulled her lips hungrily to his mouth as she came in. "I gotta see a man about a dog, know what I mean?" She stared at him quizzically; it was their code word of old.

"You mean you got another way in? Another dungeon for us to explore?"

"Yes, babes, this one's the best. We've gotta travel with my mate on the eight-fifteen from Finsbury Park, right behind him in the cab. Then when we get there, a little tap and he'll let us out at the old Brompton Road station. And on the last train, he'll pick us up just before he goes to the depot. You wanna come?" He held out his arms for her.

"Oh, Chris, you are fabby!" She jumped into his arms and ran to change into her army trousers and Dockers. Time to go underground again. What better setting than the disused Brompton Road station, which they had never explored, to proclaim her pregnancy?

When they caught the bus to Finsbury Park station, darkness was falling. It was a cold autumn night, the trees slowly dying in the battered streets. They made an odd couple. Chris painfully tall, his skin so white it looked gray. He was wearing his work clothes just in case; it was easier if there were any awkward questions. Rhonda wore her own uniform of slick black over her trim, short frame, with the familiar orange waistcoat over it. A fake London Transport VIS-ITOR badge completed the deception.

They spent a long time on the platform, nervously waiting for Pete to turn up and give them a lift. The other passengers, perhaps thinking they were checking tickets, avoided them like the plague. They stood near the mouth of the tunnel, talked without looking at each other. Going to these disused stations was something they had always done together; now she felt guilty after her own private forays into this domain. Near the watching eye of the closed-circuit TV camera, she felt like an insect in an open glass. If they waited much longer, someone on station control would get suspicious.

The sound of bumping, painful searing, the gears of a large train slowing, caught their attention. They craned their necks looking.

Was it him? The window of the driver's cab was smeared with something, but Pete's cheery face came into view. His warm brown eyes and laughing smile were a real charmer. He opened the door with a flourish. "Come on, lovebirds, get yourself in. You wouldn't want to miss this extra-special experience now, would you?"

It was really too small inside for three. Chris wedged himself on the floor by the controls, and she stood by the shaking door. The train gave a little wheeze and teetered backward for a fraction before rushing forward into the darkened tunnel.

"Wow," said Rhonda, her eyes wide with shock. "In here it looks so different. I can't believe I go this way every day! Is there anything to see down here?"

"Not much," said Pete airily, "that's why we get so bored. You see the odd rat scurrying off the tracks. Once I thought I saw a fox, but nah, there's just lots of rubbish that gets blown through the system. Sometimes you get to thinking you see things, though!"

Chris was no longer smiling. His voice, when it came out, didn't sound like him at all.

"It's the people who do the weird shit. You should see some of the CCTV footage—fucking, shitting, you name it." For half a second, her heart jumped into her mouth. But he couldn't, could he?

His flat voice continued, "Golden lads and girls all must, as chimney sweepers come to dust."

"Yeah," said Pete, "and after doing a double shift again, I'm halfway there!"

It was an old joke; working underground was akin to being buried alive in the heart of the city. She'd heard that some of the workers felt weirder on the surface when they scurried home.

The endless enclosure of the tunnel distracted them. It was an eternal penis that stretched for miles. The train bucked along at a pace, eating up the stations one by one: Piccadilly Circus, Green Park, Hyde Park Corner, familiar London just meters above. At Knightsbridge, Chris said, "Get ready, babe." His voice was still uneven, as if he needed to wash out his throat. Normally he was high now, anticipation dancing in his veins. But she would show him. The train slowed down. Through the window the colors of the tiles changed. Pete, hand on the brake stick, said, "On the count of three."

She had the door in her hand and it was half open before the train had even come to a halt. Heart racing, she jumped out into blackness, careful to keep away from the rail. She pointed her torch at a recent wall that had been built over the old platform and cut her hands trying to clamber over it. Ouch! There was something sharp on its edges, some barrier trying to keep them out. Behind her the train door was slamming, just seconds to get out of the way before being seen by one of the punters. The train groaned onward.

"Chris?" she shone her torch at the empty space where the train had been. Impossible, surely?

For some reason, she'd been left alone in the dark.

At first she sat and waited, indignation filling her with hate energy. She felt hot and stupid, panicking in the dust. Why had he done this? The idiot, dumb fuck! She'd kill him when she saw him. The remains of the platform were indistinct, half rebuilt with a raised area, the rest in disarray. Now she was here, it didn't feel real. She'd always descended below with another man, first Chris, then the others. Alone, it had a different feel. The only thing she longed for was to be out of there.

The strangest thing was, it wasn't pitch black. Although it hadn't been used as a station since 1934, the lights were on, although their color was dusty, sepialike. The curve of the walls seemed about to fall and engulf her. Torchlight was more romantic—you didn't get to notice the asbestos dust from the brake linings, the rat droppings and oozing mildew. An ancient track plate remained in place. If she ignored the abandoned building project that cluttered the platform, she could imagine she really was waiting for a train, and not for Chris to reclaim her. Perhaps she should start counting the passing trains that galloped dangerously close, buffeting her hair with their passage of air. The noise, like the trains, came and went. She could have been here minutes or hours.

How many trains had gone by? Ten? Twelve? Noise travels differently underground. Already she was disorientated. It was hard to breathe the musty old air. Her eyes were aching with the dust. Her mask, water, mobile, and extra provisions were all in Chris's rucksack. And there was no exit now. The Ministry of Defense and the Territorial Army had locked shut all access to the entrance above. If Chris didn't come back, she was trapped. She'd punch him when he turned up. In the gloom, her mind worked overtime, trying to work out the meaning of his voice in the cab. Lately, they'd grown apart. She was no longer sure she could trust her instincts about him. But he was a bastard to do this! Her seething temper kept her company for a while, but as her anger cooled, and she could feel the station's dampness entering into her throat, she started to feel the first chill fingers of fear.

And then the sounds started. Up there, right above her! A clank, like an iron pail being hit with a hammer. The air seemed to get even thicker. Now a scraping, quick footsteps—but who could it be? The walls crouched over her, thick, impenetrable. Something trickled over her fingers. A spider? She jumped to her feet, not sure in which direction to run. Along the half-renovated platform a series of wooden, rotting partitions afforded a multitude of hiding places. She could still see the tiles, with their familiar brown, green, and cream paint, but underfoot, the dust was so thick it felt like wading through sand. She started running, breathing as quietly as she could, and shone her torch into each partition. Nothing but dust. What was that Chris had said? "Golden lads and girls all must, as chimney sweepers come to dust"? Could it be Chris, somehow having a laugh? Secretly filming her panic? She stood pensively, shining her torch on the corridor ahead. Abandoned rooms gaped empty from off the corridor, each entrance painted a familiar green. Chris had told her the military had taken over this complex during the war. She moved toward the first room, noting how inside here the dust was thicker. A sharp smell assailed her senses.

It was like a museum piece. Old strategy maps hung on the walls. Colored pins still clung to ancient boards. Why had they left it? Somewhere outside there was a clunk as if something had fallen. She froze, felt prickles forming on the back of her neck. She crouched by a table. Louder now, a sound like dragging steps. Was she imagining it? Perhaps this place was haunted. She'd heard that in the wartime, lots of accidents had happened, the details of which had been suppressed. There were rumors that some of the stations had been deliberately built through plague pits. And of course there were the suicide victims. But surely the noise was getting louder? Wasn't that a man's voice, talking to a woman? And another conversation, there in the corner, and there from the other room. All around her now, there was a searing singing, she could hear bubbles of noise, as if a crowd of people were talking all at once. She caught a few syllables here and there, but nothing distinct. It was as if the station were a hive of underground operation again, and she was stuck in time with her wires crossed. She crouched under the desk. If she made herself as small as possible, perhaps they wouldn't find her.

The sounds were louder now. They sounded like fireworks, way off distant. Perhaps it was bombs, like in the blitz. After each crash of sound, the silence that followed it seemed louder. The room seemed to vibrate; there was a perceptible energy in the room that frightened her. A red heat seemed to be peeling her scalp away. Her eardrums recoiled, her breaths came out ragged and harsh. Her mind was racing, like a bicycle being pedaled by a demon. Abstractly, she thought about having a cigarette and inhaling all the fumes along with the nicotine. Quick as a flash, she recalled her hands slinking into Chris's bag, taking out the photographs. She was suddenly sure that the last corpse had been her donor with the silver streaks. He'd said his name was Jimmy. And now Jimmy was dead.

The air was getting heavier, she could feel her lungs struggling to cope. These rooms hadn't been ventilated properly for decades. Scrambling out on her hands and knees, she stood up and looked around the room again. Strangely, although it was the same, its color and edges had become indistinct, and it was the shadows that pulled her eyes in. In front of her, the brown was becoming muddied, as if the very clay behind the façade of the walls were glowing. She fancied she could see shapes writhing within, taking form. Up above now, the booming resumed. She ran, choking as she went, trying not to fall over old bricks and planks of wood. Now she was really afraid, the platform stretched out even more, its uneven surface treacherous. Ugh! Something had got to her; she was spiraling out of control in the air. The pain lit her adrenaline for an instant, making it burn brighter, before her head hit the corner of a wall. A thin trickle of blood slid out of her nose.

When she came to, she thought she'd awoken in the wrong house. Her head was burning and an insane thirst coursed through her body. She pushed herself roughly to her knees. The realization hit her like a brick. She was still trapped. Alive but underground. She wandered along to the edge of the platform. She could see in the dust her footprints where she had climbed over the wall. A peculiar silence hung in the air. They must have turned off the rails by now. She stopped, made herself count to 240. Every few minutes, a train leaves on the Piccadilly Line. If she counted to 240, and no train went past, then it was safe to proceed down the tunnel.

"A hundred and one, a hundred and two."

Now she didn't care who heard. She had to get out of here. When she shone her torch at the mouth of the tunnel, it stared back at her. It would be like walking into a lion's mouth, the most dangerous thing that she had ever done. Her dry tongue tried to suck some moisture from the gaps between her teeth.

She'd run the whole length, shining her torch the whole way. It could only be three minutes to South Kensington, two and a half if she went really fast. She could press the station alarm button once she got there. Say she got drunk and must have got out at the wrong stop.

Silence. Only the settling of the dust seemed audible. Most of London must be asleep. She had to go before the first train started, otherwise she'd be trapped here for another day. And she couldn't bear that. Having counted to 240, she wanted to wait a moment, perform another ritual. But there was nothing safe to cling to; the only thing to do was run.

The first thing she noticed was that it was hard to move quickly through the tunnel. The going was tricky; she had to take care not to trip on the rail. Anyway her head hurt and she felt sick. The scorch of burned engine oil had soaked into the roof above her, and the air was acrid to breathe. She picked her way forward, steadier now. She got into a rhythm, forcing herself to move quicker. Now the tunnel was sloping sharply down; if she didn't keep her balance she might fall. Funny, it was harder going downhill than on the straight. A drip of water startled her from overhead. Could it be a leak? No, she had to keep going, she was not so desperate yet that she had to drink where that had come from. At the start, she'd thought she could see the end of the tunnel, but now it was stretching on, winding around corners, it felt like she would never get to the end of it. But it was too late to go back. Had to keep going. It was hard work, though. Her breathing was more precarious. If only she could breathe some real air, get the edge of fear out of her nerves. She was trotting like a pony, pumping her arms up and down, until at last she could see the end, the proverbial light at the end of the tunnel. Faster now, only another ten meters. It was getting light and easier to breathe every step.

She feels it before she hears it. The sound of a train galloping in the distance. Is it in front or behind? Doesn't know, runs on. The whole tunnel vibrates, as if in orgasm, as her sweating, dirt-encrusted figure struggles, makes a break for it.

Why haven't all those attempted suicides told anyone how loud it was by the track's edge? Her head will explode before her heart does. She almost dives through the edge of the tunnel, a dusty, demented thing. Instinctively, she heads into the welcoming air and light. The last train of the night rushes to greet her.

To the last few waiting passengers, it seemed that she'd lain in wait to do this all along. "Suicide dive," the papers called it. A new and growing menace. The driver was suspended until further notice, owing to reports that an unidentified friend had accompanied him on that fatal night. A friend who had laughed hysterically as Rhonda's blood splattered the cab from underneath.*

Note: Brompton Road Station really exists. To find out more about the abandoned stations of the London Underground, check out this site:
http://underground-history.co.uk

Stiff

Lisabet Sarai

We have a saying in the mortuary business: Beauty is a widow.

It sounds mysterious and philosophical, but its real meaning is a bit more prosaic. A woman is never so beautiful as when she is bereaved.

Certainly, this woman illustrates the proverb. She is exquisite, with her hair as black as her tailored garments, her face pale with longing, her eyes sparkling from her weeping. She sits quietly by the casket, tears streaming like Niobe's, long white fingers twisting her handkerchief. Every now and again she looks at me, standing in the corner in my stiff, hot suit, my collar nearly strangling me. She does not smile, but I attempt a reassuring smile in response to her glance. Professional demeanor, detached yet sympathetic.

Let me explain. I am not the undertaker. I simply work for Mr. Graves, as I have since my junior year in high school, trying to earn money for college. I began at State last fall, and now I work weekends, plus full-time in the summer. I help with the embalming, lug the coffins around, answer the phone, whatever needs to be done. I do a good job. But it's only a job.

Mr. Graves confides in me. He would like me to take over the business. Since his partner, Mr. Stone, passed on, he becomes more frail each season. But I know my destiny is elsewhere.

I plan to become a writer. I will follow in the footsteps of Jack Kerouac and Hunter Thompson. I will chronicle the road of my life, each encounter and each revelation. At the suggestion of my senior English teacher, I keep a journal, recording whatever scenes, sensations, and insights catch my attention. I practice my craft.

I wish I had my journal now. I would love to describe Mrs. Harrington's delicate features, so at odds with her voluptuous figure. I need to purge myself, through writing, of the desires she wakens in me.

Suddenly, she breaks down into a noisy fit of crying. I find myself by her side, my arm around her shoulders in what I hope is a comforting, nonthreatening gesture.

"Mrs. Harrington," I say, trying not to swoon from her perfume. "You must get hold of yourself. Your tears will not bring him back."

"No," she says, sniffling, "but I am responsible for his death."

"Please, Mrs. Harrington. Your husband died of heart failure. You are in no way responsible."

"My innocent boy," she says, smiling at me for the first time. "You have no idea."

I am innocent, I cannot deny it. I've done a lot of reading, but my actual experience is pretty limited. Suzie has made sure of that. I've asked her to marry me, and she's accepted. She lets me fondle her breasts and French-kiss her, but that's about all. When I graduate from college, I know we'll be together. In the meantime, all I have are my books and my trusty hand.

I do not reply to Mrs. Harrington's comment, but simply don my attentive listener look, and after a moment, she continues.

"My Roger was a man of amorous temperament and considerable skill in matters of the flesh. Over the last few years, though, his ability to perform—in a sexual manner, I mean—declined considerably. We employed a variety of stratagems to try to deal with the problem, some more successful than others. We tried handcuffs and blindfolds, threesomes with nubile coeds, swingers clubs, the whole gamut."

My eyes widen as I try to picture this sophisticated and elegant lady in such sordid circumstances. I must look slightly shocked, because she gives a little laugh and pats my shoulder.

"When you are young, and constantly flooded with lust, you cannot imagine the lengths that one will travel to excite desire." She sighs as if her heart will break. "The night Roger died, I had given him some Spanish fly. Do you know what that is?"

I nod my head dumbly.

"It was with his knowledge and permission, of course. But, with his cardiac history, I should have known better.

"The aphrodisiac was far more effective than we expected. Roger had a mighty erection. He mounted me and plowed me like a raging stallion. It was absolutely divine, the best sex we'd had in years. At the moment of crisis, though, his heart gave out. He died pumping his seed into me."

I can see that she is on the verge of breaking down again. Meanwhile, her strange story has quite a different effect on me. My own member swells and begins to throb at the description of her husband's tumescence. Her nearness is not helping matters.

It's a hot July afternoon, and I'm dying in my dark wool suit. Meanwhile, I can just catch a musky whiff of her sweat, underneath her gardenia fragrance. Her fitted black jacket and skirt look as confining and uncomfortable as my own clothes. She probably doesn't notice, though, overcome as she is with grief.

In fact, she suddenly wails and throws herself across the coffin, trying to embrace the rigid corpse. "Oh, Roger, forgive me! I miss you so much! I wouldn't care if we never screwed again, if only I could have you back."

"Please, Mrs. Harrington . . ." I try to pull her away, ridiculously concerned that she will spoil the cadaver's makeup. I worked for two hours to make him look full-cheeked and rosy instead of pinched and blue. I am rather proud of the results.

She throws me off, and continues to howl, tearing at her hair and her clothing like Hecuba on the ramparts of Troy. "Oh, Roger, Roger . . ." she blubbers, trailing off into hysterical incomprehensibility. There's nothing I can do except stand there stiffly like a dummy, a futile, consoling hand on her shoulder, murmuring the platitudes for which this occupation is famous.

Finally, she cries herself out. She sits down again, gasping for breath, her eyes inflamed and her hair in complete disarray. I offer her my dry handkerchief. (Hers is drenched.) She accepts gratefully. Once more she graces me with her smile.

"Thank you, young man. I'm better now. I apologize for my lack of self-control. I appreciate your kindness and your tolerance."

"Not at all, Mrs. Harrington."

"Please, call me Lydia."

"Oh, I couldn't do that, Mrs. Harrington. It would not be proper."

"As you wish," she says with a shrug. She looked at me carefully, possibly really seeing me for the first time. "What is your name?"

"Howard Marsh," I reply. "Howard Michael Marsh."

I'm not crazy about my first name; it does not sound very literary to me. But "H. M. Marsh" has a rather nice ring to it. " 'The Lure of the Unattainable,' by H. M. Marsh."

"Well, Howard, I am very pleased to make your acquaintance. I really don't know what I would have done, had I been here alone."

"I'm only doing my job, ma'am."

"Well, you are very good at your job. Come over here, sit down, and tell me more about yourself. It will distract me from thinking about Roger."

Part of me is drawn to her like a moth to flame. Part of me is reluctant to get any closer. Already my penis is straining, trapped inside my boxers like Hercules in the dungeons of King Augeus. To sit beside her would be torture. She will surely notice the growing bulge in my trousers. I hesitate, blushing, wondering how Hemingway would handle this.

She senses my resistance. "Howard," she says with hint of sternness. "I need you. Do not disappoint me." She grabs my hand and actually pulls me down onto the straight-backed chair beside hers.

When she touches me, there's a surge of something like electricity. My breath catches in my throat. My cock gives a little jump. She does not relinquish her hold on my hand. The heaviness in my groin grows more oppressive.

"Now, Howard, tell me all."

And for some reason, I do tell her, about my family, my job, my literary ambitions, even about Suzie. Now that she has calmed down, she is a good listener. Meanwhile, I find that disheveled and undone, she is even more appealing than she was when tailored and neat. Her hands are folded calmly in her lap. She leans forward, as if eager to catch my every word.

As I talk on, I notice that in the course of her frenzied weeping, she apparently popped off one of the buttons on her blouse. When she inclines her body toward me, the garment gapes open. I catch a glimpse of black lace and white skin. Now I am not thinking at all of what I am saying, but still, somehow, I ramble on, my eyes riveted on that provocative aperture.

In the midst of explaining Suzie's views on premarital sex, I notice something else. Mrs. Harrington's sober and conservative skirt seems to be gradually getting shorter. First her knees are revealed, smooth and delightfully round. When I look again, I find the hem has settled at midthigh, exposing her glistening silk hosiery. A few minutes later, her garters are peeking out from under the somber fabric, jet against her creamy flesh.

I stop in midsentence, my mouth half open. She has pulled her skirt practically to her waist. The view paralyzes me as surely as if I had looked upon Medusa.

I can see the shadowy cleft between her thighs. I can see glossy curls framing a pink mystery that takes my breath away. I can see that, though she is clearly in mourning, Mrs. Harrington has chosen to forgo wearing underwear.

She smiles at me sweetly. "Do you like me, Howard?" she asks. Obviously, this is a rhetorical question, for my penis is rearing up like Mount Olympus. "Let me make you more comfortable," she says, and the next thing I know, she unzips my trousers and sets me free.

My cock springs up from my lap, plum-purple, straight toward the ceiling. Mrs. Harrington licks her lips. "Young man," she says, "I think I can help you." Then before I can stop her, she straddles my chair and settles herself upon my organ, burying me in the hot cavern of her sex.

I cry out, half in protest, half in ecstasy. Even while I think frantically about Suzie, I am bucking beneath Mrs. Harrington's weight, trying to embed my cock more deeply in her lubricious depths.

The sensations are like nothing that I could have imagined, reading *Hustler* and stroking away alone. The slickness, the heat, the pulsing of her muscles as she clamps down on me—oh, I wish that I had my notebook, and then realize that there is no way that I could ever describe this.

She continues to ride me, harder and faster, and I match her rhythm. Suddenly she squeals, and grinds her pelvis against me. I almost come then, but by chance I remember that I am in a funeral parlor. This is slightly sobering.

Mrs. Harrington is panting, her hair hanging down into her face. I am still huge inside her. She smiles that lovely smile of hers. "Howard, dear, you are a very talented young man. You are so kind to console a poor widow."

I grin, embarrassed, twitching with pleasure every time she shifts position slightly.

"I think," she continues, "that I would really enjoy having you on top. What do you think?"

Taking my silence for the acquiescence that it is, she looks around the room. "The floor would be dreadfully uncomfortable, I fear," she says. "But what about over there?"

Horrified, I realize that she is pointing to the demo casket over in the corner. I don't think that I explained that we are not in the official viewing room. This is just an antechamber, where we lay out the bodies in advance of the funeral. Tomorrow, Mr. Graves's nephew and I will have to wheel Mr. Harrington into the chapel for the memorial service. So there is this spare coffin, sitting off to the side. As soon as she mentions it, I understand what she has in mind.

Before I can speak, she slips off of me, leaving me feeling lost and desperately horny. She raises the lid of the casket and trails her fingers approvingly over the silk lining. "Very nice," she murmurs. "Such a quality establishment." Then without any hesitation, she strips off her suit and blouse, and lies down in the mahogany box with her legs spread as wide as possible in those narrow confines.

I am frozen, caught between desire and disgust, like Odysseus between Scylla and Charybdis. "Howard," she says, a bit impatiently. "I'm waiting."

Like a zombie, I walk over and look down at her, splayed out on the padded brocade. Her eyes sparkle with mischievous lust. Her hair is tangled into black ringlets. Her pale breasts beckon, barely hidden by her lacy brassiere. Mostly, though, I look at her sex, her vermilion lips pouting toward me, moist and inviting.

"Come on!" she says, and I can't help but obey. I shed my shoes, push my pants down to my ankles, and step out of them. Then I climb awkwardly into the casket, trying not to crush her. I really do not know how to proceed, but she takes control, grasping my rock-hard penis and positioning it at her entrance. "Now, thrust, Howard," she says. "Plow me with your beautiful young cock. Fuck me the way you have always wanted to fuck your little Suzie."

With the mention of Suzie's name, something snaps. I am suddenly frenzied and without thought. I plunge my cock into her, again and again, while she whimpers and cries and writhes beneath me. My knees are pressed hard against the casket walls. Her fingernails tear at the lining. I feel the seed rising in my stalk like Icarus flying toward the sun. The heat sears me, but it is too late to turn back. One massive, final thrust, and I dissolve inside her, then fall to earth.

It's overwhelming. I never dreamed that it would be like this. There are tears in my eyes, tears that Lydia kisses away with an enigmatic smile.

We climb stiffly out of the coffin and look around for our clothes. As we survey the room, we notice the anomaly at the same instant.

Mr. Harrington's face still looks rosy and content, a testimony to my undertaking skill. His limbs are still arranged as if he were relaxed and sleeping. However, his expensive worsted suit is tented at the groin, the bulge growing larger by the minute.

Lydia looks me in the eye and gives a little laugh. "Well, you know, Roger always did like to watch."

Seven Seeds

Tobsha Learner

The pomegranate sat in a bowl beside the bed, bulbous and shiny. It was a visual pun of his, one of the mythological references he would leave scattered about the house to test her. Penelope loved this aspect of him, the literary wit; it was one of the few ways she could ever actually read his emotions, offering a subtle opening into a far gentler and bemused individual than the man he presented superficially.

At fifty-five Hector was twenty years older than her; they'd met when Penelope was doing field research for her master's degree in anthropology at the coroner's office in Sydney. Her thesis was on death and the rituals that surrounded it, a subject for which she had a morbid fascination that had begun at the age of six when she witnessed her grandfather suffer a fatal heart attack during a golf tournament. From that point on Penelope was convinced that one's experience of death (especially at an early age) was the most definitive influence on how one actually lived. It had certainly shaped her own life, and after the unexpected deaths of both her father and sister followed, she decided that by making a study of her nemesis she might avoid the same sudden demise.

Hector was a coroner. A tall, dark-haired man of eastern European background—he was half Serb, half Polish—he had arrived in Australia at the age of ten but still walked as if he were weighed down by the collective historical grievances of both his parent nations. At six foot five, he would have been handsome if he stood upright, but, embarrassed about his own stature and the craggy masculinity genetics had bestowed upon him, he stooped, whispering in a gravely half tone that he would have been mortified to know that some found him sexy.

Lighthearted he was not. He was incapable of small talk, and the diatribes Hector launched into had the density of a base metal. But it was an intensity that Penelope—accustomed to the escapist brevity of beachside Sydney—adored. Finally here was a man with gravitas, a mature worldly entity capable of commitment: political, philosophical, and sexual.

A painfully shy man, Hector was an individual whose greatest fear was to be noticed, whereas Penelope was a creature who thrived on being noticed. She came from an old Australian family. Her mother used to make jokes about their ancestors being Irish political prisoners incarcerated in the first convict ships, and there certainly was a plethora of Irish and Scottish heritage. Penelope herself, four foot eleven, had the strawberry blond hair to prove it. She was unnaturally pale, and her mother, who ran a small but successful plant nursery in the western suburbs and was paranoid about skin cancer, had kept her daughter in during the day, terrified she might lose another child to the disease. As soon as she could, Penelope had overcompensated for her childhood isolation by becoming extremely social. Constantly on the phone, she was one of those people who seemed to have an endless web of "best" friends and surrogate family, until she met Hector. Together they were day and night, light and shade, January and May, opposites that somehow managed to counterbalance each other. To meet them you never would assume such unlikely associates would be friends, never mind lovers, but then nature is wonderful when she resists a cliché.

• • •

They fell in love over the body of a female suicide. The woman had hanged herself after being left by her husband. Usually women used pills or poison to kill themselves, they did not tend to hang themselves, and it was while debating this very subject that our two protagonists bonded.

After the autopsy (which was so gruesome the young anthropology student had to excuse herself to throw up in the toilet), Penelope, using the alibi that she'd like to interview Hector for her thesis, asked him out for a coffee.

Astounded, and a little unsure about the correct etiquette of socializing with an intern, he deferred, but she insisted and so he reluctantly agreed.

Unused to seduction of any kind, Hector was amazed when the student put her hand on his knee. It had been over a year since he had had sex (and then it was with a suburban prostitute he visited annually as a begrudging concession to the fact that he had a physical dimension, whether he liked it or not), and well over ten years since he'd actually made love. And so, incredulous that any woman might actually desire him, it had taken another four dates before Hector submitted to Penelope's frenetic caresses. Ironically, this resistance, formed from confusion, worked in his favor. For, by this time, unused to being refused, Penelope assumed his reluctance was a truculent admission that he didn't desire her; naturally, such opposition only fueled her own desire.

To the amazement of Penelope's friends and Hector's colleagues at the morgue (who long ago had nicknamed him Dr. Hades) and to the strong disapproval of Penelope's forty-three-year-old mother, three months later the young student moved into the coroner's palatial postmodern apartment, which overlooked the harbor and the city.

It was an apartment utterly devoid of any fecundity, any mess, any indication of human frailty—any kind of signal that anything organic (never mind human) slept, ate, and shat within its four immaculately white walls. In a defiant challenge to such sterility, Penelope spilled one of her numerous cupboard boxes out on the polished wooden floor, releasing a jumble of makeup, old hairbrushes, half-used lipsticks, sex aids, and strange jars of skin care products.

"Hector, you're afraid of decay," she announced. "You— yourself an expert on decomposition—are terrified of your own demise. I shall be your liberator. I can promise you we shall make the most gloriously memorable messes ever. Here on this Persian rug."

To which Hector had no answer, for she already had her tongue in his mouth and her hands wound around his buttocks, her fingers trailing around to reach for his penis. Penelope's spontaneous and complete delight in all things sensual never actually gave Hector time to be appalled. It was as if she had been brought up with absolutely no inhibitions whatsoever, and Hector, after meeting her mother, June—who was a bit of an old hippie—was somewhat mortified to discover that that indeed had been the case.

Under her caresses his body seemed to straighten and return to the tautness of his youth. Unlike several women before her, Penelope, instead of being repelled by the ungainly long torso that was feathered in long straight black hair from his chest to his groin, truly reveled in Hector's scale. Everything was to proportion and Penelope was defiantly vocal in her approval.

"You have the most fantastic penis. Not only is it large, with exactly the right perimeters, it is also aesthetically pleasing—the perfect dick. You look like one of those Pompeian erotic statues— Priapus incarnate," she'd told him with wide-eyed sincerity while kneeling with the tumescent organ under discussion in hand.

A less-educated man might not have appreciated the nuances of her compliment, but Hector was well versed in classical mythology. He understood her references, but it was her appreciation of his appearance that perplexed him. All his life he had thought of himself as ill-made in every physical aspect. To imagine that a part of him was beautiful was inconceivable.

Deeply perplexed, the poor man stared down between his legs. He had never thought of a man's genitals as being attractive before, and certainly not his own—in fact, they'd only been a source of intense embarrassment for him and were indirectly responsible for his stoop, which was a vain attempt to visually neuter any movement in his crotch.

"So does this mean you are really only with me for my body?"

"Absolutely, that and your completely morbid and absurd sense of humor," Penelope concluded, grinning wickedly before taking him back into her mouth with a sensual gluttony that had him, three minutes later, swooning against the wall.

Used to younger men who hadn't the complexity of a mature man, Penelope likened her seduction of the coroner to the metaphor of prizing open an ornate coffin and discovering a well-dressed, debonair corpse, then reviving him. Much of the European's makeup remained a complete mystery to her. None of her usual seduction techniques had worked, and when she finally wangled the reluctant fifty-five-year-old to bed, the discovery that the coroner not only was a good lover but also was physically endowed confirmed to this connoisseur of men that she had great instincts.

As for poor Hector, he was a lost soul. For the first six months he would go to retire still disbelieving that Penelope was actually in his bed, and every morning he would wake terrified this would be the day she would come to her senses and leave him. But she stayed, and it was in the seventh month that he started buying her exotic fruit.

Penelope reached over and picked up the pomegranate. There was something obscenely naked about the skin; the pink and yellow shiny surface reminded her of flesh, or of one huge singular bald testicle. Hector lay sleeping on the other side of the bed, his huge bulk curled up slightly, his black hair bristling like that of an angry armadillo, his snore making a bellows of the bedroom.

The low-ceilinged open-plan room with its minimalist hard-edge furniture reminded Penelope of an expensive hotel room—a luxurious pit stop for transient executives. Had Hector, confronted, as he was daily, by the precariousness of life, concluded that his life was inherently transient? Penelope thought so. She suspected that the coroner had a great unwillingness to invest in his actual day-to-day existence, but that she the wonderful sorceress (as she regarded herself) had slowly begun to transform this reluctance.

When she first moved in she was amazed to discover that his cooking utensils were completely pristine, as if they had never been used. In fact they hadn't. Hector existed only on takeaway food. The only dish he used daily was his coffee cup—even breakfast was a croissant eaten at a local café on the way to work. He'd been completely traumatized when she cooked their first meal, and yet now he was buying fruit.

Fecundity, love, ripeness, their sex—great passionate wrestling that would begin almost arbitrarily, perhaps with a shy caress on the couch while watching a documentary. (They only ever watched documentaries, Hector having no tolerance for fiction. "Fiction is for escapists," he would mumble in his sexy accented half whisper, "for cowards who cannot swallow life's bitter pips, skin and all. We are not cowards, Penelope, we may be shadow people, my love, but our faces are always pressed against the glass, the very edge of life—this is our strength.") His hand would creep up her skirt, caressing with infinite patience and infinite finesse the soft skin of her inner thighs, circle her sex while she sat there trembling, watching the odyssey of the giant sea turtle or whatever epic was unfolding on the television screen, and pretended nothing was happening. It was their game, her way of coaxing him into becoming the initiator, the one who would do the taking. And slowly his fingers would creep closer to her clit (the running monologue in her head now screaming "Touch me touch me" against all that controlled silence), her breath an orchestrated panting through the nose to disguise her growing excitement as he encircled her—the ridges and furls of skin, her growing wetness, the hardened button. All the while their faces were still turned to the television, the façade of detachment separating their heads from the drama of their bodies. Then as he gently pushed two, three, four fingers into her, the sweetness of her excitement would rush over her and she would turn suddenly, bite his neck, and it was only then that their limbs would tear themselves out of their locked positions, and a frantic pushing back of clothes, a mad whirl of zippers, buttons, tearing nylon, as both scrambled to enter the other as soon as possible. And, oh, the size of him, lips squeezing back, the juicy stretching of tissue, the sheer bulk of him filling her.

It was an allegory, she decided, this joyful consummation as her vagina, stretched to its limitation, contained him. It was as if he filled her whole skin, inside and outside. The bulk of him arched over her like a circus tent. Her sad clown, her beanpole, big-cocked lover. She had never known such happiness, and now he had brought her fruit.

Snorting suddenly in his sleep, Hector rolled over onto his back, pushing her to the edge of the bed. She held on to the pomegranate, wondering whether she should save eating it for a special occasion. Then she remembered yesterday's news. That was a special occasion. Her hand slipped down to her belly. She was a slender woman, one of those creatures with the metabolism of a butterfly, constantly vibrating, constantly moving, but now there was a discernible arch to her belly, the faintest of swellings.

Encouraged, she slipped a nail into the pomegranate and peeled back the thick skin. The seeds glistening like small red crystal hexagons. That was one of the reasons why Penelope loved pomegranates, the peculiar mathematical logic to the seeds, as if some celestial gardener had sat down and spent an eternity calculating how to fit as many seeds into the one piece of spherical fruit as mathematically possible. Then, without thinking, she popped seven into her hand and ate them furtively while staring at her sleeping lover.

The taste of the last one still lingered in Penelope's mouth when Hector stirred, one long monkeylike arm reaching lazily across to curl itself around her waist, pulling her down to his damp, sleep-drenched torso. Burying her nose in his chest hair she inhaled deeply, the stiff rod of his penis a hot pushing bar that stretched from her pubis to above her belly button. How she loved his smell. Particularly in the mornings, when the scent of him had collected in the hollows of his body and mixed with sweat and the aroma of half-remembered dreams. The essence of Hector, she called it, appalling him again with her primal naturalness.

She watched him open his big bulbous eyes, his pale green irises dilating like a sleepy reptile's. Lowering her face, she rested her cheek against his erection. His penis (which she could barely wrap her hand around) lay like a hot rabbit against her skin. It smelled delicious as she ran her tongue along the seam that ran up to the helmet that mushroomed out into the full swollen catastrophe. Just touching him made her wet. Somewhere above her, Hector groaned. Stretching her lips over the tip, she took him as deep as she could into her mouth. It wasn't easy, the size of him would often make her gag, but she had learned to relax her throat muscles around him, taking him deeper and deeper. It gave her intense pleasure to give him pleasure, each of his buttocks clasped in her hands as she played his anus, his thighs shaking with intensity as she wound him closer and closer to orgasm.

Sensing he was close, she lifted herself up to his face and as slowly as she could manage lowered herself down onto his cock; his huge face stared up at her in a kind of perplexed bewilderment mixed in with an intense joy he couldn't hide. When she had first seen this look of his, she almost broke into laughter. Now she loved this rare expression of delight that was uniquely his.

Exhaling slowly, she closed her eyes, focusing on the sensation of him entering her. It was unbelievably pleasurable, this viscous stretching that bordered on pain, her clit pushed hard against his shaft. He didn't need to touch any other part of her as she squatted over him like a primitive earth goddess, their two sex organs making an anchor, a sculptural point of contact. Looking down, she thought that she could never leave him. She rode him vigorously, Hector closing his eyes as he tried to hold himself back. Finally he rolled her onto her back, his huge, bulky body arching over her as he pinned her beneath him. Kneeling, he pushed her legs high over each of his shoulders so that she was curled right underneath him like a split peach, each half squeezing against his cock as with a maddening slow pace he entered her over and over, his tip playing just inside her lips, teasing out her orgasm until, feeling her beginning to convulse, he plunged into her fully, burying his seed deep.

Afterward she fell asleep half lying on top of him, her head curled against his massive chest, and found herself dreaming.

She was lying on the small hillock that stretched just before her mother's nursery, a gentle slope that was covered with perfect soft grass. It was a warm spring afternoon and the scent of the newly mown grass rose up in waves around her. Sun warmed her skin and a sense of complete contentment and relaxation flooded her body, stretching all the way down to her extremities—the tips of her fingers and toes. A quiet ecstasy filled her as she snuggled closer into the earth. Suddenly somewhere beneath her was a low rumble that grew louder as the ground began to quake. Sitting up, she blinked in the strong sunlight. The juxtaposition of the innocence of the perfect clear blue sky to the earthquake that was now shaking the ground was extreme. Terrified, Penelope began to run toward her mother's house.

• • •

She woke, her limbs reaching out to an empty bed. Her brain, still pulsing with her dreaming, dimly registered that Hector must have already left for work. Her womb ached. She sat up and after placing one hand over her belly, looked across at the pomegranate. It was sitting in the same spot as before on the side table, its yellow and rose skin catching the early-morning sunlight. It was intact. Strange, she thought to herself blearily; she had the distinct memory of breaking the skin and eating seven seeds of the fruit, to be exact.

Now, it's hard to believe that it actually happened. I mean our relationship. It's like a film sequence that just ends, suspended in air, a length of my life that was so profoundly different to how I was before and how I am now.

Looking back I don't even recognize myself. Was I ever that happy? That's what she brought into my world, this vividness, this profound trust that not all was decay, not all was doomed to entropy. Maybe that's where my liberation lay, in the fact that for the first time in my life someone trusted me—with her happiness, her future, her love. Unthinkable before, unthinkable now, but it did happen, didn't it? She was real, we were lovers?

It happened, Hector. It will happen again, with somebody else.

I don't think so, not at my age.

Every day when I come back from work I have this moment, just before I put the key in the door, when I see the light shining from under the crack. My heart jumps every time before I think she's going to be there, waiting on the couch for me. Every time. I can't push her out of my mind. Even in the middle of an autopsy, what I see before me is not some dissembled poor bastard, but her skin, the twist of pale hair against white skin. Sometimes I can hear her voice, you know, whispering against my shoulder. It's pathetic, I know, I can't let her go. Instead I just lie there night after night, replaying every moment we had, the lovemaking, the conversations—I remember it all.

Sometimes I start talking out loud, right there in my bed alone, arguing some ridiculous intellectual details (we did a lot of that, you know she was always challenging what she saw as my inherent conservatism, she was a natural provocateur), recalling some debate with her, just to change the memory. And you know what's remarkable? I can hear her answering back, clear as a bell.

You have to find closure, Hector.

Closure, what the fuck is that? You don't find closure if you've loved, really loved. Love is an element that runs independent of time. Profound, eh, coming from a withered old coroner, but I should know. I see victims of both every day. Time/love/time/love. The victim of love, the one who has been found with the rope around his neck, his lover's photo fastened to the collar of his jacket with a safety pin, like some kid at a railway station in case he gets lost. That photo is an address. It's a message for the underworld. It's saying, "This is who drove me here, this is who I want to join me in eternity." Why wait?

You telling me you're suicidal?

I don't know, you're the shrink, isn't that your job? I'll tell you this much—sometimes I feel like I killed her. Like I was responsible.

It was a pregnancy that went wrong, these things happen, they are out of our control.

If there was a God and if there had to be a deal struck, I would have offered myself instead of her. Twenty-four years old is too young. No one should be a corpse at that age.

It's tomorrow, you know.

What is?

The due date. She would have given birth tomorrow. Ectopic pregnancy, that's what she died of—but you know that, a pregnancy in the wrong part of the body that burst . . . like a poison seed. We weren't to know. We just wanted to make life.

He unbuckled the Patek Philippe watch and laid it carefully on the dresser; his suit was already hung up in the wardrobe, the tailored white Egyptian cotton shirt folded in the drawer. The scent of freshly ironed and laundered pajamas drifted up and comforted Hector as he pulled back the clean, cool sheets and slipped into the bed.

This was his ritual, the routine he had adhered to every night for the past thirty years. These habits were the underpinning, the small gestures that had stopped him from floating off into a hemisphere of crushing loneliness. Now they stopped him from stumbling and hitting the ground under the avalanche of grief that had become his waking existence.

Before he switched the lamp off he stared across at the pomegranate. He hadn't the heart to remove it since her death seven months ago. Its skin now withered, it was a calcified parody of itself—a wrinkled, decaying fruit, the only organic thing left in the room.

Among the Living

Andrija Popovic

Life is wasted on the living.

Trust me. I'm dead. It gives you a little perspective on things.

I ran into a sensitive, someone who can see and hear the dead, just once. He chatted with me as if I were still alive and corporeal. "What's it like being a ghost?" he asked.

"Well, it's like being on vacation in a foreign country." He looked puzzled. I explained. "You never appreciate the familiar, mundane things in life until you're an ocean away from them."

The world barely exists for me. When I touch a flower, I feel its presence, but nothing else. I could pass my hand through the flower, but I couldn't hold it. Or smell it. Or feel the thorns prick the meat of my thumb.

Death separates you from the world.

James Van Hollen died ten years ago and was born into this world. In death I haunted the same places I knew in life. I mimicked my old existence because I knew nothing better. I left the world alone, never trying to escape my little slice of hell.

Then Anna walked into my home.

I lived in a two-level studio apartment, a wonderful place with a living area and kitchen on the first floor, an iron spiral staircase, and a spacious open bedroom area on the second floor. Massive bay windows caught every mote of light the day offered. For a late photographer like me, it was perfect.

Anna, also a photographer, thought it was perfect, too.

She shattered my world the moment she stepped through the door. Her raven-black hair bounced in long curls against the small of her back. I watched her ice-blue eyes cut the room into hundreds of tiny portraits. The sweaty movers, eyeing the lines of her black bra through her tight gray shirt, were a minor disruption compared to Anna and her things.

Everything swirled into a time-lapse photo. Walls that had held my carefully composed still-life photos and nighttime cityscapes now carried darkly erotic photographs. My simple, sparse, and mismatched furniture gave way to Persian rugs and arabesque seating arrangements.

The true work did not begin until darkness fell. She stripped down to her tiger-striped panties and scrubbed everything until it glowed. At night's end, she turned on her stereo system, fell onto her simple mattress, and played with herself.

I watched her. I crouched beside her mattress; my ethereal legs crossed, I watched her fingers vanish beneath her underwear. The fabric rose and fell in a lazy beat. Beads of sweat, already dotting her naked chest from the day's exertions, deepened and ran along her skin. Her left hand cupped ample breasts and tugged at dark nipples.

"Oh, dear God," I said. I burned. My normal form, a shadow of my old body writ in dark gray smoke, glowed like a hot iron. I felt myself growing erect. The painful rigidity, long forgotten, shocked me from my seat on the floor. As I tried stumbling to my feet, my hand pressed against her bare shoulder.

I felt her. I felt her skin, hot from desire, damp from sweat, against the back of my hand. God help me, I could smell her. For the first time since I died, I could smell.

Anna, too wrapped up in her pleasures, ignored my epiphany. She moaned and thrashed, twisting in the sheets. Sweat beaded on her clavicle. I reached out and touched her with the tip of my index finger.

She shuddered as if she felt me. I ran my finger along her skin, between her breasts. Sweat parted under my touch. Anna rose beneath me. I cupped her breast. Her nipple swelled beneath my palm. She sighed and stretched, toes curling as orgasm came near. I kneeled down and kissed her left nipple. I could taste her; the sharp tang of sweat, the light rasp of erect skin against my tongue, all of it came into focus.

The moment Anna came, I felt alive again.

Anna loved baths. My simple shower was replaced with a massive twin-headed standing shower and a whirlpool tub. On busy days, she would quickly wash under the twin showerheads. Every Friday night, between returning home from the clubs and going to sleep, she would soak in the tub for an hour.

In either case, she kept a waterproof tape recorder nearby. Any images that came to mind, she recorded. She never played it back. The recording was more a comfort than a necessity.

"A thunderstorm. I can see it in the distance. She's on the rooftop, naked except for black vinyl pants—there should be raindrops on it. She watches the street. More of a landscape shot. Need to sketch it out later."

Today was a shower day—a quick one before reviewing negatives on her computer and then heading to a photo shoot in some pretentiously named club or other—and I joined her in the shower. I felt the water. Not the way I once could; if I stood in a rainstorm now, the heavy drops passed through me with ease. But with her nearby, I felt the warmth and the moisture.

"I wish you could hear me," I said under my breath. I fixed my gaze on her face. Not out of any need to be modest on my part, but because I wanted to see her eyes when she opened them. Since taking over my loft, I'd grown accustomed to seeing her in everything from full vinyl club gear to nothing but a thin sarong. Her body was beautiful, but her eyes entranced.

"A figure watches the city." She spoke into the recorder the way one would whisper into a confidant's ear. The gears clicked as she started and stopped the recording, gathering her thoughts before committing them. "A woman, bare feet, bare chest, just the long vinyl pants with rain on them, crouched like a cat as the lights go by. Night shoot. Have to do some Photoshop work to matte the time-lapse car lights and her on the roof."

"Hell, I wish there was another sane dead person I could talk to about all this," I said. I leaned against the shower walls. Cold. The tiles were cold and wet. Not a dull cold, not like death, but a sharp prick against the skin. "I don't want to become a yammerer. I met one, once, before he just faded away. He did nothing but talk to people about anything that came to his mind, just to talk to someone. He ignored me; just talked as if I weren't there. Only the living mattered to him."

"Still wish I could get Sebastian to pose for me," she said.

I blinked. "Sebastian? You mean the skinny one with the dark hair and the witch's lock?" I asked.

"I've got a whole series of photos that would be just perfect with him . . ."

"He's got a very angular face. And he's wiry. I can see why you'd find him attractive." Death did me one kindness. No physical form meant I didn't have love handles and an overhanging gut, either. It was a small kindness, but I took what I could get. "But he's wrong for those photos. Low-key, soft focus lighting with someone who looks like Iggy Pop's crackhead brother? They'll look like crap."

"Maybe I'll just do some test digital shots before I make any final decisions."

I nodded. "Smart move."

She shut off the water and wrapped herself in a towel. I followed her out, stepping where she stepped. I'd almost left a set of vague footprints the last time. I didn't want to make that mistake again. The last thing I needed was a crew of exorcists trying to discorporate me.

Anna wrapped herself in a tiny robe and went to her computer. She scanned in the latest batch of negatives the lab had returned and triaged them. Dead ten years, and photography had changed completely. I remember doing this by hand, with contact sheets and a grease pencil.

"Let's see if these are any good," she said as the images arranged themselves into a series of thumbnails.

"I can give you composition pointers," I said. "But I'm not that good with portraits." I sat down in an empty chair beside her. Not that I needed the seat—it just felt more human to me.

All of this felt more human. I understood why the yammerers did what they did. Especially near the end when they could sense they were disappearing. They felt real. In the right mind-set, you could imagine this was a real conversation, not just two monologues. And there were times I thought to myself—"Hey, she heard me" or "She saw me that time," even if it wasn't true.

She saved the digital contacts and headed for the closet. Tonight was another shoot at La Boutique Noir; another job for her clubbing outfit.

"I'm too fat," she said as she stepped into a black thong and looked at herself in the mirror.

"Oh, gods, not again," I said. She did this to herself every time she went out.

"These hips have to go." She stepped into a pair of leather pants.

"No, they don't. I like your hips. I like all your curves." One thing hadn't changed since I was alive. All the beautiful women I knew thought they were ugly. No matter what I told them, they refused to believe otherwise.

"Oh, as for where all the good men are, they're dead," I said. She'd slipped on a black bra and a long-sleeved mesh shirt with silver Celtic decorations along the belly. It matched her bomber jacket. "Well, dead or just not anorectically pretty."

Anna ran a comb through her hair, collected her camera bag and tripod, and headed out.

"But," I said, "mostly, the good guys are dead . . ."

It's all Sebastian's fault.

Life in hell teaches you to be resourceful. And the last few months had made me very resourceful. I suppose I should thank him. Ever since Anna developed a "relationship" with him, I've been forced to discover myself just to keep from going batshit.

I learned, for example, that I touch the memories items held without difficulty. Not their physical form but their emotional residue. Thus, this journal, the quill pen I'm holding in my hand, and a few books of quaint and forgotten lore are now mine to keep.

I learned that my whispers might not go unheeded. After just an hour of describing the similarities between semen and human phlegm, I drained Sebastian's erection the first time he found himself feeling "unprofessional" during a photo shoot.

Oh, and I learned how much I hated watching her be with him. She glowed. Living became an erotic experience for her. The air was charged. I touched and smelled and tasted without hindrance. I touched her. When she toyed with herself in the shower, or in bed, or while reading, I would join in. The heat of their passion let me share in her world for a brief moment. I imagined I was making love to her and that she was thinking about me, instead of her anorectic boy toy.

And I also learned that when I get angry, I could interact with the physical world. Forcefully. That was a hard lesson to learn.

"Okay, I think I might break him some nights. You happy?" Anna sat beside the bathtub; a bottle of Tilex dangled from her fingers and her cell phone nestled against her ear. Her friend Theresa called just as she was in the middle of an "I need to get things clean, so I'll strip naked and scrub every exposed surface" binge. I kept telling her that she wouldn't need the cleaning binges if she cleaned a little every day, but who listens to the dead?

"Still, I've been thinking about last night," she continued. I stepped off the bedroom balcony into the air above the living room. Another trick I discovered; when you're dead, gravity is entirely perceptual. "Yeah, I think he meant it." She brushed her hair from her eyes as she spoke.

I walked above the living room. The air felt cold against my feet, like I was walking on a thin sheet of ice.

"What am I going to say? I think I'm going to say yes," she said. Anna stood up and rested her arms against the loft's railing. "He doesn't have much. So he'll probably be able to move in soon . . ."

The ice shattered and I fell into the living room in slow motion. I saw the hardwood floor and glass-topped coffee table rise up to meet me. It would have made a beautiful photograph.

I caught myself before passing through the table. I could hear bits of her conversation drifting downward. "Sebastian . . . his things . . . sleeping with me, duh . . ."

"He's moving in," I said. "The fucker is moving in."

Without thinking, I rammed my fist through the table. Months—no, years—of frustration burned its way into the glass tabletop and left a fist-sized hole. Shards of cracked and melted glass chimed on the hardwood floor. Anna leapt to the railing and stared at the violated table. I thought she was looking right at me.

"Sorry . . ." I said.

"What?" She blinked and picked up the phone. "Wha? I dunno. The glass table broke. Probably a bolt falling from the ceiling beams . . ."

I sank into the couch and hid among the springs and cushions. "I can't believe it," I said. Not so much that I could interact with the real world—I've seen ghost movies, I know that much—but that I felt this way.

But I did feel that way. I felt jealous, angry, hurt, and a hundred other emotions. I felt the way any man would, watching a woman he loved move in with another. It was the only thing I had felt since my death. And somehow, I had to tell her.

I pushed myself out of the couch. When the fabric and stuffing cleared my vision, I saw Anna. She stood beside the table, arms crossed, looking me dead in the eye.

"Hi," she said. "I guess this means we can finally talk."

"That's it," she gasped. "Unh . . . please, harder . . ."

Anna rose and fell, like a ship on rough seas. Sweat ran down her hair. It fanned out against her naked back. She leaned forward, grabbed the bedclothes for support, and ground her pelvis against Sebastian's hips. The mattress banged the wall as the force of her thrusts slid everything back and forth on the wood floor.

"God!" Sebastian spat. His thrusts did not dent Anna's desire or energy. He lay back, pinned to the bed, and was ridden. A deathly white came over him. His pained body strained under Anna's assault.

She was close. I could feel it. Anna flipped her hair back and shot me a long look. It wouldn't be long now.

"I said yes so he would move in and I could see you more often," she said.

"You can see me? And hear me?" I blurted out. My knees gave way and I sank back inside the couch. Only my head and shoulders appeared above the cushions. "Oh, gods, you could feel me, too."

"But that's the point, James, isn't it?" She paused. "I can call you James, right?"

"You know who I am?" I said. Anna sat down on the couch beside me, toes inches away from my ethereal nose.

"It's one of the reasons I bought this loft. You're one of my favorite photographers. If I could afford them, I'd have your prints all over this place." I must have gotten more popular after my death. Typical. "So when I first heard you walking around, I had to get this place. And when you touched me—"

"Oh, God in heaven, I'm sorry about that. Please, please understand. I could touch! I could feel your skin. Not just that it was there but the texture and oh, shit, I'm making it worse." I covered my head with my hands.

"Hey?" Anna brushed her toes against my hand. "I don't think you get it. I liked it when you touched me."

Anna dangled at the edge of pleasure, every nerve afire, and he climaxed just a moment too soon. He jumped and jerked like a toad on an electrified floor, then collapsed in exhaustion, leaving Anna in a cloud of frustration. Flaccid and spent, Sebastian drifted to sleep and snored.

She slipped free of him and watched him until he slept. It was always this way. They made love with Anna as the dominant partner while Sebastian mostly sat or stood there. After a noisy and wet orgasm, he would try to be sociable, but always passed out in the end.

Anna walked into the shower. She trailed her hand through me, fingers pressing into my nebulous chest. Water sluiced onto the tiles as she spun the taps. A toe ventured inside, testing the temperature, before she stepped under the spray. I joined her. Steam collected around me; I'd gained a halo.

Shampoo drizzled into Anna's hand. She worked it through her hair. I ran my finger through the lather. Strands of wet hair clung together on my hand. I concentrated, cupping my fingers together and catching water in my palm, then splashing it down her back.

She laughed.

"So that's all that separates us? A little passion?"

"No," she said. "A lot of passion. And death."

"Death? I've learned to live with death," I said. "The passion might take getting used to."

Anna raised her hands. Water trickled down her fingertips as she toyed with the spray. I leaned close and kissed her throat. Her skin tasted a little metallic and the soapy strawberry flavor of her shampoo tickled. She curled her arms around me. Not being entirely visible, she explored by touch and taste. Her fingers dipped down my back, tracing my spine, curving with my buttocks.

With the tip of my finger, I connected the water droplets on her skin, merging one into another until they ran down her breasts. I followed the track with my mouth. She kept her hands on my head, pressing me close as I lapped at her dark and soapy areola.

"I can almost see you," she said. "You're a halo of steam. Translucent . . ."

"Double-exposure effect?" I asked before kissing her navel.

"No. More like you were airbrushed on acetate, or a very carefully done Photoshop effect—ah!" Anna stiffened as my tongue parted her labia and found her clitoris. I suckled on her, trilling my spectral tongue against her sensitive bud. She grabbed on to the shower supports with one hand and turned her tape recorder on with the other.

"Series of photo shoots designed to show off darkroom and digital techniques. Very explicit, ohhh, gods, harder . . . Um, images of people alone with ghost lovers—mmm, fuck, yes . . ."

Life is wasted on the living. Most of the time. But not on Anna. Every moment contained the raw stuff of inspiration for her.

Death is often wasted on the dead, too. They sit around and do nothing, mocking those who try to interact with the world. The lucky ones learn better and appreciate what they have.

". . . and they should be black and white—Ah, gods, don't you dare fucking stop, mmm. Uh, yeah, a lot of skin texture in the scenes. Oil and water work. Ohhh . . ."

Me, I have heaven.

A Satisfactory Resolution

Josephine Chia

My mother always told me, "Noorita, if you want to keep your husband, remember that the best way to a man's heart is through his stomach and his vital organ."

Mothers talked like that in our *kampung* out in colonial Malaya. Mak, short for Emak—"Mother" in Malay—should know. She was a cook par excellence and had sixteen children, I being the youngest. Until the day my father was nailed in his coffin, he never strayed from her side. Especially since there was no other woman as beautiful as my mother in our remote village. Our community of *attap*-thatched huts was on the east coast, whose white-sand beaches faced the South China Sea, far away from other towns and our capital, Kuala Lumpur. You would have to cross the peninsula's midsection of jungle and mountain ranges, which later became Taman Negara, our national park, to get to our *kampung*, hence we were far less accessible than the places along the west coast. This was before international hotel chains discovered our scenic spots and built their American-style hotels along the seafront, snatching the beaches from us locals and making our houses on stilts look antiquated, or, as the British colonists would say, "Oh, so charming."

I didn't know how Caucasian daughters were taught to please their men, but from puberty our mothers taught us how to cook enticing dishes and how to create a beautiful home in whatever circumstances.

"Money alone does not make a home," Mak often said. "It is love and devotion which do. Beauty is attention to all that is fine and graceful. You can create artistic ornaments from mere driftwood and seashells."

More important, we were schooled in the art of satisfying a husband. We practiced daily, squeezing our nether muscles so that we were tight enough to hold a pencil, and in some cases, even write with it. You would have to be able to squat properly with your heels flat on the floor before you could attempt this muscular feat. Cabaret girls in Hadyaii, Pattaya, and Bangkok illustrate this skill in public as if it were unique to them, calling such demonstrations tiger shows. On the streets of Patpong in Bangkok, pimps hold up signboards as if they were menus with prices: PUSSY WRITING WITH PEN, PUSSY SMOKING CIGAR, PUSSY OPENING COKE BOTTLE, and such like. For the uninitiated provincial tourist from the West, they could be talking about well-trained cats. I could just imagine a staid matron, a lover of cats from somewhere in Cornwall or Scotland, visiting Bangkok for the first time and paying to see the show, thinking it might be a feline equivalent of *Crufts* and then, after watching it, becoming suitably enlightened. For my sisters and me, the exercise was just a normal process of our education. It was no secret that Asian women had something different from their Western sisters. And I'm not talking about a slit that ran horizontally, either.

In some ways, the days before piped water and electricity were idyllic; rustic life was congenial and contained. Life for our fishermen fathers, husbands, and brothers revolved around the weather at sea and their skills in drawing in the nets, mending them, and maintaining the sampans that took them out to sea. Our tasks as females were to plant and grow fruits and vegetables for our table and to clean the fish and to provide nocturnal recreation for our seafarers. Occasionally, we might have a glimpse of fair skin and blond hair belonging to the adventurous who had braved the jungles to our distant shores. They were so fair that our term for them was *orang putih*, literally "white people." As more and more of them arrived, we made straw mats and boxes, cane baskets and fancy kites to sell. We were known for our colorful kites that were shaped like all sorts of birds and mythological creatures and when they were up in the sky in a kite-fighting competition, it was truly a sight to behold. When our national airline broke away in partnership from Singapore's national airline, our new logo consisted of a kite. The winds on our shores were very strong and kite flying was a great pastime with an annual competition to boot.

"We are ruined," the elder of our village lamented when hotel chains started building their luxurious hotels along our beaches and forbade us to enter areas that used to be our own private hideaways. "The white people will destroy our way of life and infiltrate our culture."

In this world, nothing is white or black. Good could come out of bad and vice versa. With the emergence of smart hotels came electricity and piped water for the villages. And then came television, the Pandora's box that showed me the attractions of the world outside our *kampung*. I was just entering my teenage years and the sight of all that luxury and smart people in smart clothes moving around in luxurious automobiles in a world that was not subjected to the vagaries of the weather or smelly fish made me restless. I longed to be like Emma Peel, living a life of adventure, entirely in control of her fate, rather than letting a father or brother or husband dictate how she should live. Then again, maybe I would opt to be like Joan Collins's Alexis with all her millions and her life of pure luxury, her beautiful clothes. Or maybe I would just be happy if I fell madly in love with a handsome white man who would take me to that world, away from this small village, which had suddenly became claustrophobic and provincial.

More and more white people came, lying on the beach for hours, like fish being dried in the sun. We were deep brown by nature and when it was possible, we tried to escape from the harsh tropical sun so that we might get the chance to whiten. And here were people doing exactly the opposite, coveting the sun, oiling themselves as if they were about to be roasted over burning coals to brown themselves. It was an interesting phenomenon for us watching these people whom we secretly thought were mad. And what was more exciting for our men was that some of the young white women were unabashed at taking off their bikini tops to offer their breasts to the sun and to the hungry gaze of our men's eyes. The men sat by these women's feet, pretending to sell them our home-made crafts or to engage them in conversation about local folklore, when all the time, they were staring at their large exposed breasts. And one thing that *was* different about our Western sisters was that they do have breasts that are sizable, compared to our own pathetic mounds of nothing. They made us feel inadequate. But I soon discovered that our dark complexion was considered an asset.

"You are beautiful," people kept saying to me. And strangely, I grew beautiful in my own mind. This was a change from the vision I had of myself as a thin, flat-chested, dark girl that nobody would look at twice. It was amazing how you could be both ugly and beautiful all at once, just by a change of perspective and viewpoint. Of course, we humans have the inclination to go where we are wanted, needed, accepted, or praised, so it was no wonder that I gravitated toward the *orang putih* in my search for the romance of my life.

One early morning when the boats were in and everyone was busy helping to bring the catch in, I hurried away from the hustle and bustle to my favorite spot in a quiet corner of the beach, to sit on a uprooted trunk of a coconut tree to watch the sun rising. I loved the way the sun slipped out of the horizon in haste as if it were late and rushing upward into the sky like a ball someone had thrown.

"Hi," he said, appearing by my side.

Startled, I looked up to see a shock of blond hair and amazing blue eyes, and my knees turned to jelly. Lightning zapped through my entire being. Both clichéd but true. Love can happen. Stories in storybooks don't materialize from nothing. Whatever is not true must have been conjured up from the depth of the writer's desires that fuel her imagination. Life without such hope, without such yearning for the fanciful and impossible, is rational but arid.

I dropped my eyes quickly like a good girl, as I had been trained to do. Mak always said, "Never look directly at a man. He will think you are bold."

"You are the most beautiful girl I have ever seen," he said with that voice of his that had the capacity to make my nether regions react in a way that all the exercises I had done before had not. Was that a sign that I had fallen madly in love with him? Or was it madly in lust? I had never been so turned on by someone before. It was the way he focused totally on me, as if no one existed but me. As I bent my head to look down, my long hair fell across my face. Without pausing, he brushed my hair aside so that he could look at me. As his hand brushed across my forehead, I swore it was like fire rushing across a dry field of *lallang*.

"I'm James," he said. "What's your name?"

"Noorita," I mumbled. And when asked, repeated it again.

"Your voice is like the ocean," he said, and I took this to mean it sounded good. Everything he said about me sounded good. He asked me questions, told me about himself. But all I was aware of was his body. I had never been so conscious of another's body before, or of my own needs. Perhaps he sensed it, too, because he took my chin.

"Don't look away," he said. "You have such deep brown pools for your eyes, I could drown in them."

You must be aware that I was not used to such fancy talk and was completely convinced and smitten. Then he did the unspeakable, at least in my society in that era. He took my lips in his! I reacted instinctively by attempting to free myself, but he was not easily dissuaded. His arms went around me and his lips gripped mine with a measure of force but also with a profound sweetness I had never known before. My nether region was throbbing like crazy! I had never known what it was like to desire a man. Now I did and I was ecstatic. So I started to kiss him back. He pushed his body into mine and I liked the feel of it and pushed myself into him. He started to grow in his trousers, hardening—this was magic! I, who was considered dark and ugly, could wield this power in a man! Surely this must be the greatest thing that could happen to a woman. His breath was quickening, I could feel it on the side of my face. He started to unbutton my blouse. Thinking of all those Western women with their beautiful large breasts, I was suddenly ashamed and grabbed his hands to stop him.

"No," I said. "I have nothing there. I'm so ugly."

"Let me be the judge of that," he said as he gently moved my hands away and for the first time in my life, someone other than me looked upon my miserable mounds that passed as breasts.

"They're perfect," he said as he put his mouth to my nipples.

From those words, from that moment, I was his. Yet I played hard to get. After all, my mother had always said, "If you give of yourself completely, why should he marry you? *Kalau sudah dapat makan, tak kan dia nak beli.* If the food is already eaten, why should he have to buy it?" Besides, men enjoyed the chase, the hunter in them surfacing. Offering everything to them easily takes away the thrill. So I let James pursue me, return again and again to the village, our courtship getting more daring each time, but I ensured that it remained unconsummated until we were married and he took me back to his own country.

"Jesus! That was well worth waiting for!" he exclaimed at our first consummation. "How on earth did you do that?"

"It's my specialty," I said, using my newly learned humor.

"God, I've never had anything like it. The orgasm was so strong I nearly passed out. No wonder the French call an orgasm *la petite mort*. 'Little death!' How did you manage it?"

"Well, it's a case of being able to control the sets of muscles down there. Most women simply clench the first set of muscles near the opening of the vagina. We were taught to squeeze each set of muscles in turn with the penis inside so that it gets a rhythmic pulsation right along its length. It requires practice."

"I'll bet! What may I ask do you practice on?"

"Oh, necks of bottles. But mainly fruits and vegetables. We had not heard of vibrators then. At least our mothers hadn't."

"Pray tell."

"Well, for bottles, the strong glass type with long necks. But the hazard there was that if you squeezed too hard, the bottle could break. Picking shards of glass out of there isn't much fun, I can tell you. Fruits and vegetables are much safer. The obvious one is the banana with its skin on. But after a lot of exercises on it, the banana does become squashy and makes a mess. Carrot is okay but not wonderful. Moolie is a good one because it has better thickness than the carrot. But the best one of all is the aubergine. Aubergines here are not of the right shape, but in Asia we get the long variety with a suitable curve and an excellent head. The greatest advantage is that it is smooth-skinned and so it's comfortable. Unlike the solidity of carrots and moolie, the aubergine has a little give in its texture which is very much like flesh. I must show you it next time we're out there."

"I wouldn't be able to keep a straight face if I am served it at a meal."

It was his sense of humor I liked best. And his blue eyes, which were sprinkled with laughter dust.

Alas, fairy tales do end. Beautiful princesses do wake up from their long-drugged sleep. But Prince Charming usually endures. A bit older and grayer perhaps, but these are not disadvantageous in a man. Especially *not* in a man who has vintage cars, yachts, and an easily accessible Platinum credit card.

"Are you coming home for dinner, James?" I asked as I saw him busy himself showering and picking out his best clothes. I hate the despair in my own voice at the prospect of another evening without him. He was oblivious to my mood. Having the children for company was wonderful, but it was not the same.

"How can I keep you to the lifestyle you've become used to if I don't work all the hours that God gave me?"

"It's Saturday, James. I don't want this lifestyle if you have to be away all the time. It would be nice if you are around more. You hardly ever see the children."

"That's your job, isn't it, to take care of them? Mine is to feed them. Four is a lot to educate, you know. Don't you want to see them in the best schools, the best universities? How will we pay for this if I don't work like I do? You think I do this for fun?"

"Are you having an affair, James? You promised me that we will be honest with each other. It's the one thing I cannot bear. I can take the kids back to Malaysia. They can be with their grandparents and cousins, spend more time outdoors, live a different kind of life than here in London."

"Don't be ridiculous. You are getting paranoid."

I could stomach poverty, entertain loneliness in a new country, be subjected to a foreign culture and foreign habits and customs, weather the miserable rain. But the one thing I would not be tolerant of was a husband's unfaithfulness. After all, I gave up so much to be with James, created a beautiful home for him, gave him lovely children, cooked for him, was available for constant and good sex, was the companion he wanted—everything that was expected of a good wife. He had no reason to be dissatisfied. But if he fell in love with another, I could understand, because love is not a conscious thing, it can happen. But I wanted to be told.

Maybe I was getting paranoid, but I observed that his moods were changing; there were less smiles and laughter for me. Everything I said or did made him testy. He was coming home late more and more often, was away most weekends. I found receipts of purchases and credit cards left inadvertently in pockets that had no bearing on our life; he was taking or making calls on his mobile in the garden. All these were taking their toll on my mental constitution. But the thing was that even if he were getting something from someone out there, our sex life never faltered. It was the one thing that reassured me that he still loved me or assured me that he had not found anyone else to make ripples of pleasure along the whole of his penis. When the day came when he did find someone, I was sure I'd be thrown out like an unwanted old shoe. Even after being married for ten years, we still went at it like dogs in heat. Mostly a morning glory session these days because he would be too tired by the time he came home. My training in working the nether region had been worth it. At least so I told myself. It was possible that he did love me but could not cope with monogamy, or he might be a sex athlete, or worse, one of those who had a sex addiction.

"James," I called before he stepped out the door in his best silk shirt and smelling of Givenchy for yet another evening at some dinner that I was not invited to.

"What?"

"Remember what I told you before. If you come home to tell me you are in love with someone else, I shall be reasonable. We can part amicably and you can move out and live with your lover. You only need to tell me. But if I find out that you've been seeing someone else and have been lying to me, I will cut it off. No questions asked. It's the Asian way."

In our summery love days, I had recounted to him tales of such incidents where such things happened in the Far East. Crimes of passion. Mrs. Bobbit was not the first one to make tabloid history, only the first one to hit the Western media with her deed. Betrayed and scorned Asian women have been known to drug their husbands, which put them in a half stupor, then they would cut off their husbands' penises. There was never any intention to poison the men or to knock them out completely, for they had to suffer for their sin: they had to be made to watch the decapitation of the object of betrayal. Mothers have been known to assist with glee, brewing the tea that held the opiate. Surgeons were geared to stitching these things back on.

"Make sure you wrap your dismembered part in ice to keep it alive on your journey to the hospital," they advised.

James used to laugh and say, "Ouch! You make me shrivel with such talk. But you'd better be sure before you do such a thing."

"You have nothing to worry about if you remain faithful."

This time, though, he gave a slightly nervous laugh and said, "You know, I could have you put away. You're crazy! Mad."

"I'm not joking," I warned him.

He turned his back to me, walked out, and slammed the door in my face.

Of course, he was cheating, the bastard! I hacked into his e-mails. He was not aware that even deleted e-mails could be read. Love letters, sexy outpourings that were so intense I could have come myself if I had not been so furious! Sweat ran from my brow. He was truly a dirty rat. He had not been faithful since he brought me back to this country. One girlfriend for every pregnancy. I could just imagine him using his persuasive voice to tell some young girl how his wife did not want sex as soon as she got pregnant. How overweight she was. Men have a way of putting themselves forward as the injured party, the one requiring lots of TLC and sympathy. "You are the most beautiful girl I have ever seen!"; "What perfect breasts!"; "What gorgeous eyes!" Bloody hell! Even his vocabulary was limited. Words that he once used to me that I thought were precious were handed out like sweets to these other paramours. Nothing was sacred to him. *That* really hurt. Bastard. I could kill him. But he was not worthy of a quick death. Besides, he was still the father of my children.

But I had an idea. He must be made to be hoisted with his own petard. Pretty simple, really. Down to more exercises for my nether region. Having given birth naturally to the children instead of opting for the designer cesarean section that was popular these days had taken a bit of a toll, and I had some catching-up work to do—and more, for what I had in mind. Contract and release. Contract and release. In the interim period, James would enjoy extra-stimulating sex. I would make sure of that. He must not suspect a thing. I would go about as if I did not know of his betrayal. If I confronted him and started a quarrel, he would be put off with having sex with me. Of course, now that I knew about his affairs, I could no longer see it as lovemaking. The deed first, then I will serve the divorce papers on him. Meanwhile, it was of paramount importance that we continued to have sex. My plan was hinged on this taking place. I would make sure that when the time came, I would be on top of him—it was one of his favorite positions. He said he could go in deeper like that and he could fondle my breasts, which were now made larger by having the children and breast-feeding. In that position, it was I who controlled the penetration. I would make doubly sure that he was very, very erect—that would make the deed easier. A flaccid penis with loose skin like a turkey's neck was more difficult to slice into. He would be in such ecstasy; he wouldn't know what hit him—until after. *La petite mort* indeed. It would be a satisfactory resolution for me.

All manner of things have been inserted into a woman's vagina in the pursuit of erotic pleasure. But the thing I was going to put in mine for James was going to be extra special. Yes, very special indeed. Inserting the thing would require diligent practice if I was not going to nick myself. It had to be a hinged ring with blades and a spring so that it could be inserted like a Dutch cap, with the two semicircular halves folded over, and once it was secure in its position could be opened out into a full circle, the blades facing inward, like a circular guillotine. I would have to have it specially designed and made, of course, find some craftsman or engineer. It would have to be a device that I could control with my nether muscles. When the moment came, with James inside me at the height of orgasm, all I needed to do was squeeze tight the inner set of muscles and the spring would be activated to clamp it shut around his penis. A rat trap. The more I squeezed my muscles, the tighter the vice would be. It might require superhuman effort to force the blades to meet, but I would certainly give it my best shot. Of course, the edges had to be sharp. Exceedingly sharp. Something that could easily and efficiently top a carrot.

Garden of Earthly Delights

Adréana Robbins

I am seated at an outdoor café in Madrid. Across the street is the Museo del Prado, where I have spent the entire morning admiring the phenomenal collection of old masters. As a souvenir, I have purchased art postcards of my favorite paintings—*The Naked Maja*, by Goya, a pale and sensuous nude. Then there is *The Maids of Honor*, by Diego Velázquez, where the painter has placed himself in the royal portrait. Lastly, and perhaps my favorite of all, is *The Garden of Earthly Delights*, by Hieronymus Bosch. The first time I saw the surrealistic late-fifteenth-century masterpiece, I was on my honeymoon, and my husband leaned over to kiss me and whispered, "I promise to show you thousands of delights." That he did. But now my fond memories can no longer sustain me, for it is in Madrid where I choose to die.

My table is close to a gushing fountain. My bare arms and shoulders are being splashed; my black summer dress is becoming soaked. Passersby can see the outline of my firm breasts. But I don't care. This is the hottest summer that I can remember. One hundred and ten degrees. Then again, I complain every summer when I'm working, wishing I were vacationing instead on a breezy Greek island or on the French Riviera, sailing on a yacht near Saint-Jean-Cap-Ferrat.

A young woman with waist-length jet-black hair and a flowing crimson dress passes by my table. She looks as though she belongs on a theatrical stage, and at any moment will break into a flamenco. Instead, she stops, curtsies, and displays a collection of Spanish fans, waving them in her outstretched hands like a Balinese dancer. I must buy one and hand her several Euros. The fan I select is made of crimson satin and black lace and has an etching of a matador slaying a bull.

Once the lady is gone, I order a glass of cold sangria and play with my fan. It opens and closes with a twist of my hand and a snap of my wrist. The fan makes a bursting sound when it opens, similar to that of a peacock spreading its wings. My newfound toy occupies me until my drink arrives.

I am served an enormous goblet of sangria with slices of fresh peaches, oranges, and plums floating on the top. If only I could float away into oblivion with the sweet fruit. Before I taste my first sip, a man seated at a table behind me calls out, *"Buenos días."*

I try ignoring him for a while, until curiosity gets the best of me. Turning to look at him, I hide part of my face behind the opened fan. I have to admit that he is surprisingly attractive. And I've found no one appealing during my sojourn in Spain, but that was never my intention. The stranger has a thick mane of brown hair, flecked with amber and gold, that falls to his neck. Dressed in Levi's and a blue cotton Polo shirt, he has the mixture of vibrant health and ruggedness that would be perfect for a Marlboro man. When he smiles at me, I once again bashfully look away.

If I were living in another era, and if I *desired* him, all I would have to do is drop my fan and he'd rush to pick it up. But I don't want him, or anyone, for that matter, unless *death* is his name.

I had almost achieved the final exit in New York, London, Rome. I've stood on the edge of tall bridges, wanting to jump. I've gazed forlornly into the Hudson, the Thames, the Tiber. But the water always seemed too cold and foreign. But now, Madrid—in the peak of summer—seems satisfyingly familiar and is a finer place to die. All that is missing is a river, a deep sea. I must figure out another method of escape.

Closing my eyes, I feel a swaying ocean beneath me. I have finished my drink and exceeded my limit. Somehow I manage to pay my bill and leave my table.

It doesn't take long before he follows. Does he know I am fragile? Intoxicated? Should I say something? The sound of his boots echoes on the cobblestone streets. Who wears boots in the summer, anyway? He must be a fool. I ignore him and continue walking, entering the magnificent Buen Retiro gardens.

My first stop is by *El Angel Caido*, the monument of the fallen angel. When do we begin to fall from earth? In Bosch's painting, there is a bird-headed monster devouring damned souls. How do we know if we're damned? After taking a slow promenade through the park, I finally rest on a ledge by *El Estanque Grande*, the Big Pond. It is still hot, even under the shaded chestnut trees. I open my fan and circulate the warm air. Dipping my fingers into the pond, I stare at the glaucous green water. The enormous lake is teeming with trout. Schools of fish rush toward my fingers, thinking I'm food. Hundreds of hungry, shimmering mouths open for me. Fish, like people, are never satisfied. We always want more of something good, especially once it's gone.

I reach into my purse and hunt for a cigarette. The Marlboro man has one ready before I can find my pack of Merits. He slides in next to me, sits down, and strikes a match.

"I thought I was alone," I say.

"Would you like one?" he asks, patiently holding out his pack.

I'm too tired to search for my own. "Okay. Thank you. You followed me," I say.

He pauses after a drag of his cigarette. "I had to. When something or someone captures me, I go for it. Anyway, you left these on your table." He hands me my art postcards.

"I can't believe I did that. Thank you."

"What's your name?" he asks.

"Christine," I reply.

"Cool. I'm Luc."

"Cool Hand Luc?" I tease.

"Yeah, sure," he says with a peevish smile. "I've got a big gun in my pocket and boy am I happy to see you!"

I don't want to look at the bulge in his blue jeans. Yet I can't help but notice that which I'm trying to avoid.

"Where you from?" I ask.

"L.A. And you?"

"Paris."

"I thought so. French girls are so elegant and sexy."

I don't bother explaining that I'm only half French, on my mother's side; the other half is English from a line of dukes and earls. As for being sexy, well, lovemaking was the furthest thing from my mind. At thirty-five, I feel as though my days of excitement and danger and sex have ended. To be with a man seems like a monumental effort, simply too much work. I refuse to look at him and return my gaze to the hungry fish.

"What brings you to Madrid?" he inquires.

"Death."

"You came for a funeral."

"Not exactly."

I can't bring myself to tell him that I was married for ten years, until a sacred love turned to a devouring cancer, a death—scattered ashes. Now I spend the nights alone with a ghost. I came here to Madrid to meet with publishers and to fulfill a promise. Opening my fan again, I turn away from the basin and admire the crystal palace: a palatial greenhouse made of iron and glass that is overgrown with exotic plants and flowers.

"What about you? What brings you to Madrid?" I ask.

"Vacation. I needed a break from the Hollywood rat race."

"Actor?"

"Nope. Stuntman. *Mission Impossible*, the movies and all the James Bond films in the past five years. I've done them all."

"You must like to take risks."

"You bet! What about you?"

"I rarely take risks."

"No, I mean what do you do for a living?" he asks.

I pull out a guidebook and read. Without looking at him I say, "I'm a book translator, Spanish and French to English."

"Books, very cool."

"According to this guidebook, which could have used better translating, the park was built in the seventeenth century for the Spanish nobility. Philip IV used to come here and ride horseback in the nude," I inform him.

"Now that's a stunt I've never done," he admits.

"Yet," I reply.

A young girl runs in front of us. She is adorable, with flowing blond hair, blue eyes, lily-white skin. She reminds me of the maidens in Velazquez's painting. The child's arms and the hem of her frilly pink dress brush past my calf. I want to grab her, hold her, feel the softness of her skin—the purity and the life emanating from her warm little body.

I want her to forgive me. She could have been ours, mine. Eight years ago, I was expecting—a life growing inside me, an unplanned child, whom I chose to abort because of my career. And now I don't give a damn about my career. I think of her and wish I had something of my husband left behind. Instead, all I have are his clothes, still left untouched in his closet, his books, the cards and the poetry he wrote to me on birthdays and anniversaries, his voice on our answering machine (I haven't been able to erase it), and his ashes. I keep them in a gold silk jewelry box and take them with me wherever I go. The ashes are exactly seven and a half pounds in weight, the same as when he was born. . . .

Luc touches my arm. "Are you okay?" he inquires.

My eyes are fixed on the basin, on the school of wriggling fish; bubbles float up to the surface and then vanish into the murky water. Finally I speak, but refuse to make eye contact.

"We came here on our honeymoon. We sat by this basin. Everything in this park looks exactly the same, the crystal palace, the mimes, the daring lovers hidden in the bushes. Nothing has changed in ten years except for me."

Luc has enough tact not to ask more questions. He listens and reaches for the tight chignon on the back of my head. Unpinning my freshly washed hair, he says, "I bet you're more beautiful." My hair is still damp and falls loose, cascading past my shoulders. He spreads his thick fingers and combs through my long strands. Turning his palm toward the patches of sunlight, he admires my coppery gold hair entwined in his fingers.

"Why hide this?" he asks.

My long hair is one of my best features. I rarely take it down except in the privacy of my own home. Luc continues to run his fingers through it, as if practicing *tai chi*, or a slow-moving prayer. He continues this soothing gesture, touching my scalp and then moving out toward the ends; I tilt my head to one side, and for a second, let my head rest in his opened palm. He is content, just as I am—to stay by this pond, to stroke my hair, to say nothing. I study his muscular forearm; his skin is smooth and bronzed. He stops for a moment, rolls up his shirtsleeves, and reveals a tattoo, an image of four human skulls.

"What does that signify?" I ask.

"I used to be a Dead head. You know, the music of the Grateful Dead."

"Yes, of course."

"I'll cover it if it bothers you," he adds.

"No, it's fine. It just reminds me of . . ." I swallow for a second and clear my throat.

"You don't have to say," he interrupts.

"It's okay. I want to. My husband loved Madrid and always wanted to return after our honeymoon. We talked about retiring one day along the coast, near Tarragona, finding an old *castillo*—turning it into a bed and breakfast."

"That sounds awesome."

"It is his wish for me to scatter his ashes in this park," I continue, "on this lake. But I just can't bring myself to let go of him." Tears stream down my face. I glance at my purse, which contains the box of ashes. Luc wipes away my tears with his fingertips.

"Please forgive me," I mutter. "I'm so embarrassed. You don't need to hear all this."

"Go on. It's okay," he says, reaching for my hand. His touch is reassuring, comforting. It has been a long time since I've felt a man's strength. My husband was so weak and frail toward the end, unrecognizable.

Luc leans over to kiss my wet cheek. His lips are warm, soft—inviting. I tilt my head back and offer him my neck, my throat. That moment, I want to believe in the supernatural—in what most cannot see or imagine. I want Luc to bite me, turn into a vampire, sink his perfect Hollywood teeth into my flesh, give me pain and pleasure, and then slowly drain my blood until I die in his arms. I want to become the color red like the bleeding Christ in El Greco's paintings. . . .

He grazes my neck with his wet lips, but moves away to take hold of my hand again, leading me toward a section of the park shaded with Japanese maple trees and lined with pots of geraniums, birds of paradise, and red hibiscus. Sweet fragrances waft toward us, a blend of honeysuckle and jasmine.

Kneeling down on a patch of soft grass, Luc removes his shirt and spreads it down on the ground for us to lounge on. I cannot take my eyes off his magnificently sculpted torso. His body is more chiseled than Michelangelo's *David*. His physique is unblemished and perfect in every way, except for another tattoo on his bulging right tricep.

In any other circumstance, I would have fended off this stranger, whom I know nothing of, other than his being an American stunt-man. Gently, he guides me closer. His skin smells as if he has just bathed in the sea and then soaked in a tub filled with sangria and limes. I recline on my right side with my head propped in my hand. My elbow rests on the ground. We face one another, sharing the width of his cotton shirt.

"Do I frighten you?" he asks.

"No," I lie, staring at his right arm with its tattoo.

"This one's a Vedic symbol, a lotus blossom in a ring of fire," he says, touching the tattoo. "My parents were hippies and got me into Middle Eastern philosophy. I teach martial arts," he goes on.

Closing my eyes, I inhale more of him. Nothing matters any-more, not the tattoos, the stunts, or his Hollywood background. I *want him* and imagine being on a beach with him, perhaps on the coast of Marbella, where we'd ride horses at midnight and swim by moonlight.

Fuck! What am I doing? I don't want to be romantic, nor do I want to hope for anything. Yet a force is guiding me back to the pleasures of seduction—of men—further distancing me from my dance of death. Luc caresses my face and says, "Don't worry, I won't hurt you."

Secretly, I want him to hurt me. Turn into Bruce Lee. Or a serial killer. Please! Take me with a sharp knife, a sword. Cut me deep. Slash my throat. I tilt my head back, displaying my delicate clavicle. Instead, his hands reach down and slide up the arch of my foot, brushing against my ankle. His fingers climb up my calf, my inner thigh, and then rest on the seam of my cotton panties, landing there, not knowing yet if he should dare enter. His hands commu-nicate that he has loved women before, perhaps even adored them. There is skill and sensitivity in his touch. With agile hands, he glides my panties down my legs and begins to explore my sex, touching the lips, the soft inner folds of skin, the moisture. A wave of desire washes over me, cleansing and awakening my senses.

To my surprise, my death wish is vanishing and so is the grieving widow. Instead, I become the dahlias and the orchids planted in the crystal palace, petals opening, soft and fragrant, luring bees into their sweet centers. It doesn't take long before his head vanishes under my dress. A breeze is blowing on my parted lips. I realize it is his warm breath.

"Yes," I coo softly. There is nothing like a man who loves the taste of women and isn't afraid to express it. And then, while he is licking me with his cool tongue, I feel a tap on my shoulder, a lighter and gentler touch, as if a songbird has just landed. We are no longer alone. There is someone beside us, watching. Spirit? Angel or demon? My past. My pain. The ghost of my husband appears.

Charles is lying on his side before me, elongated like a sleeping Buddha. He glances at me with half-closed eyes. His tranquil expression reminds me of the many times when we lay on the floor of our Saint-Germain apartment, reading or making love by the fireplace. Afterward he would pause to look at me with such serenity and adoration in his eyes that I often wept.

"Where are you?" Luc asks, departing from under my dress. He leans his head on my thigh. "I can tell you're not with me. Is there something wrong?" he continues. I fear if I tell him about Charles, he'll think I'm mad.

"Do you want to stop?"

Unable to answer in words, I can only shake my head. Even so, my clit is speaking and becoming a stronger part of me. I am warm, wet—burning. I *want* Luc. Sex. In French the word *mort*—death— is part of the phrase for orgasm, *petite mort*—small death. The ghost of my husband is still beside us; his hands are now touching my forehead, running his fingers through my hair, the way Luc was just doing. I turn to Charles and ask if I should go further with this man.

"You're still so beautiful, Christine," he whispers. "Don't give up on life. Allow yourself to enjoy all that it has to offer."

Impassively MY husband watches me with this stranger, this Luc from Los Angeles. Then, it is as if he reads my thoughts and desires when the ghost says, "Be with him. He is good. Kind. Go where he wants to take you. I must travel alone now. I'm finally at peace, released from the bondage of my body, from pain. You don't have to join me. Look at what your senses are capable of. Enjoy, my darling, enjoy. . . ."

The ghost stands up and begins to walk away, heading toward the Big Pond. Pearl-white wings appear as his feet touch the water.

"Luc," I say.

"Yes," he replies.

"I've been talking to a ghost."

"Huh?"

"A ghost," I repeat.

Luc moves on top of me and looks directly at me. I smooth out my dress and gaze deeply into his clear blue eyes. I had forgotten the intoxicating sensation of a man lying over me. His arms and thighs are rock hard. I can't stop touching his bulging quadriceps, and naturally my legs begin to part. His right knee begins spreading me wider. I want to feel his hard gun and reach for the fly of his jeans. As I unzip him, he touches his wet lips against mine. Finally, we kiss. Mouth to mouth. His tongue is curious, yet delicate in its probing.

"Is the ghost still there?" he asks between deep kisses. I look behind my shoulder and see the enormous lake with its sea-green water, along with the silver painted mimes decorated before it, the skipping girl, the faded statues.

"No. He's gone."

Luc kisses me again. The first cool breeze of the day drifts over us. Clouds begin to shelter the scorching sun as I'm surrendering to his touch.

The Good Place

Ashley Lister

I've heard psychologists refer to "the good place."

It's not a specific location, or a town you can visit. It's a state of mind where, instead of being glum about your lack of prospects or miserable because you're lonely, you're content with life and all it has to offer. I was there once and I know it's a good place. It's a better place than where I am now. But as I'm currently sitting on death row, in Waverley, Virginia, with less than a week to go before execution, I think any other place might be considered better.

Not that I should be on death row.

I'm an innocent man.

And, while I did kill Katy and although I do hear voices in my head, I'm not one of your crazy murderers.

Have I just rushed ahead too fast? Should I slow this down a pace and start from the beginning?

I first fell in love with Katy's voice. She spoke with a throaty chuckle set deep into her Virginia drawl. There was the hint of mischief dripping from every word and the sultry promise of passion in each syllable. She breathed every sentence, speaking from the swell of her breasts and projecting with the competence of the finest opera singer. It would only take the simplest invitation—"Are you coming for dinner?" "Can I do anything special for you?"—and the mere timbre of her suggestion had me besotted.

And she chose her vocabulary with a deliberation that was always delightful. She had a risqué way of phrasing every question or response, so you never knew if she was teasing, talking straight, or deliberately flirting. When I fixed her dilapidated runabout, she gave me a kiss and told me she "appreciated the services of a capable man." Each time I saw her at the diner, where she faithfully waited tables, Katy would ask if she could "try to satisfy my appetite."

Not that it was just her voice or her wordplay that I loved.

She was a good person—kindhearted, intelligent, and fun—and the sexiest woman I've ever had the good fortune to encounter. Petite, brunette, perfectly formed, and invariably dressed in shorts and a T-shirt: she was blessed with a figure to die for.

I guess that last observation is an irony.

I genuinely do regret killing her.

But it wasn't murder, and . . .

I'm getting ahead of myself again, aren't I? Things didn't happen slowly between Katy and me. The sultry tone of her voice was enough to tempt me to her side, and as soon as we were alone together, I discovered another quality to her words aside from the rich accent or the clever wordplay. She could make the air crackle with the electric taste of promise. Using no more expression than a flutter of dark lashes over large eyes, she had me enlisted as a willing partner to her every sordid fantasy.

Now that we're talking about Katy's fantasies, it's only fair to mention that she had more than a few. The first time we made love it happened on a balmy summer's evening. I found her sitting on the porch, with a V of sweat molding her T-shirt to her breasts and giving her sun-kissed skin a glossy luster. The fading light of the day caught auburn flecks in her brunette tresses. Beads of perspiration on her neck and collarbone glistened like diamonds.

"I'm hot," she breathed.

And there it was again. The casual inflection in her tone that said more than those two words should be able to say. It was a double entendre that was maddeningly appropriate, regardless of which way I chose to interpret what she'd said. The day was sweltering, admittedly. But the glint in her eye, and that perplexing way she spoke, suggested that she wasn't discussing the clemency of the weather.

The electricity in the air made it hard for me to breathe. I tried to shift my legs so as not to embarrass her about the effect her declaration had stirred in me. Not wanting to appear stupid, or incapable of matching her banter, I struggled to find a suitable retort. Swallowing thickly, nervous that such a specimen of feminine perfection could show an interest in a lummock like me, I observed, "Hot suits you."

"You don't think all this sweat makes my skin look clammy and unattractive?"

"Hell! No!"

"You don't think it makes my skin feel unattractive?"

I hesitated, aware that she was taking my hand, watching as she guided the tips of my fingers to the slick skin of her collarbone. The heel of my palm was mere millimeters above the thrust of one nipple. I had noticed they stood erect, their shapes defined through the fabric of the clinging T-shirt. The ghosts of her areolae were deliciously obvious beneath the flimsy material. Touching her body—and painfully aware of how close I was to properly touching her breasts—I came near to shivering in spite of the sweltering heat.

"Well?" Katy prompted. She stroked my hand back and forth over her chest. Her skin was moist velvet with perspiration lubricating my caress. The ball of my thumb glanced against her breast and I was sure I felt the nipple stiffen. "Do you think that feels unattractive?" she asked.

"I don't recall touching anything that ever felt better," I answered honestly.

Her questioning expression turned into a mischievous grin. She lowered my hand to one breast so I was cupping her through a film of damp cotton. In the stillness of that moment I could feel her pulse through the hard bead of flesh that sat at the center of my palm. "In that case," she whispered, "if perspiration suits me so much, why don't you see if you can make me sweat a little more?"

It was the beginning of a beautiful relationship.

Maybe there was something appropriate about the fact that it began at the end of the day? I don't know. I only know that once we'd started, our passion quickly became boundless.

Perhaps I should have noticed there was something a little kinky in her desire to excite me on the porch. The exhibitionism of what we were doing didn't cross my mind until afterward, when I realized that any passing neighbor could have seen us and been shocked or offended by our intimacy. But at the time it simply felt natural to do everything Katy asked. I was content to bury myself deep inside her smoldering depths and bask in the cries of her approaching orgasm. Once again it was her beautiful voice—that musical cadence and enchanting lilt—mesmerizing me and blinding me to everything except Katy. And from that moment on, I was oblivious to everything except the pleasure that came from being with her.

I only began to suspect that she had unusual appetites after a month of our relationship. We'd tried a million and one variations on the traditional themes of sex, going from her porch to the bedroom, detouring via the kitchen-diner, and the stairs on the way there. She invited me into every recess of her body, welcoming me with her mouth, sex lips, and other places. She worshipped my erection with caresses from her breasts, tongue, hair, and hands, and we took each other to climax after climax in a splendor of shared bliss. I spent endless, happy hours watching her tease herself. And I particularly adored the way she would trill her fingers against the beautiful split of her sex—parting the dense, dark curls that covered her labia—while she charmed me back to arousal with the whispered promises of what we would do next. Each step further in our relationship seemed more like a declaration of our love rather than another jolt down on some descent toward a perverted conclusion.

We made love in semipublic places—under the stars and sometimes under the noon sun. We played power games and water sports, screwed while we were drunk, fucked while we were high, then made love when we were grounded and stone-cold sober. We confessed our wildest fantasies, then endeavored to make them reality for the pleasure of each other. And, although I'm probably wrong with saying we did everything, it's true to say: *we did everything we wanted.*

Which is why I had no problems with the ropes Katy brought to the bedroom. The contrast of coarsely woven hemp against her dainty wrists was ugly, but somehow exciting. The vulnerability of her naked form, spread-eagled for me and available for the satisfaction of my every whim, was infuriatingly arousing. When I placed myself between her legs, then rode her helpless frame as she sobbed and moaned through a multiple orgasm, I could totally understand what those psychologists meant when they referred to "the good place." At those moments, when Katy was screaming with joy and her inner muscles convulsed around me in the throes of ecstasy, I knew we were both in the good place.

But, I suppose, good places were never meant to last, and ours ended two nights after Katy first suggested we bring another rope into the bedroom. The term "anoxia" is cold and clinical—a million miles removed from the joy of Katy's last moments or the liberating release of her final climax—but it was bandied around a lot by my defense lawyers in court. It was usually lumped with a string of other fancy words and supported by dry accounts of the reported stimulation that comes from autoerotic asphyxiation.

The prosecution simply called me a strangler. The jurors were won over by their succinct use of words and, because I was convicted of first-degree murder with more than one of nine aggravating circumstances, I found myself a resident on death row.

Which, until last week, had been the total antithesis of the good place Katy and I had known. But on the morning when I was ready to meet the attorney handling my final appeal, Katy decided to speak to me again. At first I thought I was dreaming—I hadn't properly climbed out of my bunk and was enjoying the sounds of the morning calls from blue jays and chickadees—when she whispered in my ear.

"What's a nice guy like you doing in a place like this?"

I could hear her voice as clearly as when she used to nibble on my lobe while we were locked in a postcoital embrace. It was that familiar Virginia drawl, deep-set with a throaty chuckle of mischief. Death hadn't killed her sensuous way of speaking, nor had it stifled the effect she had on me. As my erection grew I began to wonder if I was either insane, or mistaken, or still asleep. Unable to stop myself, I spoke her name aloud. "Katy?"

"Do you like being inside?" she breathed.

And, in that moment, I knew it was her. I didn't know how she was talking to me. I didn't know why she was talking to me. But I knew my own imagination could never have supplied such a perfect Katyesque innuendo. With that one question I was beyond being skeptical that the voice was the product of my own diminishing faculties. I knew that Katy was back by my side.

"I've missed you, lummock," she confided.

"I've missed you, too," I admitted.

Her words were a balm, soothing and massaging away the tension I had suffered since incarceration. She hadn't said anything overtly sexual, yet already she had excited me to the point of full arousal. An appreciation of my responses told me that it would only take another couple of sentences and she would have me ejaculating like some overexcited schoolboy on his first real date.

I closed my eyes and easily pictured the way she had looked

when she was speaking. The fullness of her lips was easy to recall, the sensuous pout of her mouth was invariably glossed each time she trailed the tip of her tongue across her Cupid's bow. When she had used her tongue on my length I always remembered the thrill of pleasure that came from hearing her words and feeling them reverberate through my shaft. On this occasion, when she first spoke to me from beyond the grave, the pleasure was every bit as intense as it had been during those fondly recollected times.

"I've come to help with your release," she giggled.

It was another of her double entendres, and hearing that sly humor made me simultaneously excited, relieved, and delighted that she was back in my life. I had missed her and I had quietly mourned her passing. But the pressing demands of death row and impending execution had urged my focus to slip away from such important things. "How can you help?" I asked. I wasn't doubting her ability: I was simply curious to know. "My lawyers are qualified and alive," I pointed out. "At the moment, you're neither."

She laughed. With my eyes closed I could picture the way her breasts always trembled with mirth and her entire body shook. If I kept my eyes closed I could have believed she was in the room with me. It was all too easy to imagine she was struggling to lie by my side in the cell's single bunk and squeezing her body close to mine. With only the effort of a little concentration I could feel her bare flesh pressing against me. She had one long, muscular leg curled around my waist, and her bare crotch kissed at my thigh. The scrub of her pubic bush scratched wickedly at the top of my leg and rekindled the eager thrust of my arousal.

"I've been talking to the state's governor," Katy explained. "He has the power of clemency—the right to say whether you live or die—so I thought it best to go to the man who makes those decisions. I made a special plea for him to personally consider your case."

The statement was too unexpected for me to comprehend. I was still being enchanted by the lull of her words and teased by the seductive lilt of her voice. The meaning behind what she said took a full minute to register. Disembodied, with no more presence than her voice, she was still able to excite me more fully than any other woman I had previously met. My body ached for her and the threat of climax throbbed in my groin. If she'd had a physical presence I knew I wouldn't have been able to resist. Passion would have overwhelmed me and we would have revisited the halcyon days of our brief time together. Because I was only listening to her sultry whispers I managed to contain my impulse—but it was still a challenge.

"You've spoken to the governor?" I repeated. "How did you manage that? You're dead."

Again, she laughed. I didn't realize how much I had missed the sound of that merriment. As comforting as the sex, as exciting as the most daring of her propositions, Katy's laughter was almost enough to make me cry for what we had lost. "I know that I'm dead," she agreed. "But I spoke to the governor the same way I'm speaking to you now, you lummock: with words."

My mind glanced over the technicalities with a simple rationalization. If the disembodied voice of my lover could speak to me, why couldn't she also speak to the governor? "What did you tell him?" I asked. "Is my sentence being commuted? Are the charges being dropped? Or am I being released?"

Katy didn't get the chance to respond. The crashing of gates being thrown open and the hollow stamp of boots from the corridor outside announced the arrival of my attorney. I leaped from my bunk and pulled on my uniform of garish orange overalls. Judging from the heavy clomp of feet I could hear there were three of them. And, after Katy's revelation, I wasn't surprised to see my attorney and the guard were accompanied by the state's governor.

Our meeting was surprisingly swift.

The guard was dismissed.

My attorney started to speak.

Then the governor drove his fist into my nose. He called me a murdering son of a bitch, turned around, and left the cell before I had finished falling to the floor. On his way out I heard him say I was going to fry. Unnecessarily, he added, "and fucking soon." Clearly startled, my attorney shrugged an apology and hurried off to pursue the chief executive.

"That went kind of well," Katy said guardedly.

"Yeah!" I had a hand over my nose, collecting a stream of blood while I struggled to decide whether I was angry, surprised, or simply confused. All three emotions were vying for control of my reaction, but sarcasm eventually won. "That went so well I think the governor's going to go and check the wiring on the electric chair so there's no danger of a mistake. What did you tell him, Katy? I thought you said you'd explained what happened on the night you died."

"I didn't stick to the truth," she mumbled. "I said you'd killed me in a vicious and deliberate attack. I mentioned that your diabolical assault has left me walking in limbo for all eternity. And I demanded that he avenge me, or else I'll haunt him forever." She laughed, the sound tinged with nervousness this time. "None of it is true," she said quickly. "But I didn't think it would matter if I lied a little on this occasion."

Closing my eyes, trying to show patience and restraint when all I could really feel were confusion, disappointment, and betrayal, I asked, "Didn't you think that sort of statement would be likely to make him believe I was guilty? Didn't you think that sort of statement was likely to expedite my execution?"

"But that was my plan, lover," she whispered. "I thought you understood."

For the first time since Katy's death a smile stretched along my lips.

"You're going to get out of here," she promised. "And, this way, we'll be together again, where we should be."

As the understanding continued to dawn I realized exactly what she was telling me. I wasn't just going to get away from death row: I was going to be with Katy. In the good place.

Rain

Harriet Scott

Ellie was magnificent. Her hair was black, curly, and long, and in her eyes was something close to transcendence. She peered at me that first day, in Spencer's Bar, like a teacher inspecting a new pupil and deprecating what she saw. With a flicker of the eye she moved farther down the bar, and I admired the casual simplicity of her putdown.

But it was too late: I would not be put down. I had fallen in love.

Crass, I know, ridiculous. How can you fall in love with someone who has done nothing but give a disdainful look? Well, she did; and I did.

"Can I buy you a drink?" I asked.

"I don't know. Can you?" Her voice was hard, enunciation precise.

"*May* I buy you a drink?"

"And why would you want to do that?"

"Because I've had a good day and I'd like to share it with someone."

"Tell it to the barman. He's paid to do that shit." She took her wine and retreated to a seat at the rear of the bar. My cheeks reddened.

The barman leaned toward me. "Don't worry, miss. She's like that with everyone."

"She's a regular, then?"

"Yeah, most evenings."

That was all the information I needed.

It was two days before she returned. I was waiting. "May I buy you a drink?" I asked.

"And why would you want to do that?"

"Look on it as a prelude to fucking your brains out."

She turned and stared, her eyes focusing sharply on mine. I could tell I was being appraised. Finally, she nodded. "White wine, dry, large." She wheeled and walked to the same seat as before. I began to shake, that wonderful churn of fear starting up in my stomach. Smiling to hide my nervousness, I gathered the drinks and turned toward her. She watched me approach, her lip curled in a curious grimace, and nodded as I laid the glass before her. The coldness of her expression was breathtaking, her eyes dark and unwavering, mouth set forbiddingly. She was the antithesis of romance—and as such, the embodiment of sexuality. My body was tingling.

"So," she said, staring into my eyes, "you want to fuck my brains out. What makes you think I'm into that sort of thing?"

"Instinct, guesswork, hope."

"Sounds a bit desperate to me."

"Maybe I am desperate."

"Oh, dear. I do hope not."

"Maybe I've fallen in love with you."

"Again, I do hope not."

"Sorry to disappoint, but I think I have."

"You know nothing about me."

"I don't need to."

Her expression betrayed derision as her eyes wandered around the bar. "Grow up, little girl."

I felt like I'd been slapped. "Maybe it's just lust, then."

"That's better. More credible." She settled back in her chair, observing me casually. "And what would it be like, having you fuck my brains out? Sell it to me. As a concept."

I stared into my wineglass. "Rough," I said. "Raw. Hard. I'll use my nails on you. Strafe your body with them. And I bite, and suck. I'll sit on you and make you lick me until you're dizzy with lack of oxygen. You'll scream for me to stop, and as soon as I do you'll scream for me to start again." I looked up, registering the merest flicker of surprise in her expression. "And then I will." I dropped my hand to her thigh, resting it against her stocking, feeling the sleek roughness of its texture on my fingertips. My nail grazed across her thigh and hand slid beneath her skirt. "I'll keep on fucking you till you explode. And then I'll eat the pieces."

She swallowed hard, but I was impressed by how well she maintained her composure. Gripping my hand, she eased it from her thigh. "Not today, thank you, sweetie. An interesting scenario, but I think you'll find it's me who does the fucking." And she rose and left.

"May I buy you a drink?" I asked the following evening.

"No, you may not." She retired to her usual seat and I sat at the bar, watching as she sipped her wine. She was tough, that was for sure. She refused to display any weakness, facing me out with icy hauteur. I liked a challenge: my love increased.

"I may buy you a drink," I said the following evening. "Sit down and I'll bring it to you." Quietly, she acquiesced. A frisson of anticipation shivered through me: she was mine. The barman served my drinks and I sashayed toward her, easing myself into the next chair.

"Thank you," she said. She took the glass and raised it. At first, I thought she was about to declare a toast, but she continued until her hand was poised over my head. After a melodramatic pause, she tipped it and poured the contents over me, chilled wine cascading down my hair and neck and chest. I spluttered and wiped my eyes, shivering with shock. "Don't you ever give me an order again," she said. "I don't take kindly to orders. Stick to your own league, little girl." She rose once more and left me, sodden and humiliated.

I should have conceded. None of what subsequently happened would have occurred if I had heeded her warning, but I was obsessed. It was a battle of wills, and I was determined to prevail. Visions of her filled my mind. I lost myself in the luster of her hair—at once an enticement and a barrier. The mask which concealed her thoughts—blank eyes, cold mouth—came to torment me as I alternated between trying to understand it and wanting to penetrate it.

I had to have her. I returned on the next three evenings and on each occasion she arrived, sidled to the bar and pointedly ignored me. Each time, I offered to buy her a drink and each time she refused. From her seat she would stare, confronting me, and I was gradually drawn into her web. It was clear she was toying with me, relishing my discomfort, testing my resolve. "I think you'll find it's me who does the fucking," she had said. That was the key. As I watched her watch me, I knew she was vying for control.

And if that was the case, let her have it. At first, anyway.

"Would you buy me a drink?" I asked the following evening. I felt sickened by the deference in my tone, but forced myself to smile.

She stopped and turned, and for an instant I saw triumph cast across her face, before, once more, she assumed her mask of impenetrability. "Certainly," she replied. "Joe, one wine—large, dry—and one small, sweet."

I was about to correct her, but realized I would be falling into her trap. "May I join you?" I asked. Nodding crisply, she turned toward her table. She walked with exaggerated grace, swinging her hips expansively, and I was transfixed by the sight of her backside—

beautiful, perfect, encased in a sleek, black skirt, shaped for ardor and heartache.

"Okay," she said, indicating with a nod that I should take my drink. I swallowed a small mouthful, trying not to cringe at its cloyingness. "Do you still want to fuck my brains out?"

My heart was hammering. My senses were betraying my mind. "No," I replied. "I want you to fuck mine out."

She smiled. It was an expansive smile, but cold and calculating. I felt inconsequential. "What a very good answer," she said. "Cinderella, you shall go to the ball."

There was a hint of rain as we walked to my house, spots shifting in the wind, sizzling against the coldness of my cheeks. I had to admire the way Ellie took control. I almost felt grateful as I swung open my front door and stood aside to let her enter. Wordlessly, she swept past and headed straight for my bedroom, sliding off her coat and draping it across the back of my chair.

"Take off your clothes," she said. Her nipples showed beneath her blouse, but otherwise she betrayed no excitement. Her impassivity served only to increase my own arousal: she was playing with me, using my desire as a leash with which to control me. I hated myself for succumbing to such feelings, but, perversely, the discovery of such weakness within me merely fueled my desire. I stripped, self-consciously and with decreasing confidence, all the time watched by this inscrutable woman. I began to feel afraid as I unclasped my bra and let it fall to reveal my bare breasts. She showed no emotion, and a dart of dismay pricked my consciousness: I wanted to please her.

It was almost a physical effort to force myself to take off my panties. Fear was giving way to a sense of panic as I bent and slid them over my hips and dropped them to the floor. Stepping from them, I looked up, trying to mask my apprehension. Still, she exhibited no emotion and I began to feel foolish.

"Very nice," she said baldly. "You'll make a pretty plaything." I should have been outraged, but instead a warmness gurgled through me, and I was shocked to realize that what I was experiencing was gratitude. The notion was humiliating, but that humiliation was, I discovered, intoxicating. I didn't want to be treated like this, but at the same time it excited me.

"Lie on the bed. Play with yourself. Show me." I stood my ground. This was a step too far, something close to abasement. She stared at me icily. Her dark hair shimmered in the light and her mouth was fixed. I looked into her eyes and saw the reflection of my defeat. "Show me your cunt," she spat and pushed me onto the bed. I succumbed and spread myself wide, sliding my hand downward and cringing as I explored the root of my arousal.

She watched me. She watched my fingers, my cunt, my climax, my surrender. And through it all I watched myself, and hated it, and loved it. I forced my eyes open as I climaxed and sought her approval.

It didn't come.

"Very nice show." Without another word, she picked up her coat and walked out. When the front door slammed I crumpled into tears.

I didn't go back to the bar. I felt crushed by what happened that night. My sense of humiliation was overwhelming—I had been used like some performing animal, made to display myself in the most demeaning manner. That in itself was bad enough, but what made it infinitely worse was that I had secretly enjoyed it. And worse still, I knew, if I saw her again, I would do it all over.

It had rained all day. Driving from the north, it battered my windows relentlessly and I felt as though I were under siege. The noise began to settle into my brain, fixed and dull, a permanent rhythm that underscored the mood of the day. I couldn't get her out of my thoughts. The sound of the storm pulsed in my head as memories of that night ran and reran, quickening and slowing with the tempo of the rain, awakening those feelings of humiliation and arousal and despair and excitement. The air was humid, heavy with failure, summer lost to the fickle power of nature, just as I was to the power of lust.

I thought I was going mad.

The noise was spiking through my head and pulsing in my ears, and it took some time before I realized there was a new rhythm—a peremptory knocking—vying for attention. It was someone at the front door, and I knew instinctively it would be her. She swished past me and swept into the living room.

"Tidying up. How quaint. Just like little Cinderella."

"Don't speak to me like that."

"Like what, darling?"

"Don't patronize me."

She stared at me for some moments. "You're quite right. I apologize. That was uncalled for."

I nodded, grateful to have gained some measure of equilibrium. Making coffee, I composed myself, ignoring the echoes of rain and trepidation in my head.

"I don't think I treated you very well the other night."

"No."

There was a long pause as we stared at one another, trying to guess the other's thoughts.

"But did you enjoy it?"

Did I? Can you enjoy something you hate? Despite myself, I knew the answer. "It ended rather abruptly."

"Yes, it did rather. Again, I apologize."

She was wearing a sleeveless black dress, the neckline plunging toward her breasts. Only the thinnest of bodies could carry such a dress with elegance, but she looked stunning. Two-inch stilettos helped define the shape of her ankles and drew my gaze up her legs, toward her thighs, her hips, her breasts. Dark hair hung lush around her bare shoulders, draping demurely so that when it moved and her flesh was exposed, it was as though I were seeing a moment of revelation. Her fingernails were deepest purple, livid, as if she had been tearing raw flesh.

"And if it weren't to end so abruptly, would you do it again?"

"I don't know. Possibly." Outside, the rain was growing heavier, sleeting against the window as though impatient for action.

"Would you do it now?" The rain's rhythm and the beating of my heart began to merge to form the sound of desire. I knew I wanted it. I wanted her.

"Yes."

She led me to my bedroom and once more I stripped, once more I revealed myself to the woman I wanted to call my lover. I lay on the bed and stroked myself wet. There was longing in my loins such as I had never known, a craving to be touched, to touch, to know. "Please," I said, and stretched my hand toward her.

She smiled and began to undress. I watched, rapt, as she unzipped her dress and stepped from it to reveal that underneath she was naked but for her stockings. The flare of her hip, the symmetry of her thighs, the slenderness of her waist imprinted themselves on my mind. Her breasts were small, delicately shaped, nipples dark and upturned. She was shaved, her slit pink and hairless and I was breathless as she began to walk toward me.

"Do you want me?" she asked.

"You know I do."

She leaned over, her breast grazing my face, nipple sliding against my mouth. I sought it with my tongue but she pulled away. She stroked my cheek with her hand, purple nails dragging against my skin. Her flank was against mine, and the electric clash of skin on skin erupted in my senses. She traced her hand down my cheek and across my neck, toward my breast, and rolled her palm across it, dragging against my nipple. With her eyes fixed on mine she gripped my nipple and squeezed, rolling it viciously between her fingers. She smiled as I winced.

"Will you do anything for me?"

The rain continued unabated, slamming against the window, insinuating itself into my mind. It was relentless, the noise sludging through my brain, leaving me weary and mesmerized. I couldn't fight it. I couldn't fight her. However much I hated ceding control, she had me in her grip. She was undeniable, unconquerable. Even then, part of me wanted to rebel and fight back, to win her for myself. But only a part of me.

"Yes," I replied. She smiled and bent to kiss my breast.

Bursts of light flashed with growing intensity, the electric spark of nature in its glory, control lost to elemental fury. The storm was long and livid, vibrant and vivid, constantly circling, refusing to dissipate. On it went, two hours or more, the air impossibly heavy, fat rain plumping straight down, the smooth, dark sky scarred over and over to the beat of a constant thunder.

The senses must eventually submit to ceaseless assault: it was a night for madness. Ellie and I had been together for around six weeks, our relationship growing daily more torrid. I needed her. I had long overcome my reluctance to admit to such a need, letting myself slide into submission, following where my enigmatic Ellie led. She taught me about myself, introduced me to places I didn't know existed, opened my mind to emotions and feelings which were too beautiful to be earthly. The pleasure of pain and the pain of pleasure were my constant, cherished aspirations.

I had sought control all my life, but, somehow, Ellie persuaded me to cede it. She tested me, chased the boundaries of my obedience, but each time she did, I performed to her satisfaction, and I began to think I had no boundaries. She spanked me, tied me, dressed me like a tart, and paraded me through town. She even bought me a collar, which I proudly wore, panting with quiet restraint as she slipped a lead onto it and trailed me behind her. Truly, I was the hunter tamed. Our games became increasingly wild.

There was a three-week period, in late July, when only we existed, where our lives were consumed by sex and experimentation.

I submitted totally. When she took my hand and led me outside—into the storm—with the rain thrashing my naked body, it seemed more natural than if she had walked me to the bedroom. In the blackness of our garden, I knelt before her, gasping in the flaying rain. A pulse of lightning cracked the night, throwing electric light on the world. Ghostly blue, Ellie stood above me, smiling, and raised her dress. I bent toward her, groping, hoping, sliding my tongue in search of its home. She waited until I was within touching distance and then roughly pushed forward, sending me sprawling backward onto the sodden grass. Before I could settle she was astride me, yanking my hair, pushing me hard against the ground. Another flash of lightning streaked overhead, shading her skin peach and silver. She sank to her knees, sliding herself over my face.

My ears thrummed with low energy as thunder rumbled incessantly. Ellie was pressing hard, her knees pinning my arms, leaving me helpless. Rain speared onto my bared stomach and legs. Twice in as many seconds her face was revealed by the night's magic, silver and severe, her eyes lost to expression, focused on an inner journey. She seemed to be in a daze, quite unaware of me except as a tool for her own pleasure.

I was becoming genuinely frightened, struggling beneath her weight, trying to free myself, as all around the elements colluded in my assault. My chest was convulsing uselessly in protest at the lack of air, and my head was full of noise. It was a pulsing fear, and yet even in my alarm I remember one thing, and it is the thing of which I am most ashamed and most proud: throughout, as I struggled for air, hovering on the verges of panic, my tongue remained in Ellie's cunt.

How low had I fallen?

In another lightning flash I saw her reach back and felt her hand on my breast. She gripped my nipple and twisted violently. I tried

to scream as shock slithered through my body. Somehow it afforded me unwonted strength and I bucked beneath her, thrusting my
shoulders upward. Off balance, she fell forward and I felt a surge of
air enter my mouth.

Ellie quickly composed herself. She slid her knees sideways and
fell on top of me once more. She was soaking, her velvet juices sliding into my mouth, and I flashed my tongue against her clitoris.
Again, I felt the delirious dizziness of suffocation as she pressed herself to me. She rode me ever harder and faster, rough and truculent.
I was on the verge of passing out when I heard her scream and felt
her body tense to a climax. My mouth enclosed her clitoris and I
sucked fiercely. Ellie screamed once more, the storm darkened, its
noise engulfing me, and I fainted into ecstasy.

The night it began to fall apart there was gargantuan rain, too—
huge, oozing rods suffused with such certainty you began to doubt
they would ever stop. We had had an argument—something trivial,
but the day had been tense and sex-laden: we were both exhausted
and it was obvious that only violence would resolve it.

"Bitch," she said and slapped me hard across the cheek.
Refusing to cry, I stood my ground. I wanted to see love in her
eyes, but that night, for the first time, it wasn't there. I think I knew
then it was the end for us. Seeing my resolve, she began to waver.
"I'm sorry," she said.

"No, you're not."

"No, I'm not. Do you mind?"

Walk away, walk away. If only I'd walked away.

"Why should I? I'm just a bitch."

Even now, I don't know what I meant by that: fantasy and reality were becoming too blurred. She grabbed my hand and pulled
me outside, into the embrace of the rain. Facing me, she slapped me
again and waited for a response. I made none. Rain slid down my
face, like a balm against the sting of her hand.

"Thank you," I said.

Enraged, she slapped me again, and again and again. Five in all, each time searching for the limits of my endurance, each time seeking affirmation of her own dominance. And each time I thanked her, refusing to be cowed, and her control receded. She pushed me to the ground and fell on me, snarling and pulling my hair. Wrestling herself into position, she sat astride me once more.

"Bitch," she repeated.

"Bitch," I replied.

She pulled up her skirt and slid forward onto my face, and once more I felt myself entombed by her crushing weight. Despite my anger, I slid my tongue into action, parting her lips and darting inside, but this wasn't about sex, or love, or control. At first, I didn't understand what was happening. A burst of warmth filled my mouth, and it was a moment before I realized it was liquid. Confusion gave way to disbelief, and disbelief to anger, and anger to impotent fury as my mouth was filled by a stream of piss. I struggled, but Ellie held my head fast. Frantically, I swallowed and swallowed, feeling her piss rise up through my nose and gather helplessly in my mouth like a rain-flooded drain. At first I tried to gulp it down, but that merely triggered a gag reflex and made me choke. Finally, I relaxed and let it wash into my stomach, a rain which broke my heart.

I told her it was over. There was nothing else to say, and she didn't argue as she gathered her belongings. The trouble with searching for boundaries is that eventually you find them and, once found, they scream to be crossed. I was miserable. For days I didn't go out, didn't speak, barely lived. When I swallowed I could taste her piss, so I chose not to eat.

July turned to late August and gradually the wounds healed. I began to visit the bar again and formed a friendship with the barman. We never mentioned Ellie and her memory faded.

Until she appeared.

"May I buy you a drink?" she asked. Her voice was thin, uncertain. She was smiling, but her smile revealed nervousness.

"No, you may not," I replied and swung away from her. I meant it, too. But then she said the words which sealed our fate.

"Would you buy me a drink, then? Please?"

You can't control your emotions. It's the downfall of us all, eventually. A burst of sexual excitement rushed through me, a momentary surge of lust which filled me with dread. I tried to fight it but I knew I was lost. I turned to her, already assuming my role in the game.

"And why would I do that?"

"I owe you a huge apology. I behaved atrociously." She paused, her eyes pleading. "I deserve to be punished."

I was stunned. Ellie, the control freak, was offering herself to me. I wanted to fight, but it was pointless: without a battle, lust won. I smiled. "Joe, two wines. One large, dry, and one small, sweet for my little lady."

As soon as we returned home I made her strip—in the hallway, with the front door open. I knew she hated it, but she obeyed meekly. I left her there while I fixed a drink. In truth, my mind was in turmoil. I could never forgive her for what she had done, and part of me wanted to throw her out; but equally, there was a thirst for revenge, a sexual urge to finally control the woman who had so entranced me. And more than that, although I fought to deny it, I knew that I loved her. It was a reckless love—ruinous, doomed—but love nonetheless, and you can lie to anyone but yourself.

"Come here," I snapped. Silently, she padded into the living room and stood before me, naked and vulnerable. I sat in my armchair and appraised her. "So you're sorry?" She nodded. "And you want to be punished?" Again, she nodded. "I don't know. I don't know if this can work, Ellie."

"Yes it can, please."

"Why?"

"Because I don't want to lose you."

"Why?"

"Because I love you."

We were alike, Ellie and me. Neither of us liked to show vulnerability and I doubted she had ever said those words before. I shook my head. "But things are different now."

"Yes, I know."

"And you don't mind?"

"Not if it means keeping you."

"So will you do anything for me?"

"Anything."

I smiled, in relief rather than triumph. "Get over my knee, bitch."

I spanked her until she screamed. I spanked anger and frustration out of my body. With each stroke I felt my fury decrease and love grow until, by the end, I knew that I loved Ellie more than anything in the world. We would surely destroy each other, but we couldn't be parted. She slid off my thighs and crumpled to the floor. Taking her face in my hands, I soothed her tears into her red-soft skin.

"If you ever do anything that comes between us again, I'll kill you," I said.

She smiled. "Never. Never."

We were together, and she was mine. There was happiness in the world.

Love blossomed the second time around. We fell in love again and it was magical, a mix of domination and devotion. Ellie was my girl, my plaything, squealing at my spanks, screaming for my licks, squirming beneath my touch. Summer dripped by, August into September, and every day was an exploration. But gradually—and I can only really see this in hindsight—the tone of our relationship began to change. It had always been a game played at the edges of decency, but increasingly it became personal and bitter: arguments that had once had an element of contrivance were now full-throated; punishments that before had a spark of mischief now reeked of rancor; and mute obedience sullenly slipped toward dumb insolence.

We lost the joy.

It was clear Ellie was struggling with a submissive role. She was exotic, a bird of paradise, and in captivity her soul died little deaths with each passing day. I wanted to set her free, but I needed her too much.

Rain. Rain like I'd never seen, never heard, never felt. It was alive, a sobbing, seething mass, pulsing through the air and through my head and mind and consciousness. It was the rain that drove me mad.

We were barbecuing in the garden when it arrived. With it came ill temper and incaution.

"You're going to leave me." I didn't look at her as I spoke. I didn't want to see her lies.

"Really, sweetie? What makes you think that?"

Her words confirmed it, and my heart sank. She hadn't spoken to me like that for weeks, condescension dripping from every syllable. I looked into her eyes and saw the blank look of someone who had already made a decision.

"Oh, Ellie, you really are, aren't you?"

She denied it for some minutes, her voice shrill but unconvincing. I pressed her and finally she snapped. She hurled herself from her chair and stood before me furiously, and finally it seemed as though a weight had been lifted from her.

"And why would I do that?" she spat. "What would drive me to leave, do you think?" Her voice was cold and challenging, as it had been in the bar those months before. "What causes someone to leave? Because they're happy? Fulfilled?"

"You should have talked to me if you weren't happy. . . ."

"Oh, grow up!"

"No, you grow up! Don't patronize me every time you go on the defensive and can't think what else to say. It's a coward's way of arguing."

"Oh, I'm sorry, sweetie. Have I been naughty? Do you want to spank me?"

I slapped her hard, the crack echoing around the garden like a rallying call for indignation. Instantly, she slapped me back, and in that moment love died.

Her voice was heavy with sarcasm, lip curled in a dismissive sneer. I felt a surge of anger as she spoke. "You haven't a clue, darling. You stride about, playing the madam, showing off your 'dominant' personality. Can't you see, that's not dominance? It's just your insecurities calling. It's a subterfuge, little girl, concealing your inadequacy. You're just too vanilla, sweet Harriet. No imagination, no adventure." Her voice was rising to a shout. "Do you know how boring it is, being bent over your lap every fucking day, same crap, same dreary, dismal rubbish? Do you know how boring it is? Really? How boring *you* are?"

I tried to say something but no words came. My hand was on the barbecue knife and I gripped it unthinkingly. Rain was thundering on my head, its pulse driving dementedly into my mind. A slew of madness slushed over my thoughts.

"I tried, I really tried," she continued. "But frankly, I don't think you're worth the effort."

"Bitch!" I yelled.

"Temper, temper."

Her patronizing voice was the catalyst. Almost blinded by rain, I swung my arm at her. I don't know whether or not I knew the knife was in my hand at that moment, but it doesn't matter: I'm not making excuses. It slid through her skin so easily, so beautifully, it was almost a moment of poetry. Ellie stared at me, open-eyed, then slid to the ground. Keeling over, she lay on the grass and looked up at me, smiling.

"You silly bitch," she whispered. There was a fleck of mud on her mouth. I eased it away before caressing her cheek. "I still loved you. Still do."

I shook my head, crying. "You don't. You love what you want me to be. But I'm not that."

I've never known whether she heard me or not.

Her face was creased with pain, smile erased by a mask of death. People look so vulnerable in the seconds before dying—it's the moment when you can truly read a soul. I stood and watched her life depart, pooling in a viscous sludge at her side, then walked inside, out of the rain.

I felt numb. Ellie's words speared me, her accusations of inadequacy firing my indignation while at the same time finding some resonance. We all play games, and I more than most. But how do you know when your mind is playing games with you? I stood at the window and watched her lifeless body cool to oblivion, drenched by the dying rain, and tried to determine what to do next. To control or be controlled—the central dichotomy of my life.

So tell me, what would you have me do?

Nona Take Five

Lene Taylor

Los Angeles, 1960

Let us get one thing straight from the beginning, you dig: Texas Matt was one sexy bitch.

Tall and dark-haired, dark-eyed, but with skin white like bone. Tall, yes, but narrow shoulders, not much to grab hold of anywhere except where it mattered, and the first time I saw him, a thousand years ago, I knew I wanted everything in those faded worn-out jeans. Oh, my.

Saturday. Hot day. Nothing to do. Like every day in L.A. Drinking helped. But the days must be spent, time must be killed, so I sat with the other bored rats in the parking lot of Harper's, baking in the sun, watching the bikers drift in and out on their Harleys and hoping to God for a fight. It is a strange and true thing that you can go a thousand miles west in a straight line and end up right back where you started.

The car cruised by once, then twice, then slowly pulled into the lot. Five heads and ten eyes followed its progress till it rolled to a stop close to where the rats were staked out: me, Scotty, Tom, José, and Jamie. A beat-up hot-rod monster with Texas plates. Oh, lord, save me from another redneck, I prayed.

I watched him walk over to where Scotty had his H-D in several pieces, like he always did, thinking he could fix it or jazz it or just not break it, nice white boy that he is. Nobody ever helped him, because nobody wanted to have to do it all over again tomorrow. Texas Matt came walking up slow and stiff like he'd just gotten off his horse, hands jammed in his pockets, head down.

"Nice. This year's?" he asked, all nasal twang.

"Nope. Last year's, Fifty-nine Special. She runs like a tiger, when she runs at all," Scotty said.

"Y'all need a hand?" Scotty looked up at him, grateful.

"Matt," the stranger drawled by way of introduction, and stuck out his hand.

He had that beast back together in no time, working quiet, lost in his machine-world trip. I watched him, enjoying the view. Tom watched me. Jealous bastard, but what can you do?

When Humpty Dumpty was back together again, I picked a bottle out of the ice bucket and tossed it to Mister Matt. He popped the cap with his belt buckle and took a long swallow. Sweat ran down into the open collar of his checked shirt.

"Thank you kindly, ma'am." He took a step closer and touched my face, trailing his fingers down to my chin. "Man, those are some *feral* cheekbones."

I watched him suck down the rest of that beer, holding the bottle with his long fingers, and when he was done he looked right at me again, all smiles and dark brown eyes with long black lashes. Have mercy. I slid down off my perch on the flatbed of someone's pickup truck and started toward his car.

"Where you going, Red?" Tom called. I flipped the cigarette I'd just lit on the ground.

"Smokes."

I heard Matt's feet crunch on the gravel behind me, dog on the scent. Inside his old car it was even hotter. I twisted my hair over my shoulder so I wouldn't have to sit on it, but he pulled it loose into his hand and held it up to his face, breathing deep.

"Your hair is sure pretty," he said, but from his rose-colored Texas mouth it came out "shore purdy." He inhaled again, like he was taking a hit of ether. "I never seen hair so black. How come he called you Red?"

"Don't you have eyes, baby? I'm an Indian princess," I snapped.

"Oh," he said, moving closer. "Well, what *is* your name, girl? You don't look like no Red to me."

"Nona. Call me Nona."

"Let's go for a ride, Nona."

So we drove down the coast for about an hour—don't know how far, if I'm not walking on my own two bare feet I don't know the distance—and he bought us dinner at a little beach place, good cheap Mexican food and more cold beer. By the time we got back to L.A. and to the scary-looking house by the beach where he rented a room, it was purple dark and velvety out. Inside it was straight past the people sitting in the living room listening to music and smoking dope, up the stairs and into his bedroom, first on the left.

And then he took off my clothes very slow, and kissed me like he meant it, and we fucked the night away like everyone should get to fuck at least once in their lives. Naked he was sharp bones and tough muscle and his hands were callused and strong, strong enough to lift me and flip me over and handle me like I wanted to be handled. Seemed like his cock was always big and hard, and mostly inside me, which was where it belonged, and between that and his lips and fingers I stopped counting how many times I came and just rolled along on the pleasure groove till the sun started to come up. We fell asleep and he held on to me real real tight.

He woke me up later, sun streaming yellow through the dirty window, and his fingertips tickling the back of my knees. Again? There was much to look forward to, but my cunt needed a break from fucking, that was for damn sure. He was lying close to me, grinning, a smile that showed his crooked teeth.

"Mornin', beautiful," he murmured.

I put the pillow over my head. Matt laughed and started to pull the sheet off me.

Then the door creaked open. "Matt, I need to ask you . . ."

Who in the hell comes walking in without knocking on a Sunday morning? The high-pitched voiced trailed off into silence. I lifted the pillow some and saw curly hair and a face that would have been cute if its owner didn't look like he'd just been sucker-punched in the gut. Yes, a boy, I decided, though he could have passed for a girl, with his arms wrapped around his skinny body. He looked at me and looked at Matt, who sat up, and the boy shifted nervously from foot to foot.

"Can I talk to you, Matt?" he asked, and he sounded desperate now.

"Later," Matt said, and turned back to me.

"But Matt—" the boy tried again. Well, he was a persistent little elf, that was the truth. Was he even legal?

"I said later." End of conversation, time's up, better get out while you have the chance. The sprite shot me a look of pure jealousy and shut the door.

"What the hell was that?" I asked. Matt wrapped himself around me and slid a hand between my legs.

"He lives down the hall. Probably wanted to borrow a cup of sugar."

"It's like that, is it? Listen, baby, do us all a favor and let me sleep for another couple of hours, dig? I can't take warfare so early in the morning." He laughed into my neck, and kissed me, and we slept a long cozy time.

Later, later, much later, we rose and dressed and went out for food, some local place where they seemed to know him. First it was coffee and breakfast (even though it was afternoon) and then time went by and we switched to beer and dinner and when we left it was dark out again. He talked the whole time. Like Old Man River, the words just kept rolling along, and every now and then I'd step into that stream to see what flowed by. The rest of the time I didn't bother to listen, just kept a watch on his hands, his face, and the grin that he couldn't seem to get rid of.

He told me he'd hitched from Texas out to California to see the ocean and stayed to work; he was a carpenter and that was much in demand. New houses, old houses that needed work, and there sure were enough rich folk who had the money to burn. The hand that held his coffee cup was pale but scars showed red-brown on the knuckles; clean fingernails, and I remembered how those fingers had tasted last night after they'd been inside me. The story had gone somewhere else, now, back to Texas, where his sister lived, and there was some piece of land near Dallas that his daddy had left to him. Grass and trees, not like here, a place to build a house and ride horses.

"You know how to ride?" he asked suddenly.

"'Course I do. It's in my blood." I said it hard and mean so that he would feel some pain, but he leaned forward and grabbed my arms.

"I bet you look fuckin' fantastic on a horse. I bet you ride like you was flyin'. That's where you belong, Nona." Dammit, how did he know where to aim? I needed to be more careful with this one, that was for damn sure. "How come you ended up in L.A.?"

I had to light a cigarette to waste time. "It's a long, sad story, baby, and maybe I'll tell you one day when I'm too drunk to care. I'm just looking for kicks. This will do till something better comes along."

He relaxed. "Yeah," he said. "I reckon you're right." He stared into his coffee for a while, a whole minute of silence. Then he looked up again and the grin was back in place. "You know what would be better? Listen, I got this all worked out . . ." and he was off again, as the sun set slowly in the west and I tried hard not to think about horses.

Back in his car. I didn't much care where we went, and I had the feeling nobody told Texas Matt how to drive.

"Where you stayin'?" he asked, twining a thick strand of my hair around his fingers: black on white, very artistic.

"With friends." Spare bed if I was lucky, couch or floor if I wasn't.

He got up close to me and his eyes got soft and serious. "Let's get your stuff. You can stay with me." He must have seen something in my face, so real quick he added, "If you like."

I thought about his clean white bed, neat little room, sunshine through the windows, ocean out the back. "Righteous, baby. Let's go."

Through the house in a rush again, only this time I saw the little elf all alone in the living room, looking miserable. Oh well. Texas Matt took his time fucking, slow and familiar with me like we'd been doing this all our lives. He pushed into me as soon as I was ready and stayed there a long time, sometimes moving, sometimes not, first on top and then under me. I liked it. I liked fucking him. I liked his mouth on me and his hands on me and the way he buried his face in my hair. When we were done, sweaty and breathless, he told me he had to go to work in the morning and that he'd be home at six. Then he quick fell asleep, his arms tight around my waist.

Next morning I was alone. Can you take a vacation from nothing at all? This felt like one. Sleeping till I wanted to get up, in a big bed, quiet; bathroom with an iron tub, and clean towel waiting for me, like I was his guest and not his personal whore. Hello, old house: Thanks for keeping the night spirits away.

Clothes, makeup, boots. Downstairs. In the tidy little kitchen there was coffee and a good-looking cat sitting at the table, reading. Blond, very blond with brown-golden skin, handsome in that movie-star way, white teeth showing when he smiled at me. I never saw blond people till I was ten and I thought they were ghosts.

"Nona," I said, pulling out a chair.

"Nicholas," he replied. "Want some coffee?"

It was good and strong, just what I needed. He watched me blow on the steam rising out of the cup.

"You staying?" he asked, and I nodded. "As long as Matt pays his rent we're cool. Kick in some when you can, for food and electricity. I've been here the longest, so I sort of run the house. It's quiet most of the time—everybody has day jobs—but weekends can be wild."

"You are not working," I observed. "In fact, you don't look like you ever worked a real job. Too good-looking."

"You sound like my parents," he laughed. "They work in Hollywood. That's why I left." Nicholas went over to a big old wing chair by the fireplace and started strumming a guitar. Twelve-bar blues, my favorite. He grooved for a while and it was good.

"My parents sent me to music school, dancing school, finishing school—all those factories. They still think I'm going to make something of myself." He played a few more chords, but he was smiling gently.

"Blond college boy plays the blues. What a trip." That made him laugh.

"What about you? Something tells me you're not a sorority girl."

"I just roll with the flow, baby. Sometimes I mind the bar at Harper's, but I am on probation now, since some jackass called me a squaw and I broke his nose." I finished the coffee and started a cig. "Who's the boy with the wild hair?"

"Denny? He's Matt's dog. Denny just followed him home one day and he's been here ever since. Matt even got him a job in the wood shop. At least he doesn't eat much."

We sat in comfortable silence for a while, till I got the call to touch the water. "Later," I told him, and headed down to the ocean.

• • •

The pattern of days. I never could get used to clocks and appointments, and now I didn't need either. Lying in bed. Smelling the ocean wind. Walking for miles on the beach. Sitting on the couch, listening to Nicholas playing his guitar; he was very very good at letting his eyes follow me around without moving his head. Matt and Denny would come home when the sun was low in the sky, most days; sometimes a little later, sometimes a lot, and on those days Denny would hang a nasty smirk on his baby face.

Nights we spent together, always. Matt talked and I let him talk. About everything—work, Texas, his dreams, what he liked about me. It all ran together, like a warm blanket that I wrapped around myself. One thread was always woven into his talk, his big plan of going back to Texas with money, to build himself a house on that piece of land. That's what made it all worthwhile, he said, going back with money so he could be a man and live his man's life. I wondered if that included screwing a teenage boy on the side, but I did not say this.

And even after a couple of weeks Denny hadn't said word one to me. Not during parties, not during dinners, not no way, nohow. I could feel him watching me when I was in the room, and once in a while our eyes would meet and he'd shoot poisoned arrows in my direction.

One afternoon I looked out the back window and saw them sitting together on the beach; Matt was talking, and Denny listened, his face shining pink with excitement. Matt cracked a wise one, and Denny's laughter, high-pitched, too loud, too intense, ricocheted around for a while. Then Matt got up and wandered away, waving. Denny smiled but his body deflated slow like a leaky balloon.

I went down to the beach. When I sat down next to him, he shrank away from me. But he wasn't mad, he was afraid. I put my arm around his thin shoulders. "Little brother, we're on the same side of the river, you dig? No cause for you to be mad at me."

"What do you mean?" he asked, sharp and suspicious. His eyes were brown and tilted up a little, like mine. Real.

"Baby, you know what I mean. I am not here to take him away from you." Now he was embarrassed. He looked down at his hands, and the words started, slow at first, then a rush like he'd been waiting to tell somebody, anybody, what he'd been hauling around.

"Matt has been so nice to me. Nobody was ever that nice. I ran away from home and I came here and when I ran out of money I had to do something. That's where I met him, in Griffith Park. It's a good place to hustle in the summer. And he . . . well, he said I should get a decent job, and he could help me, and he did, Nona! Now I have a job and a place to live and, well, you know. And I thought—I guess I thought maybe—well, anyway, things are different now that you're here. Now he only wants to be with you." He looked just adorable when he pouted.

"Don't worry, boy, it's only for a little while. You can believe me on this—you will be with him long after I am gone and forgotten."

He turned back to me. "You think?"

"I know it. Nobody could love him like you do." And that made him blush furiously.

"Aw, c'mon, Nona! Quit it! It's not like—well, it's just that—I just want—I just want . . . I just like to be with him. I never felt—I mean, there were people at school but it wasn't like—like Matt is. I know he thinks I'm just a kid, but sometimes, you know, it's so different . . ." he trailed off. I knew what he was talking about. I could have cried for him then, but since that was not possible I just squeezed him a little harder. He came back to the present and the spark inside him jumped and he grinned, happy to forget Matt and talk about something else, I think.

"So what about you? Where did you grow up?" Nobody had posed that question in an awfully long time and it took me a minute to remember what the answer was.

"On a reservation. In Texas. It was hard there."

"Matt is from Texas. How come you don't talk like him? Did you tell him you're from there, too?"

"I don't talk like him because I am not a redneck cracker. I did not tell him because he never asked."

"Oh." He seemed disappointed for about two seconds and then it was back to twenty questions. "Where was the reservation? What was it like? Do you ever go back there?" If any other cat had grilled me like that I would have slapped him into next week, but some crazy thing inside made me want to be nice to him.

"It was outside a little town called Waxahachie and it was very hot in the summer and very cold in the winter. We were all poor. And we were beaten for not speaking English in school. And so," I said, getting up and holding out my hand, "there is no reason to go back. Come on, little brother, let's go inside and get Nicholas to play us a song."

A night on the beach. Denny, Matt, Nicholas, and me sitting around a little fire, drinking, singing, talking. So much wanting, greedy sneaky looks bouncing around; I was surprised that the fire didn't explode and knock us all on our asses. Denny was trying to show Matt some shells he'd picked up on the beach, but Matt was more interested in his beer.

"Look at the silver stripes on these. Aren't they cool?" Denny asked.

"Yep."

Denny tried again. "I never saw these before. I wonder what they're called. I wonder if they have a name."

"Hell if I know." Matt went back to poking the fire with a stick.

Such a world of hurt in Denny's pretty face. I took the shells out of his hand.

"They have a name. Everything alive has a name. The easy part, you dig, is the names people give things. The hard part is grooving on the real, true name of something . . . or somebody," I told him.

"What do you mean? My name isn't real?" Nicholas asked. It was the first time he'd talked to me in an hour. Texas Matt must have made him real nervous.

"This shell," I said, holding it up so that it glittered in the firelight, "belongs to a snail that some scientist cat named. Before that it had a different name, probably Spanish. And before that, names in languages nobody talks anymore. All the way back. But not one of them the real name."

"So how do I find out what it is?" Denny asked as I gave it back to him. I shrugged.

"Ask the snail." They laughed at that, know-it-all white boys. "It's the same with people. Your parents named you Nicholas," I said to him, "but that's not who you are. Your real name is probably something that means 'overeducated ego-tripping lazy son of a bitch,' a rich preppy name like Biff or Skip."

Nicholas looked hurt, then pissed, but Matt was laughing so hard he had to let it go. Smart.

"And you," I said, throwing my empty bottle at Matt's feet, "Matt is pretty close, but I think *your* real name will turn out to be Skeeter or Delbert, you know, one of those backwoods barefoot sister-fucking lynch-mob kind of names." Mean, mean laughter all around. Nicholas looked like he was speeding, eyes all intense; Matt looked like he couldn't decide who to hit.

But they were ready for me to get the elf now. "What about Denny?" Nicholas asked.

"Yeah, you ain't said nothin' about him, yet. Go on!" Matt barked.

I turned to the boy and saw he was trembling. In the red firelight his brown slant eyes were big and liquid and afraid again. I grabbed his cold hand and then zap! looking into his eyes I knew his name, his secret name, and all it meant and would ever mean. Blood reaching to blood, maybe. Wild. The fire spit loud in the silence. So I smiled.

"I don't know yours. You'll find out one day. But Denny will do just fine for now." He let out a breath and grinned back at me as the other two bastards groaned, disappointed. Enough of this fuck-ing game. I got up and brushed the sand off my ass.

"Hey, now, what about you? Ain't Nona your real name? What's it supposed to mean?" Matt just wouldn't give up; this time dog looking for a fight.

"What it is, Delbert, is short for 'none a your fuckin' business,' you dig?" I said, and walked away into the dark.

When he came to bed I was asleep, but not for long. There he was, curled up behind me, sniffing my skin and licking my ear.

"Damn, we're out on the beach all night and you still smell like the desert," he murmured. He used his fingers and his lips and it was good. "You are much woman," he said, his big hands cupping my breasts, not big enough to cover them, but just the size to hold them close, with authority.

I reached back and stroked his cock. The skin stuck to my hand and at the base it felt wet. Maybe sweat, maybe spit, maybe come, or maybe all three.

"You're such a sweet-talker, Delbert," I said. He laughed as he moved and now he had me pinned on my back, hands on my wrists, his cock pressed against my belly.

"Now you stop that. And you tell me your real name." His lips were smiling but his voice was not.

I shook my head. He frowned at that.

"Can't?" he asked. I nodded.

"Is it on account of I'm not Indian like you?" I nodded again. Then his face softened up and he leaned in to kiss me deep and sweet. "I reckon—well, I reckon it ain't none of my damn business."

He slid into me, deep and sweet, and later, much later, he fell asleep with his lips pressed against my neck. Wrapped around me like ivy on a tree.

Then, as it will, everything happened at once.

One day M&D came home, like usual, but then Matt disappeared upstairs to his room and we all heard a lot of banging around. I looked at Denny. He gave me a how-the-hell-should-I-know look and went to fix something to eat. When Matt came down he acted like none of that had happened and started talking to Nicholas about cars.

I knew he'd tell me eventually, because Matt, you dig, could not keep a secret if he locked it in a cage. Nicholas knew, that was obvious; they kept disappearing for tense little chats, and spending much time on the phone. It would be drugs or money, they being the two most important things in our cheap little lives, and sure enough, it wasn't long till Matt couldn't stand it anymore and spilled.

His room, at night, late. He went to the closet and moved a loose panel in the ceiling, then took out an old cigar box with a rubber band around it. Watching his long fine muscles move under his pale skin as he did this was a treat. He sat on the bed next to me and gave me what was in the box.

Pictures, black and white, some color. Naked women. "Dirty pictures. So what?" I said, handing them back to him.

"No, look again. Not your standard dirty pictures." I looked again. Pretty women. And then I recognized one of them, two of them, lots of them—actresses all, from the thirties and forties, ones I'd seen in that movie house in Waxahachie when they'd take us into town. All in the altogether, posing sweetly and smiling for the photographer.

"Quite a collection, Delbert. What does this mean?" It was coming out in a minute, I could see it in the way his hands twitched.

"It means I'm gonna be rich. Remember how I told you we're always findin' stuff on these restore jobs? Coupla weeks ago we were in this old Hollywood house, owned by this big-time producer. Used to be, anyway. He kicked and his son moved in, and the first thing Junior has us do is start tearing out the old woodwork, all this

beautiful carved stuff, just ripped the place right down to the skeleton. And Junior was always pokin' around, askin' if we found anything interesting. Like he was lookin' for somethin'. Well, I reckon
he was, only I found it first—in a box, way back behind a trick panel
in a closet."

"You stole them."

"I removed them to a place of safety."

"Too clever for your own good, baby. So now what? How are
you gonna translate them into bread?" I placed the photos carefully
back in the box. Holding them was sending bad vibes up my arm.

"Nicholas. He knows people, people who collect stuff like this.
We're gonna split the take right down the middle." His eyes were
burning with excitement. "Now, ain't that somethin'?"

"It surely is."

And the wild thing was, he was right. It took only a week and
Nicholas had set up the deal, which was supposed to take place in
some restaurant, for protection. Matt was the driver and I was the
window dressing. Everyone was nervous except Nicholas, who went
in cool and calm to meet the collector and came out just as cool and
twenty thousand dollars heavier. He didn't even crack a smile till we
got back to the house and locked the door. Then they spread it all
out on the floor and counted it, counted it, made me watch them
count it, and Matt took his half and put it in the cigar box and said
nothing to Denny when he got home.

Two nights later I asked him why there was something under
the mattress, because he sure wasn't hiding it from anyone like that,
and when he showed me the gun he'd bought "for protection" I
lost it.

"No gun," I told him. It looked awful, black, scarred. And Matt
would keep it loaded, that I knew.

"I need it now, can't you see? No thieves in this house, but I
ain't gonna take no chances."

"I don't want it in the room with me. I do not like guns. I mean it." I folded my arms and glared at him. Don't they ever get the message? He moved to his side of the bed.

"Don't you worry, I'll keep it on this side and you won't never know it's here." He started to lift the mattress again but I slammed my fist down on it. He jumped back in surprise.

"Here, let me say it so you understand. I ain't sleeping in *no* bed with *no* gun under *no* mattress! You GOT that, Delbert?" I shouted.

"All right, calm down, Nona. I'll find some other place. It ain't a big deal," he mumbled.

"Good, 'cause neither are you," I said, and went out for a walk.

Nicholas never told us the collector's name, just that he bought this kind of stuff for himself and was real happy to get the goods; he'd been looking for those pictures for a hell of a long time. So had Junior, and of course—of *course*—he found out: that Hollywood grapevine works like lightning. The first thing Junior did was pay a little visit to the carpenter's shop with a couple of his hired goons and pointed to Matt and said this hillbilly son of a bitch stole things from my house, and Matt being Matt he had to turn it into a fight and get himself fired—not for stealing, but for taking a swing at Junior and connecting in a big way. Denny told me later all he could think about was how he was going to get to work now, because he couldn't drive. He hadn't been around the house much lately, and I missed him.

So Texas Matt threw himself a party, a getting-fired party, and he invited everyone he'd ever met and then some. People everywhere, endless booze, and a band set up in the corner that grooved all night long. A good party, maybe even a great one. If you like that sort of thing.

Somewhere around midnight I lost track of them. I had three shadows that night: Matt, cruising through the crowd but coming back to me every couple of minutes, running his hands through my hair; Denny, always a few steps behind Matt; and Nicholas, watching from a distance and pretending he didn't care. I got involved with talking to some chick about making bread and then Matt was nowhere to be found. Denny neither. But I saw Nicholas open the back door and then stare at me hard and then he went back to pouring drinks in the kitchen.

Down the back stairs to the hard-packed sand behind the house. Too close to the water to have a basement, so there was a big extra room built onto the house for storing whatever shit you didn't want to have inside. It was a good hiding place for drugs and other interesting items. No windows, but the catch on the door was long since broken, and now I could see a glow of light coming through the gap between door and frame. Curiosity never killed this cat, you dig, so I edged close; the music was still so loud that you couldn't have heard fireworks, even outside. And I looked.

Junk and more junk in there. There was a dim, bare lightbulb hanging in the far corner, just enough light so I could see them but they couldn't see me, I guessed. Not that Denny could have spared one bit of his attention, anyway, not when Texas Matt was standing in front of him, so easy and confident, one arm around Denny's waist and the other draped over his shoulder. Smiling. Denny lunged at him and planted a powerful hot kiss on that smile, and so they stayed like that, and Matt's hands were busy busy busy roaming over Denny's skinny body.

It didn't take long before Denny was down on his knees on the dirty floor, sucking Matt's big, stiff cock for all he was worth. All I could see was his curly head bobbing up and down, and the quick glimpse of wet, shiny skin when he paused to take a breath—lord, that boy was working, working it hard and fast and when Texas Matt looked over at me, he was grinning. Then he closed his eyes and got that look I knew so well, and he threw his head back and opened his mouth and thrust hard, hips jerking with every spike when he came. I could almost taste it in Denny's mouth, salty and bitter. The boy got up off the floor and fell into Matt's arms, looking beautiful and wanton and ecstatic and I wondered why I was part of this equation.

When I crept away they were lip-locked. The party was going strong, music so loud it shook the floor, and people, people everywhere; and Nicholas, of course, watching me like he always did but without the balls enough to come right up to me and say whatever was on his goddamned mind. I boosted a whiskey bottle out of the jerry-rigged bar in the kitchen and sat out on the front porch where it was cool.

It wasn't till later that I heard Matt's voice, when the music stopped. He was holding forth like he always did, only this time he was telling his same old story about going back to Texas to the whole crowd, telling them that it was finally gonna happen now, because he had more fucking money than he'd need for the rest of his life and he was ready, damn ready, to get the hell out of L.A. Cheering, lots of it—especially since the booze and the band and the food were all courtesy of him—and then he jumped up on the kitchen table and raised his glass to the ceiling in a toast. I saw Denny gazing up at him, his soft mouth open just a touch, and his lips looked swollen and maybe a little bruised. Matt let out a rebel yell.

"Waxahachie, Texas, here I come!" he shouted, and everyone shouted with him except Denny, who looked at me like he'd never seen me before.

The party ended when the cops came and cleared everyone out. For once Texas Matt was too drunk to fuck, and knew it, and just fell into bed. I lay there next to him, all night, staring at the wall, and when morning came he got up to take Denny to work and I pretended to sleep. I got to Harper's just as it opened and said hello to my old friend firewater. Cold. Like the way I felt inside.

I could not go to Texas. I could not go back. I knew what it would be like, because that shit never changes, and even with Texas

Matt to back me up I could not bear to go through it all again. All those years. They had looked at us, those hard white faces with cold eyes, and we would know what they were thinking, even though they'd never say it to our faces. They never did, not on the reservation, not in school, not at any of the awful jobs I had—those nice polite white people who didn't know that we could read them like we could read the clouds on a windy day. Look at an Indian boy and think *drunken bum*; look at an Indian girl and think *dumb slut*. All those angry white folks, and nobody to take it out on but us poor backward Injuns.

And Matt would never understand. That man was some freak of nature, you dig, because he was a hillbilly through and through in every other way and yet he did not see that I was different. Or that Denny was different. It was what made Denny fall in love with him, and me put up with him for as long as I had, but it only worked as long as we were together alone. Texas would kick my ass and pound me into the dirt for coming back with Matt.

Three beers later my mind was made up. If Nicholas let me stay, that would be good; if he didn't, well, no matter, the door was always open at Harper's. If I waited till Matt left, I could get my stuff and avoid the scene that would end with a lot of swearing, that I knew.

Just then Saint Nicholas himself came screaming into the lot and almost ran me over. I just sat there and looked at him, until he yelled at me through the open window.

"Christ almighty! I've been looking all over for you! Get in the car!" He flung the door open and revved the engine. So this wasn't quite over yet. Might as well see how the movie ends.

"Did they come here?" Nicholas asked. He was sweating, and he kept looking around like he thought something big and bad might show up.

"Skip, all I can tell you is that nobody named 'they' has been here all day. But you had better tell me what the fuck you're talking about."

"Junior's boys. They showed up at my fucking *parents'* house looking for me. We have to tell Matt that they'll find us soon." He put the car in gear and tore out of the parking lot.

"Oh, lordy," I said, hanging on to the door for dear life. "This is bad news and no mistake."

"This would be a very good time to disappear. If you and Matt are really going to Texas, you should leave today."

I managed to light a cigarette. "He's going. I am not."

"Oh. Well, you'd better lay low for a while, till this blows over. I think I'm going to take a little vacation in New Orleans or someplace." He looked at me kind of sideways-like, thinking he was being all sly. Then something occurred to me.

"What about Denny?" I asked.

"What about him? He's not my pet," he said flatly. All of a sudden I felt like I had to do something—everyone taking off and leaving him like that, poor little queer boy with nowhere to go and nobody to love him.

"And a good thing, too," I said softly. Nicholas didn't hear me, he was too busy being paranoid. When we got to the house he stopped at the curb and turned the headlights on; it was getting dark.

"Matt's car is here. You go in and tell him what's going down, Nona. I've got something to deal with."

"Be careful, Skip," I said.

"Don't worry. Just going to pay a visit to the collector." And he roared away. I swear I could see anger coming out that tailpipe.

The house was dark. Denny sat on the sagging old couch, staring at nothing in front of him; he ducked his head down when I came in, like he always did when he didn't want to look at me.

"Hey, boy, you're home early," I said, trying hard to be friendly. "Is Matt around?"

"Upstairs," he said, and his voice sounded like he was being strangled. Bells went off in my head. There was something awful going on, that I knew.

"Did they come here? Junior's muscle?"

"Just me." His voice faded to a whisper and I took the stairs two at a time till I saw the light spilling out of the bedroom.

Texas Matt was very, very dead. I had seen dead bodies before, you dig, back on the rez, but I did not get used to them. Blood all over his white bedsheets, bright red where it had fallen in drops, dark and almost purple in the stain under him, and in the great big hole in his chest. Eyes open. And I could not move for a long bitter while.

Then I saw the cigar box on his dresser and the thought came to me that he wasn't going to need it anymore, was he, so I stuffed it in my bag and backed out of the room, careful not to touch anything else. Denny was still sitting where I had left him.

"Boy," I said quietly. "What happened here, boy?"

He turned to face me and now I could see the big, nasty bruise on his face and the blood on his mouth. Oh, lord.

"He said he was leaving. He told me I couldn't go. And I said, I said I could pay my own way, I had the money now, and he said how did you get that money and I said it was just a few more tricks and then he got so mad. And he said he wasn't going to take care of me anymore and I tried to hold him, to kiss him, so he would know how much I loved him . . . and then . . . he hit me . . . and then he told me to get out." His voice cracked and shook. "Were you going with him, Nona?"

"No, baby," I said, truthfully. He pulled the gun out from between the cushions of the sofa. Matt's gun. He held it in his lap and stroked it.

"I just wanted him to love me back. But he wouldn't listen to me," Denny said, and then the tears started to fall. I was still standing on the last step and I wished that if he was going to kill me too he would get it over with, and soon.

He looked down at the gun and back up at me, and now his face, his sweet baby face so full of hurt, was calm. "Sorry," he said. "You better go now."

I let out the breath I'd been holding. "I'm gone."

Out the back door, down the stairs, and then I ran down the beach as fast as I could, tripping over rocks, slipping on seaweed that grabbed at my feet. The waves were angry and loud, but the sound of that last lonely gunshot was like the end of the world.

So now I am lying on the grass in Waxahachie, Texas, looking up into the hard blue sky. Nicholas is walking around the edge of the land, Matt's land, looking for something we can take with us. I gave the money to his sister when we got here; she didn't look too broken up that he was dead, but she said thank you for his stuff and took the money without asking where it came from. I could see her rug rats lurking behind her in the kitchen. The oldest boy, dark-haired, dark-eyed, peered out at us warily, looking and acting too much like his uncle.

In L.A. there were cops and newspapers and the most god-awful circus you ever lived through, so when Nicholas asked me to go with him I said yes in a heartbeat. Nobody asked about the money, and I don't know whether that was through divine or earthly intervention.

We're headed for New Orleans, or Baton Rouge, or someplace like that. Nicholas's money, Nicholas's car, and I can't read a map. Nicholas says he's in love with me. He's a fool, but what can you do? Some scenes are better, some are worse; I can't go back, I can't stay here, and nothing surprises me anymore.

Texas Matt made it back here, but in a box. Is that luck or fate?

Time to go. I turn over and press my face into the ground, hoping he will hear me, or feel me near him. All I can give him now are words.

I whisper to the earth my name, my real, true name, and then there is nothing left to say but good-bye.

Corrida

Jan Levi

My name is Carmen Batista de la Fuente.

You must have heard of me. Last year, did I not fight at all the top festivals? Did I not star at Las Ventas in Madrid, at the height of the season? They say I looked no different from the others in my jacket embroidered with gold and sequins, skin-tight trousers, a black *montera* on my head, and my hair in a pigtail.

Today is the fiesta of Our Lady of Hope and Sorrow and I am here at the famous ring of San Lorenzo de la Torre. But this year, the band does not play for me. I do not enter the ring. Instead, I wait in the hot afternoon sun, I watch. My seat overlooks the barrier where the matadors await their appointment with the bull.

My old friend, Ana Maria Benitez Perez, sits next to me. She cannot understand why I insist on baking out here, instead of sitting comfortably in the shade. Ana Maria comes from an old bull-fighting family. "Too much politics in the ring these days," she says. She has no stomach to be a matador, and prefers to be a spectator. Unlike me.

Applause breaks out. It is for Emilio Romero José Fernandez. This year, you, Emilio, lead the procession that is the official start of the *corrida*. You hold your head high. Your suit of lights is ornate, turquoise and gold. You raise your hands to acknowledge the crowd. You gyrate your hips. You sweep the cape from around your shoulders and bow. You take a fold of cape in your mouth and lower your eyes. Then you break into a wide smile for the ladies. They shout and clap. Oh, yes, there are many out there who would shed a tear for you. Not I.

Not so long ago, Emilio, we were together at the Madrid Academy of Bullfighting. Isn't that true? We graduated at the same time, remember? Felipe, the first in our class of a hundred, died in the ring soon after. I took second place, you third. Since that time, we have kept our distance, wouldn't you say? But at the end of last season you started to speak out against me. You said that women in the ring were unlucky. You and your friends boycotted the fiestas where I appeared. All of you, you mounted a campaign against me. Carmen Batista de la Fuente has not made the grade, you said. She is not good enough to rank among the stars. She never learned to kill well enough. In all the fights of the season, she has not even sustained one injury. And anyway, you joked, breasts get in the way.

That wasn't the case during those long moonlit nights at the ranch, was it, Emilio?

The three matadors are taking their places now. You will be the last to fight. The music ends. The crowd waits. You are directly below me, hidden, watching the action through the eye slot. I can see the movement of your breathing, even from the back. Suddenly the bull bursts through the gate, black and sleek, with a bright rosette. It runs this way and that, confused. Its hooves pound the dry earth. At first, it heads for the *picador*, on horseback, but then swings around and charges the matador. The crowd gets excited. He makes a pass. The horns of the bull nudge his body and the crowd cheers. This is what they came to see. I wriggle in my seat, imagining myself down there. I was not made to sit and watch.

They play out the old ritual. The *picadors*, on horseback, make the first lancing, the second, the third. Blood runs from the flanks of the bull. But this one shows spirit. It bellows in anger. Its tail thrashes and slices the air. It paws the sand and readies itself for a charge. The trumpet sounds. The matador's assistants, the *bander-illeros*, run out with their barbed sticks. The matador beckons, taunts, tricks. The bull begins to weaken. Its head lowers. It hurtles toward the matador, but he casually steps aside with a sweep of his cape, and courts the bull some more. The crowd can't get enough. The trumpet calls again, to mark the *faena*, the final act. The bull skids one way and the other, ever more desperate. The matador is on his knees now, making the pass of the *trincherazo*, and then up again, standing still in the *pase de la firma*, with the cape almost touching the bull's nose, and once more holds the *muleta* behind him in the *manoletina*. I have to admit, he is not bad. I wipe the sweat from my face, almost forgetting why I am here. Suddenly the bull hesitates, eyeing the man. The matador takes his chance. He hurls himself at the bull, plunging the *estoque*, a short sword, deep between its shoulder blades. The crowd roars. The bull falls. More blood stains the pale sand of the ring as the matador slices off horns, one ear, a tail. The band starts up. The bull is bound and dragged away. The matador makes a circuit of the arena, throwing his tro-phies to the crowd. I understand his expression only too well. Triumph, relief. I, too, have worn it many times.

The next fight begins. But this time the crowd is disappointed. Ana Maria pronounces the matador a wimp. I offer her some almonds and nibble a few myself. I check how you are getting on, Emilio. You still have your eye pressed to the hole in the barrier, weighing up the situation. Why did things change? I want to know why. Do you not remember the night you first asked me to practice caping at the ranch with you? When you made me swear not to tell anyone? For everyone knows it's forbidden. Forbidden, secret, and romantic.

We drove for two hours from Madrid to the ranch. We talked of the training and our plans for the future. The moon was full that night, and you took my hand, Emilio, as we walked through the scrub toward the bulls. You picked one out and lured it through the gate into an empty field. There was no music, no applause, just the sweet smell of grass in the warm night, and the dark, looming shape of the bull as it charged under the stars. That first time I watched. You fought as if in a trance. You forgot I was there, and it was only when I shouted your name that you stopped and jumped over the gate. You kissed me. You laid down your cape for me. You caressed me with your tongue and voice for a long, long time, your blue eyes and dark curls framed by starlight. Oh, yes, you knew exactly how to play me, your fingers deep inside. You brought me to the threshold again and again, then stopped and smiled and shook your head, until I begged for release.

"I am going to drive you wild," you whispered, and turned me over and drew me onto my knees. "And then I am going to tame you." And then you thrust deep and hard until you were satisfied, while I clutched the grass and my cries were muffled in the dark folds of your cape.

Those outings became an addiction. We made all kinds of excuses to our families, but it was the best way, the only way, to get the practice we needed with the bull. Back in Madrid, we behaved as if there was nothing going on, as if we were simply colleagues. That added to the excitement, of course. Not even our best friends knew.

But after six months things changed. We set off as usual. You drove. I offered you some cakes left over from my birthday celebrations. You took one bite and stopped the car.

"What is this?" you demanded.

"Just a marzipan cake," I said. "Is something the matter?"

"Never give me it again."

Your eyes were wild, the whites showing.

"I cannot go to the ranch tonight," you said. "Drive me home."

I had no choice. We went to the ranch only once more after that. I trained hard, driving the bull to a frenzy of frustration, luring it in close. But you gave up early, and I had to stop. I lay down on the cape then, aroused, ready for you. I drew you on top of me. But even when I held you and licked you and tried every trick I knew, still you could not manage the final act. Afterward you whispered, "If you were my wife, it would be the end of bullfighting for you."

I was shocked. "I wouldn't dream of being your wife," I spat. I got up and walked away. We drove back to Madrid in silence. A week later I saw you with that flamenco dancer, Isabella, the one who always thrusts her huge tits in your face.

He's been gored! Yes, the second matador has been gored in the thigh. He tries to carry on, but clearly, he's had it. You are raring to take his place, Emilio, I can see that. You run out onto the sand, to massive cheers. The limping matador is escorted out, and quickly forgotten. It's you they want to see, Emilio. Because you are so poised and graceful and courageous. You are such a showman. True to form, you make short work of the bull, and do a lap of honor around the arena. Then you retire briefly to await the next fight, your own.

I've been thinking about you, Emilio, since the end of last season. You always said you were on a diet, and brought food prepared at home rather than snack with the rest of us in the cafeteria. Why was that, Emilio? I did a little research. Almendratoxicosis is an interesting and unusual condition, don't you think? What a nuisance it must be to feel so nauseated and disoriented when you have the smallest taste of almonds. Even the smell makes you sufferers feel so very ill. It can make you hallucinate. What a shame. I, myself, bathed in sweet almond oil this very morning, and I so enjoyed it.

The third show has begun. And you are out there, Emilio, making some truly daring *veronicas*. The crowd cries out for more. You posture. You take your time. You play with the bull. To the ladies you are such a hero. They dream of being rescued by you. They dream of being snatched from the horns of peril at the very last moment by your strong arms. Oh, yes, you are a master, but I am better. I am nimbler and quicker. I have an equal amount of stamina, as we have proved. And I am cleverer. I follow your every move.

The bull is weakened. Your team of assistants is slick, for you can pick the best. The *banderilleros* pierce the bull's flesh. The final act will soon begin. I lean over to where you left your *muleta* and *estoque*. I sprinkle them both with the powder of ground almonds. I spray them with almond essence. I sit down and fan myself.

"What are you doing?" Ana Maria asks.

"Mosquitoes," I say. "Particularly bad today, aren't they? Must be the blood."

For isn't this a game of trickery and subterfuge, Emilio? You return and grab the tools of your trade. The sweat is running off you. Your smell reminds me of when we made love in the moonlight. It wasn't so long ago, was it? I catch a glimpse of your face, drawn and tense. But that soon changes, of course, when you go back to your audience. You move in with the smaller cape now, ready for the kill. The crowd eggs you on. You're still swaggering. No, you're not. You're stumbling. The bull's head goes down to charge. For a moment you stand transfixed. You drop your cape. The crowd gasps. You stare ahead, unseeing, as if you can't remember who your adversary is. Suddenly you are up in the air. The crowd groans. The bull tosses you once, twice, three times. Then you land on the floor with a thump. The bull turns to gore you with its horns, and tramples you for good measure. What style! The crowd is in uproar.

"Fantastico," I shout, adding my voice to the general pandemonium. *"Estupendo!"*

Ana Maria looks at me. She gives me a nudge.

It's so sad that we have to part like this, Emilio—you, lying on the ground like a puppet, broken and squashed, while your blood flows onto the sand. The bull is lured out of the ring and leaves with a flick of its tail. You are taken away on a stretcher. *Adiós*, Emilio.

My name is Carmen Batista de la Fuente. I am a matador. Soon, I will be the star attraction once again. You will see. So, my friends, next time you are in Spain, make sure you book early for the *corrida* in Madrid.

Woman-in-a-Box

Roberta Beach Jacobson

It was in downtown Amsterdam that Ron first saw the woman of his dreams. In a sex shop. Of course.

It was love at first sight, or so he claimed. And so it was that my old college friend Ron bought the woman-in-a-box and took her home to share his apartment and his life. He decided her name was Tiffany and he treated her like royalty. He sang to her, he wrote her love poetry. He didn't seem to mind that his partner was not exactly a living, breathing human.

Ron explained that their sex life was "gentle, yet wild." I could imagine Tiffany would be cool and smooth to the touch. She was special in many ways. Face it, she would never gripe about PMS, she would never start an argument, and her figure would not balloon up as she approached middle age. Ron probably had found every delight in Tiffany, the woman who would never get wrinkles and who would never complain about his mother. Even better, she could take as much sex as Ron could give! He'd never hear a single "Not tonight, dear" out of her!

"Tiffany is everything I could want," he told me. "What a woman!" He bought the brunette doll-of-a-woman a wardrobe to die for. She was decked out in designer frocks, lovely hats, lacy underthings, uncomfortable-looking pumps. The works.

"Do you think that shade of blue would look right on Tiffany?" Ron asked me one day as we passed a Chanel shop. Though Ron was not a wealthy man, when it came to his woman, money was apparently no object.

Come to think of it, I might enjoy being a passive blow-up doll for a change—if it would mean my husband would do everything for me. Aside from the fantastic wardrobe, it can't be half bad for Tiffany to get so many sensual back rubs and foot massages after her bath. Also, Ron swears he's careful not to press hard on her when thrusting from his missionary position and I know a lot of other women friends who would sure appreciate this thoughtfulness for our comfort during lovemaking. The constant *slap-slap* of a heavy male belly tends to be distracting—if not uncomfortable.

Ron had no hobbies. He worked his thirty-eight hours a week in an Amsterdam bank, and then he went home. To Tiffany. He put ribbons in her hair and kept the volume on the TV low so she wouldn't be bothered. As if to prove his love, every Saturday, no matter what the weather, Ron walked to the florist on the corner and bought Tiffany a white rose. She was pampered from the moment she entered his life.

Ron bought a queen-size waterbed. "It's a surprise for Tiffany," he told me on the phone. "She usually stays in bed while I'm at work."

I had to admit, Ron and Tiffany outlasted every marriage I knew. Maybe he was on to something after all.

Since Tiffany had come into his life, Ron refused to eat in restaurants, fearing that people would stare at them. So for their fifth anniversary, I arrived with a bottle of champagne and Chinese carry-out. I debated getting two or three entrées and decided on three. What the heck.

"Perfect timing. We're fresh out of the bubble bath," Ron announced as I arrived. Tiffany, delicately perched by the window, was dressed to the nines. I felt a little scruffy in my rumpled pantsuit. I hadn't thought to change after work. Ron shook my hand. I waved over at HRH Tiffany, never really being sure how to address her. I felt no sense of female bonding with her.

"How about that haircut?" asked Ron, beaming. "I did it myself."

I was lost in thought. I couldn't even remember the last time I'd been treated to a romantic and leisurely bubble bath. Years ago, for sure! What a fantastic lover Ron must be to tend to Tiffany in so many ways. Sighing, I evaluated the hairdo. "Great look, Tiff. I like the shorter cut on you. Very attractive."

Ron chatted away all during our dinner, which meant I did not need to struggle with any one-way conversations with Tiffany. We each had a plate at the table. As always, Tiffany didn't eat a bite. Ron wolfed down his egg roll and half the cashew chicken before thinking to pop open the champagne.

"To my Tiffany," he toasted. "I couldn't ask for a more perfect partner. Thank you for these last five years, the happiest of my life."

Who was I to argue? I knew Ron had been miserable with some of his girlfriends. Most of his more serious relationships had lasted only two or three months. One smoked too much, another was hooked on cocaine. Another not only crashed his car and lied about doing it, but ran up his credit card to the limit buying presents for her other boyfriends. Most women in his past had pressured him to get married, as he seemed to be the last bachelor in the city. Let's face it, Ron had actually found his fantasy woman (a one-in-a-million chance), and he was treating her right. There seemed to be no limit on how much he could give—or on how much Tiffany could take.

Ron had rented a video, and that's how we spent the rest of the anniversary evening, laughing at an old comedy classic. About midnight, I could see his longing glances in Tiffany's direction and took my cue to leave the lovebirds alone.

Because of my having to travel for business, I didn't see much of Ron for a few years. We'd catch up on the phone when we could. I showed up in great style for their eighth anniversary. I brought sixteen long-stemmed red roses, eight for each of them.

Ron had never looked happier. A watercolor of Tiffany hung over his fireplace in an ornate frame. I'd known Ron since grade school and didn't even realize he could wield a brush. But there she was, captured in her dark-haired splendor, mouth perpetually open.

"See how love in the soul and a waterbed in the bedroom brings out the best in a man?" he asked me, proud of his painting achievement. "Here's to another year together!" He raised his glass.

I would love for my husband to ask to paint me. I'm sure I could pose on a waterbed for hours, but I'd only do it on the promise he would never display the painting over our fireplace. Or anywhere. But it might be something fun to try.

I turned toward the ever-silent Tiffany. Though dressed in a short lavender gown that would have been perfect for a night out at the opera, she looked slightly down. Had she lost weight? I tried not to stare at the patch just below her knee.

"Yep, my darling isn't as robust as she used to be," Ron explained. "But who of us is? We age, it's a fact of life. Now she's all doctored up. No problem."

I had my doubts about that, but the patched old girl still hung around, as if to prove me wrong.

We met up in Ron's living room for the big tenth anniversary, and what a celebration it was. A cheese platter, a selection of fine wines, a huge roast beef with the works. Salads, breads. He had gone all out, sparing no catering expense for the three of us—possibly suspecting this would be the last such celebration.

Tiffany's designer clothes no longer fit properly and her rings wouldn't stay on. She was down, way down. Ron realized it and it pained him. I could see it in his eyes. I visited them occasionally to see how things were going, but Tiffany was a mere wisp of the alluring woman in the painting.

Was it suicide? Nobody can say. One day, not long after their tenth anniversary party, when Ron was at the office, Tiffany blew out an open window and soared over the city. Only her stilettos remained behind.

About the Authors

Kelley Armstrong is the author of the *Otherworld* paranormal suspense series. The series begins with *Bitten*, the story of a female werewolf, then branches out to witches and ghosts. The sixth installment, *Broken*, will be published in May 2006. Armstrong lives in Canada with her family. For more information, check out her Web site at http://www.kelleyarmstrong.com.

John Barfoot lives in Newcastle upon Tyne, England, recently voted the eighth most popular party city in the world. Fortunately, he doesn't have to go to parties anymore, and can devote more time to doing less writing than he should. Recent publication includes Issue 10 of *Interpoetry* (http://www.interpoetry.com/index.html), Issue J of *The Printer's Devil*, and the anthology *The Unexpected Pond* (Route, 2000). His Max Ernst-inspired collages and accompanying tiny tales can be seen at http://uk.geocities.com/j.barfoot2@btopenworld.com.

Laurent Boulanger has been Australian Correspondent for the UK's *Writers News* (the UK's largest circulating magazine for writers) since 1995. He has published tens of articles in a variety of publications, including *Independent Filmmaker*, *Motor News,* and *Australian Small Business & Investment*. His short novel *Murder on*

45th Street was published in 2002, and his first full-length novel, *The Girl from France,* was published in 2005. He teaches in the postgraduate writing program at Swinburne University and is currently completing his Ph.D. in writing at the same institution.

Josephine Chia, 54, is a Peranakan or Straits Chinese and is originally from Singapore. She migrated to England in 1985. Her second novel, *Shadows across the Sun,* has just been released in August 2005. Josephine was one of the winners of UK's prestigious Ian St. James awards for short fiction in 1992. Her short story was published together with the other winners by HarperCollins in an anthology, *Blood, Sweat, and Tears.* Josephine has another winning short story published in an anthology. Her other published books include a novel, *Singaporean Cookery*, a book on yoga, memoirs, and a collection of short stories. Full details of her books can be found on her Web site: http://www.josephinechia.com. She is a tutor in Creative Writing, yoga for health, and cookery. She has an M.A. in Creative Writing and is also a yoga teacher trained by the British Wheel of Yoga.

Clare Colvin has published three critically acclaimed novels, *The Mirror Makers* (Hutchinson, 2003), *Masque of the Gonzagas* (Arcadia Books, 1999), and *A Fatal Season* (Duckworth, 1996). Her short stories have appeared in many anthologies. She was born in the UK and grew up in South Africa, the Lebanon, and India. She now lives in London, and is completing her fourth novel, set in Italy.

Muthoni Garland is a Kenyan writer based in Nairobi. Her stories have been published in Kenyan, South African, and American literary journals. "Odor of Fate" was inspired by a visit to the Kenyan coast. She wondered about the background of older expatriate men from relatively wealthy backgrounds who'd turned native and now lived in "dubious" circumstances. Muthoni is fascinated by smell. Certain smells provoke memories one can almost taste. They can even make one gag or hyperventilate with fear.

Decadent, devilish, and delightful are just three words that have been used to describe the work of **K. L. Gillespie.** She wrote her first published story, aged seven, about a child-eating nun and since then she has worked as a music journalist, gallery curator, and screenwriter. She is a regular contributor to *TANK* magazine and has most recently been published in *Wicked: Sexy Tales of Legendary Lovers* and *Best Women's Erotica 2006.* Her eagerly awaited first novel, *Jesus Loves Penge,* is out later this year.

Niall Griffiths was born in Liverpool and has lived at the foot of a mountain in mid-Wales for about twelve years. He has had five novels published, the latest being *Wreckage.* A novella, *Runt,* and a collection of short stories, *Further Education,* will appear in 2006. Two of his novels are being filmed, and his work has been translated into several languages.

Lauren Henderson was born in London, where she worked as a journalist before moving to Tuscany and then to Manhattan, where she now lives. She has written seven books in her Sam Jones mystery series, which has been optioned for American TV, many short stories, and three romantic comedies—"My Lurid Past," "Don't Even Think About It," and "Exes Anonymous." Her latest book is *Jane Austen's Guide to Dating,* which has been optioned as a feature film and is published in the US by Hyperion. Her books have been translated into over 20 languages. Together with Stella Duffy she has edited an anthology of women-behaving-badly crime stories, *Tart Noir,* and their joint Web site is http://www.tartcity.com.

Vicki Hendricks is the author of noir novels *Miami Purity, Iguana*

Love, Voluntary Madness, and *Sky Blues.* Her short stories appear in collections and periodicals, including *Murder for Revenge, Best American Erotica 2000, Flesh and Blood, Tart Noir, Nerve.com,* and *Mississippi Review Online.* Upcoming in 2006 are stories in *Deadly Housewives* and *Miami Noir.* She lives in Hollywood, Florida, and teaches writing at Broward Community College. Her work reflects interest in adventure and sports, such as skydiving and scuba, and knowledge of South Florida environment. Her latest novel of murder and obsession, *Cruel Poetry,* set in South Beach, Miami, will be published in 2006.

Roberta Beach Jacobson is an American writer who makes her home in Greece. Her credits include *Playgirl, True Confessions,* and *True Experience.* Her Web site: http://www.travelwriters.com/Roberta.

Teresa Lamai started writing in 2003. This year, you can find her work in *Best Women's Erotica, Best of Best Lesbian Erotica,* and *Lips Like Sugar: Erotic Fantasies by Women;* as well as in *Mammoth Book of Best New Erotica 5.* A former dancer, she's just completed a collection of dance-inspired erotic stories entitled *Swayed to Music,* and is working on her first novel.

Tobsha Learner's books include *Quiver, The Witch of Cologne, Tremble—Sensual Fables of the Mystical and Sinister.* Her new novel, *Soul,* will be published in mid-2006. She divides her time among Sydney, London, and California.

Jan Levi lives in Leeds, England, where she is a founder member of *Women, Mountains, Words.* Her work has been published in a number of anthologies and magazines and has been read out on Radio 4. She is currently working on a biography about a Lakeland climber entitled *And Nobody Woke Up Dead,* due to be published in 2006, and hopes to finish her novel, *The Tightrope Walker,* in the near future.

Under a variety of pseudonyms (including Lisette Ashton) **Ashley Lister** is the author of around thirty erotic fiction novels as well as countless short stories and articles. A regular columnist for the Erotic Readers & Writers Association, and a frequent contributor to the *The International Journal of Erotica*, Ashley lives in the coastal resort of Blackpool, England. Virgin Books, London, has just released Ashley's first non-fiction title *Swingers: True Confessions from Today's Swinging Scene*, which is gaining international attention.

Michael Mahoney is a recent graduate from Lancaster University in the UK, where his progression through their creative writing program developed his craft and helped him achieve publication. His work has also recently appeared on the Internet magazine *Muse Apprentice Guild*. He has moved to the US, where he plans to continue his studies and his writing.

Kevin Mullins lives and works in the wastes of Slough, England. He has had stories published in *Darklands*, *Darklands 2*, *The Tiger Garden*, *Peeping Tom*, and *Squane's Journal*. His most recent piece is an article in PS Publishing's *Cinema Macabre* discussing the film *Don't Look Now*, another great tale of sex and death. "Underneath" is Kevin's second collaboration with Marcelle Perks. Their first is a dark tale of soiled photographs and pubic hair called "Strawberry Pink."

Marcelle Perks spent her twenties in London and has lived in Hanover, North Germany, since 2001. She is the author of *Incredible Orgasms* and her short fiction has appeared in *Sex Macabre*, *Three-Way*, *The A-Z of Naughty Spanking Stories*, and *The Mammoth Book of Best New Erotica 2005*. She also writes for *Fangoria*, *Nerve.com*, *Gay Times*, and *Kamera* and has contributed to *Alternative Europe*, *The Goth Bible*, *The BFI Companion to*

Horror, and *British Horror Cinema.* She's liked the idea of the underground since seeing the film *Death Line* and previously used to work there on location as a photographic coordinator for London Transport Advertising.

Edward Picot was born in 1958 and lives in Kent, England with his wife and daughter. He studied English Literature at Peterhouse, Cambridge, and later took a Ph.D. in English at the University of Kent. His Ph.D. thesis was published in 1997 by the University of Liverpool Press as *Outcasts from Eden: Ideas of Landscape in British Poetry since 1945.* In 2000 he set up his own Web site and soon became interested in hyperliterature (literature designed for computers). In 2003 he guest-edited the Slope Hyperliterature Feature for the online magazine *Slope* (http://www.slope.org). Later the same year he launched *The Hyperliterature Exchange,* an online directory and review of hyperliterature for sale on the Web, with links to the places where it can be bought. He has published numerous articles about hyperliterature and other aspects of new media arts in *The P N Review,* *trAce* (http://trace.ntu.ac.uk), and *The Hyperliterature Exchange.* He has also published numerous creative works online, notably *Heronsbrook* (2002), *Flower Story* (2003), *The Recycling Bins* (2004), *Linesland* (2004), *Chicks* (2005), and *The Greyhound Murder* (2005). Personal Web site: http://edwardpicot.com. The Hyperliterature Exchange: http://hyperex.co.uk.

Half Serbian, half Venezuelan, **Andrija Popovic** is a product of the unique cultural stew found in the Washington, D.C., metropolitan area. Now a resident of northern Virginia, Andrija spends his days helping people contact their elected officials for a living. He has written for several small press magazines, but this is his first publication in an anthology of short tales. An amateur photographer, he has yet to capture anything supernatural with his camera besides the cats in his house.

Jendi Reiter's first book, *A Talent for Sadness*, was published in 2003 by Turning Point Books (http://www.turningpointbooks.com). Her work has appeared in such journals as *Ellery Queen's Mystery Magazine*, *Hanging Loose*, *Mudfish*, *Alligator Juniper*, and *Clackamas Literary Review*. She is the editor of *Poetry Contest Insider*, an online guide to over 750 writing contests, published by http://www.winningwriters.com. Born in New York City, she currently lives in Northampton, MA, with her husband (the other half of Winning Writers) in a Victorian house next door to a cemetery.

Adréana Robbins is a freelance writer and author of the novel *Paris Never Leaves You*. She has been published in the *LA Weekly*, *Brentwood News*, *Hustler*, and has written erotic fiction for *Leg World* and *Hustler Fantasies*. Ms. Robbins was born in the south of France and was also raised part of her life in Hollywood, California. It is not surprising that she took up the pen; her father was the bestselling novelist Harold Robbins. As the daughter of a famous parent, her childhood was at times indulgent, as well as chaotic, but some of her fondest memories were spent exploring the Mediterranean by boat. She took a lot of Dramamine and traveled to Malta, Gibraltar, Morocco, Barcelona, Greece, Turkey, Venice, Sicily, Ibiza, Majorca, Capri, and Sardegna. A love of art, travel, and literature ensued; she studied creative writing and French literature at the American College in Paris. "Garden of Earthly Delights" was inspired by a trip to Madrid, where she visited the Prado and Buen Retiro Park. When she first composed the story, it came to her entirely in French. Ms. Robbins lives in Los Angeles and is working on another novel.

Lisabet Sarai has been writing fiction and poetry ever since she learned how to hold a pencil. Her latest work, a short story collection entitled *Fire*, was released in June 2005 by Blue Moon Books. She is the author of three erotic novels, *Raw Silk*, *Incognito*, and

Ruby's Rules, and the coeditor, with S.F. Mayfair, of the anthology *Sacred Exchange*, which explores the spiritual aspects of BDSM relationships. Lisabet also reviews erotic books and films for the Erotica Readers and Writers Association (http://www.erotica-readers.com) and Sliptongue.com. For more information on Lisabet and her writing visit Lisabet Sarai's Fantasy Factory (http://www.lisabet-sarai.com).

Harriet Scott lives in England but is proud of her Scottish roots. She works in education, mostly with reluctant learners. She has been writing for a number of years and has been published in anthologies including *The Mammoth Book of Women's Fantasies* and *Skin Deep 2*, as well as magazines and e-zines. Her writing tends to explore areas of control and submission and in particular the mental processes involved.

Lene Taylor is an author and editor. Her writing has been published in many venues, both online and in print. She currently produces two podcasts: *I Read Comics*, devoted to the first love of her life, comic books; and *Look At His Butt!*, which combines the second and third—*Star Trek* and sex. When she's not talking to herself, she's writing for the Lincoln Heights Literary Society (liheliso.com). She lives and works in northern California.

Jan Wildt (janwildt@sff.net), whose "A Son of the Revolution" (*New Genre* 1, 2000) started the "erratica" movement in slipstream fiction, wrote this volume's contribution ("Hate Mate Awaits Fate") in a sudden fit of linearity. More typical are "Wonderfreaks" (*Northwest Passages*, Fandom Press, 2005), the typographer's nightmare "Bink Is Luv" (*New Genre* 4, 2006), and "Apology" (some future, doubtless groundbreaking, collection). Wildt lives in a Southern California monastery and is delighted to find himself between these covers in this distinguished company.

About the Editor

Mitzi Szereto is the editor of *The World's Best Sex Writing 2005*, *Wicked: Sexy Tales of Legendary Lovers*, and the Erotic Travel Tales anthology series (volumes 1, 2, and 3). She is the author of *Erotic Fairy Tales: A Romp Through the Classics*, and the M. S. Valentine erotic novels. She has pioneered erotic writing workshops in the United Kingdom and Europe, and has conducted them from the Cheltenham Festival of Literature to the Greek islands. She and her work have been featured in the *Sunday Telegraph* (London), *The Independent* (London), *Toronto Star*, *Family Circle*, *Writing Magazine*, and *Forum*, as well as on Bravo UK Television BBC Radio, and on Madrid's Telecinco TV 5. Mitzi Szereto's work as an anthology editor has earned her the American Society of Authors and Writers' Meritorious Achievement Award. Born in the United States, she now lives (and occasionally dies) in England.

Permissions